"I AM NOT AFRAID OF YOU, GRIFFYN RENAUD."

"I did not say you were afraid of *me*." A darkened spiral of hair had sprung forward over her forehead and he brushed it aside with a breath of a kiss. "You are afraid of this," he whispered, trailing the caress to her temple and down to the curl of her ear. "And this." He bent his head and she felt the black silk of his hair on her cheek. His lips were on her throat, in the crook of her neck, and she closed her eyes, her breath coming even hotter and faster than before. Her heart beat with a wildness that frightened her, and she felt as if she were standing on the edge of a cliff, the hypnotic lure of danger pulling her forward and the safe sanctuary of solid ground calling her back.

"How . . . can you expect me to believe you?" she gasped. "After everything that has happened . . . the lies, the dishonesty, the cruel games—"

"That night we spent together at Gaillard was no game."

With her tears spilling faster than she could blink them free, she watched the dark outline of his face bend toward her.

"Tell me," he rasped, "you do not believe this. . . ."

STRAIGHT FOR THE HEART

IN THE SHADOW OF MIDNIGHT

Also by Marsha Canham

Across a Moonlit Sea
In the Shadow of Midnight
Straight for the Heart
Through a Dark Mist
Under the Desert Moon

MARSHA CANHAM

THE LAST ARROW

A DELL BOOK

Published by
Dell Publishing
a division of
Bantam Doubleday Dell Publishing Group, Inc.
1540 Broadway
New York, New York 10036

The trademark Dell® is registered in the U.S. Patent and Trademark Office.

ISBN: 0-440-22257-5

Printed in the United States of America

Published simultaneously in Canada

May 1997

10 9 8 7 6 5 4 3 2 1

OPM

About eight centuries ago, an unknown bard sat under a tree in the vast expanse of Sherwood Forest and composed a ballad about a hooded outlaw who robbed from the rich to give to the poor. How could he know he was creating a legend? This book is dedicated to him, and to all the writers before and since who have made history an exciting and romantic visit in our imaginations.

Prologue

Marienne FitzWilliam had blossomed into a beautiful young woman. Because she had not taken any vow of seclusion, she was often sent to the market in Nottingham to trade the linens woven by the nuns of Kirklees. It happened one day, she was caught in a circle of sunlight, frowning in concentration over a selection of needles and spindles, when the bored and lecherous eyes of a town official came to settle on the abundance of glossy chestnut curls. His name was Reginald de Braose and he was in the service of the Sheriff of Nottingham, Guy de Gisbourne.

An ugly man, short of height, overbulked in stature, de Braose's face was ravaged with the scars of a childhood disease. One eye was coated in a milky-white film, red-rimmed, and leaked fluids that more often than not were left to dry to a yellow crust in the corners. His hair, brown as dung, lay in greasy spikes against his neck and poked out from beneath the battered iron dome of his helm. His armor was not the finest. He wore no coif to protect his neck—not that any common man would be fool enough to attack him. His mail hauberk bore definite signs of combat and was ill repaired in the sleeves and hem; a sorry chain of broken links hung like a frayed iron thread down his thigh. The surcoat he wore was dull blue with more patches stained from food and drink than were clean. His hose bagged at the knee. The blade of his sword was pitted and chipped and betrayed no gleam, not even in the bright midday sun.

He looked to the left and to the right, casually nodding

to the half-dozen soldiers who lurked in the shadows. Only one was too preoccupied to nod back. He had a hand down the front of a blowsy wench and was too busy fondling and pinching to notice his captain's glare.

De Braose and his men had been at the market since dawn. It was the fourth Saturday they had been up before the crowing of the rooster, turned out of warm beds with empty bellies and foul tempers; this day, like most others, they had positioned themselves at various vantage points in the market square watching for strangers, following them, hoping one might lead them to rich rewards. This was not the first time de Braose had seen the little dark-haired maid. She lived and worked for the nuns at Kirklees Abbey, but she was the most interesting morsel to come into view so far since the villagers had taken to hiding most of their wives and daughters—even the ugly ones—whenever there were soldiers around.

Yeomen and peasants had started taking to the forests as well, especially those likely to be picked up by the soldiers and dragged off to the castle for work details. Overtaxed and half starving, they hid what little of value they had; it was up to the king's men to find it and pry it out of them by whatever methods they deemed necessary. Men forced to work in the castle could pay a fine and free themselves. Women forced to whore could pay a fine—after their usefulness was fully exhausted—and return to their mud-and-wattle homes. Those who thought to struggle or resist found themselves missing ears or fingers, toes or tongues by way of example to others. It was the same everywhere in England. The king's treasury was empty and he demanded it be filled. Whether he had to steal taxes from the rich or bleed it from the poor, it mattered not so long as his stores of jewels and gold were replenished.

In the eleven years since he had taken the throne, John Plantagenet had emptied the treasury many times over. He had lost the hereditary Angevin lands in Normandy and Brittany to his ineffectual leadership, and turned most of the English barons against him by using cruelty, repression, and murder as a means of ruling. Anyone who possessed anything of value found himself robbed of it, or fined for having it. The king's men scoured the land, inventing new tortures, confiscating properties, ravaging women, and more and more nobles were questioning their wisdom all those years ago in having supported John's claim to the throne when they might have had the young and malleable Arthur of Brittany.

Their self-doubts only raised more rumbles of dissent. Where was Prince Arthur? What had happened to him? What had happened to his sister Eleanor? They were the offspring of John's older brother Geoffrey, and, by right of succession, Arthur should have inherited the throne upon King Richard's death. Instead, John had snatched the crown for himself and had thrown Arthur and his sister in prison. Neither had been seen since. There had been rumors and speculation, of course. A body had been found floating in the River Seine not six months after Arthur's disappearance. Badly decomposed, it could not be readily identified, but it had bright golden hair and the scraps of clothing it wore were of the finest, richest quality. Then and now there were murmured convictions that John had had his nephew murdered, even that he had committed the abhorrent crime himself in one of his fits of rage.

As to the sister Eleanor, she had simply vanished off the face of the earth. There was one whispered tale of her confinement in Corfe Castle, of a daring rescue staged by unknown knights, but the whispers faded when it came to the end of the tale. If she had been rescued, where had she been taken? Who could have possibly kept her hidden for so many years, and why, *why*, when England was embroiled in civil unrest, would she not have been brought forth out of obscurity to lay her rightful claim to the throne?

The king was well aware of the resentment and hostility brewing around him. He had tried, and failed, to gather an army this past spring to cross the Channel and reclaim his lost territories in Normandy from King Philip of France. Less than a third of his barons had answered his call to arms, and to repay them for the insult, he had sent them home in disgrace and hired mercenaries in their stead at a great cost to England's treasury. Defeated by indifference before he began, he had suffered an abysmal loss in Flanders, at the Battle of Bouvines, and had once again been sent scurrying back to England, his tail firmly tucked between his legs.

His rage was then focused on his barons, namely those who had refused to join the ill-fated venture. He was the king! All of his subjects—nobles, clergy, knights, and peasants alike—were at his mercy, and he was determined to prove it, even if it meant fining every noble, burning every castle in England, and placing their inhabitants in prison!

To that end, he put vicious, brutal men in positions of power, giving them free rein to rape, steal, murder at whim. Guy de Gisbourne was one such tyrant who laid no claim to the possession of either a conscience or a willingness to show mercy. One of his first tasks, upon taking command of Nottingham Castle, had been to fill the donjons with men and women who owed a tax or were suspected of hoarding profits. His was a garrison of misfits and brutes, his authority was fire and sword, and few who defied him by word or deed lived to see another dawn. Those meager few swelled the ranks of the outlaws who had begun to live in the surrounding forests. Gisbourne had put high prices on their heads, and when they were caught, he had their bodies drawn and quartered, their various parts hung in the village square until the flesh turned black and fell off the bones.

Only last week Reginald de Braose and his men had caught an outlaw trying to visit his blind sister in the village of Edwinstow. They had taken both the outlaw and the sister to the sheriff's court, where one had been sentenced to hang, the other to service the men of the garrison by way of an example to those relatives who might think to offer succor to their fugitive kinsmen.

* * *

Reginald de Braose watched the maid, Marienne, move away from the milliner's stall and signaled his men. She would not waste time returning to the abbey now that her linens were sold and her purchases made. Kirklees was a two-hour walk from the village, most of it through forest thick enough to tint the air green, dense enough to muffle the loudest screams from unyielding virgins.

A friar was waiting at the edge of the village to escort her back to the abbey, but de Braose was not concerned; most of the graycloaks flew away like startled moths at the first glint of a sword blade. His men were another matter, for none of the soldiers in Nottingham liked to venture too deep into Sherwood. The trees seemed taller here, thicker, denser than anywhere else in England. It was said they were filled with ghostly sentries who whispered alarms and brought forth demons to slit the throats and spill the entrails of all those who came uninvited into the greenwood.

De Braose did not believe in ghosts or demons. He believed the woods were filled with outlaws and misfits, and he believed strongly in the reward of a thousand marks Gisbourne was offering for the capture of their leader. No one had ever seen him without the trademark hood that concealed his features, nor, in truth, could they tell one outlaw from another, for they all moved like silent, shapeless shadows through the trees. They dressed in drab greens and browns to blend with the undergrowth, their soft leather jerkins and linsey woolsey making them *seem* to be apparitions, moving from one glade to another like mist. The only warning of their presence was the faint *hiss* that came before their arrows struck.

Still, it was a warm day and the thought of sinking himself into such a tender morsel as this dark-haired novitiate was too sweet to resist. He pushed away from the airless patch of shade that had harbored him, signaling his men to follow.

* * *

"You seem distracted today, Friar," Marienne remarked as she adjusted the weight of the package under her arm.

The monk turned and held her eyes a moment before responding with a self-conscious smile. "You were longer in the market than you should have been."

"I had a difficult time finding everything on the abbess's list," she said, indicating the two bulky parcels he was carrying for her. "The sisters were short of many things—needles, spices, seed and such. And the tailor haggled longer than usual over the price he was willing to pay for the linens."

"Everyone is suffering for the king's greed these days. Coins are scarce, generosity a thing of the past. Did you get the herbs you needed for Sister Bertal?"

She nodded. "Thankfully, yes."

He cast another veiled glance over his shoulder, and this time Marienne joined him in looking back at the tree-lined road. She could see nothing but the quiet stillness of the greenwood, the majesty of the tall oaks that stretched their leafy boughs high into the blue vault of the sky. So thick were the branches overhead that not much of the blue could be seen. Here and there, mottled patches allowed bright streamers of sunlight to slash through the latticework of branches and leaves, but by the time it reached the earth so far below, the light was diffused to a soft, blurry haze. And there were so many shades of green! The apple of young saplings, the emerald of ferns, the staunch vert of the firs, the varying jades, mosses, and olives of the towering oaks, ash, and yew. The air itself seemed shaded, lush with dew, shimmering like a jewel where the light touched upon it.

So many feared the unearthly silence, the cool shadows, the pungent scent of isolation, but Marienne loved it. She loved the long walk to Nottingham from Kirklees, and she had hoped this day, like many others, her companion might be cajoled into veering off the road and taking her deeper into the living heart of Sherwood.

One look at the worried frown on his face that morning

had dispelled her hopes. He had tried his best to talk her out of going to Nottingham at all, claiming the sheriff's spies were everywhere, thick as fleas in an old man's beard. Any other time the abbess might have agreed with his prudence, but several of the sisters had broken out in a high fever and painful rash, and their limited supplies of medicine had run perilously low.

The friar had capitulated, but not gracefully, for his feet had moved so quickly on the road Marienne's shorter strides had been hard pressed to keep his pace. She looked over at him and once more marveled to herself how unlike a friar he appeared. Over the past decade he had never once dropped his guard or taken any manner of precaution for granted. Nor had he allowed any of his knightly skills to wane. He was lean and hard, his limbs were like iron from living off the land. Where he might have missed the power of a destrier beneath him, he more than made up for the lack in sheer strength and stamina. He could run for miles without taking a heavy breath. He could and did practice for hours with sword, mace, and stave with hardly a trace of sweat on his brow to show for it.

Like Marienne, he had taken no formal vows with the church, nor was he inclined to offer a prayer in lieu of a cut from his sword should his back come against a wall. He was one of the deadliest swordsmen in Sherwood and had his monk's robes specially fashioned to afford access to the weapon he always wore strapped to his waist. He had earned the familiar name Tuck because of the assortment of knives, daggers, and blades he kept hidden in various folds and pockets of his garments, and this was just as well, because his real name, should it ever slip from an unguarded tongue, would have brought the wrath of the crown down on all their heads.

With the forest filling with outlaws, and those outlaws becoming bolder in their actions against the sheriff and his henchmen, it was becoming more difficult to remain anonymous. Luckily they all had secrets to keep, and the quickest way to earn a blade across the throat was to ask too many questions or offer up too much unwanted information. The outlaws of Sherwood were successful because no one man knew too much about another. Their leader insisted on keeping it that way, preferring to use nicknames rather than proper surnames, or names that identified them by skill, like Derwint the Fletcher or Edgar the Cobbler. They neither made nor passed judgment on any member of the band, and strangely enough, because loyalty and trust were not *demanded*, they were given freely and fiercely, even unto death.

"Why do you keep looking over your shoulder?" Marienne asked, huffing a bit as they started up an incline. "Is there someone following us?"

"I think there may be an excess of vermin in the woods today, aye. You will, of course, oblige me by running whither I send you if I deem their presence to become too annoying?"

"I would sooner not have to run anywhere at all today." She sighed, then added shyly, "I would rather find a soft glade and a cool stream and practice the lessons you were teaching me."

Haste had made the short hairs at her temple curl damply against her skin and put a rosy blush in her cheeks. She was at the far end of three and twenty but looked much younger, and her simple wool tunic could not completely conceal the ripe curves of the body beneath. On several occasions, Tuck had caught himself looking longer and harder than he should, most recently when he had taken the foolish notion into his head to teach her how to swim. It had happened all very innocently, for she had fallen off a cracked log and surprised him by panicking in water that was scarcely over her shoulders. He had taught her then and there how to make a few strokes and hold herself up by kicking and paddling, but the sheer act of supporting her wet and shapely body had left his own aching in ways that made him flush with hot guilt every time he thought of it. To repeat the exercise any time soon would have tested the fortitude of a real monk.

Avoiding her gaze, he frowned over his shoulder again, unable to rid himself of the feeling he should have been more insistent that morning with the abbess.

"I am as quick on my feet as you are, good friar," she said, not knowing where his thoughts had drifted, but drawing his eyes back. "And if you have another sword tucked beneath your cassock, I will prove I can be just as good at ridding the forest of vermin."

"I know full well your skill with blade and bow," he said grimly. "And those were lessons I should *never* have been extorted into teaching you."

"They have come in handy on more than one occasion," she reminded him, "when you were not there to watch over the abbey like a tarnished archangel."

Tuck's tawny hair caught a glint of sunlight and for a moment resembled threads of pure gold. His skin was weathered a healthy bronze, and, not for the first time, Marienne found herself smiling at the comparison.

"You should never have strayed outside the abbey walls," he grumbled, "regardless how many of the sisters went with you, how sunny a day it was, or how ripe the berries were for picking. You were lucky it was just two errant knights looking to do a little mischief in the grass."

"Well, they spent the rest of the day looking for the arrowheads I buried in their hides."

Tuck started to give his head a rueful shake but froze when he detected a faint stirring in the sea of ferns that grew alongside the road. They had crested the hill and started on their way down and for the moment, the view of the road behind them was blocked from sight.

His footsteps slowed measurably.

Twenty feet ahead, the road took a sharp turn to the left, the gully too thick with evergreens to see what lay beyond. It was, he realized at once, the perfect spot for an ambush, with blind spots ahead and behind. He was at a further disadvantage, having a canvas-wrapped parcel cradled under each arm. As casually as he could, he transferred the one to free his sword arm.

"Marienne—"

The whisper barely left his lips when the impatient nicker of a horse justified the scratching on his neck. The unmistakable clank of armor followed close by, and with sudden certainty he knew they had been caught in a trap. He did not have to see the row of gleaming steel helmets that rose above the crest of underbrush, nor did he have to hear the muffled command and subsequent pounding of hoofbeats on the beaten earth ahead. A dozen or more horsemen had been waiting around the bend in the road, the same number of foot soldiers, armed with crossbows, had been secreted in the bushes waiting to cut off their escape. Even as he whirled around, dropping his packages to the road, the two lines of soldiers closed in behind them like a pincer.

Marienne's hand went to her waist and found the hilt of the dagger she wore sheathed in her belt. Beside her, Tuck had his sword in his hand and was turning in a slow, shocked circle, his teeth bared over a steady stream of curses.

The mounted knights drew to a halt behind the ring of foot soldiers. They wore plain gray tunics devoid of any crests or blazons. They carried no pennons, no shields embossed with identifiable markings. Their mail was made of the finest Damascene steel, polished to a professional gleam. The horses were huge, well fed, well blooded, and, to judge by the utter lack of movement, exceptionally well trained.

They had the hardened look of mercenaries about them, and Tuck's grip tightened on his sword, raising the point to chest level, wondering if this was Gisbourne's work . . . or the king's.

Before he could divine any answer, one of them nudged his warhorse forward a few paces, his way of announcing himself as the leader. For all of two full minutes he said nothing. Dark, keen eyes glittered out from behind the steel nasal of his helm, giving Marienne but a cursory inspection before settling intently upon Tuck.

"Of all the remarkable sights we have encountered of late"—his voice was a low, sinister rasp—"that of a monk wielding a fine Toledo blade must needs rank as one of the oddest."

"Try your hand at taking it from me," Tuck said bluntly, "and you might rethink the ranking."

"Boastful words, Friar," the knight hissed. "And ones that will likely require testing some time in the near future. For the moment, however, you might want to simply set the weapon aside instead."

"Why would I want to do that?"

"Because, as you can plainly see, I have twenty men with twenty fingers itchy to pull the trigger on twenty crossbows."

Tuck's sword wavered not an inch. "Who the devil are you?"

"Of more pressing interest, friend, is the question: Who the devil are you?"

"Obviously not who you think I am."

"You deny you are a member of the band of outlaws who populate the forests of Sherwood?"

Tuck's jaw clenched. "I am but a humble mendicant going about God's business."

The knight eyed the finely honed sword again. "Not so humble, I think, and judging by the number of robberies in these woods, not as much God's business as that of the King of Sherwood."

"The sword was a gift. I carry it for defense against those selfsame robbers you accuse me of knowing."

"That is good," the knight mused. "Very good." He leaned forward with a soft creak of leather and crossed his arm over the frontispiece of his saddle. "And if I believed you, Priest, it would be even better."

"What would it take to convince you?" Tuck asked tautly.

"More than you have to offer. Although if you persist in wasting my time"—the knight's eyes slid over to rest on

Marienne—"we may be pressed to seek some form of compensation."

Tuck delayed another fraction of a moment, then lowered the tip of his sword.

The dark eyes returned. "Ahh. You concede the point."

"Before I concede anything, I would call upon your honor as a knight to let the maid pass unharmed. She is but a simple child of God and carries medicines for the nuns at her convent."

The knight weighed Tuck's words against the pale, stricken look on Marienne's face and agreed with a curt nod of his head.

"Let her pass," he said to his men. "We can always find her again if we need her."

Marienne, her skin the color of old wax, was conscious of Tuck drawing her down to retrieve the contents of one parcel that had split open.

"Do not spare a single breath getting back to the abbey." His voice was raw with urgency, the words barely loud enough for her to understand. They came through bloodless, unmoving lips and frightened her more than any threat of rape or ravishment. "Lock and bar the gates. Let no one inside. *No one*, do you understand!"

Her eyes were as wide and dark as those of a doe facing a hunter's arrow and Tuck knew what she was thinking. He was thinking it too. If they took him to Guy de Gisbourne and if the sheriff recognized his face . . .

He groaned and bowed his head. "If you do not hear from me in two days' time," he said tersely, wondering if he could even last that long under torture, "get word to Amboise. Tell them the Pearl may be in grave danger and needs their help."

PART ONE
Château d'Amboise

I

Lady Brenna Wardieu raised her head ever so slowly,
lifting her two startlingly clear violet eyes and the tip of her
nose barely above the lush sweep of ferns. Her hair was
braided in a thick rope that hung almost to her waist.
Golden wisps had sprung free to surround her face in a soft
halo of straggled curls, and she had lost her peaked felt cap
somewhere in the chase, snagged by a low-lying branch as
she had darted through the tangled underbrush. Her heart
was still slamming against her ribs with the urgency of
her flight, and she knew her adversary was out there somewhere, camouflaged by the same sea of green that protected her.

She sank back down into the cocoon of foliage that
skirted the base of the oak tree. This part of the forest was
dense, the shadows kinder to the prey than the hunter,
darkest in the gullies and culverts that offered sanctuary
from searching eyes, yet each whisper of the leaves was sinister, each scratch of a squirrel's claw a potential threat.

She had lost all sense of time and knew only that it must
be growing late in the afternoon. There was already a fine
layer of mist curling around the tree trunks, swirling filmy
fingers into small pockets of open air. The branches were so
tightly woven overhead the sky was only a distant impression of pale blue. Brenna could not even be certain of the
direction she had been running, for she had concentrated
on keeping her head down and her ears trained for sounds
of pursuit. She was not overly worried about getting lost.
She had grown up in these woods and would have had to
run without a break for two days and two nights before

entering unfamiliar tracts of forest. But she held no advantage there over her pursuer. He had been hunting deer and boar and hare in these vast tracts since he was a child. Moreover, because he hunted her now, his senses would be at their peak, his instincts honed for blood, his determination a rival only for her own.

The ground underfoot was soft and loamy, scenting the air with the rich decay of several centuries' worth of fallen leaves. Her skin was damp and cool. She had been running almost steadily for over an hour trying to keep ahead, trying to keep from being caught out in the open. She would have liked to strip off the doeskin jerkin she wore, for it was holding the sweat next to her skin. Her shirt was plastered uncomfortably across her back and breasts despite the brisk nip in the autumn air. Her leggings and tall kidskin boots were crusted with mud where she had splashed through a stream—her toes still squeaked with water when she rubbed them together—and one knee was split where she had ripped it on a thorn.

She fingered aside the torn edges of chamois and cursed at the deep scratch in her flesh. It had stopped bleeding but it still stung like the devil, and she struggled to calm her heartbeat, to *think*, as she flicked out the bits of dirt that clung to the drying blood.

Somewhere *very* close-by a twig snapped.

It was only a faint sound, easily attributed to a rodent burrowing in a rotted tree trunk . . . if one did not imagine the silently mouthed curse that instantly followed.

Brenna parted her lips, drawing breath as quietly as possible. The sound had come from behind her, and luckily, she had the bulk of the ancient oak to shield any soft ripple of movement she might make. Inch by inch she maneuvered her bow off her shoulder—*not* an easy feat to accomplish in a cramped position. The weapon was nearly five feet in length, made of seasoned yew, and could fire an arrow with enough power to pierce through chain mail and with such swift, deadly accuracy a graceful *fwoosh* was usually the last sound its victim heard.

She plucked a slender ashwood arrow out of her quiver and, keeping her back against the tree, slid herself upward until she stood waist deep in the ferns. He was there, all right. The narrowest sliver of a violet eye peeked around the gnarled bark and marked the shock of bright red hair visible through the labyrinth of tangled saplings. Fool. It was the only splash of color in an otherwise green world, and he thought to trip *her* up on errors.

The initial sound had seemed deceptively close, distorted by the almost liquid silence of the forest. In reality her quarry stood more than fifty yards away, frozen himself against his own clumsiness, his golden hawk's eyes searching the surrounding woods even as Brenna slowly ran her tongue along the arrow's fletching, dampening the vanes to ensure there were no gaps or breaks in the feathers. The shaft itself was three feet long, tipped with a twice-tempered iron head that could, at this distance, penetrate clothing, flesh, bone, and muscle from shoulder to shoulder and pin him fast to the tree. The shot had to be perfect. Precise. She would not have a second chance.

Brenna nocked the arrow, blew out a final breath, then wasted no time in setting herself. She stepped out from behind the tree, her bow arm already raised and straight, her feet planted solidly apart for balance. She drew the fletching back to her cheek, took a split second to aim, then snapped her fingers away from the string and sped the shaft clean and true to the target.

Habit sent her fingers to her quiver for another arrow, but she knew she did not need it. She knew from the yelp of surprise and the stunned look on William FitzAthelstan's handsome face as the bolt streaked past his nose, close enough for a lick of hot air to tickle his skin. The resounding *f-f-bungg* left the arrow buried nearly six inches in the wood and the shaft humming with lingering, resonant vibrations.

"Christ Jesus God, and all the Saints!" He whirled in time to see Brenna give a small whoop of victory as she held up their scores on her fingers—two clean wins for her, only one for him.

"You could have cut off my nose!" he shouted.

"You should be more careful where you put it," she countered, wading through the ferns toward him. The smile was wide and fixed on her face. It was the first time she had outfoxed him two straight strikes in a row.

His complexion stayed as red as his hair for the full minute it took for her to weave her way through the saplings to join him. The dark copper brows remained crushed together in a frown, the normally placid set to his mouth was distorted by a scowl.

"Cheer up, Will'um," she said over a laugh. "We all have our bad days."

He bent his head forward by a breath and tapped his forehead lightly on the shaft of the arrow. "Good shot, Bren. A damned good shot. All of them today have been damned good."

"I know." She slung her bow over her shoulder and laughed again—it was difficult not to, seeing the abject look on Will's face. "And you, Sir Archer, are a far better sport than I would have been were our positions reversed. Ooooh . . ." She reached out a slender finger and touched the end of his nose. "Is that a feather burn I see?"

"You could have put out my eye if you had missed," he said sourly.

"How could I miss such a fine, bold target?"

"It has been known to happen."

"Not since I grew breasts and improved my balance."

He looked up from under his brows and could not help responding to her teasing smile. A moment later, he sighed and shouldered his bow. "I suppose we should start back. Dag and Richard likely gave the game up long ago, but Robin seemed in a particularly stubborn mood this day. Do you recall where we lost him?"

Brenna shook her head as she glanced back at the deepening shadows. It was true her brothers Richard and Dagobert would have long ago lost interest in chasing elusive targets through the woods. No doubt they were back at the château quaffing mead and bickering over comely milch maids. Robin, on the other hand, could be anywhere. He had also tallied two hits this day, but not solely due to his own skill. He was a keen enough archer to be sure, but both Will and Brenna tended to cheat a little in his favor if he had gone too long without a win. He was far more comfortable on the back of his enormous warhorse, Sir Tristan, leading a company of knights into battle. Only this past July he had, with his brothers and the men of Amboise, joined forces with Philip of France to offer the mercenary army of King John a crushing defeat at Roche-au-Moine.

"Dearest Robin. On a battlefield or in a jousting run, he is undefeatable. Put him in lincoln green and fit a bow to his hand and . . . well . . ."

"Some men are suited to wear shining armor and do battle with demons and dragons. Others possess more human qualities, like a tendency to bleed, quake at the heels, and recognize their own limitations."

"Then as long as he has you at his back, he has no need to fear such mortal failings," Brenna added with an affectionate smile.

Will's face mirrored her wry expression, but she knew he was thinking the same thing. He had been squire to her father, Lord Randwulf de la Seyne Sur Mer, since the age of ten, but it was Robin with whom he had developed a close, fast friendship. At four and twenty, Robin was six years his senior, yet there were times the younger man's wisdom and patience far exceeded that of the passionate, impulsive heir to Amboise. In that much, it was said, they resembled their respective fathers, for Alaric FitzAthelstan had always been content to stand in the shadow of Lord Randwulf, letting the legendary Black Wolf establish himself as the champion and slayer of dragons while he himself sought only the position of friend, ally, and closest advisor. It was a role that suited Will as much as it suited Lord Alaric, for although he had trained as hard as any of the sons to earn his spurs and showed as much ability and courage to wade wholeheartedly into battle, his quick mind, instincts, and powers of perception had proved far more lethal. He was a brilliant strategist. He could look at a problem and see three solutions where others were left scratching their heads in search of one. Lord Randwulf had had no qualms sending him to Maine with the rest of the men from Amboise. It had been Will's quiet advice and Robin's genuine respect for it that had, as much as the brazen courage of the thousand knights who fought under the pennons of the Black Wolf, won the day at Roche-au-Moines.

With only eighteen years to his credit, however, he had not been among those knighted on the field by King Philip as a reward for their services. It had been a bitter disappointment, but as Brenna had been quick to point out upon his return to Amboise: "Your time will come. Even Robin was nineteen before the king took notice of him, though I am not sure he would not have ridden Sir Tristan straight into the royal bedchamber if all else had failed. Why are men in such a hurry to have their brains bashed out anyway?"

"You would not understand."

"Indeed, I admit that quite freely. I most certainly do *not* understand. Richard and Dag have no brains to speak of, therefore they would hardly feel the loss. But you—you have the best bow arm . . . with one obvious exception of course . . . in all of Normandy, Brittany, Poitou, and Touraine, yet you fever with eagerness to clamber up on a horse, burden yourself under a few hundredweight of armor, then hurl yourself down a course knowing there is a good likelihood of breaking every bone in your body."

Will had scowled. "Your confidence in my ability is touching."

"It is not my goal to encourage you. Nor is it my father's, I warrant. And before you puff up like a weed pod, I am not saying he is less than proud to bursting that you came this close"—she had pressed her thumb and forefinger together by way of emphasis—"to wearing your spurs home from Maine, but he has four sons who would sleep in their armor if they could find a way to do so without making eunuchs of themselves. What he needs and what they need is a cool, level head to guide them."

"Now you think too *much* of my abilities."

"Your modesty is commendable, truly it is. But who else in this or any other demesne within a ten-day ride can speak six languages fluently and quote great boring passages of Sophocles when it is least expected?"

" 'It is not the powerful arm, but the soft enchanting tongue that governs all,' " he mused.

"There. You see? Even he agrees and he has been dead for a few hundred years."

Will had only laughed and shaken his head at her unaffected lack of reverence.

Less than four months separated them in age and they were as close as they could possibly be without becoming intimate. She suspected both sets of parents had always harbored the secret hope that a lifetime spent in each other's company would naturally have progressed into something more. There was no denying Will was painless on the eyes. He was long-limbed and well muscled, handsome enough to draw second glances from women of all ages and situations. From his father he had inherited his scholarly mind and an easygoing nature that hid a devilish humor and deep sense of honor. From his mother, Lady Gillian, had come the shock of red hair and the gilt-colored eyes, the keen sight and rock-steady nerve that had made her one of the best and most feared archers in all of Christendom.

To no one's surprise, Lady Gillian had fit a bow to his hand as soon as he could stand. Brenna, because she was always underfoot and could not bear to be left out of anything, had stood alongside him learning how to find her balance, to sight along the shaft of the arrow, to listen to what the bow string was saying if the fingers plucked too hard or too soft. Under Gil's expert tutelage they had become master archers in their own right with neither able to claim consistent superiority over the other. The game they had played today, they had been enjoying since they were children, and while they retraced their steps through the forest, it would be her pleasure to annoy him by verbally replaying each of the five winning shots, pointing out the errors made or the particular cleverness required to score the winning point.

As far as seeking a deeper intimacy, she could not deny she had thought about it, wondered about it. The trouble was they had been so close for so many years, their affection for one another was more like that of a brother and sister. To make more of it would have felt like incest—something both had acknowledged long ago despite their parents' lingering hopes.

All was not completely lost, however. Brenna's younger sister, Rhiannon, was only in her eleventh year, but just last month had presented their father with a petition, a contract of marriage for herself, drawn in her own hand with every word and phrase labored over as if it were going before the king to be made into law. In it she insisted Lord Randwulf and Lady Servanne recognize the immediate and pressing need to insure the future alliance of their noble house with that of FitzAthelstan. Since both Eleanor and Isobel had chosen to marry indiscreetly (meaning they had fallen in love with the landless brothers LaFer), and Brenna showed no inclination to marry whatsoever, she considered herself, Lady Rhiannon Wardieu d'Amboise, the last hope of salvation. Further to the point, she was the perfect match in temperament and passion for the more reticent William.

Upon hearing it, the prospective groom had remained oddly silent on the matter. He had not laughed aloud when Brenna had told him of the petition, nor had he suffered any prolonged teasing with his usual display of good humor. If anything, he grew downright prickly whenever she broached the subject, and of late, she had even caught him flushing whenever his duties caused him to be in Rhiannon's company.

From a sister's perspective, Brenna supposed she could not fault him for his taste. Rhiannon, like their two older sisters, shared their mother's white-blond hair, cornflower blue eyes, and complexion as pure as milk on snow. Their figures were slender and delicate, their hands unblemished by any labor more damaging than the weaving of threads in a tapestry.

By contrast, Brenna had tough yellow calluses on the pads of her fingers and arms that were more like iron than velvet. Her complexion tended to be more in keeping with nature, lightly tanned with a spray of freckles across the bridge of her nose. Her hair was an equal blending of gold and brown threads, her eyes were a darker, more exotic shade of blue with hints of violet and flecks of indigo to suggest an underlying temper not precisely in keeping with the expected sweet compliance of someone groomed to be the chatelaine of some noble lord's household.

In truth, she had tried to learn patience, she had even tried to learn embroidery once. That had been when Goodwife Biddy had still been alive and in charge of the nursery. Old Blister had known all of Brenna's hiding places and had not shown the least bit of hesitation in storming the male bastions of the castle to root out her charge and drag her back to the classroom. But Brenna had never stayed put for long. She loved her sisters and admired their maidenly skills, but she had preferred the company of her brothers as far back as she could remember. She would sneak off to join them in the tilting yards, buckling on a sword and challenging them in the practice fields despite the dangers and risks that could not be avoided regardless how careful or indulgent the boys might be. After a while, indulgence was a long-forgotten sentiment as she proved she could hold her own with dagger, mace, and sword. A further challenge from Dagobert had put her up on the back of a destrier for the first time when she was but ten years old, and in spite of the rigid social conventions forbidding a woman to ride, much less own, a blooded warhorse, she had so impressed and pleased her father, he had presented her with a stallion sired by his own great champion steed.

As for her supposed indifference to marriage, it wasn't that she didn't want a husband. It was just that she had not yet met the man whose life and destiny she would willingly trade her freedom to share. She had never experienced the warm fuzziness her sisters trilled about constantly, nor had she felt the earth shift beneath her feet or the blood run cold and hot through her veins. And she certainly had never suffered the queasiness of a flock of butterflies let loose in her belly, as Eleanor had described it. Love, in fact, sounded like more of a malady than a happy circumstance anyway, and there were times she watched Isobel and Eleanor—even Rhiannon who circled poor Will like a bird of prey—and wondered at the nonsense of it all. A kiss was nothing more spectacular than a pressing together of lips. What a man and woman did together in bed sounded like an uncomfortable chore, looked like an ignoble thrashing of arms and legs, and inspired only vague feelings of disgust when she saw how slack-lipped, dull-eyed, and witless a man became in the throes of lust.

Mercifully, neither of her parents were strong advocates of contracted marriages, and Lord Randwulf was certainly no ordinary father bent on using his daughters to make sound political unions. Kings already quailed at the sound of his name. Whole armies shrank at the sight of the black-and-gold. Troubadours as far north as Scotland, as far east as Jerusalem retold glorious *chansons de geste* boasting his accomplishments as Crusader, warrior, and sworn enemy of King John. They sang of his years as loyal champion to the dowager Queen Eleanor, and they spoke in awe of his seeming return from the dead to avenge his wrath upon a treacherous bastard brother. And they whispered, even to this day, of his adventures in the forests of England— whispers that had begun to take on the quality of legend, especially in the greenwood of Lincolnshire where there were deeds of outlawry still being attributed to a hooded man who fought like a demon to right the wrongs perpetrated by the king and his evil disciples. This, despite the fact that Black Wolf had not set foot across the Channel in over twenty-five years.

How could a man like that trade his daughter's happiness for mere political gain?

Moreover, Will's mother, Lady Gillian, had taught her more than just how to shoot an arrow. She had been branded and made a guest of the king's prisons when she was not much older than Brenna was now. After escaping, she'd had nowhere to go but the forest, where she had joined the Wolf's band of outlaws and lived among them with no one the wiser for her more delicate attributes until her love for Alaric FitzAthelstan had made her sex difficult to conceal. Even so, she had not relinquished her position of trust or responsibility simply because she had unbound her breasts and allowed her hair to grow. In disguise as Gil of the Golden Eyes, she had proved time and again her skill and deadly accuracy with the Welsh longbow. As Lady Gillian FitzAthelstan, she had personally trained every knight and foot soldier who fought under the blazon of Amboise to have a healthy and lethal respect for the weapon.

"When I saw you just now," Brenna said quietly, "just for a moment, I saw your lady mother standing behind your shoulder."

Will rubbed a hand across the nape of his neck. "Mother would never have been caught out in the open like that. I felt her presence too, more than the heat of your arrow, pinching my nose in reprobation."

"It has only been three months, yet it feels like three years since we lost her. I miss her dreadfully. She was like . . . like a second mother to me."

Will nodded but said nothing. There was nothing to say. Gil Golden had died as she had lived: proud, stubborn, defiant, determined to stand by her husband's side as his peer, not just his bedmate. She had taken a company of the best archers to Roche-au-Moines and led them in the assault against the English mercenary forces. When they had searched the bloody remains of the battlefield, they had found her body, blessedly unmarked save for the single bolt that had pierced her brave heart.

Brenna had been *this close* to winning her father's permission to accompany Lady Gillian and her archers. Only her age—she had not yet turned eighteen—and Lady Servanne's tears had stopped her. That and a particularly thorough search of the supply wagons before they passed through the barbican gates of Château d'Amboise.

"How is your father?" she asked.

"Still devastated. I have tried to help him but he seems to have lost the desire to keep living without her. He eats very little. He never sleeps. He is turning into an old man before my eyes, and there is naught I can do to bring him out of it."

Brenna thought of the passionate love between her own father and mother and knew either one would suffer the same agonies as Lord Alaric should one leave this earth before the other. Thankfully, Lord Randwulf's past injuries had kept him well out of any fighting this time. A knee badly crushed beneath a horse some years back could no longer be trusted to support his weight, and the whole of his right side was riddled with pain from wounds suffered long ago. In three years, he would celebrate his sixtieth birthday, a mark few men with such a violent past lived to achieve.

"And Eduard?" Will asked. "Any news from Blois?"

He was referring to the separate packet of letters usually delivered to Lady Servanne from her daughter-in-law, in which the news was not always as enthusiastic and sanguine as what the son wrote to the father.

"Only that he makes a poor invalid. Lady Ariel sent a message just yesterday begging our forgiveness in advance if she was driven to dent the side of his head with a cauldron."

"She should be thankful he still has a head to dent. Four horses were cut out from beneath him in the battle! And how many sword thrusts did he take? Ten? Twelve? I vow there was hardly any blood left in his veins when we carried him off the field."

"She says he is already trying to use his legs, though he has broken more walking sticks than she can keep supplied by his bedside. And he insists on taking his meals in the great hall so that everyone can see he is alive and still in command of his faculties."

Will nodded. "It was a concern of your father's too. Any sign of weakness and the vultures would have flocked instantly to the walls of Blois Castle. He still attracts the greedy eyes of King John's assassins once or twice a year, and no doubt the price on his head will increase substantially after the role he played in Maine."

"You would think Softsword would be too busy these days to remember old grudges," Brenna sighed. "Father, Eduard, even Robin for pity's sake."

"Once an enemy of the English king, always an enemy of the English king."

"Indeed, but he has so many on his own side of the Channel, why does he persist in plaguing us?"

"Because your father, with but a snap of his fingers, can call up another thousand men to support King Philip should he decide to invade England and drive Lackland into the North Sea. Because Eduard has already proven himself willing to go to any lengths to avenge the death of Arthur of Brittany. And because Robin, firstly, is more than equal to the mantle of all he would inherit should the unthinkable happen to your father, and secondly, because he crippled Lackland's pet viper and left him but a ruined shell of his former self."

"You are speaking of Guy de Gisbourne, of course? The one who thought Robin had such a pretty face, he wanted to splay him on the bed and swiv him?"

Will frowned again. "I might have put it in more delicate terms."

" 'Twas hardly a delicate intention against a thirteen-year-old boy."

"Nonetheless, Robin should have aimed the knife higher and killed him instead of just paring away the few inches of excess flesh that offended his tender sensibilities. Especially now that he has been made Lord High Sheriff of Nottingham."

Brenna laughed. "Gisbourne will have his hands full enough dealing with Lady Ariel's outlaw brother."

Will came to an abrupt halt and stared at her. "How the devil do you know about . . . No. Never mind. I should know better than to ask." He started walking again, his long legs scything through the ferns. Brenna walked dutifully beside him, but in her head she was counting off the paces . . . five . . . six . . . seven . . .

"All right." He stopped again. "How the devil do you know about Lord Henry?"

"Eight," she said. "Your restraint is improving."

"Your father's will dissolve completely if he thinks there are too many wagging tongues inside the castle walls."

"Only one tongue. And actually . . . it belonged to him, so he could only rail at himself if he went looking for a culprit to blame."

"Your father told you about Lord Henry?"

"Well . . . I am sure he did not *know* he was telling me. He was, in truth, having a conversation with Robin and—"

"And you just happened to get your ear caught in the door?"

"No," she said with an elaborate moue. "I was in the stable and overheard them talking."

"Dare I ask exactly what you overheard?"

"Well, Father was angry. He called Henry de Clare a young fool who had not the sense God gave a goat. He said if it were him living under the king's nose, he would surely do it quietly and discreetly, he would not join a band of thieves and misfits who go about committing all manner of mischief against the king's sheriff."

Will sighed. "He has not joined them. He has simply learned to live in harmony with them."

Brenna shrugged off the distinction. "At any rate, Father is appalled that scion of the noble house of Pembroke—the nephew of William Marshal, for heaven's sake—would resort to thievery and skulduggery to make his way in the world. More than that, he thinks Lord Henry's antics could even become . . . uhh . . . compromising to a certain progeny of royal blood who mysteriously disappeared about the same time Lord Henry took to wearing the robes of a mendicant monk."

Will's shock was complete, and he came to an abrupt halt. "Do you realize what you have just said could get you killed if you repeated it in the wrong ear?"

"I have no intentions of repeating it in anyone's ear. I only want to know if it is true, that Lord Henry remains in England because he is safeguarding the Lost Princess of Brittany."

"Brenna—" Will's hazel eyes were scanning the forest around them. It was dangerous to be speaking of lost princesses and nobles-turned-outlaw, regardless of where they were, and she held up her hand to ward off a well-deserved rebuke. The gesture was halted midway, as was whatever Will had been going to say.

"Did you hear something?"

"I thought—"

"Listen." He hissed her to silence and pointed into the trees. "It came from over there."

Neither one of them moved a muscle. Only their eyes flicked down to the black, spongy earth beneath their feet to isolate the subtle vibrations that could only be caused by thundering hoofbeats.

"Close," Will whispered. "Not a horse. A boar, perhaps. And a big one."

They both heard the distant echo of a voice then, not roaring with the challenge of a hunter but reverberating with the shock of pain.

"Robin!" Brenna gasped. "It must be."

But Will had already broken into a run, plunging through the mist and shadows, his bow unslung and an arrow nocked for action.

2

At some point Brenna and Will parted, running at divergent angles to form a wide V and thus cover more ground between them. The tearing, thrashing sound of hoofbeats grew louder, more distinct, as did the angry grunts and enraged screams of a half-mad boar. Closer still and they could smell the telltale sourness of rot and offal that clung to the filthy beast, and they could hear it panting and snorting in a frenzy of bloodlust.

The trees and shadows were a hindrance now, not a haven, and as Brenna ran along the tracts of decaying leaves, she called out Robin's name. Will was making as much noise, if not more, partly to draw Robin's attention, partly to draw that of the boar. Both Will and Brenna had their bows unslung and arrow nocked, for boars were not known for their slow wits. They were cunning and devious and could charge from the underbrush to impale a man on their tusks before the threat was even identified.

"Robin! Damn you, answer!"

"Here!" came a hollow-sounding reply. "I am here!"

Brenna veered toward the source of the shout and saw Will do the same, converging from opposite sides on a deep, narrow gully. Robin stood at one end, at the other a red-eyed, slavering brute easily eight hundred pounds in weight. Robin had his dagger clutched in his fist, the blade glinting wet and red its full length. He was covered in dirt and leaves, and there was blood running from a gash over his temple, mingling with the sweat to plaster the chestnut waves of his hair to his face and throat. His lips were curled back in a snarl that perfectly mirrored the one on the boar's face as it lowered its head and gouged its hooves into the ground in preparation for a final lunge. Each scuff of a cloved hoof caused a spray of blood to erupt from a slash in its throat, but the damage was neither painful enough nor debilitating enough to deter it from taking one last charge at his cornered quarry.

Almost as one, Will and Brenna raised their bows, took aim, and fired. Both arrows struck simultaneously, dead center on the low, furrowed brow. The impact of the steel arrowheads split the rock-hard bone of the skull and lifted the beast up and back onto its stubby hind legs. It came down hard and stood absolutely still for as long as it took a syrupy pendant of blood to run the length of its snout. It then heeled sideways, the legs buckling beneath it, the bulk of the corpse landing with a resounding thud on the gully floor.

Robin straightened slowly out of his crouch, a hand cradling his ribs. Brenna was already on her way down the steep side of the embankment, skidding her heels in the crumbling black earth to regulate the haste of her descent. Will nocked another arrow in his bow and skewered it straight through the boar's heart to insure against any chance of a miraculous recovery.

"Are you all right?" Brenna asked.

"Damned cod-sucking swine came at me from nowhere. Tore the bow right out of my hand then picked me up and tossed me into this pit. I managed to get up a tree, but the bastard kept ramming it until he brought it and me down."

"There were plenty more you could have climbed."

"Did I know where the devil you two were, or how long I might be forced to keep a perch in the boughs?"

"You could have shouted," she said. "Or whistled. We would have heard you."

"I was perfectly in control."

"Yes. We can see that. We can also hear Sparrow now: 'Addle-wit! Groutnoll! Great hulking lummock! Good St. Cyril and all the martyrs deliver me from fools and nithings!'"

Robin put a hand to the cut on his temple and scowled at the smear of blood that came away on his fingers. "It is barely a scratch."

"And that?" She pointed to a wide slash in his tunic.

He followed her finger and pulled the gap in the cloth wider to expose the well-muscled rack of ribs. The skin was broken where a tusk had grazed him, and the surrounding flesh was already starting to turn an ugly, mottled blue.

"Sparrow will, of course, praise you until your ears ring. A sennight before the last and largest tournament of the season and you break your ribs on a boar's tusk instead of seeking the safety of a high tree limb."

Robin glared at the twitching carcass. "The day I fear a boar will be the day I wrap my spurs in flour sacking and give them to my grandchildren to use as trowels. And the ribs are not broken," he added, wincing as he probed at the discolored flesh. "Only bruised."

"Bruised, broken . . . it makes little difference. You know full well Sparrow will not allow you to participate in the tourney if he suspects you are in less than prime fighting condition."

Robin's glare lost some of its ferocity. He was near the mirror image of their father, a wealth of muscled splendor carried proudly across the chest and shoulders. His hair was cut short and straight across the nape in the French fashion, too thick with waves to hold any true style, but dark enough to give his handsome face the prominence it deserved. He had been an undefeated champion in the lists these past four years, yet the very steel that made his opponents fall by the wayside like so much chaff was itself a puddle of old candlewax under the scowling despotism of the diminutive, recalcitrant seneschal of Château d'Amboise.

"Sparrow has no say one way or the other on how I choose or choose not to spend my time."

"Brave words," Brenna allowed. "Have you ever said them to his face?"

Her brother cursed and started brushing the clods of dirt

off his sleeves and hose. He flexed his arms as he did so and stretched his torso side to side to test the extent of the tenderness in his ribs. "Prince Louis himself will be at Château Gaillard to host the events. The best knights in France, Normandy, and Gascony will be in attendance, with the winner being declared champion over all. There is even a rumor the Prince of Darkness will make an appearance."

Brenna groaned and rolled her eyes as she recited, "The most feared knight in all the Holy Roman Empire, reputed to be half man, half beast, and wholly ungodly."

"He has never ventured into Normandy before," Robin said, objecting to the sarcasm in her voice. "Those who *have* seen him joust say he comes down the lists like a dark wind from hell, his claws as sharp as those on the falcon emblazoned on his shield."

"And you want to fight him?"

"I *intend* to fight him, and to send him limping back to perdition with the name of Robert Wardieu d'Amboise emblazoned on his arse forever! I have trained for it, am ready for it, and deserve it by God, and nothing so trivial as a bruised rib or an elfin demagogue will deny me my due."

"Be that as it may," Will said dryly, "I would still advise you to keep your ribs out of Sparrow's eyesight . . . at least until you are well along on the road to Rouen."

Robin spared a frosty glance for his friend. "And how do you propose I do that? He has eyes in every rafter, ears in every *garde robe*, and puts himself under my nose with less warning than a cabbage fart."

Brenna laughed. "Such was your fate to be the firstborn and *charmed* as Sparrow seems to insist. 'Tis why he feels the everpresent need to safeguard you body and soul for whatever momentous destiny he believes awaits you. We common seedlings, on the other hand, could walk through the gates bloodied and bludgeoned and he would only sniff at our carelessness."

"Your sympathy warms my heart."

"It should warm your cockles, brother dearest, since we are your two best allies at the moment, for if you are not permitted to attend Gaillard, neither of us is likely to be venturing forth either. Moreover, we have had years of experience skulking in and out of the château without the weight of all that nobility drawing an eye toward us." She stood back a pace and examined his ragged appearance. "A clean tunic, fresh hose, and no one should be the wiser for your failure to put Sir Tusker in his place."

"I will know," he said gruffly, the pride chafing in his voice.

"So will I. So will Will'um. So will the trees and the mist and the smaller beasts of the forest who still tremble and quake at your passage. But unless you spread yourself like a crucifix on the floor and confess the transgression, *Sparrow* need not know. In the meantime, you will be left in peace to heal and to contemplate the advantages of having *some* devious bones in your body."

"I can be just as devious as any of you," Robin protested.

"Faugh! Your cheek twitches like a hare's nose when you tell a falsehood," Brenna teased. "And your throat turns a most glorious shade of red. If you had a deceitful hair on your head we would be hard-pressed to find it amid all the honor and nobility."

"I will concede I do not enjoy deceiving anyone by word or deed. Nor am I as expert as either of you at evading the truth. At the same time, I am neither as virtuous or as self-righteous as you would make me out to be."

Both Will and Brenna arched an eyebrow, their silence an eloquent enough rebuttal.

"Fine," he declared. "I shall defer to your superior knowledge of chicanery."

"*And* my superior skills in the forest," Brenna added.

Robin looked askance at Will, who shrugged and admitted, "She caught me fair on the last round."

"Which makes the two of us even, by my count," Robin said. "Two wins apiece."

"I only see two arrows in Sir Tusker," she retorted smartly. "Which gives Will and me an extra hit—leaving the two of *you* tied with a brace of strikes—and me ahead with three."

Robin's steely eyes narrowed. A split second later Will's did the same as the alignment of loyalties took a noticeable shift.

"A questionable resolution at best," he murmured. "Since it was clearly *my* arrow that felled the beast."

"I think not," she argued. "I distinctly saw mine strike first."

Will looked at Robin, who held up his bloodied dagger. "It could well have been my stroke along the jugular, for all the blood he was spraying."

The three crossed to where the dead boar lay steaming on the crush of leaves. The two arrows that protruded from the skull were seated so closely together they could have been fired from the same bow. The slash in his throat was deep enough to have soaked the ground red beneath him and intoxicate a feasting swarm of black ants.

"I see nothing for it but to declare a draw," Robin said, straightening.

"A pox on your draw, brother dear. We still have a few miles of forest between here and the château. First one to reach the gates—with the biggest trophy in hand—wins the day?"

Robin spit in the palm of his hand and held it out. Brenna did likewise, and Will made it unanimous. A minute later the gully was empty but for the soft layer of mist that poured over the sides to fill the hollow.

Brenna split off and ran in the direction of the river. She guessed, by the quivering oval patches of pewter gray that broke through the uppermost layer of tree branches, there was perhaps an hour or two of daylight left in the outer world. The inner world of the forest would have far less, but she was not worried. Having seen the gully, she knew where she was, knew the location of the river, knew where to intersect the hidden tract the villagers of Amboise used when they wanted to take their wares to Blois without paying a toll. She also knew of a place on the river where great fat salmon swam into the shallow pools to feed in the quiet water. Robin would doubtless be trying for a deer—which he would not find so late in the day and reeking of sweat. Will would be clever enough to search the area around the gully to see if the boar had a family it was protecting. But if she could skewer a plump, succulent salmon, she knew it would win a resounding round of praise from her father. He particularly loved the fish poached in wine, smothered in onions and thyme, washed down with a flagon of his prized *pierrefitte*.

Since the targets were no longer two-legged, there was no need to exercise more caution than she normally would in the greenwood. No need to play the fool either, and for that she kept her ears tuned to the sound of the wind in the upper boughs, the angry squabbling of squirrels and hare in the knee-deep ferns, the chatter of birds overhead who, like old women on a fence, stopped their gossiping long enough to mark Brenna's passage, then resumed their bickering as if nothing had interrupted. Gil had taught her the forest was full of alarms if one took the time to become familiar with them. The crunch of a leaf, the snap of a twig, the sound of furry feet scrambling away were all indications of an unexpected presence.

She ran with an easy, loping gait, her bow slung over her arm and the long cable of her braid thumping between her shoulders on each step. Her breath was starting to take on a ghostly quality in the cooling air and the fine hairs that had sprung free around her neck and temples were curling against the thin sheen of moisture that slicked her skin.

She had no desire to work up another chilling sweat, and while she loped along, she unfastened the laces of her leather jerkin, letting the sides hang open so the air passed freely through the looser weave of her shirt. Force of habit made her glide to a halt every few hundred yards to listen to the forest. Once she thought she heard the echo of a church bell, a tiny, tinny sound far off in the distance. There was a monastery farther up the river, and the monks were meticulous if not downright fanatical about gathering their flock to prayer. It was likely the vespers bell, which would be bringing the mendicants off the fields and out of the gardens after a hard day's work.

Another familiar sound brought her head tilting to one side. She was within bowshot of the river, two hundred yards more or less, and could not only hear the clatter of the water passing over the rocky shoreline, she could smell the deeper, damper musk in the air.

Moving slower now, stealthier through the tangle of saplings and gorse, Brenna listened for any alarms her presence might make. Deer, hare, and other small creatures would be sidling down to the embankment for their evening drinks. If she startled them off too suddenly, any fish in the pools would heed the warning and swim into the middle of the river. In her favor, it was also the time of day when colonies of blackbirds and swallows were returning to their rookeries in the forest, and they were making enough noise to cover anything short of a shout.

Another hundred yards and she could see the River Loire through the thinning trees. It moved leisurely toward the sea, a hundred fifty miles to the west, like a wide ribbon of molten silver. The tops of the trees on the opposite bank were burnished bronze by the settling sun, and high above, the purpled bellies of wind-dragged clouds wore crowns of pink and gold and amber. Dusk would not be far behind, all grays and blues and darkest blacks.

Creeping closer to the bank, she used a fallen tree to cloak her movements as she emerged from the edge of the forest and slipped down onto the wide, shingled shoreline. The bank here was flat, not very wide—there were perhaps ten feet between the ledge of jutting roots and the silky rush of water. This particular pool was tucked into an elbow of rocks, shadowed by the huge oaks and pines that crowded the shore, the trapped water so still and dark it looked like spilled ink. And whether it was because the closeness of the trees had exaggerated every squeak and snap, or because she simply felt overly exposed standing under an open sky after so many hours of moving from shadow to shadow, the sudden unearthly silence brought her to a frozen standstill.

A cool shiver rippled down her spine as she recalled a story Sparrow once told her of a pool in England, cursed for a thousand years to languish in utter silence despite being in the heart of a greenwood teeming with creatures of every size and description. He further claimed that Robin had been conceived in those magical waters, and his conception had broken the spell and brought a cacophony of sound to the forest such as had never been heard there before.

But that was England and this was France and Sparrow was always full of such tales, embellishing them shamelessly with his own exploits so that they rarely were recounted twice the same way. She certainly did not believe in faeries or magic spells (although when she was younger, she did believe that Sparrow could fly). She believed in what she saw, and in this case it was only the shadows pressed hard against the water, black on black. It was likely the rocks and few sparse trees on the narrow promontory that were buffering the sounds from the wind and the water beyond. As for curses and ill-fated lovers . . .

Brenna squeezed her eyes tightly shut and opened them again quickly but this was no trick of the failing light. It was not an elf and certainly not a tragic prince agonizing over a lost love. It was a half-naked satyr bent down on one knee by the waters edge, a gleaming, bejeweled dagger clutched in his right hand, raised to strike.

3

It was not a satyr, of course. It was a man. A very big man leaning over a flat rock and using his knife to clean and gut a fish. Brenna's first instinct was to tighten her grip on her bow and pull tension into the string. She had the brief advantage, for he was not yet aware of her presence, and a clean shot, taken now, could certainly rid the forest of a poacher, if he was one, or disarm a potential threat before it had a chance to develop. She had no idea who he was. His face was turned away, his profile shielded by a long, shaggy mane of jet-black hair. His hose and boots were black as well, the latter worn high to the knee and bound with rawhide strapping. In the thickening dusk, she thought she might have been mistaken about the state of his upper body, that he wore a buff-colored hauberk of padded leather. But no. The only armor he wore was the incredible bulk of solid muscle that strained and flexed with the slightest movement he asked of it. Even the powerful thews that sculpted his thighs seemed to challenge the bounds of the stretched woolen hose, and his arms, solid and splendid, were like oak, tanned and weathered and bulging with untapped strength.

She doubted he was anything so mundane as a poacher in spite of the fact he was trespassing in a private forest miles from any common tract. Judging by the sheer size of him, he was too well fed to have been subsisting off roots and berries; he ate meat and goodly quantities of it on a regular basis to maintain his superb physique. Having grown up in a household of knights and champions, she could recognize a member of the Order if he wore sackcloth and rode an ass, yet if this man was a knight, what was he doing out here, alone, catching and cooking his own dinner?

The thought took her eyes away from the stranger for a split second but she saw no animal of any kind tethered nearby. She saw some clothes—a shirt, tunic, and surcoat by the look of it—draped over a boulder nearby, and beside it a swordbelt with an enormous double-edged blade slung through the steel and leather scabbard. Higher up on the bank was a saddle pouch propped beside what appeared to be the makings of a fire. A small pile of dried leaves and pine knots had been gathered and stacked into a smoking pyramid.

A sudden splash brought Brenna's heart pounding into her throat again, and she added more tension to her bow-string as the stranger finished rinsing the fish and rose to his feet. He rose a very long way, for he was tall. Taller than Will and possibly even Robin—either of whom she would have gladly loved to hear emerging from the woods behind her. She considered ducking and creeping back to the forest's edge, but she could see the stranger's profile now and knew that any slight move she made would draw his attention. It was a handsome profile, all planes and angles, with a deep, square jaw and a wide, sensuous mouth. He might have been whistling under his breath as he worked with the fish, for when he turned fully around, his lips were still slightly puckered, a shape they held for another two frozen seconds as he looked up and saw her standing by the skeleton of the tree.

He came to a complete, startled halt. Even his breathing seemed to become trapped somewhere, keeping his chest swelled as he stared across the ten or so paces that separated them. She was surrounded by shadows but there was enough light reflecting off the river and the distant shore-line to gild both her and the tautly held longbow in glowing detail.

She forced herself to exhale slowly and evenly. His eyes were commanding all of her attention, for they were like those of a big cat, luminous and glowing, an eerie shade somewhere between palest green and gray, given even more prominence by long ebony lashes and a bold, straight nose. His hair was very black, very thick, brushed back from a wide forehead and left to fall in careless waves over shoulders broad enough to humble two ordinary men. His jaw was chiseled from a block of granite, the chin cleft by a sharp dividing crevice that served to emphasize what could only be a perpetual shading of dark stubble, no matter how keen a blade he used to shave. It was a hard face, with an uncompromising mouth twisted now in an expression that suggested he was not a man easily amused by arrows pointed at his chest, regardless if they were held by a man or a woman.

His gaze, which had been studying Brenna's features with equal intensity, followed the smooth arch of her neck down to the open lacing of her jerkin. Her breasts were not overly large, but they were firm and well shaped, and she watched his eyes trace their obvious contours, clearly visible beneath the thin weave of her shirt. She thought she saw a flicker of surprise as they confirmed her sex, but then he was all business again, assessing the length and stoutness of her bow, weighing it against the slenderness of her arm and the strength it was taking to maintain the unwavering tension in the bowstring.

"An unusual weapon for a woman to carry about," he said quietly. "I would have thought a hunting bow more suited to size and strength."

Without communicating her intention until the last split second, Brenna drew back on the string and snapped her fingers clear, sending the arrow streaking past his ear to *f-f-thud* into the trunk of a tree half a dozen paces behind him. The fletching had barely left her fingers before she was nocking another arrow to the string. And while the echo of the strike still hummed on the air, she had it drawn back and aimed dead center of the broad, hairless chest again.

The stranger slowly turned his head, keeping his eyes locked on hers until the last possible moment before casting a glance over his shoulder. The tree was young, the trunk no more than eight inches across, but it was oak, as hard a wood as could be found in these woods, and the steel tip of the arrow had been driven cleanly through the solid core to protrude more than a hand's width on the other side.

His mouth had a slightly less casual twist to it as he looked back. "Impressive. You have my full attention, I assure you."

"Who are you? What are you doing in these woods?"

"I might ask you the same thing."

"You might," she agreed. "But I have the bow and I am in no mood to waste any more arrows on pointless demonstrations."

He considered the unspoken threat behind her words and offered up what might have been considered a dazzling smile under any other conditions. "I am in these woods because I am lost. I took a wrong turn some miles back and was beginning to think I might fall off the edge of the earth before I found my way back to the road."

"This is not the road," she pointed out.

"A road, a river." He shrugged his shoulders to indicate they were one and the same thing. "I have been following it since Orléans."

"Following it to where?"

"To where my business takes me," he answered with deliberate avoidance.

"It may take you to hell in a moment, sirrah, if you are not more candid with your answers."

"I find it difficult to be candid—or anything else for that matter—when I am speaking to the wrong end of an arrow."

"Whereas you think it more warming to the heart to speak with a knife clutched in your hand?"

He looked down and seemed genuinely surprised to see it there. "An unintentional discourtesy, I assure you. And hardly a comparable threat. In fact"—he smiled again, a truly ravishing display of strong, even teeth—"no manner of one whatsoever if you would care to relieve me of it."

He reversed the blade with a flip of his wrist and extended it, hilt first, toward her.

Brenna's skin had been undergoing all manner of unusual sensations, growing cool and tight across her breasts when he had inspected them, flushing warm and dry where his words seemed to make physical contact with her flesh. His voice was deep, his French tainted with an accent she could not quite place, but combined with the fact he was a stranger and a foreigner, it caused her to remember the conversation she and Will had been having about assassins only moments before they had gone to Robin's rescue.

The last assassin the English king had sent to Amboise had been a handsome foreigner recruited from Aragon who spoke with similarly rolled vowels and a soft burr. He had assumed the guise of a troubadour, complete with mottled hose, particolored jerkin, and a repertoire of blood-warming *chansons d'amour*. He sang well enough, and might even had made it as far as the private solar shared by Lord Randwulf and his romantic lady wife had Brenna not noticed his fingers, pink and skinless from too recent an acquaintance with his harp strings.

She looked instinctively to the stranger's hand and, expecting it to be as strong and well formed as the rest of him, she was mildly taken aback to see the extensive scarring on the fingers, knuckles, even the wrist of the one he extended, as if the flesh had been scalded in boiling oil or scorched by fire.

The iced jade eyes followed her stare then waited until it returned to his face. The knife was winking at her, reflecting points of light from the river, and she almost smiled herself. Did he really think her so foolish as to accept his casual invitation to disarm him? More than likely she would be the one who found herself weaponless and dazed, the blade held to her throat.

"You may toss it over there, beside your sword. The fish too," she added as an afterthought.

The curve in his mouth spread wider. "Indeed, a carp can be a dangerous weapon."

The calm, unnerving stare held hers long enough for a warm flush of blood to bloom in her cheeks and spread down her throat. His gaze kept her pinioned, kept the heat in her complexion at its peak as he tossed first the knife, then the fish over to where his sword rested against the boulder. Then to further mock the act of surrender, he lifted his hands and laced them together at the back of his neck.

The movement and the stance only served to embolden the massive display of muscle and brawn she had thus far managed to ignore. But now the last of the sky's fading light played across his skin like teasing gold fingers, luring her eyes down to the hard, boardlike belly, the narrow waist and hips. His legs were long and planted apart for balance, and even though her eyes did not stray there, every pore and hair on her body tingled with awareness at the size of the bulge that swelled the juncture of his thighs.

An unexpected wave of giddiness washed through her, and the irony was not lost. Here then was the first man who inspired her to stare, to really and truly stare, and he was most likely a spy or a thief or an assassin in the pay of the English king.

"Your name?" she demanded, her voice a little raspier than she would have preferred.

"Renaud. Griffyn Renaud. And yours?"

"You have no need to know it."

"Oh, but I do," he said evenly. "It has been a good many years since anyone has crept up on me unawares. Even longer since anyone has disarmed me and threatened me with impalement . . . and then lived to tell of it."

This last was said so softly she nearly missed it. She did not miss the look in his eye, or the revenge it promised. Startled by the insinuation that he was merely humoring her, biding his time until the tables could be turned, she glanced once again over her shoulder, wondering if any part of his arrogance was bolstered by way of an accomplice watching them from the woods.

"Surely you have not walked all the way from Orléans by yourself?"

The smile was back, this time with a spark of genuine humor reflected in his eyes. "Surely not. Though I am surprised you are only just inquiring now."

"You have a companion?"

"I do."

Brenna stepped closer to the river and turned so that she could cover more of the embankment while still keeping the stranger under the point of her arrow. "If he is armed, or is thinking of trying anything foolish . . ."

His eyes had the amazing ability to convey a changed expression without altering their shape in the least. Nothing on his face betrayed the fact it was only a grudging respect for her bow arm that was keeping his temper in check, yet the pale glimmer in his eyes was clearly telling her it was the height of foolishness for a woman on her own to be engaging him in a battle of wits and wills.

"I promise you, he has no carp on him. Shall I summon him hither?"

Brenna cursed the two hot patches flaring in her cheeks and nodded. The gray-green eyes shifted to the trees and he curled his lower lip between his teeth, splitting the stillness of the air with a single shrill whistle.

Almost immediately he was answered by a faint but strident response. The ground thundered with the sound of hoofbeats, and a moment later, a foreboding curtain of mist was pushed out of the trees, preceding the explosive arrival of an equally gray and demonic giant of a destrier.

He was no common forester's beast, that much could be seen in the wide breast and powerful flanks. He was fully, if somewhat plainly, caparisoned; the saddle was of good leather and the saw-toothed cloth beneath it was wool, but devoid of any trim or cresting to betray the owner's identity or origins. There was a thick, rolled bundle attached to the back of the saddle from which a few links of chain mail protruded. Both the horse and the gear could have been stolen, of course, but Brenna did not believe it any longer than it took for the stallion to prance to his master's side, the velvet nostrils flared to snort out a frothy inquiry.

"Centaur, behave yourself," Renaud murmured, unlacing one of his hands from his nape to rub it affectionately down the tapered snout. "Can you not see we are the prisoners of this bold lady archer?"

"*This* is your companion?" Brenna asked.

"The only one I have needed thus far on my journey, although"—his gaze fell once again to rove speculatively over the soft thrust of her breasts—"it looks to be a cold night ahead and I imagine I could be persuaded to share my blanket."

Brenna's fingers tightened longingly on the bowstring. "You may find yourself in a hot place sooner than you expect, M'sieur Renaud. Do you still refuse to tell me your business here in these woods?"

"You have no need to know it," he said lightly, using her own words to add insult.

"Then you leave me no choice but to take you to my father—the man whose land you happen to be trespassing upon and whose fish you happen to be poaching. *He* has every right to know, especially if your business concerns him in any way."

"Is he as likely to show the same hospitality to a lost and weary traveler as his daughter?"

"He is likely to disembowel you and toss your liver to the dogs if you give any false—or insolent—answers to his questions."

Renaud gave the horse's muzzle another scratch and stared calmly back at her. His face was handsome beyond decency, no small part of her could deny it, yet for all the warmth he exuded and friendliness he inspired, it might well have been carved from the same block of marble that shaped the rest of him. The smile that came and went so effortlessly was no more than a practiced arrangement of muscles, heart-stopping to some no doubt, but to Brenna it suggested he was dangerous and deceitful, and probably could not be trusted beyond the blink of an eye.

Even as she debated his credibility, he was studying the faint tremors that were causing the laces of her jerkin to shiver with each rise and fall of her breasts. Her arm was tiring, the muscles beginning to cramp from the strain. His mouth curved up at the corner and he started to lower his hands, but Brenna's voice cut short whatever his intentions might have been.

"If you touch your sword or your knife, or reach for a weapon of any kind, I will shoot your horse first. Then you."

The pale eyes shot back to hers and she felt their heat, their power, their fury cut clean through her flesh and scrape on her bones.

His voice, when it came to her through the gloom, was a soft snarl. "I think it would give me great pleasure to teach you some manners, demoiselle."

"It would be difficult to teach something you so obviously lack yourself," she retorted smartly. "Now get dressed. We have a long walk ahead of us."

4

The first challenge of manners came before they had cleared the campsite. They had not yet shaken the wet earth from the riverbank off their boots when Brenna announced her intention to ride the stallion home while he walked a suitable distance ahead.

A knight, armored or not, was a formidable opponent on horseback. Destriers were trained to charge, lunge, rear, pivot, and trample, all through subtle commands delivered by the rider's thighs, calves, feet. Man and beast learned to fight as one unit, and a single knight, mounted, could easily lay waste to a dozen men on foot. Stripped of his horse and weapons, however, and forced to use his feet for something other than swinging a stirrup, a knight was reduced to a mere man. And a mere man was no match for Brenna Wardieu, regardless how much she admired the breadth of his shoulders or the long, fluid strides that swallowed the miles beneath him.

Clearly, the thought of her riding while he walked was as ludicrous as the notion of her being able to control the highly strung temperament of a blooded warhorse. Just as clearly, he had expected to see her clutch at the reins and tumble out of the saddle the first time he gave his destrier a softly trilled signal. But Brenna had been anticipating his deviousness and was ready. She weathered the high, rearing lurches and kept her seat expertly through the violent twists and leaps meant to spill her on her rump. Moreover, when she proved she could still nock and fire an arrow from the back of a rampaging charger, another quiet whistle ended the confrontation.

Renaud had said nothing as he extracted the arrow from the soft earth an inch in front of his toe, but he had promised her the world through his eyes as he held the shaft in both hands and snapped it in two.

Full darkness had settled over them like a thick sable blanket by the time the man and rider made their way through the forest and emerged at the small village of Amboise. There was a single fire blazing in the square; the only other signs of life came from the glowing red halo that surrounded the open doors of the smithy. Most of the cottages had been shuttered and barred for the night and would remain steadfastly so until morning. The villagers were a superstitious lot and believed the devil roamed abroad in human guise at night, searching for souls to steal.

The gray stone fortifications of the castle dominated the high ridge above the village. Seen in daylight the tall, crenellated battlements were a comfort to those who lived and toiled in its protective shadows. At night, with its darkened ramparts, towers, and spires etched against the sky, it became the lair of its legendary master, the Black Wolf of Amboise, and none who valued the seamless contours of their throats would dare venture near the fiery maw of its gates without invitation. Two pitch-soaked torches blazed in iron cressets on either side of the barbican towers, the only lights visible from outside the forty-foot walls. There was only one entrance and only one approach. The crusader who had built the original keep over a century ago had kept the swift-running river at its back and dug a deep, wide trench to protect the remaining three sides. He had stopped short of cutting into the river to flood it, but in the past few years, with the political strife constant between England and France, and loyalties changing every day, Lord Randwulf's men had completed the work. The moat was now a vein of the River Loire, black and turbulent, with a draw that could be suspended to seal off the entrance if needed.

The outer battlement walls were twelve feet thick, faced with rough-cut limestone blocks mortared around a core of rock rubble. The encircling sentry walks were nearly a mile in length and were patrolled day and night by guards in full armor, each boldly wearing the device of Randwulf de la Seyne Sur Mer: a sinister depiction of a prowling wolf, the gold head full-faced and snarling against an ebony field.

The barbican towers that flanked the entrance were in themselves small fortresses, the walls hollowed to house passageways for archers, the roof fitted with chutes for pouring boiling oil and pitch on the heads of unwanted guests. Once inside, the castle held true to the design of most Norman strongholds, with the inner stone keep being the central structure around which other buildings and wards had been added over the generations. The keep itself was the tallest and best-fortified structure, as it would be the site of the final defense should the castle come under attack. The massive stone tower rose sixty feet from its widened base, buttressed by earthworks and protected by a second draw and moat. Crouched around the outer ring of the moat were the barracks, stables, armory, psaltery, cook house, bath house, smithy, and weavers' cottages—all comprising a small community contained within the inner curtain wall. This second wall was no easily breachable defense either, but a block-and-mortar barrier fifteen feet high and twelve feet thick, guarded by double-leaf iron doors hinged between tall, square watchtowers.

Between the outer wall and the inner was a bailey that contained, among other things, the practice yards and tilting grounds, orchards and gardens, also the pens and stables that housed the livestock. Sealed off from the outer world, the château was completely self-sufficient and had been designed to withstand a siege lasting many months.

To outsiders, the château was a menacing display of military efficiency.

To Brenna, it was simply home.

"Hold up," she called softly as she eased the destrier to a halt just before the drawbridge. She had seen movement beneath the portcullis and guessed Robin and Will were there waiting for her, wanting to see her prize and gloat over their own paltry hares and piglets. A belligerent knight and a prime warhorse should be more than adequate to claim victory, however, and she was smiling even before she saw the shadows walking hesitantly into the glare of the torchlights.

"Brenna? Is that you?"

"Indeed it is, brother dear. And see what manner of prize I have brought for you to admire? A poacher, a trespasser, a churl who refused to even give his name until I tickled him with my bow."

Robin and Will both emerged from the shadowy maw of the arched entrance. They had swords strapped to their hips and were followed by a dozen men from the castle guard who fanned out behind them, crossbows in hand, poised to defend against any intruders lurking in the darkness beyond.

"A hale and hearty evening all around," Robin murmured.

"Bright enough to chase fireflies," she said, giving the proper, specific reply to assure the Amboise men she was not being coerced into bringing a hostile inside the walls. Had she answered any other way, Griffyn Renaud would be dead.

Instead, Robin walked forward, his boots echoing on the wood planks. His gaze barely touched on the stranger as he watched Brenna swing her leg over the front of the saddle and slide nimbly to the ground.

"You certainly do take a challenge to heart," he said, admiring the huge gray stallion. "Dare I ask where you found the unlucky fellow?"

"By the river. He was poaching Father's best fishing hole."

"I was attempting to ease the rumbling in my belly," Renaud said on a sigh. "I was not aware I was trespassing, or that a single fish—and a rather small one as it happened— would have me stretched out on a rack."

"We all tend toward caution these days," Robin allowed. "Did she hurt you?"

The question was asked as if it was a normal occurrence, and Renaud's jaw flexed once before he answered. "Only my pride."

Robin laughed. "Then you have fared better than most, my friend. My sister sharpens her teeth on poachers."

"He gave his name as Renaud," Brenna offered lightly. "But because he would part with no other information, I thought it best to bring him here and give him, perhaps, to Littlejohn, who would be more than happy to loosen his tongue."

"That may well be," her brother said slowly, "for he has not cracked any heads lately and his blood is running a little high. Renaud?" He was studying the knight's face, and in this he had the benefit of the torches blazing behind him, throwing hot yellow light on the sharply defined features. "The name feels as if it should mean something to me."

The stranger, his elf-shot eyes revealing nothing, crossed his arms over his chest and smiled. "Robert Wardieu d'Amboise, as I live and breathe."

Robin's frown deepened. "I fear you still have the advantage, sirrah."

"Five years ago, the haslitude at Gascon. A single-combat match between two nineteen-year-old striplings who had just earned their spurs."

Robin drew in a deep, startled breath. "Renaud! Griffyn Renaud de Verdelay! Christ Jesus on the cross! What black pit in hell has spit you back up onto the earth?"

"The deepest, naturally."

"Naturally!" Robin reached out and clasped Renaud's forearm, laughing like a fool as he called to Will. "Come and see the prize Brenna has brought us! God's good grace, I can scarcely believe my eyes! Griffyn Renaud de Verdelay!"

He pulled the grinning knight forward into a hearty embrace and clapped him several times on the back and shoulder before releasing him.

Brenna stared at her brother as if he had gone mad, and

when Will joined them, he fared no better for he could only answer her questioning gaze with a frown and a shrug.

"Griffyn Renaud ... William FitzAthelstan, my very good friend. Will! We have here the only man in Christendom who caused me to visit an armorer after the joust to have my helm bashed back into a recognizable enough shape to pry it off my head. The only man whose rampager"—he stopped and peered again at the gray—"good God, can it be the same wily beast? The one who gave Sir Tristan as good a thumping as he got in twenty ... or was it twenty-one? ... runs!"

"Actually, it was twenty-three," Griffyn said easily. "A record that stands to this day, the last I heard. And it would have been twenty-four if the judges had not stopped it and declared it too cruel for the horses to carry on."

"They gave me the win on points," Robin said, sobering briefly. " 'Twas the only time I was discomfited being declared champion of the tourney."

"Not too discomfited to refuse your winnings," Renaud reminded him.

"I refused your horse and armor," came the retort. "And came looking for you afterward to give you half of what I earned ... but you were already gone. Vanished without a trace."

"I had ... commitments."

Robin grinned again and shook his head in happy disbelief. "And here you stand now, sprung from nowhere, as alive and fit as ever I have judged a dead man to be. You know, of course, that you are. Dead, I mean. Split in two by ... Ivo the Crippler, so we heard."

"Ivo? That larded pullet? He is taking credit for my demise? The last time we met on the field, Centaur refused to run, knowing it to be a waste of energy. A trot was all that was needed to put enough force behind the lance to roll him out of the saddle and bounce him on the ground."

Robin threw his head back and laughed. Will obviously believed the story could be true and would have laughed too if Brenna's heel had not found his toe.

"It does not change the fact he was surly and rude and trespassing," she insisted. "And too secretive even to tell me where he had been or where he was going."

Renaud's smile did not quite affect both sides of his mouth equally as he glanced her way. "If you will recall, I did mention I had been following the river from Orléans. And I would not have been alone had Fulgrin elected to remain with me instead of striking out on his own."

"Fulgrin?"

"My . . . man. I am loath to call him squire, for he rarely listens to a word I say and, more often than not, follows his own whim when it disagrees with mine. In this case, he insisted on keeping to the main road, even though I argued the route was twice as long."

"You argue with your squire then allow him to go his own way?" Brenna's eyebrow quirked at the notion of a knight tolerating such insolence.

"Allow?" His soft laugh sent a trickle of sensation down her spine. "Believe me, my lady, I have *sent* him on his way with the help of my boot more times than I can recount. He keeps finding me again, however, despite my attempts to be hanged as a poacher. We agreed to meet in Rouen by week's end, and I have no doubt he will be there waiting, as surly and bellicose as ever."

"Rouen?" It was Robin, looking surprised yet again. "To the tournament, of course?"

Renaud nodded. "*L'Emprise de la Gueule de Dragon*. There have been postings at every crossroad between here and Paris."

"We ourselves leave in three days' time," Robin announced, his grin genuine and infectious. "Indeed, who could resist a haslitude with such grand designs as 'The Enterprise of the Dragon's Mouth'?"

"Who indeed?" Renaud mused.

The instincts of the two men took brief priority and caused them to study each other with sharp new eyes. They were breathtakingly well matched in size and height, both in their prime as fighting men, and the irony was not lost on either one as they assessed the advantages and disadvantages of playing host and guest to someone they would likely be meeting as an opponent in the lists.

"Perhaps," Renaud mused, "you should simply point the way to the road."

"And perhaps," Robin replied with equal graveness, "you should come inside that we might ply you with good, stout ale and have you confess all of your weaknesses."

"But I have none. Not unless you count a pressing need for a soft bed, a hot bath, and a strong herb woman who can ease my body of"—his gaze flicked past Robin's shoulder and caught Brenna staring—"the multitude of unfamiliar aches I have earned this night, being forced to walk halfway across the country."

"Your tongue should have been as loose then as it is now," she retorted smartly. "Certes, you would have been left to your own company."

"Perhaps I would have been more forthcoming, my lady, had you not addressed me first with your bow. How was *I* to know *you* were not a thief or a poacher? You put your arrow in the tree without the slightest hesitation and suggested you were only too willing to do the same to me. You were dressed like a common peasant, giving no clue to your *gentle* breeding, and since you showed no willingness to impart your name either, how was I to know you were not there to maim or murder me?"

Brenna's mouth dropped open. He had managed to mock, insult, and reprimand her in the same breath he used to put himself forward as the poor, hapless victim!

"Murder," she said, clenching her teeth again, "was a closer possibility than your arrogance lets you realize, Sir Knight."

"I rather doubt that, my lady, although there *were* other temptations that might have proved interesting to pursue."

Two hot red spots flared in her cheeks and she was thankful for the shielding darkness. Nothing hid the look in his eyes or the path they took downward to the front of her jerkin. She had laced the halves closed again to keep out the chill on the ride home, but she might as well have been naked for all the protection the linen and leather afforded. She could *feel* his eyes probing through the layers, mocking her femininity even as he challenged it.

"Come now." Robin stepped between them. "It was a misunderstanding, nothing more. No one is murdered and you have, indeed, brought a most valuable prize home. I, for one, concede defeat. A brace of pheasants is naught compared to the resurrected Renaud de Verdelay." And to the vaunted Verdelay he added, "You will naturally do us the honor of accepting our hospitality."

"If I can offer Centaur a day's rest, gladly." The ice-washed eyes rose again to Brenna's face. "But only if I can be assured it is no inconvenience."

"It is no inconvenience whatsoever," Robin insisted, ignoring the glare on Brenna's face as he started leading the way back across the draw. "If anything, we welcome the news from . . . ah . . . where *have* you been all these years?"

"Here and there. In the east, mostly. Burgundy, the Germanys."

Brenna's skin prickled again, not pleasantly. She was no lover of coincidences, and there seemed to be a deal of them flying about this night. A knight alone, lost in the woods? A knight who was supposedly a champion, supposedly dead, suddenly come to life and prominence again, discovered on Amboise land, en route to a tournament at Château Gaillard. Was she the only one who saw something odd in all of this? Was the lump Robin had taken to his head that afternoon clouding his judgment, making him careless? Burgundy? *Burgundy*, for heaven's sake, was a land infested with assassins and mercenaries, men who wore no crests and carried no pennons, who would likely prefer the anonymity of the forest to recognition on the roads. Men went into the mountains of Burgundy when they were in disgrace or they had good reason to disappear for a time.

And when they came out again, they brought the snow and ice with them, in their eyes and in their souls.

Robin would not see it, however. Often to his greater fault, he held a rare and unassailable belief in the ideals of chivalry and was too virtuous, too trusting for his own good. He could no more believe a knight capable of treachery and deceit than he could himself spit on the Holy Grail.

Brenna was not half so trusting, and neither, thankfully, was Will, who stopped Renaud at the guardhouse where Robin would have led him straight past.

"I am afraid, my lord, you will have to submit to the normal castle procedures and surrender all of your weapons at the gate. They will be restored to you, cleaned and in good repair, when you depart."

"I was already relieved of my sword, as you can see. You will find it with another strapped to Centaur's pack."

"Merely a precaution," Robin explained with a shrug of apology. "My family is not well liked by the English king and his allies, and strangers tend to put the guards on their toes."

Griffyn grunted by way of giving response, for he was on his toes now. The man who happened to be conducting a search of his person for hidden weapons was Jean de Brevant, the captain of the Wolf's personal guard and the one to whom the safety of Amboise's residents had been entrusted for the past decade. Called Littlejohn by those who dared, he was a towering pillar of muscle, standing above seven feet in height. His face was hewn out of rock, bearded to the eyes, the cracks and fissures above arranged to give proof his favorite expression was a menacing frown.

The menace deepened noticeably when he found a thin-bladed, wickedly sharp misericorde tucked into the high cuff of Renaud's boot.

"You will get this back when you leave," he said as he handed the knife to another guard. "Lord Randwulf supplies his guests with a barber if they wish to be clean shaven."

Renaud straightened his tunic and made a small adjustment to the front seam of his hose. "You are very thorough."

"I like to earn my keep."

"Then you should probably take this." He withdrew a small knife from a sheath sewn into the collar of his surcoat. "And this." He pulled up his sleeve and removed a small crescent-shaped disc he wore strapped to his forearm.

Brenna, who had been leaning against her bow, enjoying Renaud's discomfort throughout the search, straightened and stared. She had not taken her eyes off him for more than a second or two on the ride home; how had he managed to conceal so many weapons? Even more confounding was the fact he had played the captive so well when he could obviously have overwhelmed her at any time.

Littlejohn's eyebrows were crushed together to form a single dark slash over the bridge of his nose. He was clearly as startled as Brenna, and the look he gave Griffyn Renaud should have turned his bowels to stone. But the calm, luminous eyes merely stared back, showing as much fear as a cat before a mouse.

Brevant made a sound in his throat, almost as ominous as the metallic grating of the portcullis being lowered behind them. He leaned close to Renaud and bared his huge front teeth in the flickering torchlight. "I would not try to be half so clever when you meet your host. If *he* takes a dislike to you, we will be using this little toy of yours"—he thumbed the Saracen lancet—"to pluck out your guts and make them into bowstrings."

Robin sighed and touched Griffyn on the arm, indicating he should follow across the bailey. "You will have to excuse Littlejohn's manners. Not much slips past him and, as I said, his blood is high from lack of sport."

"Whereas I think he is a wise and canny fellow," Brenna muttered, loud enough to be overheard. "And better to be rude than dead in his bed of a slit throat."

Griffyn, only two steps ahead of her, stopped so suddenly she ran up his heels and would have stumbled had he not reached out and grasped hold of her upper arms. When she was settled straight again, he released her, but not before she was made shockingly aware of the strength in his hands—hands that felt as if they ached to crush her bones to powder.

"Have no fear, my lady." His voice was so silky it slithered down her spine and pooled in her belly. "As long as I am within these walls, your throat is quite safe from anyone else's touch."

5

It was to be expected that anyone visiting Château d'Amboise would be taken first to the main keep and presented before Lord Randwulf, and Griffyn Renaud was no exception. Will loped ahead to announce their arrival and when Robin and Brenna entered the great hall, the family was assembled at the dining tables, the air rich with the smell of roasted meat and savory victuals. It was a large and cavernous chamber with a high vaulted ceiling supported by stone arches. Lacking any windows below the level of the second story, light was provided by a hundred fat wax candles set in iron stands and cressets around the room. Ventilation for the smoke and smells of the crowded room was through narrow, vertical slits cut high in the stone walls. There was a log blazing in the massive stone fireplace—a relatively new renovation to the room after a century of making do with huge iron braziers. The ten-foot log sent flame and sparks climbing halfway up the new chimney that had been incorporated into the stone and mortar, but even with this new source of venting, there was a diaphanous layer of smoke hovering overhead. Several dozens servants moved like ghostly wraiths to and from the tall woven screens that concealed the exit to the cook house. Any scraps they dropped from their platters caused a mad scramble among the wolfhounds that crouched by the long trestle tables hoping for just such a happy event.

Ornamenting the towering block walls were the multitude of pennants and captured banners, crests, and shields either taken in battle or won in the many tournaments Lord Randwulf and his sons had participated in over the years. Crossed swords, iron starbursts, strangely configured suits of heavy armor from such faraway places as Jerusalem and Syria were mounted prominently on the walls alongside lances, crossbows, targes, and large woven tapestries. Chivalry itself was on display, for the Wolf's reputation in the lists was second only to that of William Marshal, the greatest knight and soldier alive. Lord Randwulf's eldest son, Eduard, in his turn, had come close to matching his father's record of triumphs and might have done so had real battles and wars not kept him away from the fairgrounds. Now there was Robin, undefeated since his twentieth birthday, and his brothers Richard and William Dagobert whose trophies and pennons were beginning to decorate the walls on either side of the fireplace.

An enormous raised dais commanded one end of the vast chamber. This was reserved for the immediate family and guests of honor. In the middle sat Lord Randwulf de la Seyne Sur Mer and his wife, Lady Servanne. Flanking them in descending order of age and ranking were their sons and daughters along with their respective husbands, the castle seneschal when he was present, and, on this particular evening, the bishop from a nearby abbey. Stretching out from the dais were two long trestle tables covered in white linen and sagging under platters of food for the castle retainers and visiting monks, and, seated below the salt, the villagers and yeomen who had come to the château on some errand and were afforded the hospitality of their overlord's table. They would eat and make their beds on any spare part of the floor, for once darkness had fallen, few were encouraged to venture outside the walls of the castle.

It was a crowded and noisy assembly, with a score of conversations taking place at the same time and, to add to the merriment, a pair of jongleurs providing entertainment in exchange for a hearty meal.

Robin, as clean and presentable as a quick detour to his chamber could make him, led the small group down the short flight of stone steps and across the floor to the dais. He lifted a hand in greeting to several knights seated at the trestles and veered briefly over to their table to exchange a few words.

The Wolf, observing from his seat on the dais, leaned back in his chair and signaled to a varlet standing behind him to bring fresh food and wine. Despite almost six decades behind him, he was still a large, strikingly handsome man. His eyes were the same slate gray that left his enemies trembling in his wake. His hair was a dark, rich chestnut, silvered slightly at the temples but as thick and luxuriant as a youth of twenty. Recent years had seen his body start to betray the massive strength that had earned him a reputation as a fighter and champion. His right arm was useless for anything requiring more dexterity than eating and dressing, but it was a legacy of past injuries that should have killed him, and so he could not complain. His left knee had been soundly crushed in a skirmish some years back, but there too, since he had not only defied the doctor who had wanted to cut it off, but lived to box the lout's ears on the anniversary of the day each year he was supposed to have died of blood putrefaction, he could not complain about that either.

What he *could* complain about was an errant squire, an absent son, and a daughter who returned from a day in the forest looking more leafy and grimy than a lowly bumpkin.

"We were about to send the castle guard out looking for you," he said when the trio came before him.

Beside him, his wife leaned forward in her chair. Lady Servanne was in her forty-ninth year, but still a rare beauty. Her hair, beneath the filmy silk wimple, was more silver than blond and there were fine creases on her throat and the corners of her eyes, but her body was slender and willowy as ever. Her long white fingers were beringed and bejeweled with gifts her husband had given her in gratitude for providing him with three strong sons and four beautiful daughters, and they twinkled now as she tapped out her exasperation over the state of her next to youngest daughter's hair and clothing.

"Brenna dear, pray tell me those are *not* your new boots."

Brenna glanced down and scuffed some of the crusted mud off the toe. "I suppose . . . they are not new anymore," she acknowledged. "But they are well and truly comfortable. We foraged nearly to the abbey and back and I have not so much as a burn or blister to show for it."

"Surely cause for celebration by anyone's measure," her mother mused. "I warrant the cut on your leg and the scratch on your neck are also prized accomplishments?"

"I won the day. Two clean hits, both against Will. The first, I crept close enough to tap him on the shoulder, and the second, I nearly pinned his nose to a tree. 'Twas a *very* bad day for Will'um all told, since Robin's two points came at his expense as well, though I will allow he redeemed himself somewhat when we killed a boar. But since our arrows struck as one, it still put me ahead the winning point."

"I gather neither Will nor Robin scored against you?" the Wolf asked, the pride and amusement vying for an equal shine in his eyes.

"They could not have caught me today if I wore a rope around my waist and tied bells to my collar."

"Oh dear," Servanne murmured. "I feel another argument coming on."

"There are no grounds for argument, Mother, nor would there be any in the future if I were allowed to enter the archery contest at Gaillard. Winning the *fleche d'or* at Gaillard would settle the matter once and for all."

"Why you would want to stand at the line with a pack of hairy foresters and throw good arrows at a bale of hay is beyond me," said her brother Richard. "And it does no good to keep complaining about it, since women are strictly forbidded to enter anyway."

"You are already the best by my reckoning," Dag said from farther along the table. "And if it is true you won the day, I will gladly share the hundreds marks I won from *someone* who did not have as much faith."

Richard scowled and belched his opinion of Dag's foresight into the back of his hand. The two were a year apart in age, but with faces so much alike they were sometimes mistaken for twins. Close inspection revealed too many differences to fool anyone not half addled with ale; Dag's eyes were set wider apart and his chin was clean shaven. Richard's nose had been broken too many times to retain its former clean line, and his own chin bore a deep scar that he preferred to camouflage beneath a neatly trimmed and pointed beard.

"A pox on tournament rules," Brenna said. "They only exist because Lady Gillian kept putting the men of Normandy to shame each year she was declared the master archer—including the last, when she disguised herself as an urchin and won the golden arrow just to spite the judges."

"You will not be disguising yourself as anyone other than Lady Brenna Wardieu," her mother declared sternly. "I expect you to deport yourself with the utmost grace and civility."

"I will be so well behaved Robin will beg me to create some havoc just to know I am not lost forever to goodness and obedience."

"I doubt that will ever happen," Richard murmured. "But we can always hope."

The Wolf laughed. "Your mother is only concerned because you will be on your own. She cannot attend this year and Lady Ariel has enough to do to keep Eduard chained to his bed. Your sister Eleanor will be with Erek in Poitou, and Rhiannon would need a dozen chaperones of her own just to keep her from creeping into Will's tent at night."

FitzAthelstan's face flamed a wondrous shade of scarlet, but no one took notice.

"Isobel is still thinking of attending," Brenna argued. "She will be a more than adequate defense against my forgetting to wear a cotte and hide my hair beneath a wimple."

"Isobel is seven months with child," Richard said dryly. "I doubt Geoffrey, for all his tolerance, would allow her to attend a corn harvest. And besides, if I am not mistaken, those are her leggings you are wearing now."

Brenna threw her hands up in feigned exasperation. "Then in truth, there is no hope for me. That will leave only Robin and Will, Richard and Dag, Sparrow and Little-john *and* a few score of the most fearsome knights and men-at-arms to guard against my accidentally stepping in a dung heap."

"They were no help to you today," observed her sister Eleanor, who crinkled her nose and glanced pointedly at Brenna's boots.

"Fine," Brenna said on a huff of breath. "Fine. I shall go to my chamber now and return in less time than it takes you to discuss all of my *other* faults behind my back, dressed to the very image of innocence, propriety, and virtue!"

Dag coughed half a mouthful of wine back into his goblet and nodded his thanks as Eleanor thumped him between the shoulders.

"We shall keep that most intriguing thought in mind. However," Richard said dryly, "it *is* the last tourney of the season. It could also be Bren's last opportunity to shop for a husband before the winter snows set in."

"Is that why you think I want to go? To shop for a husband?"

"None have come looking of their own accord."

"Hah! I would marry the first lout who came through the door if I thought it would save me from your vast wit."

"Quick," Richard said, lifting his hand to an imaginary varlet. "Is that the redoubtable Gerome de Saintonge who comes begging at the door again even as we speak? How many times is it now he has asked and you have refused?"

Her eyes flashed murder and Lady Servanne leaned forward again.

"Brenna . . . it is not that I doubt your ability to comport yourself well, it is just that . . . well . . . I worry that perhaps this is not the best time to be straying far from home."

"Château Gaillard is but a three-day ride from here! Two if we are able to forgo the wagons and litters that are usually required to haul all of Eleanor's change of gowns. *One* if there is a matter of urgency that shouts for us to fly home with any haste. I am perfectly content on horseback. A blanket by the fire, with the boughs of a tree overhead to keep the stars from falling on us while we sleep, is a far more appealing comfort than any stuffy inn or tavern. And besides, I simply have to go. You cannot possible expect me to sit here before the hearth weaving *stockings* or some such nonsense while Robin and the others are walking the same ramparts *King Richard helped lay with his bare hands!*"

"God in heaven, no," the Wolf murmured. "How could anyone expect such a thing?"

Lady Servanne sighed and turned her cornflower-blue eyes up to her lord husband. "Am I the only one who takes the latest news from England seriously?"

"What news?" Brenna asked. "The news about the king increasing the reward on Robin's head to a thousand gold marks after the sound thrashing his army of Brabançons and misfits received at Roche-au-Moines?"

"If you announce it a little louder," Will murmured, "the men working in the stables might better to be able to hear."

Brenna looked out over the crowded tables but no one was paying any heed. On the way back, her gaze touched on the almost forgotten Griffyn Renaud, who was standing quietly to one side, content to remain in the background and observe the family amenities.

"I fail to see what all the fuss and bother is about," she continued in a more reserved tone. "If there is anyone foolish enough to try their hand at collecting any such reward, we shall simply dig a few more holes in the grave-yard and plant them alongside their fellow incompetents."

"Well said," Dag concurred. "And I for one will sleep better at night knowing Bren's canny eyes and bow arm are guarding our backs at Gaillard."

"This would not be your nose for profit speaking, would it?" the Wolf asked casually, since it was well known that there would be contests aplenty between tournament goers who shared his daughter's contempt for the official rules.

"Absolutely not," Dag protested. "Although . . . the wagering in any challenges answered outside the tourney grounds should be exceptionally heated indeed. Not like the abysmal thrift displayed by the gamblers when Robin takes to the field."

"Yes, well." Robin cleared his throat and stepped forward. "That may yet change. And before we lose claim to all of our manners, may I introduce into this bedlam Lord Griffyn Renaud de Verdelay. He fell into our hands quite by accident this afternoon and I have invited him to partake of our hospitality." He held out a hand to beckon their guest forward. "Griffyn Renaud, my father, Lord Randwulf de la Seyne Sur Mer."

"God grant you good ease, my lord," Renaud said, offering a respectful bow. "Though I warrant it to be a difficult task in such lively company as I see before me."

"I thought of giving one or two away at birth," the Wolf agreed, "but my wife insisted they would bring comfort to me in my old age." He paused and looked closer at the bold, dark face. "Verdelay. The tournament in Gascon. Are you not the rogue who gave us cause to tear our hair out by the roots then and for several months thereafter while Robin splintered a hundred lances or more trying to duplicate the way you ran against him?"

"I know nothing of what happened afterward, but I do plead guilty to the day of the event."

"Where, in God's name, did he manage to find you?"

"Actually, my lord, it was your daughter who found me. I am afraid she took umbrage to the fact I was helping myself to some of your fish."

The Wolf's grin broadened. "Then you stand before me a lucky man indeed."

"So I am beginning to believe."

"And still hungry, no doubt?"

Verdelay's eyes drifted involuntarily to the boards of shredded meat, capon, pies, and pasties. "I confess my belly is rubbing on my backbone."

"Then join us, by all means, without further delay. Isobel and Geoffrey are not with us tonight and their places are vacant. Brenna—you mentioned something about virtue and propriety? Would that come in the guise of a fresh tunic and clean boots?"

She curled her fingers back from the tender morsel of roast hare she was about to pilfer off the board. "Yes, Father. At once."

"And Robin . . . there was mention of a boar?"

"A great hulking brute, aye." His cheek twitched as he glanced at Brenna. "But it gave us no trouble. Come, Griffyn, the table waits."

Renaud turned and was about to follow Robin around to an open seat on the dais, but something barrel-chested and low to the ground blocked his way.

"Littlejohn tells me you are fond of knives."

Renaud looked down and his eyes widened. The man—elf—who stood glowering before him came no higher than his waist and bore the face of a debauched cherub with large agate eyes and froth of curly brown hair. He had planted himself firmly in the knight's path, having just come from a whispered conversation with the ruddy-faced captain of the guard.

Seeing the startled look on Renaud's face, Brenna chuckled as she passed airily by. "This is Sparrow. And if you truly want to give thanks for your luck, it should be because it was Littlejohn and not Sparrow who searched you."

"Knives," declared the seneschal. "Hidden hither and thither up a sleeve and down a collar, I am told."

Renaud looked at the little man, then at the faces on the dais, all of which showed polite disapproval of Sparrow's brusqueness in confronting a guest, but not so much so they were not interested in hearing his answer.

"They were hidden only because your man did not find them," he explained carefully. "And when I travel alone across lands I am not familiar with, I am loath to carry all of my defenses in plain sight."

"A wise practice," Robin agreed. "Now, may we eat?"

Renaud took a step to the right and Sparrow followed suit, forcing him to stop and look down again.

"I am fond of knives myself." To prove it, he withdrew two small, viciously serrated blades from beneath the folds of his tunic. He angled them into the candlelight so that an admiring eye might heed the sparkled warning, then, with a flash of carnivorous delight, he wielded them expertly into their sheaths again and crossed his arms over his chest. "Enjoy your meal. The fowl improves with salt."

Renaud followed Robin to a vacant seat on the dais and Sparrow was right behind, glaring Dag out of his chair to create three vacancies where there were only two. Thick trenchers of bread were placed before the trio at once and from behind, a varlet appeared with a basin of hot water and towels.

Brenna, paused at the top of the steps to watch, saw Renaud wash and dry his hands under the hawklike scrutiny of one of her father's most loyal and respected men. To some, Sparrow may have looked like a freak and a curiosity, but they never made the mistake of underestimating him twice. He had been in the Wolf's service for over thirty years and credited the wealth of health and happiness within the walls of Amboise to his ability to sniff out trouble before it happened. He trusted no one and aggravated everyone with his interference, but this was one time Brenna was stirred to bend down and hug him.

If the mysterious Renaud de Verdelay had something to hide or some nefarious purpose for coming here, Sparrow would ferret it out.

6

Brenna hastened along the narrow stone corridor, plucking at the laces of her jerkin as she ran. Four circular half towers had been abutted to the four corners of the main keep, one of which housed her parents' private apartments. Her brothers occupied the northeast tower, with its view of the valley and the village of Amboise. She and her sisters faced the northwest and overlooked a perilous drop down the cliffs to the river below. When Eleanor and Isobel had married two years ago, they had taken over the fourth tower, leaving the rooms they had formerly occupied to be divided between Brenna and Rhiannon, with Brenna staking claim to all of the second story and its spiral access to the upper solar and roof.

Her chamber was large, but sparsely furnished with a bed, a few chests that held her clothing, a writing table, and two chairs. Because it was above the practical line of defenses, it also boasted two long, deeply set windows with wooden benches built into the stone embrasures. Her personal serving woman, Helvise, had anticipated her arrival and already prepared a welcome. A small tub of hot water was waiting and a fire had been built in the hearth—another renovation, so recently completed the surrounding stonework of the fireplace was not uniformly blackened by smoke and heat. The walls of the chamber had been whitewashed after the masons finished, and colorful renditions of roses and fleurs-de-lis had been painted on each square to signify a feminine presence. For all that Brenna noticed or cared, they might have been target circles and put to far more practical use.

She quickly finished undressing and stepped into the steaming tub of hot water. Helvise was waiting with cloths and brushes to help scrub away the muck that had seeped through her clothes. As the layers of grime and sweat were soaped away, the perfumed contents of several more buckets were poured over her charge's head to run slick and shiny down her body. Coarse, thirsty towels of hemp were wrapped around her hair and more used to blot the water off her skin, accompanied by the occasional cluck of despair when a fresh scratch or recent bruise was discovered.

Helvise had been with the household since Brenna was a babe and had trained for her duties under the iron discipline of Goodwife Biddy. While she was forced to defend her lady's sometimes wild behavior to the other servants, in the privacy of the tower rooms she despaired over her mistress's refusal to acknowledge the natural beauty that could have had so often left men gaping after her like drooling pups. It was a rare occasion when her lady even took note of the mirror that hung on the wall.

"Do you think I look like a peasant?" Brenna asked, peering at her reflection now, trying to see herself through a pair of cool gray-green eyes.

"My lady?"

"He said I looked like a common peasant. *Do* I?"

"*Who* dared say such a thing, my lady? And surely not in front of anyone who would have cut his tongue out for the insult!"

"In truth . . . it was said in front of Robin and Will, who offered no argument at all—probably because they say it often enough themselves."

"Oh, no, my lady—"

"Or at least think it." Brenna dropped the towel she was holding under her arms and moved closer to the oval sheet of polished metal that hung beside the fireplace. Her shoulders were straight and square to be sure, not rounded by a life of humility. Her chin was held level and proud, her complexion—apart from the tanning and freckles—was clear of pocks and scars; her teeth were small and even and white from scrubbing faithfully with salt and fennel. She did not believe she could ever be called beautiful in the sense that her mother and sisters were beautiful, but neither did she think she was so ugly as to frighten small children into hiding. The rest of her body was . . . just a body, so far as she could determine. Full, firm breasts, a trim waist, hips and legs honed too taut to be truly feminine, but long and lithe and capable of a certain grace in movement.

Her hair was an entirely different matter. Graceless, wild-flown, and unruly, it was long and thick and, when not confined to braids, tended to scatter across her shoulders in an irrepressible mass of tawny curls. Between Helvise's efforts with the towels and the heat from the fire, it was drying rapidly into a golden halo around her head and spreading out like burnished angel wings down her back.

"How sharp are the scissors tonight?" she murmured, fingering the end of a rebellious curl.

"Not nearly sharp enough to combat the heat of your mother's wrath."

"Ah, but one day when you are not here to guard over me . . . *snip, snip, snip* they will go."

Helvise ignored the threat as she did almost every night and continued working with the brush and towel.

Brenna glanced at the bed. A plain white chainse and brown holland overtunic were waiting on the coverlet. Another slight twist of her head found the crisp linen wimple and boxlike coronet she loathed more than anything a free soul ought to be forced to endure.

"I think . . . I would prefer to wear something else tonight. Something . . . *Eleanor* would wear."

Helvise's arm stopped midbrushstroke. "My lady?"

"The wine silk bliaud, methinks, if it can be found on the instant. With the blue chainse beneath. And toss that wretched wimple out the window! Fetch me something that does not feel so much like a pair of hands constantly throttling me."

"My *lady?*"

"Exactly. They want a lady tonight, they shall see a lady.

Quick!" She waved her hand. "Before I change my mind and descend the stairs dressed as I am."

Helvise made a small sound in her throat and hastened to the row of wooden chests that contained all of Brenna's clothes. She passed by the first two, knowing them to be full of shirts, leggings, tunics, and hose, and went to the smallest, the one tucked farthest in the corner with its leather straps so unworn they looked new. She found the tunic and the chainse. Both had been worn but once and then carefully folded and wrapped and laid to rest alongside the other garments of silk, samite, and lustrous cendal that found as much favor in their mistress's eyes.

While Helvise shook out the creases and draped both garments across the bed, she kept glancing at Brenna, wary of being the victim of a prank. But no. She stood perfectly docile as the chainse of blue linen floated down over her head and settled like a cloud around her body. She even exhibited rare patience while Helvise took up her needle and thread and threw in a line of hidden stitches to fit the long sleeves fashionably tight to her wrists and forearms. The silk of the overtunic, so deep and rich a red as to be almost black, was designed to snugly mold the shape of her upper body, which it did with exceeding boldness. From the waist it widened gracefully in full, soft pleats so that when she walked, the hems of the both the bliaud and undertunic dragged several feet behind.

The sleeves of the burgundy silk were deliberately elongated and flared, requiring more fussing, first to tack them artfully into a cuff that would reveal the seafoam blue beneath, then to knot the trailing points into rose-shaped clusters to prevent them from trailing on the floor. An elaborately embroidered girdle of gold samite was passed around her waist, further emphasizing her decidedly feminine shape, and after crossing in back, the ends were draped forward over the hips and pinned to form a deep V over her belly.

On Brenna's impatient orders, the damp abundance of her hair was wrestled back into a long braid and wound into a coil at the nape of her neck. A delicate silk wimple was fitted loosely over her head and draped in airy folds beneath her chin. It was capped by a rose-colored veil and the whole held in place by a jeweled circlet of gold.

Helvise was holding her breath as she stepped back. The entire transformation from grimy ruffian to perfumed lady had taken just over an hour, a miracle by any church standards. To be sure there were more refinements that could have been added—jewels, brooches, rings—but the maid was not wont to press her luck by making any suggestions. She was happy just to nod her approval as Brenna fingered the hanging ends of the girdle and spun once, letting the silk lift and cream around her ankles again.

"Think you I am safe joining the rest of the household for supper now?"

"You could probably join the Dauphin of France and he would not find fault."

Brenna laughed and put on the slippers Helvise had set out. They were stiff from lack of use and pinched her toes terribly, but she donned them without complaint and hurried down the tower stairs to the lower level. Just before bursting out onto the landing of the great hall, she slowed and folded her hands demurely in front, then peeked around the corner of the block wall. There was still food on the tables, for the evening meal often lasted upward of several hours, though some of the formalities lapsed after the main courses were served. Eleanor was standing behind her mother's chair showing off some bit of embroidery on her sleeve. Richard and Dag had joined a table of knights below and were discussing the morrow's training events over full tankards of ale. Rhiannon had moved closer to the middle of the dais and was staring longingly at Will with wide puppy eyes, trying to get his attention; Will, meanwhile was studiously avoiding the temptation and stood behind the Wolf's chair in anticipation of his lord wanting to retire for the evening.

Sparrow was still seated beside Griffyn Renaud, although the major part of his attention was fixed on the pile of bones he was picking clean in front of him. Renaud's appetite had apparently not suffered either from the close quarters. There was a large quantity of bowls and boards in front of him, most of them empty but for crumbs, and as Brenna watched, he was tearing up the last few squares of his trencher and enjoying every last gravy-soaked hunk he put in his mouth. Beside him, Robin was refilling both their goblets and laughing as he pointed to another full slice of bread in the basket.

Renaud declined, however, and leaned back in his chair. He was rubbing his hands over his belly and offering up a complimentary belch of satisfaction as Brenna came down the stairs and swept past. She saw him glance over . . . then glance over again when she stopped in front of Lord Randwulf and Lady Servanne and favored them with a perfectly executed curtsy.

"My lord father, my lady mother; I trust this meets your approval?"

The Wolf stared so long and so hard—as did the rest of the gathered assembly whose silence spread like a slow wave down the length of the great hall—two pale rosettes of color bloomed on Brenna's cheeks.

"I keep forgetting how beautiful you can be when you put your mind to it," her father said finally.

"A kind thing to say, but unnecessary. I only wore this to remind you that I am perfectly capable of representing the noble house of Amboise."

He sighed and shook his head. "Neither your mother nor I would argue your capabilities, daughter. We are only leaning toward caution. These are not normal times. With all the political unrest, the plottings and intrigues of both the French and English kings . . . the tournament will draw the worst of men as well as the best. The château itself is not safe. It has too many dark niches and high ramparts, too many shadowy corners for trouble to hide."

"Trouble?" Sparrow snorted and reached across Renaud to stab the point of his eating knife into a delectable morsel of poultry left on a board. "Infested and overrun, mores the like. With scullions and fools, trulls and trollops, throat-slitters and sin-eaters who would do more for the promise of a coin than you or I could do for want of imagining. All this as well as blood sport, drunkenness, debauchery . . ."

Brenna set her jaw. "I have seen—and drawn—blood before. I have also witnessed drunkenness and debauchery right here within the walls of our own castle. A full week of it, as I recall, following the victory at Roche-au-Moines."

"Ah yes," Richard commented from behind. "But the men of Amboise know and respect your skill with a dagger and shortsword."

"The men of Château Gaillard will know it too if they press me too close."

"There will be other tournaments."

"Indeed there will," she said, glaring at him. "For you as well. There is no portentous need for you to throw yourself down a jousting run at Gaillard. Not with your head cracked and both eyes blackened."

"There is nothing wrong with my head or my eyes."

"Not at the moment there isn't," she said succinctly.

Lord Randwulf tried to take control again, but it was difficult to do with a smile tugging at the corners of his mouth. It was Lady Servanne who offered up a sigh as she slipped her hand into his. "You really should try to hold your pride a little closer to your chest, my love."

He raised her hand, kissed it, and pressed it over his heart. "It already is as close as I can possibly hold it."

Brenna wrinkled her nose in Richard's direction and walked around to take her place at the table, which happened to be only two seats away from Griffyn Renaud. She was aware of the pale jade eyes following her, but when she glanced over to challenge his impudence, he had already wisely turned away.

He had to look away. It was either that or leave the table, which would only offer up more reason for her to be suspicious and hostile. In the forest, staring down the shaft of an arrow, all he had seen were those huge violet eyes, dark and sparkling with the desire to run him through. He had not doubted for a minute that she was fully capable of doing it, and the knowledge had tempered his anger, changed it to curiosity more than anything else.

He could have overpowered her at any time, of course—at least, he told himself he could—though the demonstration with the longbow had certainly prompted him to err on the side of caution. He had called for only a small effort on Centaur's part to unseat her, and the fact she not only remained on the stallion's back but seemed damned accustomed to being there had kept him playing the game if only to find out who she was, where she had come from, how she had come by the skill and nerve needed to sneak up on him and disarm him like a petty thief.

Discovering her to be the sister of Robert Wardieu and the daughter of La Seyne Sur Mer had explained a great deal.

Discovering there was more to see beneath the forest grime than just suspicions and surly accusations had caught him off guard a second time, and he had found himself gawping at her like a fool. Her skin was smooth, flawless, and when her mouth was not flattened in a scowl it was proportioned lushly enough to evoke unhealthy thoughts in a man who had not sampled such earthly pleasures in an overly long time. He had only gained an impression of breasts beneath the mannish leather jerkin, but he could see now they were large enough and shapely enough to push impudently against the confining layers of silk. A small waist and narrow hips recalled the long, slender legs that had enough strength in them to hold the temper of a warhorse.

What could they do with a man between them?

He shifted uncomfortably on his seat. He had eaten a quantity of good, rich food and consumed far more wine than he normally permitted himself. He had to move, get away from all this stifling family camaraderie before it clogged his throat. Talk at the table had turned to the upcoming haslitude, and he knew he was expected to contribute to the enthusiasm and excitement, but frankly, he was not going to Gaillard to play any more games. And talk was just that: talk. The proof came when two men stared at each other through the slats of their visors and waited for the marshal to signal the joust to begin.

"The only things in life which can be truly counted upon," Robin was saying, "are one's faith in God, in the lady you wed, and obedience to the laws of knighthood. The only truly great pleasure is to measure your strength in honorable combat with one of equal rank and birth. And I dare swear," he added, raising his cup for a toast, "there is no sunset as lovely as the sharp, cutting edge of a sword."

"Aye!"

"Hear, hear!"

A chorus of similar sentiments gave the men an excuse to drain and refill their cups. It also signaled the end of a relatively long dinner hour, and the Wolf pushed painfully to his feet, amiably passing his hosting duties on to his sons. But instead of sitting back down when the lord and his lady wife had gone, Griffyn stretched his arms wide and feigned a hearty yawn.

Robin noticed. "You have had a tiring day."

"My legs are unaccustomed to forced marches."

"Ahh yes, you mentioned the need earlier for a hot bath and a pair of helping hands."

"I am not pressed. It can wait until tomorrow."

"Tomorrow," Robin said, grinning, "I plan to see what stuff you are made of. You will need a run or two to warm your blood before Gaillard. And I am curious to know if you are as good as I remember."

Griffyn smiled. "I would be more than happy to ease your curiosity, my lord, but I would fear the repercussions if I was too successful."

Robin followed his gaze to where Brenna was watching them both over the rim of her wine goblet. "You will have to excuse my sister. She is suspicious of all men by nature and even more so of strangers."

"The reward on your head?"

"Partly because of that." He nodded. "Assassins and spies have been sprouting up throughout the countryside like mushrooms, many of them well paid just to survive a night in the village."

Griffyn looked around, noting again the not altogether casual placement of guards at either end of the dais. "And she thinks I might be one or the other?"

Robin spread his hands in a gesture of complaisance. "My father carries a reward of nearly ten thousand marks on his head, dead or alive. My stepbrother Eduard and I are not so valuable dead, but there are warrants and charges of treason that would pay a great deal to someone canny enough to bring us before the King of England to stand trial."

Renaud kept his face carefully blank as he looked over at Brenna. "Has your opinion of me changed at all, my lady?"

"Once an opinion is formed," she said evenly, "it requires a good deal of persuasion to change it."

"Should I take that as a personal challenge?"

She shrugged. "Take it however you wish, sirrah. We have all survived quite well without your friendship thus far; it would serve no purpose to grovel for it now."

"Your lack of faith wounds me, demoiselle."

"I have no doubt you will endure without it."

Sandwiched between them, Sparrow chortled through a mouthful of sugared figs. "If you think to win a war of words with a woman, you have indeed been in the wilds of Burgundy overlong."

"In this, we concur," Griffyn murmured, and turned to Robin again. "If I give my oath not to kill anyone or spy through any keyholes, could one of your men show me where I might put my head down for the night?"

Robin laughed and beckoned to his squire, the fourteen-year-old son of a neighboring lord who had been fostered into his care to train for knighthood. "Timkin here will take you first to the bath house and see that you are provided with everything you need to ease the sting of my sister's tongue. We have an excellent herb woman—

Margery—with knuckles like small hammers and unguents that can burn away the most persistent aches. I myself will probably call upon her services later tonight."

"Why?" Sparrow demanded. "You seem hardy enough aside from the glowing egg on your head. How did it come to be there anyway? You were unmarked when you left my care this morning."

Robin touched the scabbed gash on his forehead. " 'Tis nothing. A small clumsiness."

"Hah! A tree, no doubt, caught you looking the other way?"

"Something like that." Robin's cheek gave another small twitch. "At any rate—"

"At any rate you could have found better things to do a sennight before a tourney than running out your legs and cracking trees with your head. For that, you will belong to *me* on the morrow. I do not like the way you have been waving the lance thither and yon at the quintain; you missed the mark three times this week!"

"Out of forty passes!"

"Do you think you will have an easier time at Gaillard? Every clanking booby with a sword to rattle will be thrumping the challenge shield to have at you! One miss there will put your arse over the palisade and your teeth through your tongue before you can clap a hand to your face and decry the forty good passes that went before!"

Robin cursed under his breath and shrugged at Griffyn. "You see what *I* must endure? Escape while you have the chance and enjoy your solitude. Timkin, certes, has never been known to talk an ear off."

Verdelay offered no protest. He took his leave and followed the boy out of the great hall, half expecting the dwarf and a dozen guards to accompany them. As they stepped into the crisp night air, he looked about him with a fresh eye toward the castle's defenses. There were sentries armed with swords and crossbows positioned every twenty paces or so along the wall-walks, and a fire blazing in the bailey, bright enough to wash out any shadows in front of the only way in and out of the keep. There was no need to keep him under heavy escort. His every move would be watched and noted by a score of anonymous faces above.

Ten thousand marks was a lot of money. He was surprised he had made it this far without having to kill someone.

7

Brenna watched the dark knight leave the great hall and she was more convinced than ever that his smile was too shallow, his pale eyes too full of secrets. She was glad, in a way, that Robin had let him know of her suspicions; he would know also that she would be keeping a close watch over him even if no one else did.

She finished her meal and her wine and snatched a last morsel of meat off a platter before it was taken away. Robin and Sparrow were squabbling over the details of the training practice in the morning, Eleanor had given her husband Erek a moon-eyed signal that had him begging his leave of the other knights and following her up the stairs to their chamber. Richard and Dag were engrossed in conversation, likely to do with the rosy-cheeked serving wench who kept casting long, inviting looks in their direction. The evening was winding down and as soon as the tables were emptied, pallets would be made by the fire and the sound of contented snoring would echo up to the rafters.

Brenna glanced again at the landing. The bath house was located in a cluster of outbuildings next to the kitchens and laundry. The baths themselves were huge metal tubs set into the floor, lined with wood and heated by fires fed from below. It was late enough that Renaud probably had the place to himself, was probably sinking into the hot, waist-deep water now and leaning back to savor the rolling clouds of oak-scented steam. It was the custom in some noble houses for the hostess to formally bathe an important guest, and she wondered absently what Griffyn Renaud de

Verdelay would do if she appeared beside the tub, lye soap
and scrub brush in hand.

Smiling at the thought of scouring away some of that
bold arrogance, she made her excuses and started back
toward her tower rooms. She was more tired than she cared
to admit, and the notion of sinking into a soft feather mattress was too appealing to exchange for the brief pleasure it
would give her to plague the Burgundian. There was one
small task she did have to do first, however, and that was to
see if the castle bowyer had finished the new longbow he
had promised to have ready for her tonight. The one she
had used today had fine balance and tremendous power in
the seasoned yew, but he had been laboring for two weeks
over a weapon he vowed would outstrip any thus far.

She exited the keep through the narrow stone pentice—
the covered stairwell that gave access to the living quarters—and shielded her eyes against the bright glare of the
bonfire blazing across the draw. She could see no lights
beyond in the armory, no hunched silhouette bending over
the worktable. She would see no bow either if she ventured
inside, but that did not surprise her. Old Perigord was as
sly and secretive as a fox, and she would not catch the
smallest glimpse of it until it was finished and ready to fit to
her hand.

Some of the kitchen workers were taking a few minutes
of ease after their long workday, and as Brenna walked
across the draw, she veered toward the shadows, not
wanting to intrude. The keen eye of one of the hostlers
spied the white blur of her wimple and insisted she join
them in sharing a cup a mead. This was not the usual
behavior of most castle residents to their lords or their families. It was more the rule for humblies and common workers
to fall fearfully silent and lower their eyes whenever their
betters passed among them. The Wolf was harsh with his
discipline and expected nothing less than a full day of
honest work from his retainers, but there were no children
dressed in rags in his demesne, no hollow-eyed peasants
missing ears or hands or tongues. He was a fair and generous

overlord, as were his sons and daughters in turn; he knew every man and woman by their name and would not have refused to share a tup, regardless if it was thin and sour as vinegar.

Brenna accepted the warmed mead and complimented the brewer on its sweetness. Someone took up a lute and another started to sing, and before long there were dancers circling the fire, spinning and flirting and giving thanks for the day past. The fire was hot and sent columns of flame and glowing cinders up into the night sky. Brenna watched it for a time, watched the dancers with their bare feet and loose tunics, then reached up with impatient fingers to remove her veil and wimple. She shook out the long braid of her hair and, on a further impulse, pried her poor pinched feet out of the silk slippers. Feeling considerably less constricted, she slipped away into the shadows and circled around behind the clustered row of outbuildings. Waving to one of the sentries, she climbed up to the wall-walk and leaned between two cold stone teeth of the battlements to look out over the sleeping countryside.

Sometimes, on a very clear night when there was no moon and the stars were smeared like crushed fireflies across the heavens, a faint glow could be seen in the direction of Eduard's castle at Blois, less than thirty miles to the north and east.

There was no moon this night, but there were clouds scudding low and fast across the tops of the trees. She could taste the faint metallic dampness on the breeze, which meant there was rain heading their way, and, as if to confirm her prediction, a strong, moist gust snatched her wimple off the stone where she had rested it and sent it in a ghostly flight over the wall.

"Oh dear," she murmured. "A dreadful shame."

She would have sent her veil and slippers flying after it, but she could feel eyes on her and knew the sentries would be frowning, wondering what pagan madness was in her blood tonight. Sighing, she turned and let the wind ruffle her hair as she took a last overview of the keep, the bailey, the night sky above. She descended the steep stairs again and, with half an eye searching out the only lighted building in the yard, started walking back to the keep.

The enormous, muscular bulk of Margery, the castle herb woman, cut across the shadows in front of her. She was carrying her basket of oils and unguents and was clearly not in an amiable frame of mind. Her craggy features were grooved into a scowl and her ample bosoms heaved with the effort it took to climb the shallow incline toward the bath house.

Brenna's footsteps veered of their own accord and she followed like a silent, silk-clad wraith in the woman's wake. She heard voices inside the bath house and recognized Timkin's even before he emerged, hiding a wide grin behind his hand. She crept closer and saw that the tubs were empty. She heard a gruff voice protesting and another, equally gruff but far more militant, voice insisting that she had not been roused out of a warm bed for naught.

Brenna tiptoed right up to the open door. Griffyn Renaud was lying facedown on a wide table, naked but for a strip of toweling draped across his buttocks. Margery's large, gnarled hands were slapping pungent-smelling oil on his shoulders and back, prodding him when he attempted to move, pushing his head down on the padding of thick furs when he tried to tell her her services were not necessary.

Brenna folded her arms across her chest and leaned on the door jamb, enjoying the knight's discomfort. He was big, but Margery was bigger, with arms like truncheons and a body shaped like a sturdy pavilion. She had been tending the aches and bruises of the Wardieu men longer than Brenna could remember and was proud of her work. No black-haired devil was about to order her away, not when she had received specific orders from Lord Robert!

Brenna was no stranger to the magic of oils and massages. Nor was she particularly shy or modest when it came to viewing a man's naked body. Many a time she had joined Robin and her brothers—even Will—after a long day in the practice fields and helped them off with their armor, or listened to their boasting and bickering while they bathed. Many a time as well they had been laid out on the tables like oiled fish while she, under Margery's eagle eyes, had pounded, pummeled, and rubbed the tightness out of their bruised muscles. And if Griffyn Renaud was anything like her brothers, the manipulations would relax him almost into a state of semiconsciousness where questions were asked and answered without the faintest attempt at evasion.

Something, a stray lock of hair lifted by the wind, caused the herb woman to glance at the door, but Brenna was quick to press her finger over her mouth and shake her head. Some other wicked impulse bade her move on silent feet across the floor and wave a dismissing hand in Margery's direction. She ignored the scowl on the woman's face and hitched her oversleeves up to sit high on her shoulders. She twisted her hair into a loose tail at the nape of her neck and bound it with the folded length of her veil, then poured a dollop of oil in her hands and rubbed them together to warm it.

Margery, meanwhile, had worked most of the muscles across his shoulders and upper arms, and his protestations had faded into muffled groans of appreciation. Pacing herself to Margery's rhythm, Brenna nodded the older woman away and smoothly took over the massage. His face was turned to the wall, half buried in the furs, and the one eye she could just glimpse was closed, the lashes laying on his cheek like fallen wings.

She need not have worried about warming the oil in her hands first; his flesh gave off enough heat to liquefy lard. Her hands slid across the broad slabs of muscle, working the oil across the ridge of his shoulders and into the crook of his neck. She used her thumbs to push against the knots and tightness she found there, then stroked, kneaded, and manipulated each knuckle of his spine to pull out the adjoining tension. He had a terrific number of scars, she noted absently. They rippled by beneath her fingers like raised seams on a sheet of silk. Some were new, some old. Some were deep and long, and she lightened her touch as she traced their course; others were shallow and faded, crisscrossing behind the ribs as if . . . as if he had been lashed at some time in his youth.

"Forgive me for barking at you, Goodwife," he murmured thickly. "I shall be in your debt forever after this night."

Brenna lowered her chin and gave what she hoped was an admirably husky imitation of Margery's voice. "A coin or two is thanks enough, my lord. If you think it is well earned."

"Well earned?" He groaned again and curled his fingers into the fur. "You can have no idea how wonderful this feels."

Brenna felt a flush warm her cheeks and invade her brow, and blamed it on the steam rising from the huge vats. "You . . . do not come from these parts, my lord?"

"Mmm? No. No, I do not."

"Ahh. South, is it? I thought I heard a bit of the Gascon in you."

"I have spent time in Castile and Aragon," he conceded. "But I make my home in Burgundy."

"Burgundy? A heathen place, to be sure. Have you family there, then?"

He drew a deep breath, swelling and expanding the muscles across his back. "No. No family."

"And you earn your keep by fighting in tourneys?"

"I run a course now and then to keep my eye sharp and my lance steady."

"You plan to fight Lord Robert, do you? Four years undefeated is he. You will have to know your business if you expect to meet him. And no faults either. No weaknesses."

She said this as she was inspecting the extensive scarring on his left hand and forearm. She had seen a similar injury once before, in a test of truth before a church tribunal when a man had been forced to plunge his hand into a tub of boiling oil to retrieve a crucifix from the bottom. If the hand was scalded or the crucifix was not recovered, he had obviously lied; if the hand emerged unblemished, he told the truth. Either way, the flesh of the arm was usually cooked through and turned as hard as the bone before eventually rotting and cracking off.

Renaud's arm, by comparison, still looked strong enough beneath the smooth tightness of the skin, but it carried less bulk than the right, a detriment Robin might be able to use to his advantage if they met in the lists at Gaillard.

"Your arm, sir, does it cause you much trouble?"

"Women do not usually look at my arms when I am lying naked before them."

The blush in her cheeks grew hot enough to dry her lips, and she worked the heels of her hands into the grooves beneath his shoulder blades as a reward for his impudence. There was no give to the muscles, no corresponding grunt of pain, and she realized she would be hard-pressed to say who carried more power in their upper body—Robin or Renaud—for his back was like solid plate armor and she had not found an excess pinch of flesh anywhere.

"Lower, if you please."

"My lord?"

"Send your magic fingers lower, if you please. My arse feels like a blister and my legs like two firesticks."

Brenna looked down. She was at his waist now, kneading her thumbs into the dimples at the small of his back. He gave a low, throaty growl of approval as she set aside the narrow strip of toweling, and she was thankful his face was still turned away, his eyes closed against the welter of heat ebbing and flowing in her cheeks. The towel had somehow preserved a modicum of modesty on both their behalf, but without it, he was a gleaming, magnificently naked beast sprawled on a bed of fur, and she was a witless fool who had gone too far to back away.

She spread more oil and molded her hands to the shape of his buttocks. She stroked and kneaded and manipulated the marble-hard flesh until there was a fine sheen of moisture rising across her own brow, then ran her fingers lower again, sliding over the seemingly endless iron thews of his thighs and calves. When she worked her thumbs into the arches of his feet, he groaned like a dying man and shifted on the bed of furs as if it were a sexual encounter. When she started up the second leg, she saw his hands flex and curl into fists while he swore, then laughed softly and swore again.

"You will prove the end of me yet, Goodwife," he murmured. "Is there a price I could pay to lure you away from this place?"

"Lord Randwulf is as fine a master as ever there is, sir. No price on earth could lure me away."

"And the sons? They look an arrogant lot."

She dug her thumbs into a pocket of nerves and was happy to hear him suck in a sharp breath. "No more arrogant than those who would mock them, *my lord*."

His head, cloaked by the glossy black waves of hair, turned slightly on the furs. "Your loyalty is commendable, but what excuse do you give the daughter?"

"The daughter?"

"The hellion. She dresses like a commoner, has the manners of a fishmonger's wife, and likely could not entice a kiss out of a man without holding him at bowshot first."

Brenna's mouth dropped open.

"Even then, I doubt she would know how to kiss him properly." He added softly, "Unless, of course, she could find someone willing to teach her."

"You, I suppose?" She realized too late that she had challenged him in her own voice, but before she could react or respond, his hand reached out and closed around her upper arm. His head came up off the furs and all she could see were the cat's eyes, luminous gray-green glowering out from beneath the inky spill of his hair.

"Dare I ask what the game is this time, my lady?"

"N-no game," she stammered. "I was—"

"Yes?"

"I was . . ."

"Asking questions."

"Making polite conversation!"

"Spying on me?"

"Never! I was only helping Margery. She . . . she has a cut finger."

He scanned the room behind her and the look on his face was so blatantly skeptical, her eyes narrowed to violet slits.

"How long have you known it was me?"

"Since you stood in the doorway and watched. Your hair, I think—" His gaze raked appreciatively over the loosely flown curls. "It smells of apples."

"Lilacs, you dolt!" She wrenched her arm free and made a dash for the door. For such a big man he moved with shocking speed, and she was still two full steps away from making good her escape when she felt herself being scooped up in one strong arm. The other shot out and slammed the door shut behind her, and she found herself crowded into the shadows, her legs trapped between his, her arms caught and held immobile by her sides.

As hot as his skin had felt beneath her hands, his body was twice that. As strong as she had imagined all those muscles to be, they were breathtakingly forceful in driving all the air from her lungs and pinning her helplessly against the wall.

"I neglected to add foolish and reckless when I was listing your attributes," he murmured.

His voice chilled the nape of her neck and sprayed her arms with gooseflesh. There was only one lamp in the room and it was behind him, etching his oil-slicked shoulders and arms with a thin gold rim of fire. He towered over her, his face cloaked in shadows, but so close each breath fanned her skin and sent a shocking ribbon of heat curling down her spine and puddling somewhere deep inside her.

"Let go of me," she said, cursing the tremor in her voice. "At once."

He was silent a long moment. She could feel the renewed heat in her face, flaring as he studied her every feature in minute detail. The steam from the tubs had nowhere to go now that the door was closed, and it swirled in hot clouds around the lamp, dampening the light even more.

"Will you *please* let me go," she repeated in a stronger voice.

"Please? Now, there is a word I had not thought to hear from those lips."

Brenna offered up a futile spate of squirming, but his hands were like iron manacles around her wrists and whatever leeway she had gained by her initial submission was lost again when his hips pushed forward to restrict her squirming.

"I could scream and bring half the castle guard down around your ears," she warned on a hiss of breath.

"And what would they see? A woman intruding on the privacy of a man's bath. A woman enticing a naked man to a clearly dangerous state of arousal by stroking his body with shameful expertise."

She had avoided looking up to where she supposed his eyes to be, but she did so now and saw a faint glimmer through the shadows. "I did not intrude on your bath, nor was it my intent to arouse you."

"In that you have failed then, my lady, as you can plainly see."

She did *not* want to look down. God-a-mercy, she could feel him well enough. It should not have surprised her to discover he was big all over, and indeed, she had seen big men aroused before. But that had been from a distance, and usually from an objective point of view; sometimes with great humor, wondering at the awkwardness of carrying such a thing between the legs.

Renaud did not appear to be the least discomforted. It was she who felt the intrusion of hard, thick flesh, and where it pushed boldly between her thighs, it found all those little ribbons of heat and started spinning them together in a tight, throbbing knot.

"Shall we have the truth now?"

"The truth?"

"Did your brother send you?"

"No! No, he does not even know I am here. No one does."

"No one? Foolish again, my lady," he murmured, and now his mouth was close enough she could feel its warmth on her cheek. She drew back in an unconscious response, but there was nowhere to go, and when his mouth brushed her a second time, she knew it had been no accident.

Exhaling very carefully, she said, "If you let me go right now, right this minute, I promise I will not tell my brothers what has happened."

"Nothing *has* happened. Yet."

His breath was a feathery caress over her mouth, and she gave up a small shiver of apprehension. "Actually, I . . . I came to apologize. Yes . . . to apologize."

"Really? Whatever for?"

"Why, for my behavior this afternoon, for one thing," she said on a faint rush. "I was rude, and . . . and . . ."

"Insolent? Suspicious? Threatening?"

"I was perhaps *overcautious*, I might grant you."

"How generous. You offered to kill my horse if I did not abase myself like a common dung collector before you."

She moistened her lips and risked another glance up. "I am truly sorry for that. I would never have harmed such a superb creature. If I resorted to such a threat, it was because you . . . you looked a villainous and dangerous sort who might have taken callous advantage of the circumstances."

"Villainous *and* dangerous? I confess I have been called both on occasion, but never at the same time."

"In any case," she said with a small wriggle of impatience, "you must agree that a woman on her own must take certain precautionary measures."

"To safeguard her virginity?"

"To safeguard herself from *any* violation."

"Meaning you are not a virgin?"

"Meaning," she snapped, "it would be none of your business to know one way or the other."

He offered up a small, dry laugh and studied her face again. It was her hair that was winning most of his attention this time. The dampness in the bath house had sent the tawny curls spraying in all directions, and where they met the moisture on her temples and throat, they were coiling into tight, dark spirals.

"What are you looking at? Why are you frowning?"

"I am looking at you. And I would not have guessed . . ." His voice trailed away and she looked up again, her violet eyes reflecting pinpoints of light.

"Guessed what?"

"That there was such a beautiful woman under all that mulishness, and that there might be another reason I would have cause to regret not pulling you down off of Centaur this afternoon."

"As if you could have," she scoffed.

He bent his head closer still. "If you believe nothing else of me, my lady, believe I could have had you on the ground, your bow and your back broken if I had wanted it."

She had grown accustomed enough to the mist and shadow to distinguish the dark slash of his eyebrows, the straight line of his nose, the rugged squareness of his jaw with its deeply clefted chin. She watched his mouth as it formed the words, and the tightness in her belly became a series of little fluttering convulsions that flooded her limbs with heat and turned her bones to jelly. Her breath lodged with a suffocating tightness halfway up her throat, and she knew a challenge would be futile. She believed him. He could have overpowered her then, just as he could overpower her now with laughable ease.

"Who are you?" she asked in a whisper.

"No one you would truly want to know."

"Have you come here to kill my father?"

He did not even have the grace to look surprised at the question, but he answered it simply enough. "No."

"My brother?"

"No."

"Would you tell me the truth if you had?"

"At this precise moment, I would probably tell you anything you wanted to know."

Her limbs quivered noticeably as his dark head tilted

forward and she felt the searching warmth of his lips on her neck.

"Wh-what are you doing?"

"Being truthful," he murmured against her throat. "I do not want to argue with you anymore. And since you have apologized to me and I have apologized to you"—his tongue flicked languidly over the pulse beating rapidly beneath her ear—"I thought we might both take advantage of all this friendliness."

She tried to twist away, but the movement only bared a greater expanse of tender flesh, and his mouth was there suckling a warm, moist path from the crook of her shoulder to the soft pink curl of her ear. Her breath came out in a harsh gasp and her knees started to buckle. A streak of hot, stabbing pleasure shot from the nape of her neck to her belly, obliterating nearly every other sensation between. The only one that remained was the acutely tender eagerness that suddenly sprang to fill her breasts, gathering the nipples into tight little peaks that felt as if they could pierce through the layers of silk. There was no escaping the sinfully erotic pleasure, no comparison she could make with any other experience she had had thus far in her life. There would be no salvation for her either if she did not keep a firm grip on her senses.

"I do not recollect receiving any apology from you," she said, gasping as his tongue swirled treacherously into her ear.

"No?" He frowned and for all of two racing heartbeats she thought she had won a reprieve. With the next startled hammerblow, he raised her hands above her head and captured both wrists in one hand, freeing the other to circle her waist and support her faltering legs even as he drew her forward over the solid shaft of his flesh.

"Consider this to be it, then."

Shocked at the explicit, thrusting incursion, Brenna tried to cry out but his mouth was there to smother the sound. He did it with a thoroughness that stripped her of whatever breath and sense she had remaining, the kiss as bold and arrogant and uncompromising as the man himself. His tongue invaded her mouth, probing deep, penetrating what few defenses she could call to hand, silencing them with a bruising force that frightened her, for it was nothing at all like the chaste, chivalrous kisses she had exchanged with ignorant abandon before.

This . . . *possession* was neither chaste nor chivalrous. He was intent on ravishing, devouring, conquering every silken recess of her mouth, and while she managed to squeak out a few shivered protests, she could not summon the strength or wit to make them sound convincing. Each lavish stroke had its erotic counterpart below as he wedged a knee between her thighs and used his flesh to chafe the growing knot of sensations she had been experiencing into a fiercely vibrant, shimmering heat. The silk of her bliaud was a feeble hindrance, sheer as a whisper, and the linen chainse hardly better. If anything, the sleek abrasion intensified the heat and friction, bringing Brenna up on her toes in an effort to ease the tightness in the cloth and stop the shameless waves of pleasure.

A tremor in the massive body indicated her efforts had had the opposite effect, for now he could—and did—slide the whole length of his flesh between her thighs. He brought his hand up from her waist and molded the palm around her breast, groaning with approval when he found her nipples hard as pebbles, straining into each stroke of his long fingers. He groaned again, thick and low, and his lips slanted even more forcefully over hers, keeping and holding her breathless until her whole body was a mass of raw, trembling sensation.

"Yield to me," he whispered raggedly. "Yield to me and we can spend the night changing the opinions we have of one another."

Brenna's eyes shivered open. She was hot and dizzy, a wildness was racing through her blood, the flesh between her thighs felt swollen and distended, aching with sharp, sweet sensations that promised pleasures beyond her comprehension.

His hands were clamped around her waist, his fingers bruising in their attempt to control the desires raging through his own body. Her hands—when had he released them? When had they become tangled in the luxuriant mane of his hair? They were no less steady as she pushed . . . then pushed again, widening the gap between them.

"No." She gasped. "No, I cannot do this."

His hands tightened as he urged her lushly to and fro over the magnificence of his erection, angling himself upward so that he was, indeed, inside her if only by a silk-encased inch or two. "You can. And you want to, I can feel it."

"No." She shuddered and swallowed hard. "Please, let me go."

With a small laugh, he ignored her plea and lifted her breast, holding it cupped in his palm while the heat of his mouth and breath soaked through to her skin. Brenna stiffened involuntarily against the instant, violent thrill, and somewhere inside her, the pressure built to an exquisite peak and sent a melting rush of sensation flooding through her body. Her hands came skidding down onto the hard ridge of his shoulders in a halfhearted attempt to dislodge him, but he only laughed again and started lifting the hem of her skirts.

He had most of her leg bared before she was able to recoup enough of her strength and senses to push him away and gain a moment of freedom.

"Are you mad?" She gasped. "Or simply too full of yourself to see past your own arrogance?"

"I am full of something," he agreed blithely. "And am only too eager to share it with you."

"*I* am not eager to share it with *you*," she insisted, pushing against him. "Of course, you could rape me and take what you want. But then you would simply be proving my opinion of you was the right one all along. You would be proving yourself to be a man of little conscience and no honor; one who would force yourself on an unwilling woman, on the daughter of your host, on the sister of the man who took you in as a friend when others of more discriminating judgment would have shown more caution."

He stood in the swirling rolls of steam, his body gleaming from the moisture and the oil, his hair damp and clinging to his throat and shoulders in dark streaks. The veins in his arms stood out like thin blue snakes on top of muscles that bulged and quivered with menacing fury. His erection was rampant and throbbing and nearly brought her to her knees with the first genuinely pure shiver of fear she had experienced in his presence, for she doubted a charge of rape would cause so much as a flicker of concern in the smoldering gray-green eyes. She doubted it because, even as the thought sent her cringing back against the wall, she saw his eyes narrow and his mouth curve into a hard, cynical smile.

"Go then," he rasped. "Get out. Get out before you tempt me to show you exactly how little the words *conscience* and *honor* mean to me."

She kept her back pressed to the wall as she started inching toward the door, only a pace or two away. Her hand fumbled blindly for the rope latch, fully expecting him to intercept her long before she found it and groped her way to freedom. But he did not. He moved with her, to be sure, and the promise was there in his eyes that if she faltered or showed the slightest hesitation, there would be no second chance.

Her hand touched the coarse jute and her fingers curled around it. With a choked cry, she jerked it open and fled into the cold night air, her bare feet flying over the rough earth, her skirt whipping up around her ankles in a froth of churning silk. A moment later she heard his laughter, deep and throaty, following her across the draw and into the covered entrance to the keep. It followed her much longer than that, even though she could no longer hear it, and kept the flames of mortification burning hot in her cheeks until she was safely inside her own bedchamber with the door firmly shut behind her.

Panting, her hands clasped over her breasts, she was relieved beyond measure to see she was alone. Helvise had

been and gone, knowing her mistress rarely wanted or
needed help to ready herself for bed at night. A second
shocked glance found her own reflection in the mirror. The
elegant, regal lady who had exited the room with such confidence and conviction was gone, and in her place stood a
harridan, her hair a tangle of steamed curls, her tunic damp
over one breast and ripped at the hem, as soiled along the
bottom edge as the soles of her bare feet.

"Good sweet Jesu!"

Anxious hands tore off the burgundy silk and flung it to
the floor. She had forgotten Helvise's work with needle and
thread to stitch the cuffs of the chainse snug to her wrists
and forearms, and only managed to get the offending garment over her head and partially off her arms before she
had to find the scissors and snip away the bindings. It was
awkward work and she dropped the scissors twice before she
ended up simply slashing the linen and ripping it over her
hands. She balled the ruined garment and, feeling no sad-
ness over the loss, tossed it onto the logs blazing in the
hearth.

Naked, standing in a golden cocoon of her own hair,
she watched it smolder and char on the hot coals until the
edges caught and flared into blue flames. On a further
thought, she snatched up the burgundy silk and tossed it
into the cloud of rising cinders and black, acrid smoke as
well. Helvise would probably have spitting fits come morning to find out what she had done, but Brenna did not care;
she would never have worn either garment again.

In eighteen years, not one single man in the entire
demesne could boast of having touched her so intimately.
Griffyn Renaud had been in her life less than half a day and
he had not only kissed her witless and senseless, but he had
sent her fleeing to her room to burn the evidence of her
own shame.

She could not dispose of *him* so easily, however, and, it
occurred to her on a groan, he might have no qualms whatsoever in relating his version of the amusing incident in the
bath house. Imagine his surprise, he would say, halfway

through a most relaxing massage, when he discovered that the wickedly proficient hands ministering to his aches and bruises belonged not to Margery, the castle drab, but to one of the bold-intentioned daughters of the household!

Such extreme measures of hospitality were not unheard of where there were too many unwed daughters in a family and not enough available suitors of noble blood. *Not* that Brenna believed for an *instant* there could be a drop of anything noble or honorable flowing through the veins of Griffyn Renaud de Verdelay! From his clothes—as carefully nondescript and devoid of any crests or devices as the trappings of his horse—to his manners, from the way he had cleverly avoided answering too many questions about where he had been or what he had been doing these past years when he was supposed to have been dead . . . she no longer doubted he was anything better than a common mercenary. A man whose sword and soul were for simple hire. There could be no other explanation, no other reason why a knight would travel alone, without markings, without a squire, without the comfort of an open road in front of him. The fact he was bound for Château Gaillard only confirmed her suspicions. Where better for a fighting man to display his prowess and skill than at the largest, most prestigious tournament in Normandy? Where better to find a rich employer? What better boast to add to his name than an acquaintance with the son of the Black Wolf of Amboise?

Or a tawdry liaison with the daughter?

She groaned again and threw herself across the bed. *That* was why he had not raped her. Rape would not have curried anything but slow castration and death, whereas if she had allowed him to seduce her, he could have claimed afterward that she had flaunted herself and deliberately aroused him beyond reason, making it more of an insult to refuse her advances than to accept them.

She balled her fists and struck them on the bed, wanting to scream. The flame of her night candle flickered and went out, and she cursed as she found a taper and relit it. Staring at it, she wondered if she ought to light a second one. If the first was meant to keep the devil from slipping into the room to steal her soul while she slept, perhaps a second would keep her from dwelling on the black-haired, green-eyed demon who had already stolen her peace of mind.

Curled beneath her covers and furs, she stared unblinking at the remnants of her clothing smoldering in the fire. She did not expect to sleep a wink all night worrying about what the morning would bring, how quickly the scandal would reach Helvise's ears, and how early the maid would come into the chamber bearing the news that her father was demanding to see her.

If only she hadn't followed Margery into the bath house. If only she hadn't gone to the river, hadn't gone into the forest at all today! If only . . . if only . . . if only . . . !

The if onlys kept her awake until just before the first pearly streaks of dawn showed through the cracks in her shutters. And at the same moment the flame on her candle spluttered below the last hour mark, Brenna dreamed of a tall, naked knight with black hair bowing his mouth to her breast, sending a warm shiver of ecstasy rippling through her body.

8

When Brenna opened her eyes again, there was still a dark face filling them. Not the one she had been dreaming about, but equally ominous and just as unlikely to be put off without answers.

"Are you ill?"

Brenna blinked several times and looked around. The shutters were open, admitting bright sunlight. A small platter of bread and cheese sat on the table, and the ashes around the hearth had been swept and tidied.

"Your mother was concerned when you did not come down to chapel."

"Helvise?"

"Nor was it like you to miss the morning meal or linger in your bed like an ale-soaked trull—although, to judge by the bedsheets, you had no easy time of it."

Brenna propped herself up on one elbow and cast a surly eye over the shambles she had made of her bed coverings. A bare arm reached down and drew a second layer of blankets over the first and pulled them both over her shoulders, then her face. "I am cold. Is there a fire?"

"It was freshened three hours ago when I came the first time, then again two hours ago, and see? I have a splinter in my finger from adding another log just now. Are you ill?" she asked again. "Is it your flux?"

"No." Brenna sighed, causing a small hillock to blow up under the sheets. "And no. Can I not spend an extra hour in bed without the castle guard being alerted?"

Helvise straightened and puffed out her chest. "The guard, as it happens, *was* alerted, but not for you. It seems most of the castle was kept awake last night by your brothers and that bold-faced knight you found in the forest yesterday. Drinking and dicing and hoisting skirts they were, loud enough to waken the dead. Lord Dagobert is still puking. And someone hung Sparrow up on a peg on the wall, where he slept until your father found him there this morning and plucked him down."

Brenna peeled the sheet down from her face and eyed Helvise warily as the serving woman gathered up the lengths of bed curtain and tied them to the posters. "He is still here then?"

"Your knight? Indeed he is." Helvise chuckled. "Although if castle gossip is to be believed, his company will be sorely missed when he does go on his way."

Brenna suffered through a sudden loss of blood in her face and throat and waited for the bony, accusing finger to be thrust under her nose.

"What do you mean?" she croaked. "What have you heard?"

"Now, my lady, you know full well I do not like to listen to all the prattle that goes on between the laundry and cook house."

Only every scrap of every word, Brenna thought miserably. It had always amazed her that a servant in the main keep knew of an incident in the village practically the moment after it happened. Helvise, despite her air of disdain, had a special knack for sniffing out the lowest detail of the most insignificant event and embellishing it beyond belief in the retelling. Margery would have been at the trough long before cock's crow and unless, by some miracle of providence, she had fallen head first down the well or poisoned herself with one of her own enemata, she would have had one of the choicest contributions for the gossip mill.

"Well, at any rate, it seems the rogue drank nearly a barrel of ale by himself and got into a dicing game with Lord Richard over Tansy. It seems he won the throw *and* Tansy, and when he finished with her"—she lowered her voice and glanced at the door as if the ears of a thousand priests were pressed to the keyhole—"she could hardly walk. She fainted *three times*, she said. A rare swordsman, she said, not selfish like most men either. That was what she said. 'Like most men.' I can only think Lord Richard did not take kindly to the comparison, because he was all pricked up like a hedgehog this morning, turning ever so funny a shade of red whenever anyone chanced to smile in his direction."

Brenna stared. "Is that all? My brother's cocksman's feathers were ruffled?"

"Well." Helvise shrugged and straightened. "I have not heard tell of any maid fainting of pleasure in *his* arms. Not that I would give Tansy's story that much credence now, for she is a slut and would claim just about anything to win attention. Margery did say the rogue was a big brute, but she also said that after you finished prodding and pounding him, he would have been good for very little."

"Margery said that?"

"Indeed. And she thought it a fine joke too."

Brenna watched, visibly taken aback, as Helvise fetched a clean shirt and leggings from her wardrobe chest. Was that it then? Was there to be no feverish gossip? No pointed fingers or sly smirks? Was her reputation with men so deeply set in stone it never even occurred to anyone to think she would succumb to the lusty charms of a handsome stranger?

"I will not even waste my spittle trying to persuade you to wear a cotte today, my lady." Helvise was sighing. "Perigord has been asking for you, so I must assume that means the new bow is ready and you will be out in the fields again all day today."

"Yes. Yes, likely all day." She swung her legs over the side of the bed and walked naked into the spill of sunlight pouring through the open window.

A fine joke? And that was all there was to it? She had agonized and squirmed with torment the whole blessed night long . . . and he had been enjoying himself in the arms of a twopenny wench who boasted—*boasted* of having fainted three times beneath him?

Three times?

Faugh! If he had given the trull a penny more, she likely would have bragged a dozen!

Brenna was still fuming when she reached the practice yards. She had seen Perigord and been given the new bow—a stout length of sun-hardened Spanish yew as tall as she was, with a grip that fit her hand like a polished extension of bone and muscle. She had loosed a couple of arrows outside the armory, frightening half a dozen chickens and a brace of roosters going about their business, but the old bowyer knew her so well there was nothing that needed altering, not by so much as a thumb-shave. She carried the new bow and two others down to the outer bailey along with two full quivers of arrows, needing open space to fully test the balance and resilience.

Long before she crossed the draw, she heard the sounds of swords clashing and horses' hooves tearing up the earth in the practice yards. Richard and Dag were not preparing themselves so much for the single-combat matches as they were for the mêlée, usually the final event of the tournament wherein a pitched fight between two teams of knights took place. It was fought to settle a point of law, a case that had found no solution in the courts and had been agreed by both disputing parties to be decided by means of trial by combat. It was a common practice, though more for the spectacle than the legal satisfaction, and often limited to the very rich, since hiring champions to fight for a cause could cost a good deal more than what was paid out for bribes and lawyers.

The three Wardieu brothers along with their brother-in-law Geoffrey LaFer would be teaming up to resolve one such case in Château Gaillard. They had not been approached to do so, nor would they collect a penny for their efforts win or lose. The dispute, in fact, was not even to do with the law, it was to do with a matter of the heart. A peasant lad, son of a woodcutter, had perforce caused the niece of Hugh Luisignan—a close friend and ally to Sir Randwulf—to fall violently in love with him. Since it was inconceivable to her father that she would even *want* to marry herself to a mere woodcutter's son, the two were expressly forbidden to meet, the lad even threatened with maiming—or worse—should he dare see his love again. Heartbroken, the girl had run and taken sanctuary at a convent, vowing to remain there forever if she could not marry the man she loved.

Robin, whose heart was pudding when it came to ill-fated lovers, had heard of her plight and had tried to appeal to both the father and the uncle on the girl's behalf. Sir Hugh, more sympathetic than his brother might have preferred him to be, had arranged a meeting with Lord Randwulf wherein it was decided, over much ale and good-natured wagering, that the only convenient way to save the pride of all parties involved was through a battle-royale at Gaillard. If the Wardieu team triumphed, the girl would win her woodcutter. If Hugh the Brown's team was declared victorious, the girl would return home and marry a man of her father's choosing.

It was a ridiculous dispute to have to settle by means of combat, but since most of the senior parties involved were more stubborn than angry from the outset, and since smaller excuses than this had been found to stage a mêlée, it was deemed a worthy enough cause to stage a sporting challenge. Not that it would be a light or amiable affair. Hugh's men had fought shoulder to shoulder with the Amboise men at Roche-au-Moines and were equally fierce and fearsome in battle. Moreover, there were no rules in the mêlée, and the outcome was always uncertain and dangerous. After the first shock of running at each other, skill with a lance counted for very little and it became a perilous business of fighting in close quarters, swords bashing against swords, and, if unhorsed, sometimes fist to fist. While the weapons were limited to lance, sword, and poniard, there was no restriction put on their use. No swing was illegal, no weapon was blunted. Fighting continued until surrender was offered or, in the opinion of the tournament judges, one side was clearly defeated.

Thus, as Brenna crossed the draw and made for the practice yards, the metallic clashing of swords rang clear in the air. Dag and Richard were putting themselves through rigorous, mock battles with volunteer knights, while Jean de Brevant paced around the two pairs shouting at a sloppy foot here or a missed opening there.

Robin was in full armor and sat astride his destrier Sir Tristan. His face was bathed in sweat and his hair plastered tight to his head beneath the leather bascinet, a fitted cap worn under the helm for cushioning. His shoulders and chest were exaggerated by the bulk of a thickly padded *aketon* worn under a full-length mail hauberk and an outer shell of *cuir bouilli*—leather boiled and hardened in wax— to prevent against any mishaps. He wore no surcoat or tunic over his practice armor, and the lance Timkin was waiting to hand up was much battered and scarred from striking and scraping the quintain.

Judging by the amount of sweat shining on his face and the ruddy color in his cheeks, he had already made several runs at the small swinging target and was grabbing at an opportunity to nurse his bruised ribs while he waited for Sparrow to finish buckling Will into his aketon, a vestlike garment of thick cotton quilting, designed to absorb and deflect all but the most mortal of blows. This was just practice, and the only blow would come if he fell out of the saddle or rode headlong into the quintain. But learning to ride and balance in heavy gear was as important as any stroke with the lance, and full armor was worn until it became second nature to maneuver carrying almost two hundred pounds of added weight.

"My helm was leaking rust again," Robin was griping. "I was all but blinded by the sting in the last run."

"Endeavor not to sweat so much," Sparrow grumbled, glancing up. "More likely it is your vanity stinging at the thought of having to accept a lady's favor with orange stripes running down your face. Fear not, Lord Cockerel. Timkin is wearing his feet to the bone rolling your tourney armor in oiled sand. By the time we reach Gaillard you should glitter and gleam enough to attract the eye of any a nubile young dove you choose."

Robin glared and was about to voice a retort when he saw Brenna approaching and nodded a curt greeting. One look at his eyes told her it was not just the discomfort of his ribs causing him to seek a moment's respite; more likely it was a head the size of a barrel of ale.

Sparrow, meanwhile, had clambered up onto a stool to fit the bulky mail hauberk over Will's shoulders and was buckling the straps up the back. He was apparently in no better fettle, for his eyes were mere squints and his cherub's nose was in full blush. Will simply looked green.

"Well, and a good morrow to you all," Brenna said cheerfully. "I see the lot of you have come to the green well rested and full of vinegar."

Will belched quietly and turned to offer a sarcastic smile but was prodded out of his intention by a pudgy hand.

"Pay heed, Will-of-the-Scarlet-Eyes, and *try* to recall the lessons we have striven to impart. Carry the lance thus, supported in the palms, not the fingers, with the shaft balanced over the left arm, *not* across the mane of the steed as you did in Poitou. If you are too weary to carry it with some measure of fortitude, seek out a bed and lay your head upon it, thereby saving us all the aggravation of dragging your cockles out of the mud."

Will groaned and rolled his eyes in Robin's direction. "Once," he said. "I rested the lance once."

"And you will hear about it until the day your toes turn up," Robin assured him grimly.

"If you must rest it," Sparrow lectured, pouncing on the slip, "rest it on the leg . . . thus!" He clapped a hand to his thigh for emphasis. "From here it can be regained quickly. Or rest it on your chest, putting your hand as close to your arm as you are able, and bent in such a fashion as to offer support. But take care not to twist or lean forward"—he did both by way of demonstration—"for it defeats the purpose of trying to catch the breath, and only leaves you gasping for more."

"It would likely topple you out of the saddle as well," Robin noted dryly, pulling on his gauntlets again.

"Toppling will not happen," Sparrow decreed firmly. "Not if the lance is borne properly. Do not tilt the tip upward, especially if you have the wind in your face or if the horse is cantering. If you have no help for it but to be in a full gallop, press the heels down and *squ-eeeze* the legs tight, matching your body to the rhythm of the beast beneath you."

"Somewhat in the same fashion as you did last week with that little black-haired wench," Robin mused.

Sparrow threw his hands up in a gesture of defeat. "Lummocks, the brace of you. The saints should grant me martyrdom for even trying to breach the thickness of your skulls. Go then. Launch yourselves at shadows and see if you can hit the target at least once this day."

"Which one?" Will asked. "I see three hanging from each pole."

"No matter," Robin added. "By the time you gallop over there, your lance will feel like it has three tips as well."

Will pulled his bascinet over the flaming crop of his hair and managed a weak grin in Brenna's direction before mounting the block and swinging himself on his charger. He hovered there a wild moment while he fought not to swing right off the other side of the saddle, but then he found his balance and snatched up the gauntlets and helm Timkin handed up to him.

"Five marks says the weight of his head brings him down before the end of the second run," Brenna murmured.

"A fool's wager," Sparrow countered. "The pillock will be digging dirt out of his nose on the first pass."

"Shall I hang you up somewhere comfortable to watch?"

His face swelled and flooded crimson to the roots of his curly black hair. He muttered something under his breath—something to do with the wisdom of drowning all females at birth—then stomped after Robin and Will, shouting last-minute instructions.

Brenna was still laughing when she turned and found herself standing face to face with Griffyn Renaud. He had not made a whisper of sound to warn of his approach or presence. He was simply there, leaning his shoulder against a wooden pole, his arms folded negligently across his chest, his mouth curved in a cynical smile. He was not in armor and obviously had not taken advantage of his host's invitation to run a few practices course before Gaillard. He was watching, however, and undoubtedly noting every small nuance of Robin's style and manner. A cheap means, Brenna thought, of gaining an advantage over one's opponent.

It was the first time she had seen him without the disadvantage of shadows blunting his features. The purpling haze of dusk had softened him somewhat by the river, while torchlight and candlelight had proved inadequate for an honest evaluation in the castle and bath house. She was not exactly sure what more could have shocked her after last night, but shocked she was. In the bright, unflattering harshness of direct sunlight, he was quite simply heart-stopping. His hair was so black it glinted blue, his skin was weathered bronze, and where it covered his cheekbones and stretched over the finely chiseled flare of his nostrils, it was smooth and unmarked, stripping away the extra years intimated by his preference for shadows.

In the forest, Brenna had guessed his age to be higher than the twenty-four years he shared with Robin, but she thought she could see some hint of lost youth in him now, in the pearly gray-green sheen of his eyes and the small crinkles at the corners that seemed to be telling her they wanted to not be always on their guard but had simply forgotten how.

"God's grace to you this morning, my lady. I trust you passed a restful night and are well at ease."

Brenna watched his mouth as it formed the harmlessly polite words. He had shaved most of the rough stubble from his jaw and looked as refreshed as if he had spent the last few hours deep in sleep, not inciting a drunken night of debauchery.

"I am surprised you would even dare to mention last night. I am, in fact, surprised you are still here. Your kind usually skulk away under cover of darkness, do they not?"

"My . . . *kind*?"

She drew a shallow breath and released it on a brisk huff. "What term to do you prefer, sirrah, when you boast your profession? Routier? Brabançon? Hireling? Or will simple *mercenary* do?"

His face seemed perfectly composed, the mask of casual indifference had not altered in the least, but she thought she saw a muscle flicker in the angle of his jaw. "Are you always so quick with your judgments? What if I said I was none of those things?"

"You would," she said evenly, "be adding *liar* to your vast repertoire of attributes."

She gave him her best and coldest glare and walked past him toward the archery run.

Two boys, lounging on the green watching the knights practice, jumped quickly to attention as she approached the long, wide strip of grassy common. It ran from one end of the bailey to the other with straw butts and painted canvas targets placed at various distances along the run; the closest at fifty yards, the middle at a hundred, the last against the far wall, two hundred yards away. She leaned the two spare bows against a low wooden barricade and set her quivers on the bench, then produced a sticky-sweet confection for each of the boys, who would happily spend the next few hours fetching the spent arrows from the targets.

"May I?"

Startled, she saw a long, linen-clad arm reach past her shoulder and lift one of the bows. His sleeve brushed her shoulder with the motion and when she looked, he was standing close enough she could have counted each individual long lash that framed his eyes. Close enough she thought she detected the faint, lingering scent of the camphor oil she had rubbed so dexterously into the broad, rippling shoulders last night.

While she watched, he tested the weight and balance of the longbow, holding it with a hand obviously familiar with all manner of weaponry. Without asking her permission, he leaned against the shaft and bent it to seat the bowstring.

"I would not have thought someone as slight as yourself could handle one of these things," he murmured, glancing pointedly at her arms, "yet your brothers tell me you are quite the marksman."

He passed the compliment as if he believed her shot in the woods the previous day had been mere luck.

"Do you shoot, sirah?" she asked through her teeth.

"Only if my belly has gone too long without meat."

The comment drew her gaze downward to the powerful presentation of chest, shoulders, and flat, hard belly, and she doubted if he went without anything for too long a time. He was wearing a hunting green tunic of soft kid leather and a plain, loose-sleeved shirt beneath, but the casual ease with which he presented himself was deceiving. She had felt those muscles and found iron in those sinews; she imagined he could break half-grown trees in his hands if he put his mind to it.

He caused Tansy to faint three times in his arms, Helvise had said. *Three times . . .*

He selected an arrow out of a quiver and gave it the same intense scrutiny as the bow. The shaft was ashwood, nearly three feet long, tipped with an iron broadhead, counterbalanced with three vanes of gray goosefeather fletching. He nocked it to the string and held the bow in a horizontal position, face-on to the target as someone accustomed to firing a crossbow might do. Braced with his feet wide apart, he drew the fletching back between pinched fingers and sighted along the shaft.

A child, if he had the power in his arm to draw the string, could have launched the arrow as far as the first butt, yet Renaud appeared to be pleased with himself for doing so. He had even managed to hit the target, near the edge of the butt to be sure, but bedded an inch deep in the canvas and straw.

"Awkward," he pronounced. "But interesting."

Brenna cast a derisive glance at the bold rogue knight before she took up her new bow and selected an arrow from the quiver. She paused to put on a specially made three-fingered glove, acutely aware of Renaud's gaze on her as she did so. Was it her imagination, or did it just *seem* as though his mouth had taken a fuller shape in the daylight? The recollection of it, warm and possessive, moving over hers as if *she* were a sugared confection, sent a rash of pinpricks across the surface of her skin, and she averted her eyes quickly.

She turned sideways so that she stood at right angles to the target, her face sharply to the left, and, after expelling a soft breath to curse her own foolishness, raised the bow to a vertical position and fired, barely having to sight at all at such a paltry distance.

The arrow *hiss-ssed* straight and true to the center of the butt, but it was the explosive power behind the shot that caused the pale green eyes to narrow. The bolt struck the target with the force of an axe, sending the bale flying backward to crash and roll on the ground.

Renaud stared at it a moment, then touched a long, tapered finger to his eyebrow in a mock salute. "A fine shot. The target, like the tree yesterday, did not stand a chance."

"Had it been a man," she said calmly, "his leg would have been pinned to his horse and the bone shattered, even through armor."

"At fifty yards," Renaud conceded agreeably, "it is possible for a crossbow to accomplish the same thing."

"If the horseman agreed to bare his leg and hold himself still while the bowman set his shot. Meanwhile, I would have fired ten times and skewered ten more limbs."

"A confident enough boast, but would it hold true at a greater distance?"

"It might," she said, her eyes steady on his. "If there were enough incentive."

"That sounds like an invitation for a wager," he mused.

"How much do you have to squander?"

"In coin? Very little."

"I would settle for a few honest answers."

He gave her a lopsided smile. "A higher price than you realize. What are you willing to wager in return?"

"What do you want?"

"I doubt you would be willing to pay it."

"Try me. I have been known to bid recklessly."

"Very well then." He glanced away for a brief moment, and when he faced her again some of the tightness in his jaw had relented and the guarded look in his eyes had softened to something verging on boyish mischief. "My prize . . . would be a long, sweet, unreserved kiss. With your hair loose and"—he grinned faintly—"your feet bare."

Brenna opened her mouth, closed it, then opened it again to release a small, pent-up breath.

"Too much to ask?"

"*What?*"

"The bared feet . . . was it too much?"

Whatever she imagined she had seen in his eyes was gone, shielded again behind the hard, cynical gleam. His mouth was again set with a mocking curve and his brow assumed an ironic tilt that made her doubt she had glimpsed anything at all beneath the cold, impervious surface.

"The day you outshoot me, sirrah, I will lay naked on the grass and let you do what you will with me."

"Brave words, demoiselle."

"Backed by my oath of honor, I assure you."

"I will hold you to it," he warned gravely.

"I would expect nothing less."

He held out his hand, inviting her to shoot first. Brenna selected another arrow and moved to align herself with the target placed a hundred yards down the run. She held her bow arm rigid, nocked the arrow and drew the fletching back to her cheek, sighting but a moment before she snapped her fingers away from the string and fired at the second butt. This time she not only struck the center ring

of the target but sent the arrow clear through it and into
the grass several feet behind.

She relaxed her arms and looked at him, her own eyebrow crooked upward.

"*Damned* fine shot," he admitted reluctantly. "Difficult to
match."

"Not for a man who claims to have no weaknesses."

"When in God's name did I claim that?"

He looked so perplexed she almost smiled. "Last night at
the castle gates. Do I assume it was just an idle boast?"

He frowned and picked out another arrow, fitting it to his
bow as he approached the line. This time he altered his
stance to match Brenna's, and put all of the latent strength
in his arms to good use, drawing, sighting, and firing with a
fluid ease of motion that had her following the flight with
a quick snap of her head.

The arrow struck the butt a finger's width from the first
hole and well within the center ring. It went through the
bale of straw as well and left the tip buried in the grass
alongside Brenna's.

She stared at him and he accorded her a smile that would
have had most women's tongues sliding down their chins.

"Lucky shot," he said, shrugging his big shoulders.

Beginning to suspect there was more than mere luck
behind it, Brenna took half a dozen arrows from the quiver
this time and stuck all but one upright in the dirt by her
right foot. She fired all six, one barely leaving the string
before the next was grasped, nocked, and drawn, sending all
speeding in a slight arc toward the third and farthest butt,
two hundred broad paces away. All six, the boys were quick
to report, had struck in a cluster dead center of the target,
the arrowheads jammed so close together the iron on some
was bent.

"My compliments again," he said, bowing slightly from
the waist.

"A child's trick. I could do it before I was ten."

Something kindled in his eyes, she saw it a split second
before he took up a single arrow and walked to the shooting

line. He ground the heel of one boot into the dirt to set himself and raised the bow, the muscles across his back and in his arms bulging with the strain. At the last possible instant, the very moment his fingers released the string to launch the arrow, his gaze flicked away from the target and found Brenna. She did not look away. She did not even follow the flight of the arrow, for she suspected, even before the boys ran panting back across the green, what they would say.

Renaud's arrow, finding no space at the heart of the target, had traveled along the shaft of one of the earlier bolts, splitting it from end to tip and driving the arrowhead through the bale and into the wooden palisade behind. Proof was produced by one of the lads, a tow-headed, violently freckled youth who came scampering back with the split shaft and the two iron broadheads wedged fast together.

Brenna stared at the arrowheads, knowing on the one hand she had been duped, yet knowing also that no one— not Robin, not Will, possibly not even Gil Golden could have made that shot. Not at a hundred yards. Not even at fifty.

A gull swooped by, riding a current of air, screeching with laughter as it circled above the two unmoving figures. Higher up, a ragged veil of clouds passed across the sun, and cast a brief bluish shadow over the bailey.

Griffyn Renaud leaned on the shank of the bow to unhook the string and disarm it. He brought it back to the bench and propped it beside the other, and when he straightened, he stood shoulder to shoulder with Brenna and inclined his head so that only she could hear what he whispered in her ear. Two bright spots of color blossomed in her cheeks. She had not moved since he had loosed the arrow; she did not move now as he took the liberty of tucking an errant curl behind her ear before he strolled casually away.

9

He doubted very much she would come. He had whispered the time and place in her ear before he had left the archery run, and reminded her to come barefoot, but he had no real expectations of seeing her there, despite the oath of honor she had given. Brenna Wardieu was no scullery wench or serving girl eager to tuck an extra coin in her cheek. She was not even the type of woman who appealed to him these days. She was too outspoken, too brazen, too loose by far with her wit and her tongue. Griffyn preferred his women round and lush and eager, with open thighs and closed mouths. The plainer the better too, for they expected nothing from someone like him and showed their gratitude in ways that left his skin singed.

This one was too damned clever for her own good and had suspected he was not what he appeared to be from the outset.

Mercenary. How she had spat the word off her tongue as if the mere saying of it tainted her. Since it was not likely she had had to beg for anything more serious than a second helping of sweetmeats, it was no wonder she could only look down her decidedly uptilted nose at someone who fell measurably short of her impression of what a noble, valorous knight should be. Perhaps it was just as well she continued to think of him with such disdain and contempt, for he had come to Amboise as a dispassionate observer with never an intention of getting any closer to any member of the family than was absolutely necessary.

He had originally planned to approach the château on his own, but a brief foray into the village of Amboise had told him it would be nearly impossible to pass through the gates without drawing attention. Unlike some castles, where the sentries were so lax a man could live within the walls for months without anyone questioning his business there, it was obvious the Black Wolf guarded his privacy and took his family's safety seriously.

Griffyn had just returned to his campsite, just caught his evening meal when a bronzed forest nymph in the guise of Brenna Wardieu had stepped into the setting sun and *insisted* he accompany her to the château. Lucky for him he *had* held his instincts in check, for she had caused all manner of unforeseen reactions in his body—reactions he could not afford to let distract him.

She was not going to come to the archery run and for that he had the sense to be grateful. Experience had taught him harsh lessons against ever letting emotion govern his actions, and with Brenna Wardieu, the warning bells had gone off in his mind the first moment he had set eyes on her. They had gone off again, nearly deafening him, when the feel of her hands gliding over his oil-slicked body had all but caused him to explode into the furs. He had deliberately tried to frighten her then, to bring her to her senses and warn her away, but it had not exactly worked out the way he had anticipated. He had not expected her to taste so sweet and warm, or to have melted in his arms like a woman who had no inkling of the powers of her own sensuality. Angry with himself, he had returned to the keep and drunk himself stupid trying to clear the taste of her out of his mouth. He had diced with the brothers and won the eager services of a lusty wench, but the act had been perfunctory and unsatisfactory. Worse, the ache had still been with him, tight and fisted around his groin, when he had seen Brenna stride into the bailey that morning.

Madness had prompted him follow her to the archery run and madness had made him take up the bow and accept the smug challenge in the wide violet eyes. At least he could be thankful one of them had come to their senses and he would be able to put her out of his mind the way he put most things that spelled trouble and confusion out of his mind—things like a conscience, a soul, loyalty to anything or anyone other than himself. He needed to stay clear-headed and focused if he was going to succeed where others had failed with Robert Wardieu.

He needed to keep that bitter taste of revenge in his mouth if he was going to succeed in destroying the champion of Amboise.

To that end, he had watched Wardieu practicing in the yards today and had studied his every move. He was not deluding himself that it would be easy work or entirely without risk to his own neck. Wardieu's style of sitting, of leaning slightly forward and to the right, twisting at the last moment, had not changed much over the past five years, but Griffyn had been surprised to see how easily the champion tired, and he did not think it was all due to the quantity of ale and wine they had consumed last night.

Conversely, Wardieu would have only his memories to prepare him and five years eroded a good deal of sharpness from any man's mind, sometimes even adding embellishments that were never there. That was where Griffyn would have the distinct advantage for he had spent those same five years honing and sharpening his skills, learning to change his stance, to alter his attack to counter anything an opponent could throw at him. He could predict, just by studying the way a challenger sat in the saddle and how he held his lance, where the blow would come and how much conviction would be behind it, and after today's display, he was satisfied that Wardieu was good, but he was not unbeatable.

Griffyn looked down at the pale outline of his hand and flexed the scarred fingers, crushing them around the piece of straw he had been shredding to pass the time. She was not coming. He *knew* she was not coming, so why was he still out here in the damp midnight air leaning on a bale of hay contemplating his own foolishness?

He tossed the scrap aside and pushed away from the bale but he only managed a step or two before he stopped again.

Someone was coming across the green, staying close to the wall to avoid the sharp eyes of the sentries. Griffyn had deliberately positioned himself in the deepest shadows by a small storage hut so he could see without being seen, and he melted back against the wall now even though the slivered moon was hidden behind mist and low, heavy clouds. Instinct sent his fist curling around the hilt of a knife he had not been generous enough to hand over to Littlejohn at the gates, and he slipped down into a crouch, his muscles tensed and poised to spring.

Brenna kept her head down and the hood of her cloak pulled low over her forehead. She had decided, firmly and adamantly, not to meet Griffyn Renaud in the archery run as he had ordered. She had decided it at least a dozen times throughout the afternoon and long, endless evening. How could anyone expect her to honor such an outlandish, outrageous wager? How could a treacherous, conniving, deceitful *mercenary* expect the daughter of one of the most noble and feared barons on the continent to . . . *to lay herself naked in the grass and let him do what he would to her*?

It was ridiculous. Ludicrous. Insane. It was in no sense of the word an honest wager made to an honest man who had in any way represented himself honestly. Certes, she was under no obligation to honor any oath given under such dubious circumstances, not when he had deliberately manipulated and maneuvered her into thinking him a bumpkin with a bow. Brave words indeed. Tricked out of her by a low-bellied worm who sat at their table, ate and drank their food, wenched with their serving girls, then strove to repay their hospitality by humiliating the daughter of the household.

She owed him nothing.

She would give him nothing but an ultimatum to leave Amboise before morning else she would go to her father and denounce him for his crimes of treachery and deceit.

If he dared show his face.

The archery run was deserted, an empty stretch of grass broken only by the ghostly silhouettes of the butts. She turned full circle but there were no other shadows leaning insolently on the barricade; no vile laughter mocked her, no sound intruded on her solitude other than a faint quarrel between two dogs in the stables.

"A *cowardly* low-bellied worm," she muttered aloud, pushing her hood off her head. "Lacking even the decency to acknowledge my willingness to comply."

She turned another circle but she was alone. The mist made it difficult to see more than shadows upon shadows; the only lights were the distant flaring torches that marked the barbican gates and they were muted to a dull, watery yellow haze.

"*Damned* bloody coward," she muttered again. "I should have known he only wanted to torment me."

"Did I succeed?"

Brenna gasped and whirled around. The whispery voice had come out of the darkness behind her, so close it sounded like a shout. Moreover, the quickness of her spin, combined with the quantity of wine she had consumed since dusk, left her swaying slightly while the two sets of sheds, barricades, and benches melded back together as one.

"Where are you? Show yourself."

A tall black shadow straightened and detached itself from the side of the bothy. "I had just about given up on you, my lady. 'Tis well past midnight, by the watch bells."

" 'Tis well past the limit of my patience," she snapped. "And I am only come to tell you your presence is no longer welcome at Amboise."

"Why? Because I pricked your vanity this morning?"

"You *tricked* me. You feigned ignorance of the longbow when all along you knew damned well how to use one."

"Truly, demoiselle." He gave a wry laugh. "What manner of sword for hire would I be if I were not at least passingly familiar with so magnificent and deadly a weapon?"

"Passingly familiar?" Her shoulders dropped a moment. "You made me look like a boastful child."

"That was not my intention."

"Was it not?"

"Would you rather I had bowed to the dictates of chivalry and deliberately missed the shot so as not to offend the sensibilities of a female competitor?"

"Certainly not!"

"Well then?"

Well then, indeed. He had effectively defused her argument, for it was the last thing she wanted on this earth, to think any man patronized her in any way just because of some foolish notion of chivalry.

"If it is any consolation," he said, taking a step closer, "I have never seen another archer with such a steady hand or keen eye—man or woman. I have never had to take such care with my own shot."

The wine swam around her head for a moment, mellowing her to the compliment, but then she remembered the last split second before he loosed the arrow. He had looked away from the target. He had looked away as coolly and calmly as if he knew precisely where the arrow was going and what her reaction would be.

"Never?" she spat. "Not in all your years of selling your sword for profit?"

He sighed. "Believe me, there is little profit in selling anything, except perhaps your soul."

"Hah! Then you admit it! You admit you ply your trade as a mercenary!"

"I admit nothing. Only that I am surprised to see you here tonight."

"Why should it surprise you? I gave my word."

"And is that the only reason you came?"

"What other reason would you suppose, sirrah? That I *wanted* to come?"

His laugh was low and husky. "I was hoping it might have counted for a little."

"Not the smallest part," she insisted. "Not with a black-hearted, rapine trickster the likes of you."

"You wrong me, demoiselle. I have not raped anyone of your acquaintance that you should slander me so." He took another step and something metallic on his belt caught a reflection of light from the distant torches. "And unless your education has been sadly lacking about what a man and woman do together, you cannot possibly think I raped *you* last night. Teased you, perhaps. Possibly even gave you a taste of the pleasures you might encounter if you shed your tunics and boots and loosened your skirts a little."

"Pleasure?" She tensed and eased back a step, and although she could not see it clearly, a slow, wide grin spread across his face as he smelled the false courage on her breath. "You call pinning me up against a wall, threatening me, and frightening me half to death *pleasure?*"

"Did I frighten you? If I did, you will have to forgive me. I have been absent from courtly circles too long and my . . . manners . . . have suffered for it."

"A forced absence, or a voluntary one?"

"Tut-tut." He lifted a finger and wagged it. "I am not the one who lost the wager, remember, therefore I owe you no answers. You, on the other hand, owe me—"

"Nothing," she snapped. "I owe you nothing."

He bowed his head a moment and clasped his hands behind his back. "Ah, well, I confess you have me truly confused now. The chivalrous thing for me to have done this morning was to throw my shot and let you win—yet you disdain the notion. At the same time, had I done so, I would also have been expected to do the honorable thing by baring my soul and answering the thousands of questions fermenting in the back of your mind. But because you lost, and in spite of an oath of honor given freely and boldly, you expect chivalry to come to your rescue now, that I might release you from your bond and send you on your way with naught but a gallant bow. Do I have that clear in my mind?"

Brenna's cheeks flared red and her hands balled into fists by her sides. A mottling of small purple dots distorted her vision for a moment, rushed there by the anger boiling in her veins. The inner curtain wall was behind him and above, the darker jumble of towers and battlements were etched black against the midnight sky, shrouded in mist. She could see very little of his face, no more than a pale bluish smear slashed with the line of his black eyebrows and framed by black hair. Something hot and liquid and stinging flushed away the purple pinspots, but her anger remained, causing her to square her shoulders and hold her chin high.

"Have you chosen your square of grass, sirrah, or will any bed of thatch do?"

It was Griffyn's turn to stare. He had excellent night vision and saw more than just the pale blot of her face. He saw the dark stain on her cheeks and the silvery liquid rim forming along her lower lashes. He saw her fists and the tremors that shook the folds of her cloak and the pride that kept her back straight and her eyes fierce.

She was magnificent, and the simple truth was that he wanted her. That was why he had followed her onto the field that morning and why he had taken up her challenge. It was why he had stood out here in the dark for two hours shredding enough stalks of hay to build a nest. He wanted her . . . and at this moment, with his heart pounding and his blood raging . . . he wanted her badly enough to break every rule he had set for himself, shatter every barrier it had taken him so long to erect around his emotions.

"I would gladly lay you down in the grass, my lady." He reached over with a surprisingly steady hand and lifted a single long, loose curl, drawing it out from beneath the wool of her cloak. "I would gladly do a thousand things to you that would have you begging me to do a thousand more." He toyed with the sleek, tawny spiral and watched it slither through his fingers. "On the other hand, I am not going to hold you to something you have no wish to do. The devil may have cursed me into accepting many things I would not have thought of doing at one time; but I am no despoiler of unwilling virgins. The effort is too great," he added, hoping his sigh sounded casual, "and the satisfaction too fleeting."

Brenna's own heart was beating like a wild thing. She was prepared to honor her oath. She was prepared to shame and curse and denigrate him all the while he had his lusty way with her, but she was prepared, nonetheless, to see this thing through and emerge with her pride and honor intact. She was *not* prepared for the icy, prickling frissons of sensation washing across her nape and rippling down her spine with each gentle stroke and tug of his fingers on her hair. Nor was she expecting this eleventh-hour gesture of nobility regardless of how tartly it dripped with sarcasm.

She forced herself to look up, not certain she had heard him correctly. "You are . . . letting me go?"

"Alas, I neglected to bring my manacles and chains."

He dropped the silky curl and clasped his hands behind his back again, wondering at his own madness. Wondering at hers for continuing to stand there staring up at him like a trapped doe that does not understand a hunter's reprieve.

"Is . . . my virginity the only reason?"

"Not entirely." He chucked quietly. "But then you are not just any virgin either, my lady, but the daughter of the Black Wolf of Amboise. I would not want to speculate over the number of knives I would find stuck in my gullet come morning should the happy *dénouement* take place and my part in it be discovered."

She did not know where the next question came from, but it stumbled off her tongue anyway. "No . . . *other* reason?"

His head tilted to one side. "Such as?"

"Such as my . . . fondness for tunics and leggings over loose silk skirts."

If the ache in his groin was not so overwhelming, he might have laughed. If the note of uncertainty in her voice had been any less compelling, he might have cursed his noble intentions to hell and thrown her on the ground then and there. As it was, he was forced to stare long and hard, and to recall a similarly faint air of aspersion at the supper table the previous night when her father had remarked on how lovely she looked.

Was it *possible* she did not know how beautiful she was? How desirable? How the mere thought of lying with her anywhere—in the grass, in the bath house, in the weeds by the river—was putting such an unprecedented strain on his willpower, he was nearly coming out of his skin?

"No other reason," he said evenly. "On my oath."

Her head dipped down and he could see the sheen of mist droplets sparkling on her hair. "Given on the safe assumption you will not have to act upon it."

This was too much. He clamped his teeth together so hard his jaw made a grinding sound and when he did laugh, purely out of desperation, it sounded coarse and lusty and darkened the stains on her cheeks.

"Very well, my lady. Since you are so insistent, shall we strike a compromise? Comply with the original terms of the wager and we may both claim honor has been served."

"The original terms?"

"A kiss," he said brusquely. "Long and sweet and freely given . . . unlike your squirming, missish efforts from last night."

She looked up at him through the darkness. The wine was muddling her senses, spinning them from one extreme to the other, but they were clear enough to know he was making fun of her, mocking the frightened, trembling woman he had sent running out of the bath house, terrified as much by the responses he had roused in her as she was by his offer to introduce her to still more. He was cynical and unfeeling and would likely laugh all the harder even if she did kiss him and it failed to measure up against his talents as a debaucher of household servants. On the other hand, did she really care what he thought of her? He was arrogant and crude and ill-mannered, and if a kiss was needed to prove she was no country simpleton who would default on the demands of her honor, a kiss was what he would get.

She took a deep breath and moved close enough for the wool of her cloak to brush against his surcoat. She stood a long moment with the top of her head a silky curl away from touching his chin, then tilted her face up and elevated herself onto the tips of her toes, using one cool hand to circle his neck and coax his mouth down to within a breath of hers.

"You know, of course," she murmured through a frown, "that Tansy faints if a mouse crosses her path."

"Is that a fact? I gather you have been listening to castle gossips?"

"Not willingly, I assure you."

"You did not believe them?"

She lowered her lashes and tried not to think of how her breasts were tingling, crushed against his chest. "I do not believe a person could be made to faint three times, no."

"Actually . . . it was only twice." He grinned. "But I was somewhat tupped on your father's excellent ale and not in my best form."

She exhaled around a disparaging sigh and pressed her mouth over his. It was a tentative, nerveless effort at first, hampered by his grin and her own reluctance. But then she was more insistent, and he obliged by parting his lips and suddenly the clumsiness gave way to stubbornness and instinct. Her tongue sought the silky heat of his mouth, exploring it with the same kind of rolling, swirling intimacy that had caught her by surprise last night. It seemed to win a similar reaction from him for he stiffened and resisted the encroachment as if, all things said, it was an unwanted intrusion.

She forced his lips even wider and thrust deeper, determined to prove she could be as irreverent as he, but somewhere between the rush of smug satisfaction and the surge of unwarranted physical pleasure, she felt his arms circle her waist and lift her against him. He gathered her close enough to cause the tingling tension in her breasts to explode in a million fiery sparks, and suddenly it was his tongue doing the searching and thrusting, his lips suckling and molding and coaxing hers wider, wider, until she could scarce catch a breath through the heat and wildness.

She curled both hands around his neck as his tongue probed deep, deep, prowling and penetrating, urging . . . no, *demanding* she do the same. Her cloak slipped off her shoulders and crumpled on the ground at her feet and his hands were there, raking into the softness of her hair, crushing her to him with a hunger she could not have escaped if she had wanted to. Pleasure inundated her in waves and still he kissed her. Kissed her like a dying man asking his last favor from God. She was powerless to break away, helpless to do anything but cling to him and weather the intense, spreading heat.

The heat was all focused inward, and she acknowledged it with a violent shudder. She shuddered again when his hands cradled her hips and pulled her savagely against him, and she moaned as the insistent throbbing between her thighs began to liquefy and pulsate, inflaming her from without and within.

A jarring, familiar sound echoed across the green and Brenna pulled back, gasping, her mouth wet and open, her body shimmering and as molten as quicksilver. It was the watch bell on the outer gates. The guard was changing and fresh, wary eyes would be taking to the walls, alert to any unexpected movement in the bailey.

"I have to leave," she gasped. "I have to go back. If they see us—"

"They will not see us. And you cannot leave yet, the wager is only half paid."

"But you said—"

"A kiss. A long sweet kiss. And that"—his dark head bent to her again—"was not long enough, my lady. Not nearly long enough."

IO

Griffyn swept her into his arms as if she weighed no more than a feather. He dipped once to retrieve her cloak then carried her to the side of the bothy where the grass was thick and lush and the shadows were darkest. He spread the cloak with a flick of his wrist and set her down upon it without once lifting his mouth from hers, and although she squirmed and gasped the expected protests, they were only halfhearted, and his hands, his lips, his tongue were able to reduce them to mere whimpers.

He devoured her mouth, leaving her dazed and so near to fainting she felt a giddy rush and almost laughed. His lips plundered the length of her throat from her ear to her shoulder, finding every sensitive nerve, every shy fluttering pulse beat. His fingers found the laced fastenings of her tunic and chainse, loosening them enough to open a gap over her breasts. A husky groan sent his fingertips slipping beneath the cloth, rasping over the satiny warmth of her bare flesh.

She arched upward as his hand molded around her breast, shaping it, cupping it, lifting it into the wet, insistent heat of his mouth, and she cried out softly, shamelessly, as her hands clawed into the thick mane of his hair, holding him there. He obliged each gasp, each shivered cry, each ragged moan, tugging gently on the sensitive peak of her nipple, teasing it, caressing it with his tongue and lips, demonstrating a thoroughness that left her shaking like a leaf.

Brenna kept her eyes squeezed tightly shut. It was shattering enough just to *feel* where his breath heated her skin and his tongue lapped and rolled; where the rough stubble on his jaw abraded the silky surface and the blunt, callused tips of his fingers probed and kneaded. His hand skimmed the length of her leg and came back again dragging the hem of her skirts with it, then he sent his fingers in the same smooth movement to explore the soft thatch of golden down he found there.

Brenna's eyes flew open in shock and she tried to clench her thighs tight to bar his way, but the very act of challenging his right to be there only brought his fingers stroking deeper. Her limbs and belly quivered with involuntary spasms, and the first rush of unexpected pleasure caught her totally by surprise. The second brought her half up off the grass, her back arched, her hair thrashing the ground beneath, her hands tearing at his shoulders, his neck, the bunched muscles of his upper arms.

"I think," he murmured with genuine intrigue, "I may have been too hasty in offering to accept such a meager compromise. I think I would prefer the contest of making you faint."

She shook her head, her eyes wide and dark and frightened by her own inability to control the sweet, shuddering spasms that rippled through her body. Her thighs clenched again, this time to hold him firm as yet another deluge of wet heat shivered through her from head to toe, the fierceness and potency all but taking her breath away.

With a knowing laugh, he pushed the crush of her skirts higher and bared her limbs completely. Slick with the evidence of her desire, his fingers curled into the dewy petals of flesh, parting them with his thumbs to expose the glistening mother-of-pearl bud in their midst.

Brenna made a harsh, broken sound in her throat for she did not know what to expect, did not know what he was going to do next, only knowing she was helpless to stop him, did not *want* to stop him so long as his thumbs stroked and his fingers teased and her body fluttered with the promise of even greater pleasure to come. She flung her arms out on either side and grasped at fistfuls of grass. Her heart was drumming in her chest and her every nerve ending was so acutely sensitive she could feel each blade of grass where it tickled her skin. Through hot flares of shame, she could imagine the sight she made, her skirts bunched up around her waist, her breasts bared, the nipples dark and swollen hard as berries, her limbs glowing white and milky as he parted them wider and pressed a kiss into the soft flesh of her inner thigh.

For all of two mindless, disbelieving seconds she stared at his dark head as the heat of his breath and the rasp of stubbled jaw moved between her thighs. His tongue was there too, silky and devilish, lapping its way toward the juncture where his lips closed over the trembling petals, bold and devouring as if he had found another mouth to torment. His hands grasped her hips and she could not have pulled away if she wanted to, but it did not excuse the fact that she allowed it, even encouraged it with aggressive little thrusts that invited his tongue to even more sinful depths.

She cried out. Then cried out again as more sounds came from the direction of the gates again, this time accompanied by the harsh, jolting clatter of a dozen horses galloping over the wooden draw.

"Stop," she gasped. "Stop!"

The panic in her voice caused Griffyn to freeze, then to abandon her so swiftly she barely registered the movement as he sprang into a crouch and pressed himself against the wall of the bothy. She fumbled to cover herself and joined him just as more torchlights blazed into life in front of the barbican towers.

"What is it? Can you see what is happening?"

"It looks like you have a late-night visitor," he murmured.

"Impossible. Littlejohn allows no one inside after dark."

"He let us in."

"Only because it was me and Robin was waiting. Had you been on your own, with blood pouring off your head, he would have sent out a bandage and told you to bide until daylight."

"A comforting thought."

"These are hardly comforting times with spies and assassins lurking behind every handsome, smiling face."

He permitted himself the distraction of a glance before he looked back at the gates. The area around the main barbicans was flooded bright as the belly of a forge now, swarming with sentries armed with swords and crossbows. Littlejohn was plainly identifiable by his seven feet of glowering muscle where he stood beneath the center of the flying bridge.

Over Griffyn's shoulder, Brenna was fumbling with the laces of her tunic, her fingers tangling around one another as she hastened to cover herself and restore the modesty of her clothing. She could scarcely believe a minute ago she was sprawled in the grass with his mouth between her thighs. She could scarcely believe she had permitted such a depraved liberty, much less that her flesh was still churning and her hands shook so badly she could not fasten a simple knot.

She conquered the last one in time to see half a dozen riders dismounting inside the gates. The men looked exhausted, the horses were all flecked with white lather and stood trembling where the torchlight burned off the mist, waiting while groomsmen hastened forward to catch the reins.

"Why, it looks like . . ." Her eyes widened and she forgot all about her own indignities. "It looks like Lord Alaric!"

"FitzAthelstan's father?"

She nodded and the hand—which she had not been aware of placing on Griffyn's arm—dug so deep into the muscle, he turned again to look at her. Both their faces were dusted lightly by the glow from the distant torches, and he could see the sudden fear and concern pleating her brow.

"What is it? What is wrong?"

"Lord Alaric has been staying at Blois this past month to help my brother Eduard through his recovery. He would not have ridden all this way at night unless . . . unless something was terribly wrong."

She sprang to her feet and snatched up her cloak. "I have to go. I . . . should not have come in the first place, but I . . . I have to leave now."

His hand reached out and closed around her upper arm, delaying her before she could rush past. "I will be leaving as well. I will not be here when the sun comes up."

She looked confused. "Not be here? Where will you be?"

"On the road to Rouen, hopefully, unless I manage to lose my way again."

She glanced at the gate, then up at his face. "But . . . we are all going to the same place. Would it not make sense to travel together?"

"On the one hand, yes, I suppose it would. On the other"—he plucked a stray curl off her shoulder and let the backs of his fingers rest briefly on her cheek—"it would make none at all. I have already given thanks to your father for his hospitality and my regards to your brother should we meet again in Gaillard."

The group by the gate was breaking up, the sentries were returning to the walls, the horses were being led to the stables and the torches doused one by one when they were deemed no longer necessary. Lord Alaric and his men, with Littlejohn in the lead, were moving quickly across the common toward the inner gates. Watching this, knowing she would only have a few seconds to catch up, Brenna wrenched her arm out of his grasp and turned on him.

"When were you planning to tell me this? After you had thanked me for *my* hospitality?"

There was enough light to give substance to his eyes, making them glow out of the shadows with their peculiar luminescence. They were as cold and implacable as the chiseled beauty of his face and her cheeks flushed with resentment. Because she could think of nothing else to do to ease her frustration, she slammed both fists against his chest and backed away.

"You are absolutely right, sirrah," she cried, the anger

almost swelling her throat closed. "You had best not be here when the sun comes up. Further, you should pray sincerely that we do not meet again, here or at Gaillard, for if I had more time, or perhaps even a weapon in my hand, you would pay dearly for your mockery."

She turned and ran across the archery yard, across the practice fields, her cloak whipped hastily around her shoulders and belling out behind like a large gray sail.

Griffyn watched until she had disappeared through the inner gates. Her fists had barely dented the thickness of his surcoat, but he felt the blows as clearly as if she had used hammers. Reaching beneath the hunting green doeskin, he withdrew a small square of carefully folded silk—the veil she had left in the bath house the previous evening—and crushed his fingers around it as he looked over his shoulder at the looming silhouette of the castle keep. He started to let the silk go, to let it slide out of his palm, but at the last moment something stopped him and, cursing under his breath, he tucked the scrap of silk back inside his surcoat and started walking toward the stables. It seemed fitting, somehow, that the heavens chose that particular moment to crack open and begin spitting cold, fat raindrops on his head.

Brenna ran through the inner gate and across the wooden draw. Her footsteps earned the attention of the group ahead and several FitzAthelstan men reacted out of instinct, whirling around and drawing their swords. Seeing who it was and hearing her hail, they relaxed again, though not without a few choice words misting the air in front of their mouths.

"Lord Alaric!"

"Brenna? What the devil are you doing out this time of night?"

"I was . . . down at the stables. One of the mares is about to foal and I wanted to make sure she was all right. I saw you and your men come through the gates and I thought . . ." She stopped, caught a breath, and blurted, "Has something happened at Blois? Is it Eduard? Or Lady Ariel? Or the baby?"

"No! No, calm yourself, child. Nothing is wrong with Eduard, or Lady Ariel. The baby kicks a great deal, so I am told, but is steadfastly refusing to appear until its time."

"Oh . . . thank the sweet Mother Mary." She clasped her hand to her bosom. "You gave me such a fright!"

Tall and lean, an older version of Will, Lord Alaric was still an attractive man, not given to balding or graying, nor to cultivating a round paunch from easy living. Brenna had not seen him in over a month, and she was plainly shocked. Granted, to see a face by flickering torchlight was not always a true depiction of shadows and hollows, but his cheeks were gaunt and his soft brown eyes were heavily underscored by dark circles. Will had said he hardly ate and never slept, and she could see the truth of it before her despite the smile he forced for her benefit and the wide-shouldered mantle he wore to conceal the looseness of his clothes.

"Friar," she whispered, falling back on the name all of Amboise used out of fondness. "You look dreadful."

He stared a moment, then actually managed a laugh. "Only you and Gil would have the nerve to tell me so to my face. But I am well, truthfully. I am . . . through the worst of it, I hope."

He said his wife's name with such tenderness, Brenna's throat constricted around a reply. Her own emotions had already taken a buffeting this night and they were too raw, too near the surface to easily dismiss someone she had loved and admired so much. On an impulse, she threw her arms around Lord Alaric and clung tightly through a rush of hot tears.

"I miss her too. Not a day goes by when I do not wish she was here with us."

Alaric's arms hung helplessly by his sides, then slowly lifted and returned the squeeze. "Hush, child. Hush. I know you do. I also know Gil would not have wanted to see the two of us weeping like jaybirds every time someone mentions her name. She regretted nothing. Neither should we. Now come, let us get out of the rain before it truly comes down."

Brenna leaned back and swiped a hand across her eyes to dry them. "If there is nothing wrong at Blois, why are you here? You must have left after dark and ridden half blind through the forest."

"My men have already thanked me profusely for the experience. Several of them will want clean braies before we make the return flight."

"Not tonight, surely?"

"I left without your brother knowing it and should return before he is aware of my absence."

"Why?"

He sighed as if he had said too much already and resumed walking toward the keep. "I need to talk to your father."

"Shall I run ahead and tell him you are here?"

He shook his head. "Littlejohn has already done so. You could, however, see if there is any food or ale available for my men. I also used the excuse of a mare in foal to leave the supper table early and some of their bellies have been protesting since we crossed the river."

He said it offhandedly enough Brenna did not look up at once. When she did, he reached over just as casually to remove the long, silky tuft of grass she had inadvertently caught in the laces of her cotte. He said nothing more and they walked the rest of the way in silence, with their heads bent to protect them from the downpour and Brenna's cheeks burning furiously, wondering how it was that so few things escaped Lord Alaric's attention, however distracted he might be.

They parted company on the landing outside the great hall, but not for long. Varlets were wakened and dispatched to fetch food and drink, and with the thought that her father would likely be calling for similar refreshments for Lord Alaric, she filled a board with bread and cheese, and filched a flagon of wine from one of the servers.

Her parents' apartments occupied the whole of the east tower, with her father's audience chamber on the lower floor. An obviously masculine room, it was dominated by a huge oak table surrounded by many chairs, set before a vast canvas on which was painted a map of England and the Continent.

There were no guards in the corridor or outside the arched double doors. One of them, in fact, had been left slightly ajar, and it was a good thing too, for there were no candles lit in the wall sconces and only a weak strip of light escaped to spangle the stone floor and guide her way along the passage. She heard voices as she approached, and as she came nearer the brightening crack of light, her footsteps slowed, then stopped altogether. She had only a partial view of the room, which included the table and hearth, but she could see and hear that her father and Lord Alaric were not alone. Robin, Dag, and Richard were seated at the table looking rumpled and sleep-creased. Sparrow was snapping crossly at Will to light more candles, and Jean de Brevant was standing behind the Wolf's chair, his arms folded over his massive chest, his craggy face belligerent and unreadable as ever.

Dag had obviously been the last one to answer what must have been a hastily delivered summons, for he was still scraping his chair close to the table as Alaric FitzAthelstan took something out of a pouch and placed it in Lord Randwulf's hand. Brenna set the tray carefully on the floor and moved close enough to the door to fill the opening with a large violet eye. Only then could she see what they were all staring at, what had brought a sudden, stifling silence to the room.

It was a ring. A man's ring wrought in gold, the face of it carved in the image of a dragon rampant, the scaled jaws gaping wide and the forked tongue poised to spit flame. A single bloodred ruby marked the eye, and where it lay in her father's palm, the gem seemed to catch fire in the candlelight, making the golden beast come alive.

The Wolf stared at the ring for a long moment before looking up at the face of his friend and closest ally.

"Where did you get this?" he asked hoarsely.

"It was delivered to Blois this afternoon by a monk. He was very nearly on his last breath, frightened half out of his wits, and adamant about speaking to no one but Eduard."

"I presume you convinced him otherwise?"

Alaric nodded. "His loyalty was commendable and his tongue was stubborn, but he gave me the message. It comes from Marienne and says only: *'They have taken Lord Henry.'*"

II

Almost a full minute passed, then everyone seemed to speak at once.

"Surely there was more to the message than that?"

"*Who* has taken Lord Henry?"

"Is Marienne all right? Is she hurt or in danger?"

"Three weeks! Did he *swim* across the Channel?"

"*Where* have they taken him?"

"Was it Gisbourne?"

As suddenly as the floodtide rose, it ebbed away again to a tense silence with everyone looking to Alaric for answers.

"You heard the entire message," he said calmly. " '*They have taken Lord Henry.*' No mention of who or how or where. No mention if he is alive or dead, if it was Gisbourne or the king's men, or a simple peasant who discovered who he was and sought to collect the reward on his head."

Robin pushed angrily to his feet. "Regardless who took him, Marienne sent the ring. She would not have been able to do so had the lady not ordered it herself, and *she* would part with the dragon ring only if she thought more than just her own life was in mortal peril."

Outside in the corridor, Brenna's eyes widened almost beyond the limits of her lashes. The dragon ring! She had heard stories about it but never seen it. Around it, she knew, had evolved the history of her family—fabulous tales of a mighty battle between a Dragon Lord and a Black Wolf; of a daring rescue from the bleak donjons of Corfe Castle; of a valiant knight resigned to obscurity, who had forsworn his birthright to offer himself as protector to a lost princess . . .

Her father's voice pulled her gaze back into the room. "Does Eduard know?"

"I thought it best not to tell him yet, not when he is just beginning to mend. Knowing him, he *would* swim across the Channel if he had to, if he thought she needed him."

The Wolf nodded grimly. "You did the right thing, as always. Does anyone else at Blois know?"

"Lady Ariel. It was necessary to enlist her help to loosen the monk's tongue, for he was convinced eternal hellfire awaited him if he failed to follow his instructions absolutely."

Sparrow put a hand to the hilt of his knife. "This graycloak—think you he knows more than he is willing to tell?"

Alaric shook his head. "He was honestly terrified and vastly relieved to be free of his burden."

Sparrow's mouth twisted and his fingers curled in disappointment.

"Where is he now?" the Wolf asked.

"In a warm bed, with a full belly and a cask of wine. Lady Ariel has promised to keep him drunk and safely locked away until I return and can send him out of harm's way. In the meantime—"

"In the meantime," the Wolf said, "we must try to make sense of the message ourselves. Obviously, Lord Henry has been taken prisoner, but by whom?"

"Gisbourne?" Richard suggested. "It would be the logical answer. He seems determined to rid the forests around Nottingham of outlaws; Henry might well have been taken by accident."

"Nottingham," Dag agreed, "is surely one of the king's most loyal strongholds and, as you say, Lord Henry has been playing with fire to be keeping such bold company as these outlaws of Sherwood."

"If the Eunuch had him," Sparrow chirped, "his toes would be well crimped and his head spiked on the castle gates. Moreover, we would have heard Gisbourne's boastings by now."

"How so?"

The woodsprite glared at Richard, who had offered up the offending question. "Did the vaunted brain-biter have the smallest notion Lord Henry de Clare was within a thousand miles of his forest? And if so, would he not have razed that same forest to the ground long before now to flush him out?"

"Puck is right," Alaric said. "If the Sheriff of Nottingham knew he had Henry de Clare in his donjons, we would have heard before now."

"I should have killed him when I had the chance," Robin muttered.

"You will hear no argument from me," the seneschal retorted, folding his arms imperiously over his chest. "Heed the lesson for the future, my Bold Blade: show a viper a mort of compassion and back it will come to prick you in the arse."

Robin slammed his fist on the table, ignoring Sparrow and staring at his father. "Did I not beg you two months ago to give me leave to go to England and bring the princess and Marienne home?"

"Eleanor is happy at Kirklees; she has finally found peace there, with God. I doubt you could have persuaded her to leave."

"And Marienne?" Robin's face flushed and his fist clenched on the table. "Eduard was not the only one to make a solemn vow that night outside the abbey. He was not the only one who left a part of his heart behind, though I dare swear you believe his loyalty to the princess ranks far higher and is far more noble than the love I hold for a simple maid."

"I know how close you were to Marienne," the Wolf began, but Robin's anger cut him short.

"How close I *was*? Do you think it was just a child's love we shared?"

"No, of course not, but—"

"It was *never* a child's love. I knew the instant I set eyes upon her I would love her until I drew my last breath." His voice turned ragged with emotion. "Nothing has happened to change that. I read her letters and I can see her sweet face as she writes them. I read them a second time and I can hear her voice; a third and I can hear her love, her hopes that she has not been forsaken by everyone in this world."

"You did not forsake her," said a soft voice from the shadows behind Littlejohn. It was Lady Servanne sitting quietly and stiffly in the farthest corner of the room, her face bleached gray, her lips compressed into a thin line to keep them from trembling at the sight of her son's pain.

"I left her there," Robin said flatly. "I left her with promises and pledges, locked behind the cloistered stone walls of an abbey while I"—he snorted with self-contempt—"I played at becoming a champion of chivalry."

"She admires you all the more, and loves you all the more for the man you have become and the fame you have achieved."

"At what cost?" He looked helplessly at his mother. "Marienne has sacrificed eleven years of her own happiness and freedom that she might watch my success from a distance."

"It was her choice."

"No." He shook his head. "It was not her choice. It was the *princess*'s choice to enter the convent and serve God. It was Marienne's *duty* to remain by her lady's side, forced on her by circumstances she could not control."

"No more than you could have controlled the circumstances that bade you come back home to Amboise, out of the king's reach."

"*Safely* out of the king's reach, you mean."

"You were but thirteen years old!"

"Barely a fully year older than Marienne, yet she stayed."

"What could you have done to protect her? You could scarcely lift the weight of a sword. Do you think the king would have given up his search so soon had he suspected the firstborn son of the Black Wolf was living under his nose? No, Robin. No, my love. You would have put Marienne—and Eleanor—in the gravest danger, and well you know it."

Robin's lips quivered even as he clamped them tight against the logic of his mother's arguments.

"Nonetheless, they are both in danger now," he managed tautly. "And no one is going to stop me from going this time." He paused and his eyes blazed once around the room. "No one."

"No one is planning on stopping you," Alaric said calmly. "We are only seeking to avoid plunging you head-long into what could well be a trap."

"A trap!" Robin's eyebrows lifted with skepticism. "You said yourself the ring and the message were meant for Eduard's ears only."

"Good St. Cyril save me." Sparrow snorted. "Does a fisherman throw his net hoping to catch only one fish? Mores the more, how many nets have been thrown over the past eleven years, in the hopes of catching any one of the Wolf's brood with their eyes closed and their backs turned? Eduard may have been the one to hold the knife to Gisbourne's gullet, but it was you, Master Carver, who aimed the blade lower and lopped off his manly pride."

"All right." The Wolf spread his hands to bring order to the discussion again. "Apart from Gisbourne, who else would take an interest in the good friar?"

"Robert FitzWalter," said Will. "He is the leader of the rebelling barons. If he suspected Henry could lead them to the princess, and if he thought it would give them a legitimate claimant to the throne of England, he would kill Lackland himself and place the crown on her head."

"Is FitzWalter not already negotiating with King Philip to make Prince Louis regent in the viper's stead?" Richard asked.

"At this point," Alaric explained, "he has merely agreed in principle there is a possible link to the throne through Louis's marriage to Henry II's grandniece Blanche. It is neither as strong nor as popular a choice as would be a direct blood link through Eleanor of Brittany. After all, she does have a more legitimate claim to the throne than her uncle, John Plantagenet. Upon Arthur's death, she should have been next in line to inherit the crown."

"The English would never have accepted another queen after Bloody Matilda," Dag said.

"Eleven years ago, perhaps not. But in the interim, the nobles have endured over a decade of John's greed and corruption. They have watched their lands stripped, their wealth taxed to fill his treasury. They have had their daughters sold into unwholesome marriages and their sons imprisoned to insure their loyalty. Give them a queen now, the granddaughter of Henry Plantagenet and Eleanor of Aquitaine, a woman renowned for her innocence, virtue, and beauty, and they would not only accept her, they would raise an army behind her and carry her all the way to London on their knees."

"All this," Richard said grimly, "assuming they still think her to be innocent, virtuous, and beautiful."

"She is all those things and more," Robin insisted, his face flooding with resentment. "She is brave and loyal and spirited. Circumstances may have forced her to live the life of an exile, but by God, she is still the Pearl of Brittany, rightful Queen of England!"

Richard raised his hands in a gesture of apology. "I only meant—"

"I know what you meant. You meant that if the barons knew how her uncle had disfigured her, how he had scorched out her eyes to prevent her from ever being a real threat to his throne, they would no more consider making her queen than they would a leper."

"As I recall, it was all you could do at the time to keep Eduard from returning the favor," Alaric said grimly. "Small comfort to know Lackland often wakens screaming at night, clawing at his eyes, swearing someone has stabbed them with red-hot pokers."

"The only comfort would come if I had the pokers in my hand and his eyes at my feet. But we waste time contemplating the fanciful. The message comes to us already three weeks old. If we leave within the hour, it cannot be too soon."

"It is always too soon if you act in haste," Will cautioned. "We have named only two who could have been responsible for Henry's capture; there is a third to consider before we polish our armor and ride off in search of dragons to slay."

The Wolf looked dubious. "An errant huntsman out for the reward? I would credit Henry with more sense than to allow such a thing to happen."

"I was not thinking of a huntsman."

Lord Randwulf frowned and exchanged a glance with Alaric, who was no less forwarned of what his son was about to say. "Go on."

"I am loath to put forth the notion, my lord, but what if the earl marshal himself is behind it? It could be he was worried the outlaws were becoming too bold in the forests and would eventually draw the eye of the king. Or it could be he began to worry Henry might seek out Robert FitzWalter of his own accord and join forces against Lackland. In the last communication Dafydd ap Iowerth brought us, the earl sounded angry enough. And he has already vowed to all who would think of rising against the king that he will stand in defense of the throne, his sword in hand, though he be the only one against ten thousand."

"The old bastard," said Lord Randwulf, not altogether unkindly. "He is well into his eighth decade—must he always stand with his back against the wall?"

The gentle sarcasm won a few smiles from around the table, for William Marshal, Earl of Pembroke, was undisputably the greatest soldier, the most honored knight and respected statesman alive. He had served three kings— Henry II, Richard, and John—and had participated in every major battle and war since earning his spurs over sixty years ago. He was a true legend in the jousting fields, having won over four hundred single-combat matches, a feat few knights could boast of matching by half.

Lord Randwulf was one of those few. He and the Marshal had been friends and friendly rivals for the past forty years.

"I sincerely did not think his tolerance for Softsword's greed would last this long."

"It is not his love for the king speaking with such eloquent passion," Alaric said. "It is his love of honor. He gave his oath to protect the throne—"

"With no thought to whose arse might straddle it," Sparrow injected on a huff of breath.

"It was William Marshal, more than anyone else," Alaric reminded them, barely acknowledging the interruption, "who swayed the barons in favor of John over Arthur of Brittany all those years ago. To allow those same barons to usurp the king now, regardless of their justifications, regardless if he agrees or disagrees the tyranny must end, would require the breaking of every oath he holds sacred, the casting aside of every shred of honor he ever possessed. This he will not do, and the other barons respect him for it even though they sit and curse his integrity."

"Yes, but would that integrity extend to include killing his own nephew?"

"I believe it would," Alaric answered softly. "With tears streaming down his face, to be sure, but I believe he would order Henry's death if it was necessary to safeguard the throne."

"Before or after he determined the whereabouts of Eleanor of Brittany?"

"He has always been adamant up to now about remaining in ignorance believing, I warrant, that if he did not know where the princess was, he would not have to acknowledge his part in saving her from the executioner's blade eleven years ago. He may need the information now, however," Alaric added quietly, "if only to produce her in front of the world and show why she may never be considered for the role of queen."

"He would not do that!" Robin cried, shocked by the very notion. "He could not!"

"Then tell me what he would do," Alaric countered

smoothly. "What would he do to remove the potential threat of a legitimate claimant to the throne—kill her?"

Robin cursed under his breath, and it was the Wolf who answered.

"No. Not if he could not stand by and allow it to happen when he came here himself and appealed to Eduard to steal her out of the king's prison."

Alaric agreed with a nod. "He would not kill her, but he *might* do something that would prompt Eduard to go to her rescue again, knowing that this time she would have no choice but to come home to Brittany."

"He would remove her protector," Richard put forth.

"Just so."

"Our little Pearl," Sparrow grumbled, pacing back and forth in front of the hearth. "Think you she would have played the pawn enough already. I am with Robin. We can leave ere this hour is over, put wings to the horses' feet and be on a ship in under three days time. Fly to Nottingham. Skewer Gisbourne through the heart. Rescue the Pearl and bring her back home where she belongs." He snapped his pudgy fingers in a gesture of finality. "A fortnight for our trouble, no more."

"Skewer Gisbourne?" Alaric inquired mildly.

"He vexes me."

"An adequate enough reason, by any measure," the Wolf murmured. "Yet you do not seem happy with this solution, my old friend. Is there more?"

"You know what I know," Alaric replied, shrugging.

Lord Randwulf's slate-gray eyes did not waver. "Indeed. And you have had twelve extra hours to contemplate our course from every approach. The plight of a kingdom could have been decided in that time."

"You give me too much credit. A small duchy, perhaps."

"Then tell me what has you frowning."

Alaric took a deep breath. "We have the ring, we know who sent it. We have the message, we know who sent that as well. We do not know who has Henry or if he has revealed the whereabouts yet of the princess."

"He would never reveal it," Robin insisted. "They could peel the flesh from his body strip by strip and he would not betray her."

"Pain is a formidable tool."

"So is love, and Lord Henry loves Eleanor. He would not betray her."

"Not intentionally, no. But the very fact he has remained in Nottingham all these years living off the land like a common peasant when he could have come here with his sister and lived a life of comfort and ease . . . it would give more than one man pause to ask the question why."

"*If* they discovered who he was," Robin pointed out. "According to Marienne, he has become so adept at changing his appearance, there are times he comes right up beside her disguised as a beggar or a cripple and she feels enough pity to drop an alm in his cup. I grant you, Guy de Gisbourne might know him if they stood shoulder to shoulder together in a room and Henry was stripped of all subterfuge, but otherelse, he would have no reason to doubt the assassin he sent here ten years ago was anything but successful. Thanks to Dafydd ap Iowerth suffering to take an arrow in his shoulder, both the king and Gisbourne believe Henry de Clare is dead. If this was not the case, if the ruse was discovered, we would have been apprised long before now."

"Which leaves us with FitzWalter and his barons, or the Earl of Pembroke," the Wolf mused.

Alaric pursed his lips. "If FitzWalter had Lord Henry, either as a guest or a prisoner, he would not be able to keep it secret for long."

"And the earl?"

"If it is William Marshal's doing, he is putting you in a more unconscionable position than I would have thought him capable, regardless of his own vows and oaths."

"Explain."

"You have pledged your sword to Philip of France. If you—or any of your sons—are seen now to rush to the aid of a claimant to the English throne, you risk not only a charge of treason, but the loss of your lands, your titles, your wealth . . . even your life."

"I have risked all before."

"I know you have. And so does he. That is why I do not think he would deliberately press you again. Moreover, there is Marienne. She may be base-born, but she *is* his daughter and I do not believe he would cast her to the devil, regardless of his vows."

Sparrow splayed his fingers in a gesture of disgust. "You argue against yourself! Not this one but that one, not that one but this one. My head aches with all this hither thither. *Which one is it?*"

Alaric did not answer the mercurial seneschal at once, but turned and walked to the fireplace. He stood bathed in the yellow glare for a full minute before sharing his thoughts aloud. "If it is *not* the earl, then he will be as concerned as we are, for his part in concealing her all these years would be sure to come out if she was taken. At the same time, his web of spies is nearly as broad and sticky as the king's; if he does not have Henry, he might well know who does. When is Dafydd due back in Normandy?"

"He was just here, not a sennight ago," Robin said. "He will not return for another three weeks, at least."

"If the earl knows something, he will send someone we trust; he will send the information back with Dafydd ap Iowerth."

Robin looked aghast at his father. "Surely you are not going to suggest we wait three more weeks!"

"I doubt you will have to wait three more days," Alaric said, turning his head. "The Marshal knows you will be attending the tournament at Gaillard. If he has information, he will arrange to pass it to you there."

"You think"—Robin nearly choked at the idea—"I would attend a tournament when there are lives in danger?"

"I think you have no choice," Will said quietly. "Half of Christendom will be attending, including half the spies in the employ of both the French and English kings. The other half will be doing what they normally do, watching the ports and noting who crosses from one side of the Channel to the other, watching certain lords and nobles to see where they go, who they meet, which way their loyalties might call them if and when Philip decides to invade England in force."

Alaric applauded his son's insight. "Should the vaunted champion from Amboise not show up at Gaillard to defend his title, should the Wardieu brothers not participate in a mêlée that has been the talk of two provinces for several months, and should the lot of them be seen boarding a ship bound for England . . . ?"

"We would have more leeches on our heels than leaves on a tree," Sparrow predicted glumly.

"There is, ah, one other small thing," Will ventured hesitantly. "Assuming we still attend the tourney, I do not think Robin should participate in anything other than the mêlée."

"Not participate?" Robin whirled around. "What further madness is this?"

"Normally, it would not warrant caution, for few are foolish enough to offer up a challenge anyway, but . . . if there is the smallest possibility of injury, I think it must be avoided at all costs."

"I have never declined a challenge yet out of fear of injury and am not about to do so now," Robin declared. "Furthermore, in my present mood, I would gladly take all comers and turn them into kindling!"

"What if that same mood blinds you and you make an inadvertent slip? What if there is someone present at Gaillard who could match you through twenty-three courses and be determined to oust you on the twenty-fourth?"

"Griffyn Renaud." Dag whistled softly under his breath. "With the timing of the devil himself."

"Did you not just argue that I must attend the tourney to waylay suspicions?" Robin reminded them all icily. "Now you want me to play the coward?"

"You can claim a legitimate injury," Will said softly. "You can claim the broken ribs and let a surgeon examine you beforehand if there is any question of courage."

"Ribs?" Sparrow's ears perked. "What broken ribs?"

"Yesterday in the forest," Will explained over Robin's curses. "When the boar cornered him—"

Sparrow was by Robin's side before Will finished speaking, unfastening belts and lifting tunic hems before he could be stopped. The ribs were bound in strips of cloth but they fell by the wayside and when the entire midsection was exposed in all its black-and-blue splendor, the little man gave out a cry and clutched a fist to his heart.

"When were you planning to own to this?" he demanded. "When the bone pierced through the skin?"

"The ribs are not broken," Robin argued. "Merely bruised. I scarcely feel it now and, in a sennight, will likely not even remember the mark is there."

Sparrow glared and, without warning, jabbed a finger into the bluest part of the bruise. Robin yelped and doubled over with the pain, the color draining from his face for the few seconds it took to recover and shove Sparrow's hands away.

"A single blow from a lance, aimed true," said Will, "would not only finish the job the boar began, but end all possibility of your being any use to the princess and Marienne."

"Perhaps we could appeal to Renaud," Dag suggested. "He seems a likable enough fellow."

"When you are dicing over whores, perhaps," Will agreed. "But he has not come all the way from Burgundy to simply sit in the bowers and watch the spectacle. And even if we could get him to agree, there is the other, the rumor we have heard that the Prince of Darkness has been invited to attend as Prince Louis's champion."

"Perhaps the two will challenge each other and solve the problem for us," Richard mused, still prickly over the business with Tansy.

"We cannot count on anyone outside of this room solving any of our problems," the Wolf stated flatly. "I agree with Will, Robin. You will have to restrict yourself to the mêlée, where there will be others there to watch your back."

Robin curled his long fingers around the back of a solid oak chair and squeezed until the knuckles turned white. When he looked from one tense face to the next and saw agreement etched reluctantly on all of them, he cursed and swung the chair so hard, it hit the wall and split in two. Not satisfied, he picked the backless seat up by the legs and smashed it once, twice, thrice against the stone wall until he held only two splintered sticks and a portion of board in his fists.

"Indeed," Sparrow muttered. "Such antics should help heal the ribs."

Panting, red with impotent fury, Robin raked his hands through his hair and paced back and forth before the fire.

"As to the matter of time," the Wolf said, watching his son with one wary eye while prompting Alaric to continue with the other.

"Even assuming the worst has happened," said FitzAthelstan, "that Henry is dead and the princess's whereabouts have been discovered, I believe we still have a safe margin. Marienne knows full well what to do; she has been instructed a thousand times over. She will keep the princess safe by claiming their right, under Canon Law, to sanctuary on holy ground. Any man or woman, be they guilty of the most heinous crimes, is entitled to seek refuge under the roof of the church, where their safety is guaranteed for forty days and forty nights. Not even the king would dare violate the laws of sanctuary, not unless he wanted to see England plunged into another six-year interdict, and not unless he wanted to lose all semblance of Rome's support."

"The message is three weeks old," Robin reiterated through the grating of his teeth.

"Twenty-one days," Will agreed, "assuming they were

forced to claim sanctuary the instant the ring was sent. And if that was the case, we *surely* would have heard by now, for all of England would have been abuzz with the news and Louis himself would have canceled the tourney at Gaillard so he could prepare his army to invade at once."

"Gaillard," the Wolf said flatly. "The tournament is but three days long?"

"We will need at least that much time to make arrangements for safe—and discreet—passage across the Channel."

The towering Jean de Brevant, a silent, glowering figure until now, looked over and nodded. "My cousin smuggles wine out of Fecamp; I am sure I could convince him to smuggle a small group of worthies coming home from a long pilgrimage to the Holy Land. I will only need to know how many cowls to procure."

One after the other, without hesitation, Robin, Richard, Dag, Sparrow, and Will drew their daggers and stuck them, point down, in the top of the wooden table. Only Will's hand lingered on the hilt while he looked askance at Lord Randwulf.

"With your permission, of course, my lord."

"You have it gladly. I have no doubt they will need the guidance of at least one level head."

A last dagger, longer and sharper than the rest, sank into the wood a full inch deeper than the others. As captain of the castle guard, Jean de Brevant's presence at Château d'Amboise was not to be lightly dismissed. As a seven-foot pillar of muscle and belligerence, however, his sword at Robin's back would be indispensable.

Moreover, "I was born in Nottinghamshire," he growled. "I know the forests and villages well."

Lord Randwulf nodded again. "I warrant I can hold the castle walls for a fortnight while you are gone."

A seventh dagger pierced the top of the table, thrown the same instant the arched oaken door swung wide.

Sparrow's hands moved in an instinctive blur, as did Littlejohn's and Robin's. In less time than it took for the shock to register on everyone's face, Brenna was surrounded by the glitter of unsheathed knives and swords.

"You will need more than just a level head and a strong sword arm to guide you," she said calmly, stepping into the full light. "You will need someone with a knowledge of forest paths who can move with skill and stealth and shoot the eye out of a running squirrel at a hundred paces."

12

Growling a curse, Littlejohn pushed swiftly past her to check the shadows outside in the corridor lest there were a dozen more eyes and ears pinned to the keyhole.

"Christ Jesus, Bren," Will said under his breath. "I warned you one day you would be caught listening to something you should not hear."

"Why should I not hear it?" she demanded. "Why should I not know when my family is facing grave danger? Am I so flighty and untrustworthy? Do you think me so inept or such a useless weakling I would not be able to help?"

"No one thinks you either weak *or* inept," her father said, barely recovered from the shock of her unexpected appearance. "Nor was it a matter of trust. It was for your own safety these things were kept from you."

"They were not kept well," she said, looking pointedly at the dragon ring. "Mistress Biddy told me all the tales of how the Black Wolf ventured to England to fight his bastard brother and rescue his intended bride from the Dragon's lair. She told me how he defied a king and fought a mighty tournament to bring the regent of England to his knees, earning his wrath and enmity forever. She also told me how he saved the son he never knew he had, and how he brought that son home to Amboise and trained him to be a great knight."

"Old Blister," Sparrow grumbled in disgust. "Never was she happy keeping one lip fastened to the other."

Brenna looked accusingly in his direction. "She never said a word against you that was not coated with love and admiration. It was you, she said, who risked all to rescue my father and Eduard from the Dragon's donjons, and you who returned to England years later and took an arrow in the heart to delay the king's troops long enough for Eduard to deliver the princess from Gisbourne's clutches at Corfe Castle."

"Well, in that she only spoke the truth, of course, but—"

"*But* she had no right speaking of it at all." The Wolf's slate-gray eyes bored into Sparrow like two glowing coals, deflating the woodsprite's conceit before it had the chance to puff his chest completely.

"But she did," Brenna said quietly. "She told me most everything, even the part Lady Gillian played in it all."

"Dear God ..." Lady Servanne whispered, standing slowly, her hands clutched over her heart. "No, you cannot be suggesting ... ?"

"That I be allowed to go with Robin and the others? That is exactly what I am suggesting."

Her mother came forward out of the shadows. "Brenna ... you do not know what you are saying. This is not another escapade in the forest, not just a game of chance."

"It is not a game at all, Mother. I know this."

"You know. *You know!* What do you know? Yes, you can creep through the forest and shoot the eye out of a running squirrel at a hundred paces, but you will not be hunting squirrels in Nottingham! You will be hunting—and hunted by—the king's men, shooting at *them* if it is necessary, *killing* them if it is necessary." She paused and tears began to silver her eyes. "I loved Gil too. I loved her as dearly as a sister, and yes, I admired her courage, her boldness, her ability to meet danger in the face and spit in its eye. But I never wanted that for you. Never. Yet I have had to watch in utter terror as you grew into the very image of that same courage and boldness, and I have not known how to stop it. I have tried. God help me, I have tried. Tried and failed."

Brenna hastened to her mother's side and clasped her trembling hands. "You have not failed, Mother. Never think that. And never think that all of my boldness and courage has come from Lady Gillian alone. Biddy told me how you stood up to the Dragon Wardieu. She told me how you entered his lair and defied him despite the fact you knew he would kill you for it."

Servanne's eyes filled helplessly and she looked at her husband. "I . . . had no choice."

"Because to stand by and do nothing would have been worse than death. Mother . . . you would not let me go with Robin and the others in the spring because you said I was too young and it was too dangerous and I was needed here. Well, I am not too young to make my own choices anymore. There is danger everywhere. And I am needed, yes, but not here. I know you are thinking of Lady Gillian, and I know you loved her as desperately as you love me . . . but could you have imagined her happy sitting at home in front of a warm hearth while the family she loved above all else was fighting for her honor and safety?"

Still clutching her mother's ice-cold hands, she turned to Lord Alaric. "Forgive me my bluntness, Friar, but could you have imagined her happier dying any other way? She rode by your side for twenty years; would you have thought to deny her the right to accompany you? Nay, if you were to look back on those twenty years, could you imagine what it might have been like were she *not* by your side?"

Alaric pursed his lips and looked down at his own hands, which were not as steady as he might have liked them to be.

"I know what it is like without her now," he said quietly. "But no, I could not have denied her."

"Father?" Her courage faltered slightly but she met the smoldering gray eyes directly. "If I were a son, not a daughter, would you even hesitate to let me go? Did you ever once hesitate to call upon Lady Gillian's bow arm when it was needed?"

He lowered his gaze and stared at the dragon ring for a long moment, turning it over and over in his fingers so that the gold glittered and the ruby flashed.

"No," he admitted softly. "I never doubted her skill nor

thought twice to have her fighting under the black and gold. Perhaps if I did, however, she would be with us still."

"Or perhaps, if you had let me go with her, I might have stopped that last arrow before it struck."

The silence, heavy as water, stretched almost a full minute more before the Wolf raised his leonine head and sought his wife's shimmering blue eyes. Servanne simply stared back, too terrified to move or even breathe until he looked away again and turned to Robin.

"She would be your responsibility. Would you want to accept it?"

The heir to Amboise pursed his lips thoughtfully. "When I was but thirteen and freshly squired to Eduard, I have no doubt you asked him the same question, this despite the odds of our returning from England were slim at best."

"The circumstances were hardly comparable."

"Indeed they were not, for we traveled on open roads and trusted Eduard's sword arm to see us through any chance encounters with the king's men. I barely had the strength in my arms to lift a sword, let alone wield it with any accuracy, and the only sure target I could hit with an arrow was a tree ten paces away and twenty paces wide." He paused and met Brenna's gaze over his father's head. "When we travel to Nottingham, we will have to keep to the forests and let no one be the wiser for our passing. Will is fully capable of guiding us, but a man with two keen eyes surely sees better than a man with only one. As for her ability to handle herself at close quarters with sword or knife, look to the scar on Richard's chin and ask him the truth of how he came by it."

Richard frowned and raised his hand self-consciously to stroke his beard. "A minor skirmish in the practice yards. Hardly worth mentioning then or now."

Dag grinned and fisted his brother on the shoulder. "You squealed like a pig and bled like a leaky gourd. Moreover, if anyone would care to ask my opinion, I would give a hearty *aye!* to Bren coming with us. I, for one, have no love of forests or itchy-fingered outlaws and the sooner we are led in and led out again, the happier I will be."

Sparrow harrumphed noisily and flared his nostrils wide enough to take in all the air in the room. "Does no one give a cod's tooth about *my* opinion?"

"No," Littlejohn retorted dryly. "But we know you will offer it anyway."

The little man planted his hands on his hips and glared at the captain of the guard. "Fine. Then you will *not* get it. Not if you scorched my tongue and roasted my feet over hot coals!"

Lord Randwulf sighed. "Sparrow . . . save us the trouble of stoking the fires. I gather you are not in favor of Brenna going?"

The seneschal set his mouth in a twist that clearly questioned the sanity of such a thing even being debated. "I was not in favor of her going to Gaillard. Why should it tickle me now to think of her venturing into the viper's nest in the company of addle-wits and love-sick buffoons?"

Lord Randwulf's eyes narrowed. "Because she will have you watching over her, and I can think of no better guardian offhand . . . can you?"

Sparrow opened his mouth, then clamped it shut again. If Brenna had a thought to smile or give a whoop of excitement, the notion was stifled on one glance from the slitted agate eyes. His cheeks were flushed red with his opinion that everyone in the room had finally gone completely and absolutely mad, but he stood with his arms crossed over his barrel chest to warn and threaten her that this selfsame madness was not contagious. Further, that it would not only be his duty, but his pleasure, to watch her like a hawk and breathe down her neck like a foul gust of wind if she took one foot off the beaten path.

Lord Randwulf fared little better, although the eyes staring at him with a mixture of disbelief and horror were a bright cornflower blue.

"If that is everything," he said, the strain telling on his face, "I suggest we meet again in the morning, hopefully with clearer heads and cooler thoughts. Alaric . . . I beg you stay the night. You will be no help to any of us if your horse trips over a root and flattens you in the dark. Ariel will think of something to tell Eduard if he notices your absence."

FitzAthelstan nodded.

"Robin, Dag, Richard . . . Brenna—" His gaze touched each of them in turn. "I do not envy you the task you have before you, but by God's grace, your eagerness to do it fills me with pride. If I were but a younger man . . ." He stopped and lowered his head a moment, then, with an effort, took up the stout walking stick and held his arm out to his wife. "Come. Help this old fool to his feet. Judging by the look in your eye, you have more to say to me; best it be said in the privacy of our own chamber."

Lady Servanne walked with him to the door. Outside in the corridor, she was the one whose steps faltered, and she had to sag against her husband's strong arm for support until they were safely out of earshot.

"How could I have refused her?" he asked gently.

"You could have said no."

"It was Robin's decision. What is more, I do not think she would have obeyed either one of us had we refused her. And she was right: there is too much of her mother inside her—and you were never one to obey an order you disliked."

"Do not even think," she scolded, her throat swollen with unshed tears, "to credit me for the smallest part of her mulishness. Eleanor and Isobel were my daughters; Brenna was always yours."

"In that case—" He tucked a finger under her chin and kissed her tenderly, passionately on the lips. "You need not worry overmuch. She will come back to you, as I always did. And we can only pity whoever tries to stand in her way."

PART TWO
Château Gaillard

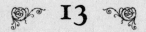

13

Château Gaillard had been the crowning achievement of King Richard's reign. Built by the supreme warrior of his time, with a master's knowledge of seigecraft and the fortifications required to repel them, it represented the efforts of the Angevin kings of England to conquer the Vexin—the territories between Rouen and Paris—and the determination of the House of Capet, ruled by Philip of France, to oust the Angevins from Normandy. Richard had situated Gaillard to command the crossing of the River Seine at Les Andelys, and command the river it did, dominating the skyline for ten miles in all directions. He had set out to construct a castle as invincible as he believed himself to be, and for the last eighteen months of his life, his boast—that he could hold his "saucy child" even if its walls had been made of butter—held true. But in April of 1199, the invincible Lionheart died of an arrow wound in his shoulder, a chance shot fired by an insolent bowman from the parapets of Chalus. And nearly five years to the day and month later, besieged and beleaguered under John's disastrous military leadership, Gaillard was surrendered to the French, her mighty walls breached by an inventive troop of men who entered through the drains of the latrines.

It was, nonetheless, an impressive fortification. Positioned atop the summit of a precipitous hill three hundred feet above the River Seine, the defenses consisted of three huge and distinct baileys enclosed by sheer, buttressed walls ten feet thick with circular towers situated every forty feet around the circumference. The first defense, the outer ward, was shaped like a wedge to take advantage of every last foot of the crag. The walls were high and sheer, with rounded towers and stone *machicolations*—extensions of the upper battlements with traps in the floor for dropping missiles, boiling oil, or buckets of red-hot sand. Surrounded completely by a deep, dry moat, this outer bailey afforded the only access into the castle from a steep and narrow approach that led up from the village of Les Andelys. The portcullis was the largest and heaviest constructed to that date, yet could be lowered within a few seconds of knocking away the chock-blocks to release the winch. A second draw joined the outer to the middle bailey and was just as heavily fortified by enormous barbican gatehouses, which, if under attack, could drop another massive portcullis gate and trap the attackers on the bridge, there to be shot from above like chickens in a pen.

The inner curtain wall rose up from a ledge of rock forty feet below the level of the middle bailey and had no proper guard towers. None were needed. The wall itself was twenty feet thick at its widest point and could be attacked or even partially destroyed without serious consequences to the rest of the structure. Inside this inner wall was the sixty-foot-high elliptical keep, its upper stories strengthened with tapering spurs and its foundation battered—sloped outward—for greater strength. Gray and lichen-covered, the keep stood with its back to the edge of the cliffs, with nary a window or door located below the second story. Entry was gained by a wooden staircase, which could easily be raised or destroyed to prevent access. Built purely for observation and as a last defense, there were no wall chambers or living quarters. Family apartments, great hall, and other domestic structures were located in buildings constructed in the courtyard and in sturdy stone outbuildings built along the inner walls.

Blame for the loss of Château Gaillard and the loss of nearly every other English possession in Normandy lay squarely upon King John's weak and spineless shoulders. Now, more than eleven years after he had taken the crown and set it upon his own head, the château was a magnificent and impregnable testament to King Philip's ever-strengthening control over Normandy, Brittany, and the Aquitaine. Despite several abysmal and failed attempts by John Plantagenet to regain possession of the Angevin legacy, Philip's armies were firmly entrenched, and the dukes, counts, and barons were pleased to pledge him homage in exchange for retaining their lands and titles. Even in the formerly intensely loyal regions of Touraine, Poitou, and Anjou, the nobles could no longer see the benefit of supporting a king who had abandoned them time and time again. John's numerous betrayals, his many tail-tucking retreats across the Channel, and his propensity for hiring black-souled mercenaries to keep his barons in line lost him old loyalties every day.

It was said by some that the ghost of Richard the Lion-heart haunted the battlements of Château Gaillard at night. Some swore they heard the long, gut-wrenching laments, the curses sent out across the land, across the moonlit sea to where his fatuous, treacherous brother ruled with such arrogant disregard for the loss of the Angevin heritage.

And on nights when the moon was too terrified to appear, when the stone ramparts were as cold and black as a tomb, Richard's form, clad in full mail armor, could be seen stalking the roof of the citadel, the legendary sword Excalibur clutched in his hand promising vengeance on all those who had forsaken his kingdom.

Lady Brenna Wardieu smoothed a hand along her stallion's neck, wondering what had spooked him. She had seen similarly nervous prancing steps from her brothers' horses up ahead and credited it to the enormous shadows thrown by the walls of Château Gaillard. The road they were on as they made their approach to the gates wound its way up the sheer slope like a snake. It had been designed deliberately without any continuously straight lengths to deter the use of any heavy siege machines that might otherwise be rolled into place to breach the fortifications. The road itself was narrow, the banks steep, and as they climbed, they could look down upon broken carts and the occasional dead rouncy who had lost its footing and slid over the edge.

With her gloved hands tight on the reins, Brenna sat back and gave her head a small toss to clear away the stray locks of hair that had blown forward across her face. She wore no headpiece or wimple, no feminine frills of any kind, preferring her doeskin leggings and a soft woolen shirt beneath a quilted surcoat of fine black velvet. Her brothers had barely batted an eye at her appearance this morning, but she knew if her mother or sisters had accompanied them and if the occasion had been normal, with no under-lying currents of tension or urgency, they would have wrung their hands in despair. But there was nothing normal about this venture. Robin was sullen and close-mouthed. Richard and Dag had gone the entire two days since their departure from Amboise without once pulling Sparrow's nose or testing the aim of his arblaster. Littlejohn was still with them, but it was his intention to see them secured in their encampment, then wait for cover of darkness to ride on ahead to Le Havre and arrange their passage across the Channel.

There was one other late addition to their group. Geof-frey LaFer had quietly offered his services to Lord Randwulf, as had his brother Erek, both hoping to repay in some small part the willingness with which the Wardieus had wel-comed them into their family. Since Geoffrey had been slated to participate in the mêlée anyway, his sword was gratefully accepted. Erek, younger by some two years and nursing a gouged leg he had earned at Roche-au-Moine, was given instead the temporary duty of filling in for Little-john as captain of the guard at Amboise. It was no small responsibility and he was flattered by the honor, though his face had been long and solemn as he watched the others ride away from the château.

Brenna was both tense and excited. It was odd how she had so looked forward to attending the tournament, but

now that they were here, it had become something merely
to endure before the real adventure could begin. It would be
her first time on a ship, her first time in the damp, mysterious reaches of England. She had heard enough stories to
know it was a rainy, forlorn place where the people were
short and dark and barbaric in their customs—those in the
far north of Scotland still dressed in furs and walked about
half naked. Food was cooked without spices or sauces and
was usually rancid for lack of proper preserving. The wine
was pitifully thin and closer to vinegar than water; the
ale was black and tasteless. She would have to eat and drink
her fill at Gaillard, for the taste of richly seasoned meats
and fine, sweet pastries would have to linger for several
weeks until they were home again.

They cleared the drawbridge and were coming under the
shadow of the enormous sixty-foot curtain wall, exchanging
the glare of bright sunlight for the more oppressing gloom
of the tunneled entrance to Château Gaillard. The black
iron spikes of the outer portcullis were thick as a man's
wrist and vibrated ominously at their passage. The sharpened teeth hovered no more than a hand's width above the
tallest head and could, if released in the urgency of an
attack, be driven a foot or more into the ground on impact.
The stone walls were mossed where the broken light from
the grating high above never warmed the earth below.
Countless slides of mud and thousands of footsteps had
packed the ground as hard as rock, causing the horses'
hooves to clatter like an old woman's teeth. Long defensive
slits—*meurtrieres*—cut in the walls of the gateway barbican
had eyes behind them, watchers who marked every rider
and could, at a moment's notice, drop both gates and trap
unwanted trespassers in between.

In keeping with polite custom, the main party from
Amboise would pay their respects to their host upon their
arrival. The bulk of their escort, comprised of four-score
knights, servants, and attendants, had broken away at the
base of the slope and, by nightfall, would have constructed
a sturdy encampment of tents and pavilions on the

meadows below. It was Robin's habit, as it had been his father's and Eduard's, rarely to accept the hospitality of lodgings inside the castle itself. It was not that he did not trust the king's custodian, Bertrand Malagane; it was simply a matter of his preferring to have all four flanks guarded by his own men. Castles were riddled with secret passageways and dark, deep donjons where a man could scream himself hoarse and never be heard. Nor was the Amboise camp the only one flowering on the common fields below the castle. Because of the sheer number of participants in the tournament, there were tents, pavilions, even pens and makeshift canvas stables for the horses being erected in every available open space. At dusk, when the cooking fires were lit, the slopes would come alive with twinkling lights and the bellies of the low-lying clouds would glow red with their reflection.

Most of the events for the tourney would be held in the flat meadow at the base of the slope. Men had been hard at work for the past several days building bowers and erecting palisades for the jousting arenas, and there was a constant stream of carpenters and laborers moving to and from the castle to the common.

They rode through the outer bailey with the smell of coal fires and raw bog iron stinging their nostrils. A vast temporary armory had been set up around the base of the walls where smithies stoked their fires and hammered sheets of red-hot iron while armorers toiled over swords, pikes, lances, and chain mail. Few looked up from their work, for they were paid by the piece and, if dexterous enough, could earn sufficient coin to see their families through the harsh winter months ahead.

Across the second moat and drawbridge was the middle bailey, crowded near to bursting with booths and stalls where every conceivable necessity or fancy was on display for sale. The huge common had been turned into a marketplace with vendors and peddlers hawking everything from ribbons and baubles to boiled eels threaded through the gills and sold by the stickful. Tinkers' wares were hung on hooks and piled on tables. The din was overwhelming as every price was scoffed at and haggled over, every knight, lord, and lady vied for the sweetest pastries, the stoutest mug of ale, the brightest bit of tinsel. At one end were the low buildings that housed the barracks where the soldiers and men-at-arms were garrisoned. At the other were the pens where fat cows and sheep waited to be slaughtered and roasted for the coming feasts, where peacocks strutted in the supposed impunity of their green-and-blue finery before they, like the flocks of hapless chickens and geese, were caught and carried squawking to the kitchens inside.

The sights, the sounds, the colors, the enthusiasm were contagious, and Brenna found herself smiling despite the grim looks on her brothers' faces. She dearly loved her life at Amboise, but there were times when she missed the bustle and confusion of big cities and towns. She even missed—though she would carve her own tongue out of her head before she would admit it to anyone else—the openly admiring glances from swarthy-faced knights and handsome chevaliers, earls and counts, even a prince or two, identifiable by the crests emblazoned on their tunics and pennons. Gathered here were the elite of Norman knighthood. They were all fighting men come to show off their skills and prowess, all come to train and practice for war in the closest thing to actual mortal combat they could devise. Their swords would be blunted and their lances fitted with coronals—crown-shaped caps with three curved points to deflect the force of a blow. But this was not to say the lists were safe or that deaths were uncommon. Far from it. Tournaments were often used to settle personal grievances between rivals. A match could be declared *à outrance* if both opponents agreed to unblunted weapons. Even *à plaisance*, a lance could splinter and skewer a man, or a blow from a dulled sword could hack with enough force to find a vulnerable weakness in armor.

For this reason, tourneys were condemned by the church. They were said to encourage the seven mortal sins of pride, envy, anger, sloth, avarice, lust, and gluttony . . . not to mention the sin of homicide, easily committed whether intentional or not.

For a knight, the chance to demonstrate his skills on the field far outweighed the risk of suffering eternal hellfire. Chivalry itself was put on display, and knights could prove their noble bloodlines as well as their worth as fighting men. Many a landless knight who might otherwise be reduced to begging his lodgings or selling his sword for bread was able to acquire considerable wealth and prestige through victories on the tournament circuit.

It was, Brenna knew, how her own father had rebuilt his lost fortunes and earned the attention of the dowager queen, Eleanor of Aquitaine. His gratitude, love, and loyalty had endured almost thirty years, up to her death and burial at Fontrevaud. Only his friendship with William Marshal, the Earl of Pembroke, had lasted longer.

"Lady Brenna?"

She had allowed her mind to drift as they crossed the middle bailey and now one of the squires had caught hold of her stallion's bridle waiting for her to dismount. The inner bailey was too small to allow for so many heavy-breasted beasts; the rest of the way would be on foot across another draw, through another gate, past another tall barbican where bull-hide–clad sentries patrolled and observed from the battlements above.

Brenna dismounted without assistance and walked forward to join her brothers, stretching the stiffness out of her spine and legs as she advanced.

"She *is* here, dammit," Richard was muttering. "I saw her by one of the food stalls, and if she were a hound, her nose would have started twitching."

Will grinned and welcomed Brenna into their midst. "You held your seat well back there. Once or twice we thought you were bound for a tumble down the earthworks."

"Many thanks for rushing to my aid," she said dryly.

"Hah. Had we done so, we would be wearing your bootprint on our rumps for our trouble," Richard noted, stripping off his gloves.

"You are looking rather more sour than usual, brother dear. Dare I ask *who* is here sniffing after your vaunted jewels?"

"No one," he grumbled.

"Lady Alice of Rouen," Dag obliged cheerfully. "She of the high, pert breasts and long, willowy limbs . . . er, was that not how you described her the last time you saw her?"

Richard glared and gave his surcoat a brief yank to smooth the creases. "High, upturned nose and greedy grasping hands, mores the like. I thought I heard the happy news she had fastened her claws into some poor lout in Anjou."

"I heard she had her heart set on you," Dag said. "And it would take naught less than your death to discourage her."

"Then I remain alive just to disappoint her."

"Tch-tch." Brenna brushed a gloved finger over Dag's arm to remove a fleck of dust. "You are both such handsome fellows, how could you expect not to earn the notice of every mewling swan within a league's distance?"

It was true. The sons of the Black Wolf were the peacocks strutting in the midst of the chickens and geese. Each wore his finest raiments, with Richard dressed all in black, as was his habit, and Dag in midnight blue. Robin wore a combination of black surcoat over sky-blue hose, the former heavily banded with gold and emblazoned with the Amboise crest. He had a slight advantage in height over his younger brothers, and a deal more fighting strength across the shoulders, but there was no denying they were all handsome, virile, tempting morsels of male flesh, and to judge by the number of ladies who stumbled over their own feet as they passed, their arrival at Gaillard had not gone unnoticed.

"Lissome little dabchicks," Dag commented, noting two swanlike creatures whose necks were put to good use craning to see behind them. "Would that I could take them all, one by one, and preen them myself."

"Bold words," came a smooth voice from over his shoulder. "But you might grow bored with the sentiment when you find yourself waking up each morning with your ballocks on fire and nothing to show for it but an empty bed and an emptier purse."

Geoffrey LaFer joined them, his mouth curved into a laconic smile. Geoffrey was a full head shorter than any of the Wardieu men, with sand-brown hair and twinkling blue eyes. He was so clearly, absolutely, and eternally in love with their sister Isobel, it humbled even Richard, the randiest cocksman of the troop.

"Ahh. The voice of our conscience," said Dag. "I for one welcome a more secular mind into our midst. In fact, I think I shall make my bed in your tent, Brother Geoffrey"—he draped an arm amiably over LaFer's shoulder— "so you can recount me my sins throughout the night and make a better man of me by morning."

"Eat dung," Geoffrey said, laughing. "You would need the services of a bishop and twenty tonsured prelates to even begin to make you see the error of your ways." He looked at Robin. "Do we pay our respects to the host first? Or should we register and find out if, by some miracle, the matter scheduled to be resolved by the mêlée has been deferred by love?"

Robin pointed to a tent festooned with a riot of colored ribbands and pennons. "We are here now, we might as well attend to business."

As he led the way across the crowded bailey, it was difficult not to notice how they had instantly become the center of attention and to hear the strident buzz that rippled through the throng as it parted to make way for the black-and-gold blazons of Amboise. The casual bystanders were suddenly not so casual anymore. Nor were the squires and servants dispatched by their masters to watch the booth and alert them to any new and important entrants. The only ones not completely enthralled to see the new arrivals were the bet-takers and speculators whose task it was to establish opening odds against each new participant. Few in their right senses took any odds at all against Robert

Wardieu d'Amboise, or if they did, it was to whether he maimed his opponent or merely humiliated him.

It was the custom to pay a token fee for the privilege of boasting one's talents in the lists, as much as twenty marks for an earl, down to two marks for a landless knight. As soon as it was paid, the knight's shield could be displayed. Those who wished to pose a specific challenge either struck the shield and declared his intent before witnesses, or left an identifiable token bound to the pole on which it hung. These were the single-combat matches where personal as well as professional disputes were settled.

Knights who bore no grudges or had no particular interest in whom they fought merely drew lots through the day. Those who won the early courses and were satisfied with their successes could withdraw any time without disgrace. Those who chose to risk more were also free to hang their shields again and advance to the next level of challengers. To the winner of each match went the horse and armor of his opponent, although a fee could be paid in lieu of forfeiting the actual beast and an armload of chain mail. To this end, there were convenient moneylenders in attendance who would pay out in coin—at a fraction of the real value—for any animals or equipment not wanted by the victor. Ordinarily these anonymous matches were perfectly suited to Richard and Dag, and to Geoffrey LaFer, for they sought no more than to keep their skills honed and earn a few trophies to hang on their walls. On this occasion, however, they would be settling for the accolades earned at the mêlée, for with Robin not entering the jousts, they could hardly be expected to show him up.

Will touched Brenna's arm. "Stay with your brothers. Do not go wandering off into the crowd or Sparrow will have my teeth hanging around his neck."

Brenna made a face and, for all of three seconds, remained exactly where she was. With the fourth came the booming, doom-laden voices of six cowled monks who walked among the crowds droning the potential fate of challengers who defied holy law. They would be forced to wear their armor through all of eternity—armor that was molten hot and nailed to their bodies so it could not be torn away! They would be given evil-smelling, sulphurous baths! And instead of the embraces of wanton young women, they would be obliged to endure the amorous advances of lascivious toads!

Brenna edged away as unobtrusively as possible. She saw—or rather, smelled—a booth nearby touting an assortment of hot, steaming meat pies. Patting her belt, she assured herself of the snugness of her money pouch as well as her falchion and dagger, then started working her way toward the food stall.

Her purchase oozed grease over her fingers as she took a large bite and chewed happily on the mix of larded hare, quail, and mashed chestnuts. She was jostled again but this time exchanged a mutually grinned apology with another satisfied patron whose mouth was equally too stuffed to speak. All around her there were pennons and flags flying. Some moved though the crowds on pikes, being carried proudly by pages who walked importantly in front of their lords and ladies. The clash of brightly colored silks was like an eruption of butterflies tainting the air with a hundred shades of vermilion, blue, green, and yellow. Some were banded, some spotted, some boasted three and four colors embroidered overall with gold and silver threads. Brenna smiled the smile of a childhood memory, the first time she had been taken to a fair, perched on the broad seat of her father's shoulders, trying to touch every streamer of silk that passed as if it was a breath of colored wind.

She had never quite lost that wide-eyed rush of excitement, nor had she outgrown the taste of sugared dates, that exotic confection first introduced by returning Crusaders. With her cheeks still bulging with meat and pastry, she wove her way through a large party of yeomen and squandered half a copper sou on a canvas pouch filled with the sticky-sweet treats.

"Hah! When your belly grows bilious and you are forced to purge it with possets of henbane and worm lips to ease the pain, do not harken to me for pity, Mistress Noddypeak!"

Brenna sighed and looked down. Sparrow was standing beside her, puffed up with indignation, the top of his felt-capped head barely reaching the level of her waist.

"Attempting to hide from me, or making me run hither and yon to search you out at every turn of the head will only make a stronger argument for tying you hand and foot to the nearest rouncy and hi-hoing you off home again! And if you think I merely vent air and bluster through these lips, ask Sir Cyril here if I am not determined to save myself the aggravation of Lady Servanne's tears."

As low as Brenna's gaze had fallen to meet Sparrow's, it rose now to Littlejohn's frowning countenance.

"You should not have slipped away without us, my lady," he growled, not happy to be agreeing with Sparrow over anything. "Lord Randwulf gave strict orders—"

"Yes, yes. That I was not to draw a breath unless it passed by you first," she finished on an exasperated huff. "Mother of Mercy, I was not trying to hide, I was only trying to avoid the crush surrounding Robin and the others. And indeed, because there is such a crowd, how could anyone work any mischief without it being seen by a hundred others?"

Littlejohn's mouth twisted into a smile. "How? Ask the freebooter who filched the elf's purse from his belt not two steps away from his horse."

Sparrow turned and hoofed his toe into the knight's trunklike shin. "It was hung there deliberately to test the honesty of Lord Malagane's minions. And see you? We have found them wanting."

"My purse is quite safe," Brenna assured him, patting her belt. "Furthermore, so am I; Will is with me."

Sparrow glared at the surrounding sea of knees and limbs. "Where?"

"I have him in my eye. He is pretending not to be showing any interest in the archery roles."

"Faugh! Another hawk of sterling attentiveness! I warrant I could strip his braies to his knees and paint his ballocks blue before he would notice anything amiss. And you, Mistress Munch, are far more valuable than any purseful of coins. Look you there. And there! A rare mort of fomenting villainy!"

He fondled his harp-shaped arblaster and glared threateningly at a few passersby until they gave him a wider berth. Brenna merely sucked the crystals of sugar off her fingers and offered the candy to Littlejohn, who greedily accepted the offering, then to Sparrow, who refused it with an imperious snort.

His declamation on the eating habits of Infidels was drowned out by a loud cheer as two wrestlers, stripped to the waist and oiled like fish, began to circle each other nearby. Brenna watched with only modest interest, for she knew most of their insults and challenges were rehearsed for the benefit of the crowd. She had already started to turn her gaze back to the archery booth when it was stopped again, this time by the face of a man in the outer ring of spectators who had gathered to watch the wrestlers.

He stood an easy head and shoulders above anyone else in the crowd, a fact she might still have missed had he not been staring directly at her. Not only staring, but studying her through eyes as pale and clear as lake water—eyes that were not only washed of color, but of manners too as he made not the smallest effort to look away or make amends for the discourtesy when he had been caught.

It was Griffyn Renaud de Verdelay.

His appearance so soon, and in the midst of hundreds of others, caught her off guard, and she all but swallowed a date whole. She lowered her gaze quickly but it was too late to prevent the dark, intense blaze of heat from flaring in her cheeks as she remembered the occasion of their last meeting. Her thighs actually shivered and the flesh between gave a single moist throb, and when she recovered enough to risk looking over again, he was still staring. If anything, he appeared to have plucked her thoughts out of the air and gave her a smile of such knowing arrogance, she nearly gasped out loud. Worse still, he was starting to circle the crowd and walk toward her. Sparrow's warnings about villains in their midst echoed inside her head, and for the spate of several wild heartbeats she was half convinced he was coming to gather her up into his arms and carry her off into the confusion, there to finish what he had begun on the archery run.

She did not want to face him or speak to him or make any attempt at a polite exchange, not while her flesh continued to prickle and her cheeks betrayed the heat of her mortification. Frantic, she turned and pushed her way through a group of strolling jongleurs, stumbling once and almost tripping headlong in her haste to put distance between her and Renaud.

She ran between two booths and circled around behind another row of stalls, coming soon upon a quieter, less congested area closer to the base of the walls. Here were empty carts and tired ponies, piles of garbage and discarded sacks. Older women bent over smoking fires to cook the pies and pasties they sold up front, and children played in the dust and mud, occasionally throwing a rock or stick at a mangy dog that crept too close to the cook pot.

Younger women with dull eyes and gaping tunics lounged in the shade resting between customers. There were no proper stews or tents set aside in which to ply their trade, but with the demand came inventiveness. As Brenna passed by a woodpile, she could hear grunting and the unmistakable slap of flesh on flesh coming from behind it.

Her head lowered, she quickened her steps and took two, three more winding turns around stalls and bothys. She guessed she must have circled half the bailey by now and should be in the approximate area back of the archery booths, but before she could head back into the noise and merriment, a tall black shadow was thrown across her path and she was brought to an abrupt, slamming halt.

14

"Well now, what do we have here?"

Brenna stumbled back a pace and looked up into the scarred face of a heavy chested, thick-nosed Fleming who wore a greasy brown beard and had a belly the size of a giant toadstool.

"By all my teeth—'tis a wench, lads, not a pretty little boy after all."

Brenna glanced to either side and saw two more men slinking out of the shadows. She put a hand to the hilt of her falchion and dropped the pouch of sugared figs on the ground.

"Keep your distance," she warned. "I want no trouble."

The Fleming arched an eyebrow. "She wants no trouble—hear that, lads?"

His comrades grinned and nodded and shifted around behind her to cut off her retreat.

" 'Tis no trouble we want to give you either. Just a slap and tickle, and mayhap a bit of a scratch to ease the itch on such a fine, festive day."

Brenna drew her shortsword and slashed it threateningly at the two men who were now in position to leap forward and grab at her arms. One of them tried and won a cut on his cheek for the effort. The other jumped back as the blade sliced the air across the tops of his thighs, but he was not unarmed himself; he produced a small leather whip that he uncoiled from around his belt.

"She cut me!" The injured man gasped. He lowered his hand from his cheek and gaped at the blood dripping off his fingers. "The bitch cut me!"

"Aye, well, mayhap we'll let you cut her back when we're finished with her," said the man with the whip as he sent it snaking out. Brenna anticipated the move and her blade flashed again, this time intercepting the leather tail and jerking it clear out of the villain's hand. Unfortunately she lost a precious second tossing the whip aside, and a second was more than enough for the Fleming to close in and grab her around the wrist and throat. He twisted her arm back and around, forcing her to release her hold on the falchion; he curled his other hand around her throat in a choke hold, exerting enough pressure to lift her off the ground and cut off her supply of air.

Brenna clawed and scratched and kicked out with the heels of her boots, but the Fleming only laughed. She tried to reach her dagger but the second man had already snatched it out of her belt along with her money purse. There was a brief scuffle while the injured freebooter rushed forward to try to take the purse from his comrade, but Brenna could not use the distraction to her advantage. She was too busy trying to breathe. Her throat was being crushed and her arm nearly ripped out of the socket. She could neither scream nor loosen the Fleming's grip even though her nails gouged his flesh and tore bloody strips into his hands and forearms.

"Aye." He grunted. "Fight as much as you like, lass. I like my cats to bite and scratch so long as they know they will receive like treatment in return."

His breath was hot and fetid where it rasped against her cheek, and his tongue left her chin coated with slime where he dragged it over her skin, trying to steal a kiss. Her lungs were burning and her vision was clouding over with huge black splotches. She was numbly aware of someone taking hold of her ankles and prying them apart as they carried her into the deeper shadows.

Something bright and silvery flashed in front of her dimming eyes and she heard the Fleming scream in her ear. The pressure around her neck relented enough for her to gasp at a breath but before she could fully fill her lungs, she was flung forward onto a heap of old rags and rotted food scraps.

Choking, sobbing for air, she scrambled onto her knees and turned in time to see the looming silhouette of a man step into the circle of sunlight. His sword flashed again and one of the villains reeled sideways, his hands clutched over his belly to catch his entrails before they spilled out onto the ground. The second man was stopped by a hammerlike fist that shattered his nose and sent splinters of bone back into his brain.

The Fleming, seeing his friends fall, snarled and lunged. He managed to get a hand around a fistful of Griffyn Renaud's surcoat before it was hacked free, whereupon blood gouted in a hot stream from the severed wrist and the thief screamed again. The sound was cut brutally short, finishing with a bloody gurgle as he crashed onto the ground, his neck split open from ear to ear.

The entire encounter had taken less than a minute, not even long enough for Brenna to catch her breath and restore her senses. Griffyn cast around until he found her sword, dagger, and money purse, then scooped her up into his arms and carried her away from the scene of carnage. With tears of pain streaming down her cheeks, she buried her face in the crook of his throat and held fast to his broad shoulders until he found a place free of two- and four-legged vermin and set her down on an overturned crate. Even then she was reluctant to let go. He let her cling to him a little longer before carefully easing her arms down from around his neck.

He looked into her eyes, at the colors and patterns that formed a nimbus around the dark centers, the vibrant blue shot through with deeper violet arrowheads. He brushed the backs of his fingers across her cheek and because he could think of nothing else to do to stop her lips from trembling, he kissed them.

The caress was ravishingly gentle and she made no move to avoid it. It was such a shocking contrast to the explosive violence she had just witnessed, she very nearly encouraged it to continue long past what might have been explained away as a brief lapse of judgment. But she recovered and pulled away. And he sat back on his heels, seeming to need a moment himself to remember where they were.

"I thought you said you knew how to take care of yourself," he chided, not unkindly.

"I do. They just . . . caught me by surprise."

"Offal like that are not usually known for issuing polite challenges beforehand."

She looked up at him, regarding him solemnly through huge, swimming eyes. "You might have been killed."

"I am not that easy to kill," he assured her, and because his hands were aching to draw her back against his body, he removed the temptation by standing and fetching a dipper of water from a nearby bucket. He held it to her lips and bade her drink a few sips, then took up a scrap of linen and gently bathed the red marks glowering down the length of her throat.

"My sword?"

"I have it."

"My money?"

"Right here."

She bowed her head and sighed, and Griffyn gave her a few more minutes. He need a few himself, for he could not have said what made him follow her. He had seen her turn and dart away into the crowd and his first instinct had been to let her go; he did not need to pursue trouble when it so obviously wanted to avoid him. But he was also all too familiar with the types of men who moved among the shadows and waited for those who wandered too far from the crowds. So he had cursed aside his own better judgment and tracked her, and for wont of not listening to those damned warning bells that were clanging in his head like broken armor, there were three dead men in the lee of the wall and here he was, a breath away from kissing her again and opening himself up to all manner of unwanted complications.

"I suppose you expect me to thank you," she said in a whispery voice.

"A simple pledge of undying gratitude—along with the soul of your firstborn child—should do nicely."

She looked up and scowled at the magnificence of his grin.

"Thank you," she muttered.

"I am ever your humble servant, my lady," he responded, bowing.

She stood up—not entirely unassisted—and resheathed her sword and dagger, and tied her money purse to her belt, tucking it back beneath the leather. She gave her throat a final, tender massage to insure it was working properly, then squared her shoulders and smoothed back the flown wisps of her hair.

"Sparrow and Littlejohn are undoubtedly laying waste to the bailey by now. They have already lectured me once for straying out of their sight."

"They are wise men, you should heed their advice. This is not the place to wander off alone. But perhaps . . . if you return in my company, they will not take as much exception to your sudden disappearance."

"I rather think they would take more."

He shrugged. "Suit yourself, but it would seem a better strategy to be able to chide them for losing sight of you instead of them discovering you emerging alone from an alley frequented by whores and sodomites."

Brenna flinched forward as if the crate she had been sitting on was crawling with contagion.

"This way, I believe," he said casually, indicating a narrow alley with his hand.

She went ahead, for the gap was not wide enough for two to walk abreast. She could feel the mocking heat of his elf-shot eyes between her shoulder blades and she was suddenly self-conscious about the tightness of her leggings and the shortness of her tunic. The taste of his mouth was still warm

on hers and the memory of how it chanced to be so caused
her to stop and turn without warning.

"Despite what has just happened, sirrah, I have absolutely no wish to renew our acquaintance. I find your character unappealing, your manner unnerving, and . . . and
your *profession* unworthy. What happened at Amboise . . ."
She stopped and started again. "What happened at Amboise was an unconscionable lapse on my part—"

"On which occasion?" he interrupted politely. "When I
was naked in the bath house or you were very nearly so on
the common?"

The breath rushed out of her lungs around an exasperated oath. "There! You see? I cannot even attempt a civil
conversation without you reminding me when you were
naked and I was naked and—"

"Almost naked."

"*What?*"

"You were *almost* naked," he murmured, lifting a finger to
tuck a stray hair behind her ear. "To my profound regret, I
might add."

She swatted his hand aside. "If you had a shred of
decency in you, you would not ever speak of either occurrence again!"

"And? If I can boast of no such shreds? If I can boast
only of extremely pleasurable memories and lingering
thoughts of what might have happened had we not been
interrupted?"

"Nothing," she gasped. "Nothing would have happened!
And if that is all you can recall, then you are indeed an ill-
mannered rogue and I see no reason to ever speak to you
again!"

She whirled and stormed into the thickening crowd but
got no farther than the mouth of alleyway before she came
to another abrupt halt and spun around again, voluntarily
seeking to press herself against the shield of Griffyn's chest.

"God love me," she moaned. "Not now!"

Finding himself suddenly with an armful of cursing

womanhood, he frowned and tipped his head down in an attempt to see her face.

"My lady? Something else is amiss?"

"It is *him*. It is the *oaf*. Of all the wretched times and places . . ." She grasped two fistfuls of Renaud's surcoat and physically wheeled him around so that his back was to the crowd and she could peek out from behind the safety of his broad shoulder. "I cannot possibly bear it now. I simply cannot!"

"What . . . or should I say *who* can you not bear?"

"*Him!* The big yellow-haired brute in the gold tunic. Gerome de Saintonge."

"Ahh." The sparks of amusement that had unwittingly flared in the pale green eyes lingered for as long as it took him to spot the designated oaf. "Not a friend of yours, I take it?"

"A friend? A *fiend* is more like it. A brute. A beast. A lecher with unclean habits and hands that never relent in seeking to go where they are not wanted."

The luminous eyes narrowed and he glanced back over his shoulder. Saintonge was broad-boned and thickly muscled, with a flat round face pitted with too small eyes and a wide sloppy mouth that resembled two slices of uncooked liver. A surplus of copper freckles and body hair ran down his arms and wrists, flowing onto the backs of his fingers, one of which was missing, bitten off at the knuckle. "He looks to be a lusty enough fellow."

"Lusty? He is more than lusty, he is perverse. And too thick-headed to take no for an answer despite the number of times I have shouted it in his face."

"He has designs on marrying you?"

She glared up again. "You say that as if it would be the last step before taking poison or falling on your own sword!"

"I assure you, that was not . . ." He stopped and frowned, but his mouth was quivering to let loose with another grin. "I gather you have refused his petition?"

"Refused him? I showed him my sword the last time he

came keening at the gates of Amboise. Good *Christ*, he is coming this way!"

She tried to push out of his arms and dart back into the alley but Griffyn caught her and led her off to one side instead. "He is not coming this way, he has not even seen you. FitzAthelstan, on the other hand, has. Here—" He took her by the arm and steered her gently toward a booth filled with colored ribbands and scarves. "Try to look as engrossed in the frippery as these other women do. This one, I think," he said, and held up a length of gossamer-sheer silk shaded the exact violet hue of her eyes.

She opened her mouth to tell him precisely where he could stuff the length of silk when she saw Will poke Robin's arm and point in their direction. Her half-formed retort curved into a less than sincere smile and she was forced to endure Renaud's company until her brother joined them.

He glared at Brenna, then held out his hand and offered Griffyn a half-relieved, half-puzzled greeting. "I see you managed to make your way to Gaillard without further incident. I see you found my sister as well."

"Found her? I did not know she had been lost. In fact, we have been wandering from booth to booth for some time with me trying unsuccessfully to convince her to accept some small token of my thanks for your family's hospitality."

Robin looked from Griffyn to Brenna to the soft lavender silk scarf. "You would have better luck visiting the armorer's row and offering to buy her arrowheads or goose feathers."

"I will keep that in mind for the next time."

Brenna clenched her fist around the scarf, mentally adding deafness to his list of character deficiencies, for had she not just finished telling him there would be no next time? There should not even have been a *this* time but for her own foolish behavior. It was bad enough just to be indebted to such a man as Griffyn Renaud for rescuing her.

She stole a sidelong glance at the dark knight as he and Robin were conversing. The breeze was plucking at fine strands of jet-black hair and curling them forward over his cheeks. The sun was lighting his face like an artist brandishing some divine creation, and she could not deny he was by far and away the most dangerously handsome rogue under the wide blue sky. If she needed any further proof, it was in the eyes of the men and women who passed by. Women stared openly, first at his face, then at the fit of his hose and the bulge of muscles across his chest and thighs. Men marked him with a keen eye to the powerful set of his body, doubtless wondering if he intended to offer himself in the lists and what it might take in strength and skill to unhorse him.

Ill mannered, unprincipled, and untrustworthy perhaps . . . but he was a superb presentation of confidence and raw sensuality. She imagined most women would have her dragged off to Bedlam for shunning him.

"Lord Robert!"

The name was shrieked not a foot from Brenna's ear, causing her to jump half out of her skin.

"Lord Robert Wardieu d'Amboise! You scoundrel! You are come at last!" A short, round, violently effeminate man capered his way past several tittering ladies and bowed over a gracefully pointed toe as he presented himself before Robin. "Indeed, how we were hoping you would grace us with your presence and look you now . . . my heart is simply *squeezed* with pleasure!"

Brenna's eyes widened to the size of medallions as she beheld the extraordinary little man, for he was easily as expansive around the girth as he was tall. Far from being shy about it, he wore his prodigiousness like a gaudy boast; his hose were bright yellow, his tunic an outrageous blue-and-orange mottle with full slashed sleeves in stripes of red and purple. A feathered cap was perched jauntily on the large, doughy ball of his head, while a collar trimmed flamboyantly in silk tassels circled the multiple levels of chins.

A bulbous nose twitched constantly as if sniffing for food, while two bright eyes flirted outrageously with every well-shaped pair of buttocks that passed, regardless if those buttocks were male or female.

They were glittering delightedly now as they flitted between Robin and Griffyn, the latter looking suddenly like an eight-point buck cornered by a line of archers.

"Rollo, you hoary rogue," Robin said, laughing. "Is business so good it brings you all the way from Tuscany?"

"My dearest friend, it is *so* good, it would bring me from the walls of *Jerusalem*, were I there on my knees *praying* for salvation. Your father did not come? A *ravaging* shame. Nor the lusty Eduard? How *cruel*." His hands fluttered in small ecstasies under his chins. "And yet I see we have a bold new face with us—a face with which, in God's truth, I am *appalled* to admit I am unfamiliar."

Robin pursed his lips to conceal his smile. "Rollo d'Albini . . . Lord Griffyn Renaud de Verdelay. If he is unfamiliar, it is because he has been buried in the mountains of Burgundy these past few years." While the rotund little man flourished another bow Robin explained, "Rollo is acting Master of the Tournament. His presence is deemed a necessity at any event worthy of note, for he is generally acknowledged to organize the most exciting and extravagant *pas d'armes* in all of Europe."

"You are so kind." D'Albini tittered modestly. "I merely share my knowledge of what I know best: good food, good wine, good entertainment. My jongleurs perform for kings and queens, and my pastrymakers"—he stopped and rolled his eyes in an expression of utter heart-stopping bliss— "have no equal *anywhere*, as I can adequately attend. But *this*, I feel"—he waved a bejeweled hand to encompass the teeming bailey—"will be my finest hour yet. *L'Emprise de la Gueule de Dragon* . . . is that not simply *delicious*? Does the name alone not just bring the thrill of *terror* to your soul?"

"I quaked when I heard it," Robin agreed.

"Fully half a hundred knights thus far have entered for

single-combat matches," he effused. "*Including*"—he paused for dramatic effect—"the Prince of Darkness himself."

Robin's smile hardened instantly. "He is here? You have seen him?"

"*With mine own eyes!* And *oh!* What a *sight* he was too! There—" He pointed a finger crusted with rubies toward the rows of pennons flying over the registration booth. "The falcon, gold on vert. He signed the role yesterday and, in a most *extraordinary* manner, declared he would entertain only *three* challenges. Three of *his* choosing, mind! Can you *imagine* it? The moneylenders are in an absolute *frenzy*, wondering which three he will accept. Ivo has smote for him already, as has that big brute, Draco the Hun, along with four or five other *reckless* souls who have no *real* wish to fight him but strike his shield anyway, knowing he will not waste his chaff on them, but they can still boast their willingness." He paused and screwed his eyes to slits as he peered myopically at Griffyn again. "*Burgundy*, did you say? Would I be erred in surmising you might have some additional knowledge of this princely rogue seeing as you both hail from the eastern provinces?"

"I have never watched him fight," Griffyn said.

"Nor fought him yourself?"

"No. No, I have never fought him myself."

"Mmm. No doubt you had your reasons." The tone of dismissal was not exactly flattering to a knight's character, but if Griffyn took it as an insult, he gave no sign.

"And yet, all is not lost," Rollo continued, switching his focus back to Robin, "for surely *you* intend to take affront at the very *notion* of such a knavish lout dictating whom he will fight and whom he will not? Surely *you* intend to give his shield the mightiest clout of all!"

"I am come only to enter the mêlée," Robin said slowly.

"The *mêlée!* It is but a trite bashing of swords to settle the differences of the lovelorn!"

"A month ago, when you begged us to resolve it this way, you did not consider it trifling."

"A month ago, a battle royale between the houses of

Hugh the Brown and the Black Wolf of Amboise was needed to draw attendance. Who could have predicted the Prince of Darkness would venture so far from his empire just to challenge you for the title of champion! We could cancel every other bout and hold only the one, and no one would ride away disappointed!"

"I am afraid they will have to wait until the next time. I . . . injured a rib not long ago and—"

"He cracked the ribs like kindling," declared an imperious voice behind them. "And it was only on the avowal of best behavior I am permitting him to attend at all."

Rollo's expression crumpled like an old parchment as he sighed and rolled his eyes downward. "Sparrow. I should have known the day was going too well. Has no one clipped your wings yet or pinned your nose to a pine knot?"

"Many have tried. None have succeeded."

"A pity. You would make an amusing trophy skewered on someone's gates."

Sparrow snorted and planted his hands on his hips. "Not half so amusing as you, Lubbergut, stuffed and larded and spitted over a cookfire."

"Such wit," Rollo said dryly. "And yet you add insult by threatening to *ruin* the entire haslitude!"

"Lord Robert will not be offering his shield," Sparrow reiterated. "And I care not if it ruins your entire *life*, sorry thing though it may be already. I will not allow a fool's vanity to ruin his."

Griffyn gave Robin a curious look. "You injured yourself? When?"

"Hunting boar," Robin admitted tautly. "It was a fool's mistake that caused it, but—" He shrugged.

"Better a live fool," Sparrow insisted, "than a dead lummock. And if anyone doubts the gravity of the wound, we will be happy to parade him about the palisades naked in all his blue-and-black glory."

"Naked?" Rollo's eyebrows lifted. "Indeed, there are *some* who might be *appeased* by such a sight."

"Anyone who cannot be appeased by our word," Richard

said tersely, coming up behind them, "we will happily satisfy with our swords."

Rollo fluttered and took a prudent step back. "*Totally* unnecessary, I am sure. It will be a disappointment, of course, but we shall survive it to look forward to the next time. Well—" He clapped his hands. "I must not tarry any longer. I am to judge some bovines—the winner has the honor of gracing Lord Malagane's table for tomorrow night's feast. And I warrant I should warn both Ivo the Crippler and Draco the Hun to sharpen their lances to a quicker point. I am told the Prince of Darkness fights *only à outrance*. Adieu then, one and all. I am certain we shall see each other soon, at the feasting if not the festivities."

Robin's face remained hard and his eyes a brittle gray long after the garish tournament master had waddled away. Within the hour it would be known throughout Gaillard that the champion from Amboise was not offering his shield, that he was pleading some paltry injury (for surely he looked strong enough to compete, did he not?), and that he was not willing to risk the loss of his title to some black-helmed paladin from Rome.

"Let it go," Will advised quietly. "As he says, there will be other tournaments to look forward to. We have far weightier matters to occupy us over the next few days."

Robin held his gaze a moment, then nodded. The ruddiness in his cheeks faded briefly as he was reminded of the primary purpose of their attendance here, and he scanned the blur of faces in the courtyard again, searching for a familiar one with dark brown eyes and long Welsh braids.

"If Dafydd was waiting for us here, he would have found us by now."

"Or he may not have risked coming inside the castle walls. He may have decided to wait until we pitched camp."

Robin glared. "Or he may not have come at all and we are wasting precious time." He started to push his way through the crowd, heading back to where they had left the horses. Sparrow was fast on his heels, as were Will and Brenna, and it was not until they were halfway across the bailey that she realized they had left Griffyn Renaud standing on his own at the booth without any attempt to explain or excuse their hasty departure. She stopped and looked over her shoulder, but there was no sign of the errant knight's broad shoulders or jet-black hair. There was nothing to catch her eye other than a gull circling in the air currents overhead, screaming at the foolish antics of the humans below.

15

Deep in the bowels of Gaillard's donjons, there was another kind of screaming. Driven by a pain so immense the sound was almost crystalline in its purity, echoing from wall to wall, reaching a high, stunning crescendo of ear-splitting agony before it shivered away in an airless paroxysm of defeat. The chamber from which the sound emanated was large, twenty paces by twenty paces, with a low vaulted ceiling comprised of several stone arches and niches that served to break it up into smaller compartments. There were no cell walls or doors, but the mortared blocks were hung with thick iron rings and shackles every few paces. Located in the center of the chamber was an array of tables, boards, a firepit, and a large circular rack on which a body could be tied and stretched until every bone and joint was separated from its neighbor. The ceiling dripped constantly with evil-smelling leachings from the floors above. Slimy black pools collected in the hollows of the uneven stone floor, the surfaces shivering with each new *ploop* of added moisture. Rats shuffled in the dark corners, huge sharp-toothed creatures crouched on fat haunches, their small, feral eyes reflecting a spark of light now and then. They were well fed and patient, content to wait for the humans to leave and take their lights with them so their feasting might resume in private.

There were three humans in the donjon today—four, counting the shattered mass of flesh and bone strapped to one of the tables. Two stood in the outer ring of pale yellow light cast by the single horn lantern, while the third bent over the table and waited for the final echoes of the scream to fade. Suspended overhead like a tinker's wares were an assortment of hooks, knives, pincers, tongs, prods, and saw-toothed instruments designed solely for inflicting pain. The table itself had open slabs for drainage and boasted deeply embedded iron manacles for the holding of wrists and ankles, plus leather straps for the chest and waist if the victim began to thrash too much to insure the subjugator's delicate touch.

One of the observers lifted his goblet of wine to his lips and enjoyed a sip. "Do you suppose he has told us all he knows?"

The thin little man beside him scratched his head with the sharpened end of the feather quill he was holding and thrust his tongue into his cheek to consider his answer. "He has spilled more than he wanted, I warrant, but I doubt he has told the half. The old Marshal picks his men well."

The first man drew a deep breath and released it through his long, fine nose. "The Black Wolf and William Marshal. After nearly forty years, the link is still there. Solange, my dear, can you not persuade our friend to simply *admit* he has been carrying messages from Pembroke to Amboise? It would save so much time and effort, not to mention the cost of a dozen spies to verify what he *has* told us."

The woman bending over the table looked up and raised her hands—which were red to the elbows in blood—in a gesture of frustration. "I can ask, but in vain, I fear. The bastard is dead."

"Really?" Bertrand Malagane, Count of Saintonge, walked forward into the light and peered down at the frozen, tormented face. Nothing much remained of the features; even his nose and ears were gone. A close acquaintance might have recognized him by the Welsh braids that hung limp and bloody over the side of the table, but nothing else. The count straightened and frowned at the extraordinarily beautiful woman who stood opposite him. "How unfortunate. But no matter." He sighed. "You kept him alive two days and nights, long enough to give us more than what we had hoped."

In a gesture of self-disgust, she jabbed the knife she had been holding in the unresponsive flesh and shook her head. Two days was hardly a record to boast, not for someone whose talents were well known throughout all of Normandy. It was said the king himself, Philip of France, had suffered vivid, sweat-soaked nightmares after once observing the pleasure Solange de Sancerre derived from her work. And while Malagane often experienced the odd cool shiver rippling across his own skin, it was not from any sense of revulsion or fear. It was because he could barely keep his eyes off the lush curves of her body, and because his own blood throbbed and raged in his veins every time her artistry was rewarded by a particularly exquisite shrill of pain.

At five and fifty years of age, Bertrand could afford to indulge his little luxuries. He was a handsome and powerful man, with a full head of iron-gray hair and a neatly groomed beard still liberally salted with the reddish-gold threads of his youth. His eyes were deep-set and heavy-lidded, blue as a lake in winter with as much inclination to reveal what lay beneath the frozen, placid surface. He had been custodian of Château Gaillard for the past seven years, five of which he had spent in thrall of the talents and pleasures of Solange de Sancerre.

Born, it was rumored, under the influence of a bloodred moon, she was feared to be half sorceress, half siren. She had the ripe, sensuous body of a voluptuary, with breasts large enough to bring a man to his knees and the carnal talents to keep him there long past the normal limits of sexual endurance. Her eyes were a clear, opaline green, slanted under thick copper-colored lashes; hair as red as flame framed a face so white it was nearly translucent. So many men, seeing a vision of such rare and striking beauty, were led to their death thinking it to be their salvation. So many screamed for the first time out of sheer horror that something so erotically beautiful could prove to be so hellishly evil.

Malagane watched her cross in front of the lantern as she went to wash her hands in a large oaken barrel.

"Aelred . . . you will, of course, transcribe all of your scribblings into something legible for me to read?"

The scrivener, who was still making furious scratching noises with quill and ink on the topmost page of parchment, looked up. "My lord?"

"By tonight?"

He blinked owlishly. "*Tonight*, my lord? There are . . . why, there are fully a score of sheets here, my lord."

"Then you had best get started, had you not?"

The little man started to stammer another protest but saw Solange look over and arch her eyebrow. "Y-yes, my lord. At once, my lord. I shall make my fingers fly, my lord."

"Just make your feet fly," Malagane said quietly. "And find my son. Tell him to meet us here."

"Here, my lord?"

Malagane turned only his head and the scrivener backed hurriedly out of the circle of light, his shoes scraping the stones in his haste to leave the airless chamber. When the count looked at Solange again, he caught his breath, for she had unfastened the thong that held the blood-spattered linen tunic closed over her shoulders and let it slide down the long, pale curves of her body. Under his unblinking stare she unbound her hair and shook it so that it spilled around her shoulders in a sleek red curtain. She raised a ladleful of water and poured it down her breasts, leaving them wet and gleaming in the dull lantern light. Another scoop slicked her thighs, but the third was gruffly intercepted and sent splashing to one side as Malagane came up behind her and cupped the heaviness of her breasts in his hands. The nipples were already hard and jutting, and as he pressed his mouth into the curve of her throat, he heard her laugh, soft and husky, and felt her hands reach up to twine around fistfuls of his hair.

"Most men would be spewing their stomachs onto the floor, had they viewed the same entertainments as you, my lord."

"I am not most men," he growled. "And you, surely, are not the slightest part like most women."

She laughed again and twisted around in his arms so that their mouths could meet. Her breasts were crushed against his chest and her belly against his groin, and he groaned as she rubbed herself over his flesh, rousing him to a painful hardness.

"Witch," he breathed into her mouth. "Only you can do this to me."

"Not your loving wife? Not the lovely Ysenne?"

Malagane cursed and thrust one of his knees between her thighs. He had married Ysenne de Boulogne for her lands and her wealth, and he had kept her for her ability to breed sons. In truth, he had broken out in a cold sweat the first time he had seen her, for she had been—and still was—broad-hipped and flat-nosed, ugly as a wart with most of her teeth lost to a childhood accident . . . likely brought about by tripping over her own clumsy feet. Thirty years ago, however, he had not had the luxury of being able to choose a bride on merit of beauty and bedroom talents alone. He had married her because her father had been counsel to the king of France, an alliance of influence Malagane could not have afforded to ignore. And in the darkness of their bedroom, he had done his duty and she had done hers, insuring his small but rich duchy of Saintonge would have heirs. There were eight of them, all sons, most of them brutish and dull to be sure, but four had already made politically sound marriages into families that could only strengthen Saintonge's ties with the Crown. The oldest was here at Gaillard serving as captain of the guard; another aspired to wear the red robes of a bishop, though there was nothing chaste or particularly holy about him. The youngest was by far the cleverest of the lot, however, and if it could be said that Malagane held any special affection for one of his sons, it would be for Lothaire, who was also here at the château, come for the tournament.

"What are these private words you would share with Gerome?" Solange breathed into his mouth.

Malagane shuddered as he felt her hands tugging at the points to release his hose. "I do have *some* business dealings I conduct without you, my dear."

"All of them dull and boring, I am sure." Malagane clenched his teeth together and tensed himself around his lover's less than tender touch as she found the opening in his braies and released the straining heat of his flesh. "Especially if they are shared with Gerome."

"And yet you yourself shared more than just words with him last night, did you not?"

Her laughter tinkled in his ear. "Oooo . . . can this be jealousy I hear in my lord's voice? For his own son?"

"My son," Malagane spat, "is a brute and a lecher who has bedded every woman inside Gaillard and half of those within a two-day ride of the walls. I am surprised you do not worry after catching some flesh-rotting disease."

"If I do," she whispered, biting his lip hard enough to draw blood, "I would be only too happy, then, to share it with you in turn."

Malagane cursed and started to push her out of his arms, but she was strong for so slender a woman, and quick. Before he could drag his focus away from the urgent throbbing in his groin and stop her, she had caught up one of his hands and snapped it into a manacle that hung from the wall. A second startled gasp was too late to forestall the iron bracelet closing around his other wrist, or the violent kicks that parted his ankles and secured them to thick, rusted shackles.

He strained instinctively against the irons, knowing the gesture was futile. A hundred men before him had tested the union of iron and mortar and had not weakened it by so much as a crumb. His chest heaving, he watched as she pulled on each chain to take up the slack and pin him flush against the rough stone wall, splayed and spread-eagled in his silk finery like an exotic bug crushed underfoot.

"Release me," he commanded. "At once."

"Not until you beg my forgiveness."

"For what? For expecting some measure of loyalty from you?"

Her eyes sparkled and her lips curled back over small white teeth. "I am as loyal to you as you are to me, my lusty lord. Your loving wife arrived last night from Taillebourg, did she not? And did you not dispatch that poxy little worm Aelred to inform me you preferred her company over mine?"

"I have not seen the ugly bitch for three months. She brought correspondence, ledgers, accounts from Saintonge. And then there was Lothaire. He kept me locked in conversation well into the small hours of the morning."

"Whereupon you came directly to me."

"Whereupon . . . I stood outside your door and listened to you keening and wailing Gerome's name in the frenzy of your pleasure."

"I wanted to be certain you knew who took your place. And with exceptional vigor, I might add."

Malagane surged against his restraints again, managing only to cut the skin of one wrist and gain a meager inch of space between himself and the wall before sagging back in defeat. He was under no illusion of fidelity where Solange was concerned. She tried other men as easily and as often as some tried different spices on their food, and Gerome was exactly the kind to appeal to her more vulgar appetites. He was big, bullish, and hung like an ox, and once he caught the scent of a wet female in his nostrils, he had little time for anything so mundane as conversation.

"Solange . . . you test my patience."

"I intend to test it a good deal more," she said evenly. "You know how I dislike jealous men. And besides, it has been a long while—too long, methinks—since I have heard you beg, *really* beg for my mercy."

"Be assured"—he snarled—"you will not hear it today."

"Be assured," she vowed softly, "I will."

She turned her back on him briefly and danced her fingers across the assortment of small metallic hooks, wires, and serrated rings that were lined up on the table behind her. Malagane's mouth went dry and his face beaded instantly with sweat. He glanced into the darkness, in the direction of the stone steps leading up out of the donjons, but he was in a place where screams went unnoticed and cries for help won hardly more than a bored yawn from the guards upstairs. Any other man, faced with such a threat from Solange de Sancerre, would have felt his bladder squirt and his blood freeze in terror. Malagane only stared through glazed, hooded eyes while she made her final selection and turned into the light, smiling and dangling a small, spiked metal ring in front of her naked breasts.

She waited for his body to shudder through several tight spasms before she frowned at the pearly ooze dripping down the front of his hose.

"As usual." She sighed disparagingly. "You are too eager, my lord. We are going to have to start all over again."

She spun the little metal ring in her fingers and melted deftly down onto her knees in front of him. He spasmed again when he felt the cold sliver of steel tighten around his flesh, and then again when her hands, tongue, and teeth began to work their torment. For half an eternity afterward he was aware of nothing. Nothing but the reverberating echoes of his own screams bouncing from one damp wall to the next.

Solange stood back and surveyed her handiwork. The elegant and distinguished Count of Saintonge hung limp from his shackles, his mouth ringed in froth, his chin hung with strings of spittle. His hose was bagged loosely around his knees and the tops of his hairy thighs were mottled red. She had upturned the hem of his tunic and tucked it into his belt, and the blotched, exposed strip of pale white flesh between his belly and thighs looked ludicrous in the midst of the fine gold silk embroidery and expensive woolen hose.

A fine hour's work, she mused, and wiped the back of her

hand across her own mouth and chin. Her gaze remained fixed on her lover's drenched, pallid face as she gently smoothed the wet locks of his hair back off his brow and bathed his skin with a damp cloth.

"Thirsty?"

His mouth worked a few moments but he had difficulty forming a coherent word. She smiled and found his wine goblet, still half full from before. She tipped up his chin and tilted it to his lips and he swallowed the contents slowly at first, then eagerly, greedily, finishing with a great, shuddering gasp.

She licked away the drops that trickled down his chin and inquired solicitously, "Shall I send for your squire to help restore you?"

"Jesu, no. No," he rasped. "We would never be able to explain . . ."

She offered up a throaty laugh. "I could explain for you, my lord. I could explain how the sight of pain and blood excites you, how the sound of screams—especially your own—bring forth a veritable floodtide of pleasure."

The cerulean blue eyes were as yet unable to focus, but he glared at her anyway. The lids were polished with moisture from his exertions, a drop of which stung his eye, and when he attempted to wipe it free, he was painfully reminded of the shackles.

"You may release me now. I believe I offered petitions to every saint and martyr whose name I could recall."

"Indeed you did. And with such frantic desperation too. I gather you liked my newest little amusement?"

He only grunted an acknowledgment as one wrist, then the other was freed from the manacles. He flinched and stiffened when he felt her hair brush his thigh, but she was only bending down to loosen his ankle rings, and when she straightened he allowed himself to breathe again. A further clutch of courage was required before he could bring himself to inspect her handiwork. His sigh was heartfelt and somewhat incredulous when he found his flesh intact.

Shriveled, drained as a dried udder and red-raw from abuse, but intact.

"Is there more wine?"

She disappeared into the shadows a moment then returned with his goblet refilled, taking a sip first to sweeten her own mouth before she passed it to him.

"A shame Gerome is taking so long to answer your summons," she mused. "He might have been the one jealous of you, for I warrant you could have filled this tankard yourself."

"God's blood," he muttered, and glanced again at the disheveled state of his clothing. "Help me, witch, then make haste to cover yourself."

Her laugh was brittle with sarcasm. "Would you not prefer to return the favor and see Gerome scald himself red with envy?"

"Cover yourself," he ordered sharply. While he fumbled to refasten his hose and straighten his tunic, Solange fetched the clean blanchet and cotte she kept hanging on a peg and slipped them over her head. Both garments were silk and clung to the curves of her body like water flowing over smooth stones. Long before she was finished braiding her hair and winding it into a regal coronet, she could feel the heat of Malagane's eyes on her, following every gleaming movement of the cloth. His own tunic was made of samite, woven with six depths of sky-blue silk that flattered the color of his eyes, and when she finally deigned to glance his way, he spread his arms and posed for her inspection, tall and elegantly lean in his restored finery.

"Well?"

She glided up to him and pushed a thick lock of silvered hair off his brow. She pressed a long, wet kiss over his lips and smiled. "Good as new. Better, in fact, for you have been looking quite dour these past few days."

His gaze went to the corpse where it still steamed faintly in the cool air. "I have been given a great deal to think about in that time. Our friend here may have inadvertently provided the clue to a puzzle that has gone unsolved for nigh on twelve years."

"A puzzle?"

"Mmm. The answer to which could bring us power and wealth beyond our wildest imaginings."

"How so?"

"As you know, I pay a great many men a goodly sum of money to keep me well informed about a great many things. I, in turn, am paid handsomely that others might profit from that information. This brave but foolhardy fellow, for example." He strolled over to the table and stared at the body for a long moment. "I have suspected for some time he has been the source of communication between Amboise and Pembroke. A seemingly simple linen merchant who traveled with regularity and ease across the Channel, always with lengthy intervals between so as not to draw too much notice, and always following an established route through Normandy and Touraine. This time, however, his ship barely docked at Portsmouth before it was turned around to catch the next tide. Even more unusual, he did not land at Cherbourge or St. Malo, where he maintains the pretense of a business, but came by way of Le Havre and Rouen.

"I have left him alone until now because frankly, both William Marshal and Randwulf de la Seyne Sur Mer have always taken great care in choosing their couriers. In most cases, you could feed them their own entrails and they would not tell you anything you wanted to know. But this . . . this sudden erratic behavior by one of their most trusted pigeons suggested something out of the ordinary, something that might have been urgent enough or important enough to cause even the bravest of tongues to fall victim to panic. The king of France pays me *exceptionally* well to know how his barons are thinking, what they are planning, how they will respond to events fomenting across the Channel, and should the Black Wolf of Amboise or any of his brood be showing any inclination to turn their sentiments toward

England's plight, our liege would want—nay, *need* to be the first to know."

"Why would you suspect La Seyne Sur Mer's loyalty at all? He has given his blood oath to Philip of France. We were there in Paris, not two months ago when he pledged homage alongside his sons, presenting his sword that it might be called upon again whenever, wherever needed to defend the sovereignty of the French king."

"They pledge homage and loyalty to Philip only because they hate John of England more, but I wonder: how soon would the echo of those pledges fade if William Marshal were to whisper four small words in their ears."

"Four words?"

"*I need your help.*"

"You believe the Marshal would appeal to the Black Wolf?"

"He has done so before with much less to lose. And I believe he would appeal to Lucifer himself if the effort were required to safeguard the throne of England. This despite the fact the devil's spawn currently resides in Whitehall." Malagane's mouth turned down in a sneer. "His own son has even turned away in disgust. I heard only last week the younger Pembroke has joined FitzWalter's rebelling barons. Indeed, there are few men with William Marshal's fortitude. Fewer still I can recount by name."

"Randwulf de la Seyne Sur Mer," Solange provided dryly. "Eduard FitzRandwulf of Blois, Robert Wardieu d'Amboise, Richard and William Dagobert Wardieu . . . and lest we forget, his ally FitzAthelstan." She paused and regarded him closely. "I am still of the opinion you credit the Marshal with too much influence. The black-and-gold will do nothing to aid the cause of the English king."

"Ahh . . ." Malagane smiled and held up a finger like a lecturing prelate. "But he might be inclined to aid the cause of an English *queen*. Especially if that queen had a more legitimate claim to the throne than John Plantagenet. Doubly so if that queen's name was Eleanor and she was the granddaughter of the old dowager, Eleanor of Aquitaine."

Solange objected with a bewildered shake of her head. "The Princess Eleanor of Brittany? She died eleven years ago with her brother."

"No." Malagane's eyes glittered in the half light. "I do not believe she did. I suspect she is very much alive and living somewhere in the north of England. Biding her time, I would imagine, quietly gathering support among the barons who have grown disenchanted with her uncle's ineptness and flagrant misuse of power."

"How the devil do you surmise that? And why have we not heard of this resurrected princess before now?"

"There have always been rumors that Eleanor survived her uncle's murderous purge. As many as there were stories of her having been tortured, beheaded, poisoned, or impregnated by Celtic faeries."

"So what makes this one worth repeating—or believing?"

Malagane gazed down at the corpse again. "Do you recall the words he babbled each time you cut off a toe?"

"He babbled a good deal of nonsense, as I recall, mainly to do with taking some jewels out of some little shire in middle England."

"One jewel," Malagane corrected her softly. "A pearl, to be precise. And his exact words were: 'There is danger. Remove the pearl from Nottingham.' I would have thought it nonsense also had he not mentioned a name at the same time—a name I had not heard in over a decade."

"He mentioned dozens of names," she remarked caustically. "Screamed them, actually, faster than Aelred could scratch them down."

"So he did—a credit to your improving techniques, I am sure. But only one—Henry de Clare—fit the puzzle."

"De Clare? Is he someone important?"

"Perhaps yes, perhaps no. Lord Henry de Clare was, according to one of the more romantic rumors, among the party of nameless knights reputed to have rescued the princess from her uncle's donjons at Corfe Castle all those years ago. There was never any proof of his involvement, naturally, and since the king never actually admitted to having taken her out of Normandy—and certes not that she had escaped his custody—the story was given little credence."

"Why give it any now?" she asked bluntly.

Malagane studied a torn nail on one of his long, tapered fingers. "Did I neglect to mention . . . Henry de Clare was the nephew of William Marshal, Earl of Pembroke?"

"Was?"

"He reputedly died too. And was buried with great pomp and ceremony . . . at Amboise." Solange's eyes narrowed and Malagane smiled.

"It could just be a happy coincidence, I suppose, but then we would have to regard the sister's circumstances as being somewhat fortuitous as well."

"The sister?"

"Lady Ariel de Clare. Some years ago—about the same time the princess disappeared—it seems she took a sudden dislike to the betrothal arrangements made for her by King John and, while on her way back from Normandy—after appealing to her uncle, William Marshal, for reprieve—she was kidnapped *just outside of Corfe Castle* and went missing for a time. She reappeared, a month or so later at Château d'Amboise, wedded and bedded to—"

"Eduard FitzRandwulf of Blois," Solange breathed. "The Wolf's bastard son."

Malagane stroked the backs of his fingers affectionately down her cheek. "The same bastard son who, as it happens, was a close, intimate friend of Princess Eleanor."

"Then this is more than just a guess. You believe the Lost Princess of Brittany is alive and living in England and about to challenge her uncle, King John, for the throne?"

"I am saying only that two dead people with such close links coming suddenly to life are two too many for my liking."

"You think the funeral at Amboise was a ruse?"

"And a good one, for it stopped the king's hounds from sniffing after him. It also gave him the freedom to assume another guise and return to England—if, indeed, he ever left."

"But if there was some question of his involvement with the princess's escape, does it not stand to reason he would want to disappear from sight?"

"Of course he would. Which makes it all the more curious for him to have remained in England, where the chance of discovery was ten times, a thousand times greater than if he had retired to France, or even remained at Blois with his sister." He touched his finger to the side of his nose. "Unless there was something . . . or some*one* of great importance keeping him there."

"The Lost Princess? But the Welshman said nothing about her. Furthermore, if what you say were true for Henry de Clare, would it not also hold true for her? Why would she remain in England when she would have been welcomed with open arms in Brittany, or Normandy, or France? My God, even Philip would have taken her in and guarded her life with his own."

Malagane gave the wine in his cup a thoughtful swirl. "I confess, I wondered about that myself, but then I reasoned: one of the strongest arguments against Arthur of Brittany becoming king was the fact he had never set foot on English soil, had never heard the voice of the English people, had never acted upon a thought that did not first come from King Philip's head. If Eleanor is indeed alive, and if she did elect to remain in England to better acquaint herself with the ways of her English subjects, it will be seen as a repudiation of her brother's French alliances; further, that she has chosen to sever ties completely with Philip. Her claim to the English throne is valid and stands before John's. The barons might well be desperate enough to accept her, especially if she agrees to marry a consort of their choosing and thus put the balance of power in their hands. In that unhappy event, England would have a beautiful young queen and Prince Louis, who is all but ready to lead his army across the Channel and assume the role of regent, would be left waving his flags from the shores of Normandy."

"William Marshal would never accept her . . . would he?"

"Pembroke is a realist. He can see the kingdom breaking apart before his eyes; civil war is inevitable if something is not done to salvage the dignity of the throne. The barons are committed to ousting John, and he has watched their numbers grow from a handful to an army, gaining strength and credibility every day. Even the common people have begun to support the notion of inviting Prince Louis to assume the throne—which is what we have been striving to accomplish these many years," he added, his eyes gleaming zealously. "To unite the people of England and France under one flag, one rule!"

Some of the gleam faded as he gazed down at the body again. "But suppose . . . just *suppose* the Marshal has been hiding and protecting a legitimate claimant to the throne all these years? Not just any claimant, mind you, but a young, innocent woman of impeccable virtue whose blood ran in the veins of the two golden kings the people so loved and admired. A spirited woman as well, brave beyond measure to have lived in England all these years when the faintest breath of her existence would have drawn an assassin's knife. A woman so beautiful in countenance she was likened to a pearl. The Pearl of Brittany she was called. A gem of incalculable value who could be used now to end the threat of civil war and unite all of England under the Plantagenet lions again."

"You think William Marshal would condone such a thing?"

"No," Malagane said bluntly. "Not himself. Not without breaking his solemn oath of fealty to the king, and that he would never do."

"Then what—?"

"Such is the curse of most men with rigid codes of honor: how do they adhere to a righteous principle when all the virtues of sentiment, reason, logic, and nobility tell them their way is wrong?"

Since Solange did not possess any of these qualities in any abundance, it was left to Malagane to supply the answer.

"They would appeal to men of similar noble qualities to help wrest them of the problem. In this case, a man not constrained by any oath to the English king, but whose life has been irrevocably bound to the queens and princesses of Aquitaine and Brittany."

"The Black Wolf," she whispered in awe. "Randwulf de la Seyne Sur Mer."

"Can you imagine," Malagane said, his voice strained beyond comprehension itself, "the power he would have if Eleanor of Brittany became Queen of England? Between him and his bastard son FitzRandwulf, they already control most of Blois and Touraine. The Aquitaine would instantly pledge loyalty to the English throne, as would Brittany, Poitou, Maine, and Angouleme. With the black-and-gold leading her armies, Eleanor would take back all of Normandy and Philip would be driven back behind the borders of Paris."

Solange looked appalled. "Surely . . . we cannot let this happen! There must be something we can do to prevent it!"

"The only way to prevent it," he said tautly, "is to insure Eleanor of Brittany never becomes queen, is never given the opportunity to rally the English barons, is never permitted to become more than the romantic, tragic Lost Princess of legend."

"We have to find the bitch and kill her," Solange said succinctly.

"Crudely put, but wisely said, for by the same token, if we remove any hope of a rallying point for the barons, they will have no choice but to accept Louis as king."

"John has a son," Solange pointed out.

"A seven-year-old child! Where would the logic be in deposing a king and putting a babe on the throne? No, the barons want John out of the way and strong leadership restored to the throne. They have watched him squander almost all of their possessions and territories in Normandy and France, and may see the possibility of having their castles and lands here returned if Louis takes the throne. Conversely, there will be lands, castles, titles *falling* into the hands of those who have remained steadfast and loyal to the French cause all these years. Men like ... me," he added proudly, "who have never faltered in our efforts to see the two countries united under the House of Capet! For that"—he slammed his fist on the table, scattering a small clutch of rats that were feeding beneath—"I will *not* let some half-forgotten princess spoil our plans now!"

"Half forgotten and well hidden all these years," Solange reminded him.

"Your next question, of course, is how do we find her?"

"It would seem to pose a small problem," she agreed.

"Not if you know where to look."

She puzzled over his smug smile for a moment then a green light suddenly flared in her eyes and she joined him in staring down at the body. " 'Remove the pearl from Nottingham,' " she quoted. "The pearl ... the Pearl of Brittany! They have hidden the Pearl of Brittany in Nottingham!" Her exuberance suffered a momentary setback as she looked up at him. "But where in Nottingham?"

"Where could a woman remain hidden away for eleven years, isolated from intrusion by the outside world?"

"A convent? But there must be hundreds of them in middle England."

"Ahh, but how many would have once come under the patronage of Lucien Wardieu, Baron de Gournay?"

"Wardieu? There is *another* plague of Wardieus in England?"

He laughed. "Only the one plague, my dear, but of course you are too young to know Lucien Wardieu as anything other than Randwulf de la Seyne Sur Mer."

"Christ Jesus!" She gasped. "Is there no end to this web?"

"None. Unless we tear it down and insure it can never be spun again."

"To do that, you would have to destroy the Black Wolf."

"The Wolf is all but a cripple," Malagane said, dismissing

his importance with a flick of his wrist. "He needs sticks to walk with and barely has the strength to stand on his own and piss. The *real* power of the black-and-gold is held in the hands of his sons, the vaunted heroes of Roche-au-Moines, the shining pantheon of chivalry and courage in mortal guise—three of whom, as it happens, could well be inside the walls of the château as we speak."

"They have come to Gaillard to play at jousting while their precious Pearl is in danger?"

"They may not know it yet."

She looked dubious. "We may have intercepted the Welshman, but would a message of this importance be entrusted to only one courier? For all we know, another has already been delivered to Amboise and the heroes are halfway to England!"

"If there were any changes to their plans, I would have known by now. And besides, their pennons were seen on the road early this morning. They are here, all right. I can feel their arrogance in the air."

Solange regarded him closely. "You are not thinking of doing anything foolhardy, are you, my love? Cripple or not, if the Black Wolf of Amboise even suspected you of plotting to kill his sons, he would raze Gaillard to the ground and roast your liver over the rubble."

"I have no intentions of killing *all* of them; only the one who poses the greatest threat to our immediate plans."

"Robert Wardieu," she surmised.

"The heir and champion of champions," he concurred dryly. "Without him to control them, the other two are hot-headed and careless; they will get themselves killed cuckolding some intolerant husband and spare us the bother. Lord Robert is their anchor. Cut him loose and the others will drift wildly into the wind."

"Have you someone in mind capable—or willing—to wield the axe?"

"As it happens, the matter is already well in hand." His gaze was drawn to the arched stone portal at the far side of the vast chamber. There, a soft bloom of light could be seen growing brighter, accompanied by the sound of footsteps grating on the stone steps. "Behold, my dear. Gerome has come at last. And with him, hopefully, the solution to our little problem."

As if on cue, two men came through the entryway, but only Gerome de Saintonge came forward out of the shadows. He carried a smoking pitch torch in front of him, the glare from the sputtering flame caused his yellow hair and gold surcoat to blaze brilliantly against the gloom and to temporarily blind both Solange and Malagane as he approached.

Eyes that were a dull blue imitation of his father's went first to the lifeless body on the table, then to Solange, who had moved discreetly behind Malagane's shoulder to shield herself from the bright torchlight.

"Forgive me," he said, offering a mock bow. "I forget you prefer the comfort of darkness."

He doused the offending instrument in the water barrel, releasing a boiling foment of hissing bubbles and a huge cloud of steam into the air. "Still toying with the Welshman?"

"Until a short while ago," Malagane nodded. "Alas, he did not bear up very well."

"Few men do under the skillful renderings of our *demoiselle tortionnaire*."

Malagane's eyes were still scorched by the effects of the light, and he could distinguish little more than the vague outline of a man standing back in the shadows. "You were successful? You had no trouble finding him?"

"He found me, actually." Gerome turned and raised his hand. "Come, my lord. Meet your host and my father, Bertrand Malagane, Count of Saintonge."

Malagane waited, unaware he was holding his breath as the newcomer entered the dull ring of light cast by the horn lantern. He had been given a rough description for identification sake, but nothing had prepared him for the sheer menacing size of the man. He was dressed all in black, from his boots to his hose to his tunic. His hair was black as well, carelessly cut and left loose to flow around his massive shoulders. A stray reflection, or some other trick of the light, caused his eyes to glow out of the dark long before the rest of him took shape. Like a big cat emerging from the shadows, the eyes were all that were visible, steady and unblinking. A pale gray-green they were, like the luminous phosphorescence on a moon-washed sea.

16

"Griffyn Renaud de Verdelay." Malagane reined in his excitement with an effort. "I have heard a great deal about you. We are flattered you could find your way to accept our invitation to attend."

"The invitation did not come without flattery of its own," Griffyn replied.

"Ah, yes." The count gave Gerome a curt nod and the yellow-haired knight melted back into the shadows, returning with a helmet-sized leather chest he had retrieved from a nearby table. A flick of a squared thumbnail freed the hasp and he lifted the lid, tilting the contents into the warm glow of light from the horn lantern. It was filled with coins. Hundreds of them. All minted with the curly-haired likeness of Henry II.

"A thousand marks was the agreed price, I believe? I trust you have no objection to receiving it in English sterling rather than Norman deniers?"

"Why would I object to receiving greater value for my coin?"

Malagane chuckled. "Why indeed?"

He saw where the knight's gaze had strayed and he invited Solange forward for an introduction. For her part, she had already finished her inspection and decided this was no ordinary mercenary, no ordinary sword for hire. The wool of his hose was as tight and smooth a weave as Malagane's, his tunic was a dark hunting green, not black, and made of such tender doeskin it could be mistaken for velvet. His skin was as bronzed as a peasant's, yet the face ... the face was anything but common or loutish. It was handsome in a way that almost stripped the breath from her throat, and she reacted the way she always reacted to an object of such obvious sexual promise. The flesh across her breasts grew taut, the nipples puckered and stiffened into visible prominence beneath the silk of her cotte, and her murmured greeting came out in a low, rasping growl.

"May we offer you some wine, my lord?"

"Wine would sweeten the mood considerably, thank you."

She crossed deliberately in front of him and slipped into the shadows, the hem of her cotte reduced to a transparent mist around her ankles. The cotte itself was made of the finest cream-colored Syrian baudekin, a delicate cloth woven with threads of pure gold that caught what little light there was and shimmered around every curve and indent of her body.

Griffyn's eyes started to follow her, as she expected they would, but when she turned, he was not looking at her but at the ravaged body splayed limp upon the table.

Malagane laughed at his expression. "Be at ease, we are all friends here."

"I have no friends." Griffyn's mouth flattened. "And I prefer to take my ease in small increments. Even if that were not the case"—he paused and glanced around the torture chamber—"I doubt it would have been possible for you to have chosen a more *comforting* place to meet."

"There are few places inside Gaillard where one can guarantee absolute privacy," Malagane replied easily. "If it disturbs you, however . . . ?"

The dark knight waved a hand dismissively and extended the gesture to accept the goblet of wine Solange offered. As their fingers touched, the texture of the scarred skin drew her attention downward for a moment and when she looked up again, there was more than a hint of curiosity in her eyes.

"I tried to retrieve my soul from hell once," he explained blithely. "It preferred to stay where it was."

The clear, opaline eyes widened.

"I think I like him, Bertrand," she breathed. "He has wit."

Malagane had watched the exchange but now addressed his son. "Did you notice any new arrivals in the bailey?"

"He is come." Gerome nodded, knowing whom he meant. "Surrounded by at least four-score knights to boast the grand occasion of his presence."

"We are speaking, of course, of Robert Wardieu d'Amboise," Malagane said to Griffyn. "Do you know him?"

"We have met in the lists before . . . but then you must have known that already before you sent all the way to Burgundy inviting me to attend your little gathering."

"Gascon, was it not?" Malagane asked. "You fought to a draw."

"The judges did not see it that way."

"No. No, in sooth they did not. They called the win in Wardieu's favor despite the fact you landed far more solid strikes than he."

"You were there?"

"As a spectator only," he said with a deprecatory shrug. "But tell me, Lord Griffyn: why have you never ventured back into Normandy to demand a rematch?"

"One of us would likely have killed the other long ere now, if I had."

"And now? Which one of you would emerge the victor, do you suppose?"

Griffyn swirled the wine around the bottom of the goblet. "I would not rush to affix a price on my armor any too soon."

It was not said as a boast nor with any measure of false conceit. Any knight worthy of wearing his spurs entered the lists confident of his power and prowess, yet was still cautious enough to have visited the moneylenders in advance to put a fair trophy value on his horse and armor.

"Wardieu has not seen the belly of a horse in five years," Malagane argued guardedly.

"The last belly I saw"—the pale eyes flicked to Solange—"was soft and white and quivered at my touch."

She stared at his mouth and her own slackened as a spray of gooseflesh shivered into prominence down her arms.

"The thousand marks was your invitation to attend," Malagane said, returning to the issue at hand. "But it is only half of what I am willing to pay should you run the lists against Robert Wardieu and defeat him." He waited for Griffyn's gaze to return, narrowed with interest. "Do you think you could do it?"

"For that much, I could feign holy vows and split the Pope out of his pulpit . . . but all the English sterling in the realm will not put me into the lists with Robert Wardieu if he himself has chosen not to fight."

"Not fight?" Gerome de Saintonge sneered. "Where did you hear such nonsense?"

"From his own lips, not an hour ago when our paths crossed in the bailey. Just before I met up with you, as a matter of fact. He claims to have injured himself hunting boar and while he is still entered in the mêlée, he is taking no challenges for single-combat matches."

This was unexpected news to Malagane, and he paced slowly to the wall, needing time to absorb it.

"I find it difficult to believe," he murmured. But then his sharply pinched nostrils flared as if scenting prey and he nodded to himself. "Yet it makes perfect sense. He would not want to run the risk of injuring himself more seriously—*too seriously to venture abroad, for instance.* On the other hand . . ." He reached up and gripped one of the iron shackles hanging from the wall, studying it with a thoughtful frown. "On the other hand, he is a proud man. A proud champion. At four and twenty he is in his prime in body and spirit, and holds a rare, unassailable belief in the ideals of chivalry. Do you know the history of his family, Verdelay?"

Griffyn shrugged as if such things were of no interest to him. "I know his father was once called the Scourge of Mirebeau and, if the legends are to be believed, had a penchant for slaying dragons and salvaging lost souls."

Malagane laughed. "Indeed, where else but at Amboise

would you find a lord who has a dwarf for a seneschal and a
giant for a castellan? But did you know the first dragon he
slew was his own brother? A bastard, to be sure, but so alike
in face and form they were said to be as twins. As the story
goes, the brother—Etienne Wardieu—sought to eliminate
the bastardy in his blood and followed the Wolf on Crusade
to Jerusalem, where he ambushed him and left him for
dead, then returned to England and assumed his guise as
Lucien Wardieu, Baron de Gournay.

"The baron did not die, of course, but was sufficiently
damaged and disillusioned to forestall an eager return to
Lincoln. He sought to start a new life for himself in France
instead, where he applied his rage to the tourney circuit and
eventually won the attention of the old dowager, Eleanor of
Aquitaine. She, in turn, used him with immeasurable success to keep her greedy sons in line. He actually fought
Geoffrey Plantagenet in a joust to teach him some humility,
although if memory serves, it was but a brief month later
that the duke was killed in another tournament, so the
lesson was not well learned.

"The queen next called upon her scarred champion
when the Lionheart was off slaying Infidels and John was
acting as regent in his absence. It was then that Lackland
made his first feeble attempt to eliminate Geoffrey's children as an obstacle—he was convinced, you see, that Sal-
adin could accomplish what he had been unable to bolster
the nerve to do up to then; namely, kill his brother and
clear the path to the throne. His ploy to kidnap Arthur and
Eleanor was thwarted by the Black Wolf, who managed to
rescue the boy before he could be smuggled on board a ship
bound for England, and then to retrieve the young Princess
Eleanor when she was carried off to Lincoln and entrusted
to the care of none other than" . . . he paused for effect . . .
"Wardieu's own bastard brother, who was by then one of
Prince John's favorite pet dragons.

"Subsequently, there came a mighty confrontation
between the Wolf and the Dragon. When the flames
cleared, the little princess was rescued and safely returned

to her grandmother at Mirebeau. The Wolf not only slew his brother, but married the Dragon's intended bride and discovered a son—Eduard—he never knew he had. All quite romantic and awe-inspiring, I assure you. You may even have heard one particular *chanson d'amour* that recounts the story of how Robert Wardieu was conceived by the waters of a magic pool, the product of a wolf and a virgin maiden, destined for some great and glorious enterprise that will have men singing his praises until the end of all time."

"I rarely have the time or patience to listen to songs," Griffyn said dryly. "Or romantic stories."

"Nevertheless, a man should know his enemy. In this case, you should know that the blood of both the Wolf and the Dragon flow in Robert Wardieu's veins. To him, the virtues of courage, courtliness, and largesse are not just noble notions to strive toward; they are a way of life and guide his every footstep. The need to triumph absolutely over evil fuels his passions, feeds his ambitions as it did his father and brother before him. I will not bore you with the details of Eduard FitzRandwulf's championing days; suffice it to say John Lackland would not be king today, nor probably even alive, had Eduard been given free rein over his emotions eleven years ago. He was very close to Arthur of Brittany and would have ridden in support of his quest for the throne had the foolish young duke not chosen, for his first act of war, to lead his army against Mirebeau and the dowager queen. Chivalry again, you see. Honor, pride, loyalty—the downfall of every man of such strident principles. Think of the trouble they could have saved us all," he added with a sigh of genuine regret, "had there been but a drop more ambition and greed in their veins."

Griffyn's voice began to grate with impatience. "I am still at a loss as to where all this is leading."

"It is leading, my lord, to the fact that I am willing to pay quite handsomely to see the great champion from Amboise humbled."

"Humbled?" Griffyn asked pointedly. "Or killed?"

Malagane's eyes narrowed, which caused the tall knight
to offer up a wry laugh.

"I stepped unknowingly on a hornet's nest once," Griffyn
said, "and did not enjoy the experience. If there is something more going on here, I would know it before I agree to
do this thing or not."

"I was not aware, in such a violent profession as yours,
that you needed a *reason* to kill. I assumed it was merely a
natural *denouement*. And that I would be paying enough to
avert your curiosity."

"Actually . . . you are paying too much for a simple
killing. And that makes me extremely curious indeed."

Malagane pursed his lips. "I would have to know I could
count upon your absolute discretion."

"I would have to know I could count upon yours,"
Griffyn countered smoothly.

Gerome's spine stiffened and his hand went to the hilt of
his sword. The pale eyes barely flickered to acknowledge
the movement, yet a split second later, a soft whisper of
steel cut through the air and, in the next instant, Gerome
de Saintonge stood with his back against the wall, his neck
stretched taut against the gleaming threat of Griffyn's
blade.

"You objected to something I said?"

"You dare to question my father's integrity?" Gerome
spat.

"He dared to question mine," Griffyn countered silkily.

Malagane saw a line of blood forming on his son's throat
and raised his hand. "Let him go. He sometimes . . . acts in
haste, without thinking."

Griffyn fixed the count with an icy stare. "Surround yourself with fools, my lord, and they will find themselves
making foolish mistakes."

"Let him go. He was only following my orders."

"Which were?"

"Not to let you leave here until we came to an amicable
agreement."

Griffyn's grin was slow to form. "And you thought *he* could have stopped me?"

"A slight . . . miscalculation," Bertrand admitted.

Griffyn relaxed some of the tension in the blade, not enough to remove the threat of a severed jugular completely, but enough to put a promise in the dull blue eyes as a steady trickle of blood started to run down under the collar of Saintonge's fine gold tunic.

"You were about to tell me why you want Robert Wardieu dead," he said.

Malagane sighed with obvious reluctance. "We have reason to suspect he may be making plans to interfere with King Philip's invasion of England this coming spring. Further, we suspect he intends to leave here immediately after the tournament and cross the Channel; once there, to join forces with the Earl of Pembroke."

"The earl is Lackland's man, is he not?"

"Alone and unto death, so he claims."

"And you are afraid of letting one man join him?"

"One man who can rally an army of thousands upon his command."

"Why in God's name would he rally a thousand *fleas* to help the English cause? Did he not just lead his army into Maine to drive Lackland *back* across the Channel?" He saw the frown crease Malagane's forehead and his mouth twisted down. "Burgundy is not poised on the edge of the abyss, nor do we wear rough hides and gaze in awe at the wheel."

The count made a placating gesture with his hand. "I did not mean to imply ignorance, simply that there are matters that cannot possibly hold any meaning or importance for you."

"Such as?"

"Such as . . ." Malagane's jaw tightened again. "Wardieu's claim to estates in Lincolnshire. They were stripped from his father by King John in an act of retaliation, and with the barons now in revolt, Wardieu may have it in his mind to return and lay claim to what is rightfully his."

"*Land?*"

"And the barony that goes with it, yes."

"For that you would kill him?"

"If I wanted it for myself, yes, I would kill him ten times over. It is an extremely rich tract of land situated between Lincoln and Nottingham, ideally positioned to defend both the north and south. If you doubt its strategic value, ask Prince Louis—he is here, in the château—if I have not pledged to hold middle England for him once he has wrested the throne from its current occupant. This"—he indicated the chest of coins—"is but a pittance compared to what I have already invested in men and bribes and time, and I am not about to see it all lost over the whims of one disseized baron."

Griffyn drew a deep breath and exhaled it around a curse.

"Simple greed," he said as he lowered his sword, "is always far easier to understand when politics are set aside."

Gerome choked out a coarse oath and held a hand against his throat. The fingers came away inky wet with blood and he cursed again. "The next time you draw your sword on me, you had best be prepared to use it."

"I am prepared now," Griffyn said easily, "if you are prepared to die."

"Gerome! Enough! Do not make a greater fool of yourself than you already have. Who *exactly* do you think this man is that I would send so far and pay so much?" Malagane looked at Griffyn and his eyes glittered like two shards of blue glass. "I warrant Wardieu himself is still in ignorance, is he not? This despite the fact you recently passed a night and day inside the walls of Amboise?"

Griffyn tipped his head in grudging admiration. "Your spies keep you well informed."

"Well enough that I could tell you what you dined on if you like, or ... ah ... how many times a certain young minx was reputed to swoon in appreciation of your *stamina*? I believe in being well informed, you see. Unlike those who would rely too heavily on others being forthright and honest. Wardieu, for example. Does he know to whom he played host? Does he know," Malagane asked with relish of someone savoring a rare and sinfully delicious sweetmeat, "that his old rival Griffyn Renaud de Verdelay has run havoc in every tournament east of Champagne as . . . the *Prince of Darkness?*"

In the utter silence that followed, only the hollow echo of dripping of water could be heard and the faint sputter of the candle burning in the lantern. Both Solange and Gerome stared at Bertrand, then at Griffyn Renaud, with the latter drawing most of the awe and disbelief.

"The Prince of Darkness?" Solange whispered. "You?"

"Christ Jesus." Gerome's hand went to his throat again—in thanks this time that there was still something there to clutch.

"Well?" Malagane asked. "Does he know?"

"I saw no need to volunteer the information," Griffyn admitted quietly. "Though I thought it might have come out today when the tournament master claimed to have seen me registering."

"Rollo d'Albini? His eyes are rarely focused on a man's face, and when they are, the face needs to be closer than arm's reach for him to see more than a vague blur. Wardieu, on the other hand, has perfect vision. What do you suppose his reaction will be when he sees you take to the field wearing the blazon of the Prince of Darkness?"

"He will foul himself getting into his armor," Gerome predicted with an almost giddy laugh.

Griffyn shot him a glance that would have curdled milk, but Malagane was quick to intercede.

"I understand you have declared your intent to accept only three challenges. Why is that?"

"Because I dislike wasting my time. Moreover, it has become the usual practice in the tournaments I have frequented to set a limit on the number of broken bodies they want carried from the field."

Malagane's smile was pure malevolence. "Well, we have

no limits here. In fact, the more bodies they drag from the palisades, the more anxious Wardieu will become to avenge the carnage. Change your declaration, my lord. Accept all comers. I doubt you will get more than two or three anyway after the first broken head, but we must give the appearance of willingness. As for your time, it will not be wasted. An additional hundred marks for each joust should alleviate your boredom. At the same time, an additional five hundred," he said to Gerome, "added to the total prize monies, should heat the blood of a few who might otherwise err on the side of caution."

"But ... the prize is only a hundred now!" Gerome objected.

"Exactly so. Think of all the brave but foolhardy young cocks who will think the risk well worth the chance to ride away with ten years' worth of earnings jangling in their purse! Well? What say you, my lord? Are you with us?"

"If I agree to this," Griffyn said slowly, "there can be no further contact between us."

Malagane's face flushed with excitement. "I have good men I can put at your disposal."

"I have a man of my own, but he will cost you another hundred marks."

Gerome opened his mouth to protest the audacity, but a gesture from Malagane cut him short. "Agreed. Is there anything else?"

Griffyn smiled grimly. "The name of a good armorer. I expect I will need to reassess my supply of lances."

He turned to leave, delaying only long enough to exchange his empty goblet for the chest of coins.

"Lord Verdelay?"

He stopped and glanced back over his shoulder.

"You will, of course, have no further contact with Wardieu ... *or any of his kin.*"

Griffyn's eyes glowed eerily out of the shadows. He did not answer. He merely broadened his smile at the corners and carried on across the blackness of the chamber, departing the way he had come, with only the scrape of his boots echoing on the stone stairs.

Solange released a pent-up breath and was the first to speak. "You were very naughty, Bertrand, to keep such a delicious secret from me. The Prince of Darkness! I have heard he comes down the course like the very devil himself. But all that money, my love." She turned and looked up at him. "You have two of the finest assassins in Europe in your employ. Engelard Cigogni and Andrew de Chanceas would gladly see to Wardieu's demise for half the price you are offering this dark princeling."

"They are also *known* to be in my employ, and what we do here must be accomplished with the utmost discretion, with no possibility of any blame falling in our direction. Nor will de Chanceas and Cigogni rust from lack of use, for once Wardieu is dead, Renaud's usefulness will also be at an end."

Solange looked up at Malagane and her eyes burned like green fire. "In that case . . . may I have him, Bertrand? He should be made to answer for the insults he has rendered you here today."

He reached out and stroked the pad of his thumb across her lower lip. "I am touched by your sensitivity, my dear. It will be a shame to destroy such noble savagery, but we will want no loose ends, no witnesses to trouble us later."

17

As soon as he was in the sunlight again, Griffyn filled his lungs several times, yet the lingering taint of the musty donjon air stayed with him until he was across the inner bailey and through the gates to the middle ward. There, the crowds were still as thick and boisterous as before, though the colors seemed more vivid, the smells sweeter as he passed by booths of meat, spices, and exotic scents.

His long strides carried him straight on through to the outer bailey without stopping, and it took him another fifteen minutes to make his way out the massive double barbicans and down the winding road to the encampments below. Since his arrival the previous day, the numbers of tents and pavilions had easily doubled. Firepits had been dug and pocked the ground at every turn; iron tripods balanced huge black cauldrons over the flames, the bubbling contents sending up clouds of steam to mingle with the clouds of milky woodsmoke. There was also garbage and offal collecting everywhere—the hazards of a large, temporary bivouac—and he narrowly missed treading in several fresh heaps of steaming dung as he made his way toward the river.

He located his own pavilions, relieved to see they were still somewhat isolated from the others by a patch of rough gorse, but was not surprised to see only bare, rocky ground in front of them. His belly reminded him he had not eaten anything but a handful of roasted chestnuts since early morning, and as he flung aside the canvas flap to the main tent, he cursed when he saw the comfortable, curled form of his squire fast asleep on a pile of blankets.

"Fulgrin!"

His voice boomed like a clap of thunder and brought the sleeper straight up off the bedding, his arms and legs splayed wide, his hair stiffened into spikes for the few seconds it took him to blink his eyes into focus and identify the storm-cloud looming in the entryway.

"Christ-a-mercy!" He clapped his hands together over his heart. "I could have swallowed my tongue!"

"You should give thanks I do not carve it out and make a pie of it. Have you nothing better to do than foul the air with your snores?"

Fulgrin was short, wiry, and villainous in appearance, with one eye scarred permanently in a squint. The other was usually red around the rim from pure belligerence.

"Fine thanks I get for staying up half the blessed night long unpacking the rouncies and building you these splendid lodgings!"

Griffyn glanced wryly around the walls, which sagged, and at the canvas ceiling that was not quite balanced on the two center poles.

"I meant to fix it by daylight," Fulgrin snapped. "Even to spread a carpet of fennel to soothe your delicate senses, but my head was thick from lack of sleep and from drinking my way into genial camaraderie with the squires of a dozen other nobles and knights."

"And?" Griffyn unbuckled his swordbelt and set it aside. "What did you learn?"

"That the ale is sour and the company full of itself." He scowled and wagged a finger. "Do you not lay that there. Everything has a place, as well you should know by now. Of course, if you loosed the strings of your purse once in a while, we could languish in willful extravagance and add a pace worth of canvas at either end so that we did not rub noses each time we passed . . . but nay, nay. Let me not be the one to find fault in your penurious ways."

Renaud sighed and hung his belt on one of the poles. "Remind me again why I tolerate your company?"

"Because I tolerate yours. And because," he added succinctly, "you need me."

"Like the pox," Griffyn muttered.

"I heard that."

"You were supposed to."

"Hmph. Ask me, then, what I have done this morning to deserve such scorn. Ask me!"

Griffyn glared across the width of the tent as he stripped off his surcoat and shirt.

"I have hired three grooms, an armorer, a lad to run errands, and found excellent stabling for Centaur and Centurion—the latter is in a most foul temper, by the way, being separated from Centaur so long and then dragged ignobly behind the wheels of a cart."

"I was planning to take him through his paces later today."

"Better you do it earlier. He will no doubt bite you to show his gratitude anyway, and I would not blame him. Was the detour through Amboise so necessary as to upset the most truculent piece of horseflesh this side of Hades?"

"I thought it was. And he will recover. Is there anything else *useful* you have to tell me?"

"Besides the proximity of the wagonful of evening beauties camped nearby?" He sucked in some air through the gap between his front teeth and whistled it free. "Well, you might find it of some value to know there is no other way in or out of Gaillard except through the main gates. The Lionheart saw no need for posterns, since they were too commonly used by uninvited guests. There is one small portal on the west wall, but it opens onto the spill of cliffs and invites a clumsy fellow to tumble nearly four hundred feet down a sheer drop to the river. I could not determine its purpose other than for the ready disposal of, er, refuse from the donjons."

"Guards?"

"Are as guards everywhere. They have sticky hands and spates of blindness when it is worth their while. They do, however, share a fulsome respect for the custodian,

Bertrand Malagane, and for his bloodless mistress, Solange de Sancerre."

"I have just come from making their acquaintance and a healthy respect is due. What about the son?"

"Which one? He has eight."

"The captain of the guard."

"Gerome de Saintonge? They give him the prisoners first to soften with his fists. Prisoners *and* women from what I gather; he likes to leave both broken and bleeding after he has had his fun. Dangerous, but in a predictable way, whereas the father is more cunning up here." He poked his temple with a finger, narrowly missing his eye. "The count is the eyes and ears of King Philip. He has leagues of spies here and in England, and I doubt a goat could shite without him knowing the how and where of it."

Griffyn nodded. "He knew I was at Amboise. He even offered to tell me what I ate and who I kissed."

"You kissed someone at Amboise?" Fulgrin's brows shot up.

"Merely a figure of speech. The fact is he must be exceedingly well informed if he has spies inside the Wolf's lair. For that matter, he knew who I was before he even dispatched his man with a personal *invitation* to participate in his tournament."

"I would not be in any great hurry to cross him— knowing how well you take to orders—or refuse him outright anything he asks you to do. He . . . *has* asked you to do something, has he not?"

"Indeed he has." Griffyn fetched the cask. Eager fingers lifted the hasp and opened the lid, but when he saw the small fortune in coins, Fulgrin's jaw gaped and his hands actually suffered a tremor.

"God's liver," he gasped. "How much?"

"A thousand here," Griffyn mused, "and a thousand more when I kill Robert Wardieu."

Fulgrin looked up. "Two thousand marks to do what you have come here to do anyway?"

The irony drew the sides of Griffyn's mouth upward, and

he walked barechested to where two large trunks were set side by side against the tent wall. The first contained an assortment of swords, daggers, and other wicked-looking implements of his trade; the second contained a carefully oiled suit of heavy chain mail. From the first chest he selected a double-edged sword, the blade nearly four feet long, wrought of twice-tempered steel with very little taper and a shallow blood gutter that ran the full length. In truth, the gutter was not for blood but for the balancing of the blade, and as he cut it expertly left to right, an admiring smile curved his lips. It was a thing of beauty; not a pit, not a scratch marred the surface. The pommel had serpentine guards to protect his hand, the hilt was deeply scored with a diamond pattern to insure a firm grip. The metal seemed to warm instantly to his touch, while the light danced along the surface like blue fire, revealing the finely etched words that read: *You need not hope that you will ever see heaven, for I have come to take you to the other side.*

"A Welshman died rather painfully today," he murmured, the sparks from the blade reflecting in the luminous depths of his eyes. "Prove how indispensable you are to me. Find out who he was and if his death has anything to do with Saintonge's desire for Wardieu's demise."

He reached into the second chest and withdrew a large square of carefully folded silk. The pennon spread open in his hand, the light once again catching the threads of the deep green background, making it shimmer like the still waters of a pond. Emblazoned on the green was a gold falcon in full flight, the wings outspread, the talons extending forward as if about to strike.

"Have you seen where Amboise is camped?"

"On the far side of the meadow, nearer the road than the river. Four-, five-score tents at least. Shall I hang your pennon, sire?"

Griffyn smiled grimly at the sudden note of respect that had crept into Fulgrin's voice. It was, indeed, as if he stepped into the guise of another man whenever the falcon's wings were unfurled. A man who had no conscience, no loyalties, no qualms about destroying everything that lay in his path.

"Why not?" he said. "It is only a courtesy to let them know death is in their midst."

The word spread quickly, carried on the smoke that drifted up from the cookfires. It came to Brenna's ears just as the sun was slipping down behind the silhouette of Gaillard's battlements, forming a coronet of red and pink spikes behind the stark black outline of towers and ramparts. The temperature had dropped noticeably and she had donned a heavier quilted surcoat to ward off the chill and dampness.

Robin, Richard, Dag, and Geoffrey LaFer were in their own tents changing into their finery for the evening feasts. The château's great hall held seating for a thousand and more, and it was likely all the long trestle tables would be filled to overflowing with knights, nobles, and visiting dignitaries. Brenna had declined Robin's invitation to join them for the spectacle. Her throat ached and her pride was still bruised. Since the occasion was specifically intended to welcome all to the tournament, she suspected Griffyn Renaud de Verdelay would be in attendance, and she was simply not in the mood to cater to his misguided sense of humor, or to even see him again for that matter.

Sparrow had been clinging to her like paint all afternoon. He meant well and she knew he would defend her with his life if need be—despite threats to give her to the first marriageable man who passed by—but occasions like this brought out the most aggravating characteristics in him: the pacing, the strutting, the flashing of knives if some poor lout did happen to stray too near the boundaries of the Amboise encampment to pay his respects. He would naturally be accompanying Robin and the others to see that they stayed out of trouble and did not addle their wits on too much wine, and she was looking forward to an evening of peace and quiet.

Littlejohn had left camp. He had a hard night's ride

ahead of him to reach the coast, where he would arrange passage to England on his cousin's smuggling ship. He had insisted he would be back at Gaillard in time for the mêlée, but Robin had done his best to dissuade him. Even giants had to rest sometime, and Littlejohn's strength would be far more vital to them in the uncertain days ahead.

Will was helping Timkin polish armor. All four suits of mail had been rolled in barrels of oiled sand before they left Amboise, but the iron hauberks and chausses would be polished and oiled again before the brothers took to the field, as would every blade and sword, helm and shield. Those who were not attending the feast or bending over last-minute preparations for the morrow's events were wandering between enclaves of tents, hailing familiar faces and catching up on gossip. Fires blazed everywhere, and as the sunset faded to a dull pewter, torches were lit and stuck into the ground to form wide circles wherein goliards and minstrels put on impromptu shows for their dinner and a sup of wine.

There was activity outside the torchlit boundaries as well. The men-at-arms who were left behind to guard the pavilions and equipment were quick to find the whores and camp followers who did the most in the shortest span of time for the least amount of coin. There were always more men than willing women and business was brisk, with lines of cheering, jeering customers forming in front of the more popular wagons. Occasionally they could not wait and tried to push ahead, which led to fights and brawling and the odd broken head.

Brenna sat with her eyes closed, using only her ears to pinpoint and identify the different sounds that were so completely different from the odd hooting of an owl heard over the battlements of Amboise. The hundreds of ribald conversations blended together and sounded like flocks of geese. The fires snapped and crackled. The river swept by in a rush in the background, and women's laughter was everywhere. From somewhere high on the crenellated walls, a bell was rung to signify the hour of vespers and she crossed herself instinctively. She murmured a quick prayer and wondered if it would be a moonless night tonight, if she would catch a glimpse of the Lionheart's ghost stalking the walls.

Or a glimpse of the devil stalking through camp.

"—by the river, did you hear? Everyone moved their tents back as soon as they saw his pennons go up."

Brenna opened her eyes in time to see a group of yeomen walking by the rear of her tent, their footsteps crunching on the pebbled ground.

"But did you *see* him? Did you actually *see* the Prince of Darkness?"

"No, but I heard he is as tall as an oak, with brown hair—"

"Gold hair," one stout fellow objected. "And yellow eyes, like a mad dog."

"*Green*. His eyes are green and glow red in the dark."

Another laughed. "And he has writhing snakes for hair, no doubt."

"I heard he had a scar on his face—thus—and speaks in a foreign tongue."

"Is he a Saracen, do you suppose?"

"Why else do you think he never lifts his visor on the field or shows his face? He is either ugly as the devil, or he *is* the devil."

Their voices passed out of earshot and Brenna fed another stick onto her fire. It was the fourth . . . or fifth? . . . such conversation she had overheard, and she felt she was getting to know this dark prince rather well. He was young, old, tall, short, stout, solid, blue-eyed, green-eyed, brown-eyed, *one*-eyed, with long hair, short hair, curly hair, dark hair, light hair . . . hair with snakes! He had black skin, white skin, yellow skin with hideous tattoos, scars, and various disfigurements. One creative fellow even swore he had six fingers on each hand and cloven feet.

"Bren?"

She saw Robin approaching and stood up to greet him.

"We are going now. Are you certain you do not want to come with us?"

"I am quite content leaving the civilities up to you," she said, smoothing a crease in his rich royal-blue velvet tunic. "And besides, Will has promised to ply me with wine and dice away my clothes. Perhaps even sell me into the camp wagons for the night. I shall not be bored."

He regarded her closely for a moment, then tucked his hand beneath her chin, tilting it upward. "Take nothing less than a zechin for your services. No halves or cut coppers."

She laughed, "I shall probably be fast asleep before you reach the top of the road."

He leaned forward and kissed her lightly on the forehead. "There are men every ten feet. If so much as a worm disturbs you, call out."

"I will. You have not had any word of Dafydd yet?"

His expression hardened in the glare of the firelight. "No. Nothing. Someone said they think they remember seeing him the day before last ... or it may just be they saw someone who looked like him, but ..." He shrugged. "If he is here, we will find him. It is the only reason *I* am willing to endure all the pomp and ceremony tonight."

She returned the favor and pointed a stern finger under his nose. "Do not let yourself be talked into anything foolhardy. The mêlée and nothing more. If you feel yourself wavering, just think of Marienne waiting for you in Nottingham. She has waited a long time, and I am sure she would like to see you all in one piece."

Robin chucked her under the chin and rejoined Richard and Dag, who were impatient to depart. Sparrow was waiting farther up the slope, haranguing Geoffrey LaFer at length about some finer point of combat strategy, and Brenna tried not to look too cheerful as she waved to her brother-in-law and silently wished him luck. Geoffrey was a patient man—almost saintly compared to the quick, hot temperament of the Wardieu brothers—but Brenna suspected nine-tenths of the time Sparrow found himself hung on a peg or turned upside down in a bink of onions, Geoffrey's large hands had played a part in it. Isobel was truly a lucky woman to have found someone so genial, so compassionate, so brave, so thoughtful. And so passionate. He had wept openly and unashamedly when she had given birth to their first child, and attended on them hand and foot until Isobel herself had finally scolded him back to more warlike matters.

A sudden picture of Griffyn Renaud de Verdelay popped into Brenna's mind and the comparison was not favorable. Arrogance and constant mockery could hardly be considered genial. Compassion? He probably kicked small dogs and frightened children half to death if they crossed his path. Thoughtful? To his own ends, perhaps. Brave? Well, she had only the one incident this afternoon to liken his behavior to and that had been against three ruffians with nary more than a couple of dull blades between them. Animal lust was not passion. A well-executed kiss was not a sign of devotion, and bathing a bruised throat with cool water was no proof of enduring tenderness. As for sainthood . . . he was probably dicing over some blowsy wench right now, or lying naked on a bed of furs urging some silly girl to rub lower . . .

Brenna returned to sit by the fire, but her cheeks were warm enough and she kept walking, nodding at a group of Amboise guardsmen who looked up from their conversations as she drew near. Two of the burliest accompanied her to the riverbank and guarded her privacy while she washed and tended herself, and when they escorted her back to her tent, she yawned and bade them good night, then doused the lantern and crawled onto her pallet of soft furs. Another yawn sent her snuggling deeper but her eyes remained wide open. She lay there in the semidarkness listening to the voices, the laughter, the singing, the clink of tankards and ever-present grinding of whetstones . . . and felt more wide awake than she had all day.

Blaming the cold river water for revitalizing her, she curled herself into an even tighter ball and forced her eyes to close, determined there would be at least one fully refreshed, clear head in camp come daylight. Moreover, it would likely be one of the last chances for a good night's sleep before they departed for England.

"Ivo is boasting he will snap this Prince of Darkness in two like a dried twig."

Brenna groaned into the furs as more eager speculators passed by the tent.

"More than that, he says he will do it on the first pass and spit this golden falcon on his lance like a trussed capon."

"Hah! I have two deniers to wager—think you I would squander them on the boastings of a fat dolt?"

"Boastings? Did you hear that women have been forming lines outside *his* tent, some of them just to see the size of his cod?"

"Whose . . . Ivo's or the Prince's?"

The sound of a fist clouting a shoulder drifted through the canvas. "The Prince of Darkness, of course. He is taking on all comers now, in the lists and out."

Brenna sighed and sat up. Lines of women, indeed. Snakes for hair. Eyes that flashed fire. What in God's name did they say about Robin behind his back?

She drew her boots on again and went to the door. No one was showing any interest in her darkened tent, and she felt suddenly rebellious enough to take advantage. She wound the braid of her hair tight to her scalp and stuffed it under a felt cap pulled low over her forehead. Then she slipped out and moved quickly to the rear of the tent where the firelight would not betray her. She had her dagger and her shortsword, as well as a small blade in her boot, and as she made her way toward the river again, she kept her head down and her shoulders squared to give the impression of more manly bulk.

Once away from the Amboise encampment, she followed the curving bank of the river. There were lights and tents and people everywhere so she was not overly worried about a repeat of what had happened earlier in the day. There was nothing about her appearance to tempt anyone into taking a second glance anyway. If anything she looked like a squire or a page out running an errand for his master.

She had no clear destination in mind and was not even aware of where her footsteps had carried her until the brightest sector of camp came to an abrupt and noticeable break. There could be no mistaking which tents belonged to the Prince of Darkness, for there were only two— somewhat innocuous-looking, she thought as she stared at them—set well apart from the others on a narrow spit of land. There were no lines of women waiting their turn for a tumble, nor any brave souls waiting to catch a glimpse of the devil's disciple. There was a small fire to mark the camp, but otherwise, no signs of life or movement at all. Only the soft rustle of silk pennon waving in the breeze, vert with a gold falcon, its outstretched talons warning the curious to stay their distance.

Brenna did not know whether to be disappointed or annoyed. She stood there in the shadows with the long grass tangled around her ankles, aware only of the water rushing by beside her and the bright pinpoints of light twinkling on the walls of the château high in the background. She did not hear the approach of another set of footsteps along the riverbank. Nor did she mark the presence of anyone behind her until she felt an ominous stillness at her back, blocking the breeze that had been blowing steady since she left the encampment.

She twisted around but, with the glow of the sprawling camp full in her face, all she could see was the shape of a tall, broad-shouldered man who had a knife glinting in his fist and a curse hissing between his lips.

18

Griffyn cursed again. "You! What the devil are you doing out here? I would have thought you had learned your lesson this afternoon and not gone wandering off on your own again."

She swallowed hard to force her heart out of her throat and back down into her chest. "I . . . could not sleep. I thought a walk might help. What are *you* doing here? *I* would have thought you would be up at the château feasting and wining and wenching along with the others."

"I am not one for feasting or wining on the eve of a tournament. In fact"—he paused while he resheathed his dagger—"I usually walk the night away myself. I have had enough close brushes with death to appreciate the importance of savoring a night like this, since it could well be the last I see." He glanced wryly at the isolated tents ahead. "Tell me you are not come to ogle and swoon over the Prince of Darkness?"

"*No.* I am not. I was merely following the river, with no thought to where it led."

His face angled briefly into the light and she could see the skepticism on his lips. "Well, another twenty paces or so and it follows straight into a rocky gorge. Come, I will walk you back to your own camp."

"I do not need your company, sirrah. I can find my way on my own."

"Suit yourself." He started to walk away, then stopped. "To answer your question, I was just going to check on my horses. If you would care to come along, I would vouchsafe my best behavior."

She followed the direction of his nod and saw long, low rows of canvas stables strung out along the curving base of the slope.

"Horses? You have more than one destrier?"

"I would make for a pretty poor soldier of fortune if I did not." She let the comment pass without a rejoinder and he smiled again. "Fulgrin brought the others with him, along with the wagon and supplies."

"Fulgrin . . . the squire with the mind of his own? I take it you found him without difficulty."

"He is always difficult, but refuses to go missing for very long. Come. I stole some excellent apples and would not want my efforts wasted."

She frowned at his broad back for a moment and, against her better judgment, fell into step beside him. The make-shift stables were lit by torchlight, filled with the warm, musky smell of horse. He walked to the far end of the row of divided stalls, startling a boy who was seated on the ground, dozing.

"Sire!" The lad scrambled to his feet, his face blanching white. "The beasts are fed and watered, sire. I groomed them myself and have let no one else near them."

"See that you do not. Go down to the river and douse yourself in cold water. I want you awake and alert all night."

The lad nodded, his neck stiff with terror. "I will be, sire. I swear it."

Brenna watched the boy stumble away and arched an eyebrow, recalling her opinion of Griffyn Renaud's tolerance for underlings. "You do seem to have a warming effect on people, do you not?"

He ignored her sarcasm and went into the first stall. The big gray destrier, Centaur, had swung his head around at the first sound of Renaud's voice and nickered softly now as he accepted a fat, juicy apple. He was a beautiful animal, fully eighteen hands high, and Brenna had admired him in the forest outside of Amboise. But the stallion that drew her attention now was tied in the next stall, taller even than the gray, a darker shade of coal ash with mottled black spots across the rump and hindquarters, with one snow-white cuff banding a foreleg. He was so thickly muscled across the withers and flanks, it prompted her to take a precautionary step back, uncertain the rope would hold him if he took to balking around strangers.

Griffyn noted her wariness and stepped around Centaur's rump into the next stall. "This is Centurion; Centaur's son. His dignity is a little bruised from having only Fulgrin's company for the past few days."

He held out another apple, which was snorted at with disdain.

"Fine," said Griffyn, and took a bite. The stallion reared his noble head and stamped his forelegs, but his master did not even flinch. He calmly chewed and swallowed and took another bite before offering the remainder of the apple.

The snort was quieter, but the fruit was snatched between the huge white teeth before it could be withdrawn again. Griffyn rubbed the velvety snout with obvious affection, then ran his hands along the neck, across the withers, and down the solid forelegs, checking every muscle and tendon for tenderness. He did the same to the hindquarters and back legs, ending his inspection with a robust pat on the rump.

He had two more apples tucked into the front of his surcoat, which he fed to the pair of short, scruffy-haired rouncies stabled next in line that had watched the entire proceedings with rounded, eager eyes. Both neighed softly when he rubbed their snouts and gave them their treat, and one plucked gratefully at his sleeve when he stopped to frown over a sore on his flanks.

"If Fulgrin has been using leather on you again," he murmured, "I will ply it across his own worthless back."

Brenna was mildly taken aback by his gentleness, though she supposed a mercenary still had to show some consideration for his animals. A knight, even a poor excuse for a knight, would be helpless without a good horse beneath him. And a knight who came to a tournament with only one mount most definitely did not have high expectations.

Griffyn returned to the first stall and gave Centaur the same meticulous inspection he had given Centurion. Brenna moved closer and smoothed her hand along the stallion's flank, watching how carefully, how gently, yet how expertly Renaud probed and stroked and kneaded his way down one foreleg, then the other. She followed the movement of his right hand, the fingers long and tapered and so precise in their search, she felt her own skin responding to each careful, sliding stroke. Beneath the bulky layers of her surcoat she could feel her flesh prickling and tightening as she remembered how that same hand had shaped itself around her naked breast, chasing after every shiver and shudder.

Her gaze was drawn to the scarred left hand, and something else shuddered deep within her. It was not fear, nor pity, nor sympathy, for she had seen far more heinous wounds on men returning from war. It was something else that she could not quite identify.

"It is probably none of my affair to know, but . . . how did you burn your hand?"

He glanced at her, glanced at the hand, then returned to his inspection. "You are right. It is none of your affair."

She said nothing and after a moment, he sighed and straightened. "Forgive me. I am not accustomed to anyone showing any concern for my well-being."

"It was not concern," she said archly, refusing to admit it, even to herself. "Merely curiosity."

He splayed the fingers of the scarred left hand and turned it over, studying it as if seeing it for the first time. "It is not a very pretty sight, is it?"

"It does not hamper you in any way?"

He flexed the strong fingers and rested them on Centaur's shoulder. "No. Were you hoping it did?"

"Of course not. Why would I hope such a thing?"

"Indeed, why would you? Your brother is not fighting tomorrow, his own injury is keeping him amongst the spectators. I would think you would be looking forward to the pleasure and the possibility of my getting spitted and spilled."

"I do not particularly relish seeing anyone get spitted."

"Not even a . . . what was it you called me? A low-bellied worm?"

She flushed. "I was angry when I said that."

"So you were," he mused. "And very, very beautiful with your face all flushed with indignation and your eyes snapping fire."

"It was dark," she said, swallowing. "How could you know how I looked?"

With his left hand still on the stallion's shoulder, he moved his right to the rump, effectively trapping Brenna between. Warmed by the heat of two formidable bodies, she could only stare at the cleft in Griffyn's chin, not daring to look any higher up or any lower down.

"I know how you looked in the forest," he murmured. "I know how you looked in the bath house. And I know how you look right now."

His lips came almost close enough to brush her temple, and she held her breath.

"Beautiful," he whispered. "Whether you believe it or not."

He straightened and she risked a glance up at his chin again. He had shaved recently, bathed too to judge by the clean, earthy scent of him. His hair gleamed like ebony under the torchlight, full and thick and silky. If anyone was beautiful . . .

"I . . . I am plain and awkward," she stammered softly. "My hair is unruly and my nose has spots, and . . . and . . . I will never have soft hands or pale skin. Mother despairs of my ever behaving the way a proper lady should."

"Thank God for that," he said sincerely. "Proper ladies are nice to look at, but I for one prefer the company of someone who can stop a poacher dead in his tracks or rouse the curiosity of a man who is careful not to be curious about too many things—especially women. As for your spots, I find them charming. And your hair . . ." The words trailed away on a frown as he plucked the cap off her head and cast it into the shadows. His strong fingers started to untangle the glossy braid, spreading the curly profusion around her shoulders, spreading ripples of sensation through her body and down into her limbs. When he was finished working his mischief, he waited for her to open her eyes, to raise them up to his and acknowledge the heat coursing through her veins. He waited, and when he saw it, he cradled one hand on either side of her neck and brought her mouth up to his, the kiss so deep and long and tender, the end of it was marked with a soft, shuddering sigh.

"I thought you said you would vouchsafe your behavior."

"I lied." He smiled rakishly enough to send a shiver shooting straight down to her toes. When he kissed her again, the tremors spread into her arms, to the very tips of her fingers where they curled into his surcoat.

She should have known, of course, coming with him to the stable, envying the motion of his hands, envying the way she had seen the other women staring at him earlier in the day, ruing the way she had pushed him away when he had kissed her in the alleyway . . . she should have known this would happen.

And she supposed she did, for there was no thought of denying him. There was not even a modest attempt to refuse him as her hands crept up to his shoulders and her lips parted wider beneath his, inviting him into the warmth and wetness. Her eyes closed tight and she sighed again, the sound as soft and grateful as that from the rouncies. She kissed him back, not even caring that the front of the tent was open to whoever happened to walk past, or that the torchlight was bright, or that she was playing the fool for someone who must thrive on fools. Fools like Tansy who fainted three times in his arms. Fools like the women who followed his stark beauty with hungry eyes.

His tongue traced delicate patterns in and around her mouth, and she shivered helplessly beneath its seductive power. His body crowded her against Centaur and his hands raked deeper into her hair, angling her head this way and that so that her cheeks, her temples, her eyes, the tenderest stretches of her throat were exposed to his roving lips.

She leaned shamelessly into each caress and her hands crawled upward to his shoulders, to his neck, to the lush thickness of his hair. She sought the generous curves of his mouth and kissed him, knowing full well where it would lead this time. She knew and pressed eagerly against him, wanting to feel his heat on her body, between her thighs.

"There is an excellent patch of grass by the river," he whispered. "Soft and lush . . . I would gladly take you there if you would let me."

Her body was pure liquid, flowing and silky and smooth, and she felt weightless, lightheaded, not caring that it was madness, sheer madness to agree. She tightened her hands, dragging his mouth back down to hers, and he took this as assent, picking her up in his arms and carrying her out into the darkness of the night.

He walked until the torchlight faded and the camp sounds dimmed, until they were knee deep, waist deep in the grasses by the river, and only then did he set her down. Only then did he release her and stand back, showing the smallest bit of uncertainty for the first time, as if he were afraid to acknowledge the strength of his own desire. This sudden glimpse of vulnerability brought Brenna forward, her whole body trembling with the brilliant madness.

"A thousand things you promised me," she whispered. "A thousand things that would have me begging for a thousand more. I intend to hold you to it, sirrah, unless it was all simple boasting."

She caught her breath as his arms went around her and his lips were hers again. His hands were everywhere at once, stripping away her tunic and padded surcoat, her belts and weapons and inhibitions. He lifted the hem of her shirt and drew it up over her head, leaving her standing in a shimmer of sheer silk, an abbreviated chemise laced in front with tiny ribbons and embroidered with clusters of ivy leaves and delicate blue flowers. The ribbons were torn without a thought and she stood like a pagan in front of him, bare from the waist up, with the night air puckering her breasts, chilling them so that when his mouth claimed the roseate nipples, she groaned and held him close, her fingers buried in his hair, her head bowed over his.

She watched him, on his knees now, peeling down her leggings, pushing them only as far as the tops of her boots before the hunger and impatience bade him press his mouth to her belly, to her thighs, to the soft thatch of tawny curls between. She held his shoulders and her knees buckled, and then she was lying in the grass and her arms were stretched out flat on either side, and his lips were *there*. His mouth was *there* and she could not breathe or think or reason. The heat and pleasure washed through her in long sweeping waves, deep and intense, and she clutched at fistfuls of grass, tearing it out by the root. There was more, and more, and more, and she opened her body wider, wider still, and she arched her back, arched her hips into the exquisite ravishment as the sweet, stinging rush of her first orgasm lifted her off the grass, pressed her into his mouth, and begged him to hold her there, his tongue and lips taking her to places she had never been before.

A stunned, breathless shudder brought her melting back to earth again, and he took his mouth away only long enough to cast his own clothing aside. With the disbelief shining in her eyes she watched as he lowered himself over her again, this time with flesh pressing flesh, with his hands bracing her thighs and his heat thrusting into the lush wetness he had so ably prepared. She felt the tender, inward stretching and she gasped as he pushed forward, throbbing and hard and uncompromisingly virile. He thrust past the flimsy barrier that was no barrier at all but a floodgate . . . a floodgate that opened and welcomed him with warm spasms of moist heat.

Lacking the wit or sense of what to do next, Brenna could only trust his strength, his power, and cling to him as he began to move within her, to withdraw and thrust, withdraw and thrust with long, silky strokes. He was inside her!

He was inside her and she could feel him moving, flesh into flesh, heat into heat, sliding and probing, making her gasp and writhe in utter disbelief. His dark head was bowed over her breast. His lips were working their magic on her tormented flesh and she begged again, without shame or modesty, urging him to plunge deeper, thrust harder. The waves of pleasure seemed to ripple back into themselves, now hot, now cool, and it was like nothing she could have imagined, nothing she could have prepared for, and when the ecstasy came, she rose to meet it, her eyes shocked wide and glazed with astonishment. It was there, just within her grasp, and she clawed her hands into the plunging motion of his hips, thrilling in the primitive savagery of the act even as she dug her heels into the soft earth and sought to match him thrust for thrust.

Bright, raging torrents of pleasure swept through her and her senses dissolved in a rushing, white-hot orgasm. Her body tightened around one mighty spasm after another and she was vaguely aware of Griffyn arching his head back and crying out in the grips of some similar cataclysm. It held him there for an eternity and more, the pleasure pure and undiluted and unrelenting in its intensity. It held them locked together, their bodies straining for more . . . more . . .

A final massive shudder gave way to the finer ecstasies of whispered words and urgent, pressing closeness. He tried to hold her but his arms were without strength. He tried to reassure her but his own body was quaking with shock, with breathlessness, with awe. He tried to fake bravado, as if such a monumental explosion of the senses was commonplace and routine, but his own body betrayed him, thrusting again and again in decreasing increments, not wanting to admit she had shattered him as much as he had shattered her.

But she had. The proof was in the deep, thudding pulsations as he melted into her arms, melted into her body, confirming he still had a soul, that he was a man who could feel and want and need.

* * *

Griffyn did not move for several minutes. He needed that long to catch his breath and collect his wits about him. When he was finally able to lift his head out of the crook of her neck, it was only to kiss her mouth, her throat, the valley between her breasts.

Brenna kept her arms wrapped tightly around him. Her heart was drumming so loudly in her chest she was sure he could hear it, certain that was why he laid his head upon her breast. He was still a formidable presence inside her, a huge and heated presence above her, and she tried not to picture the sight they made, his black hair scattered over her naked breasts, her legs gleaming white and hooked over his like pincers, surely looking utterly heathen on their bed of grass.

She blushed so hot it hurt. Hot enough he must have felt it for he stirred and roused himself enough to lever some of his weight onto his elbows. He brushed the back of his fingers across her cheek and traced the flow of warmth down her chin, her throat, and onto the satiny curve of her shoulder. Tight, damp tendrils of hair were curled forward on her temples, and as he toyed with them, he studied her face, seeing it as if he had the benefit of a hundred blazing candles to light the way.

Suddenly self-conscious, she let her limbs ease down onto the grass. She half expected him to move as well, or to at least detach himself and allow her to redeem a semblance of her dignity, but he did not. He seemed quite content to keep himself wedged comfortably between her thighs, to keep himself cocooned inside her and his fingers stroking absently down the side of her neck. Each stroke sent a corresponding shiver down her spine and across her breasts, gathering and tightening the flesh so that he could hardly help but notice the reaction . . . notice it and take advantage of her defenselessness by kissing a warm path from one puckered crown to the other.

"Wh-what are you doing?"

"Obeying your command, demoiselle. You ordered a thousand pleasures; we have nine hundred and ninety-nine to go."

"I was . . . only jesting," she stammered.

"I was not."

She sucked a breath through her teeth as his hand slid under her hips and raised her so that she could feel he was not nearly as depleted as she had supposed him to be. His naked legs slid against her inner thighs as he positioned himself more deeply and she made a soft, helpless sound in her throat.

"Let yourself go," he whispered. "Trust me."

Let go? she thought wildly. What was there left to hold on to? She was lying naked in the grass with a man she barely knew. She had sacrificed her virginity and her common sense for a few moments of reckless passion with someone too dangerous and too unscrupulous to trust with the smallest part of her heart.

He held her tight, pushing into her with ever-strengthening thrusts, and she had no choice but to trust him. She let his hands guide her knees up to his waist and she shook with the deep, explicit friction, championing it with such stunning proficiency, she felt his body stretch and stiffen and flood her with a welter of shimmering heat. He held her tight and showed her how to move, how to create her own friction where she needed it most, and this time, when she cried out, she cried out his name, and they swept over the brink together, their release long and splendid and scalding in its intensity.

It was noisy as well, and the watcher high up on the river-bank smiled and closed his eyes, fitting pictures to the groans and shivered sobs, the damp sound of flesh sliding into flesh. He felt himself growing too hard to remain crouched in the bushes much longer and, besides, he had found out what he wanted to know. The sister of Robert Wardieu d'Amboise rutting with the vaunted Prince of Darkness! It was enough to make him want to laugh out loud.

Gerome de Saintonge had scarcely believed his eyes when he had seen them together in the stable. He had been keeping a close watch on Griffyn Renaud at his father's request and had seen him meet with what he thought was a young boy on the edge of the encampment. That would have been interesting in itself, though not altogether unheard of in men who fought like demons to prove their manliness in other ways. The Lionheart himself, according to some old Crusaders, had spent more time choosing his pages than he had his bride.

But the torchlight had revealed curves and shapes beneath the leather surcoat and leggings and when the hat had come off, the recognizable cloud of tarnished gold hair made the long crawl through the dew-slicked grass all the more rewarding.

The haughty little bitch!

Who was she to laugh in his face and refuse his offer of marriage! Who was she to stab him with an eating knife when he tried to steal a kiss, and how many more offers was she likely to have at the lofty age of eighteen? Most women were married and breeding at fourteen; few had anywhere to go after nineteen but a convent!

Or a grassy riverbank like a common slut.

The noises stopped and Gerome raised his head above the tall bank of grass. They were still lying there, a tangle of naked arms and legs, collapsed in blissful exhaustion. On a smiling thought, he ignored his own discomfort and crept a few feet closer. The breeze was ruffling the grass, camouflaging any sounds he made, and he was able to inch right up to where the bank leveled and the grass became thick as a carpet underfoot. They had obviously been in a hurry, for there were clothes strewn in a wide circle around them, and he was able to use the tip of his sword to pluck a particularly feminine article off a nearby rock and fish it back to where he crouched in the darkness.

For a moment, he debated simply standing up and

shouting out his discovery, but he remembered Renaud's quickness and cold, deadly instincts, and he decided to keep his skin intact. He tucked the scrap of silk beneath his surcoat and retreated the way he had come, careful not to step on any twig or root that might disturb the dozing lovers.

19

Brenna heard voices nearby and they wakened her. At first she did not know where she was, she was only aware of a strong, warm body curved around her and deep, even breathing against her nape. She was curled like a child in his strong arms, shoulders to chest, back to belly, rump to hip, cradled there in the languid fatigue that had claimed them both. Some time during the night he had covered them loosely with their discarded clothing, but she did not notice the cool air where it touched her exposed skin; it was a welcome relief after the extravagance of heat and energy they had expended. She had not fainted, but she had come perilously close on more than one occasion when the sheer magnitude of her pleasure had become almost too much to bear.

The voices faded and Brenna risked lifting her head to peek over the thick wall of grass. She was shocked to see a watery blue film of light along the horizon and to realize the voices she had heard belonged to early risers, not late revelers.

She glanced down at Griffyn and his eyes were open, waiting.

"I have to go," she gasped. "I have to get back to camp before I am missed . . . if I have not been already."

She scrambled to sort out the various articles of clothing and cursed when she could not find her chemise among the scattered trappings. She dressed without it, shivering when the coarse linen of her shirt chafed skin that had become far too sensitive to the slightest touch. Her hair flew in an untamed mass of curls over her shoulders; she made a few futile attempts to comb it with her fingers before giving up and cursing it back into a tail.

"Here," he said, "let me help."

"I can do it myself," she insisted, recoiling from his hands.

He watched her fumble with the laces of her surcoat and when all she managed to do was tangle them in knots, he gently grasped hold of her wrists and moved them away, then took up the thongs himself and fastened them with silent efficiency.

"I had best walk you back."

"No!" She looked up in mild horror. "No. My God, what would Robin or the others think if they saw us together?"

He stared at her a moment, as if she had reached out unexpectedly and cut him with a knife. As if, after the night they had just spent together, he was surprised she still had the arrogance to remind him of his unsuitability to be the lover of a nobleman's daughter.

"Forgive me, my lady," he murmured, bowing. "I forgot myself."

"I did not mean that the way it sounded," she said quickly. "I only meant . . ."

"I know what you meant. And you are absolutely right. Your brother would likely kill both of us if he knew."

He finished tying off the last knot and gave her a perfunctory smile as he bent over to retrieve his own clothes. He had pulled on his braies and hose but was still magnificently bare from the waist up, and as she watched him push his arms into the sleeves of his shirt, all she wanted to do was lean into his heat again, feel those arms go around her that they might protect her against the waves of anxiety and guilt that were threatening to overwhelm her. As it was, she could hardly believe it had not just been some wild, other-worldly dream she had experienced and she would waken and find it had not really happened. She had not really crept away from camp. She had not really allowed him to seduce her and then given so freely of herself, doing things . . . begging to have things done that would, indeed, keep her pink with mortification all day long.

"Perhaps this should not have happened," she agreed on a ragged whisper. "But I am not sorry it did. I do not regret a single moment of last night . . . I . . . I only wish . . ."

He stopped tugging on the hem of his shirt and glanced at her intently. "You wish what?"

"I wish . . ." She moistened her lips and glanced at the growing bloom of dawn light. "I wish we had more time. I wish . . . we had the chance to know each other better."

He seemed surprised. "Why? I thought you had already made up your mind as to who and what I was—a common mercenary with few scruples and no conscience. Good God," he muttered through a half smile, "you were not expecting more from me, were you? You were not expecting me to turn out to be something more than what I am?"

Her heart tripped over a single poignant beat and she had to look away, look down at her hands, look over at the flattened grass that marked her initiation into all these strange new emotions surfacing within her. She was not expecting anything from him at all and was certainly under no illusions of any obligations owed. In two days' time they would be going their separate ways, and the likelihood of ever seeing one another again was too remote to even contemplate. But she did not want to think about that, not with her body aching in places it had never ached before, wanting more of what she had never wanted before.

"I warrant it would be easier to change a stone into pudding," she whispered. "And yet I do not think there is anything common about you at all. Confusing, confounding, vexatious, yes, but not common."

"Is that a compliment . . . or a complaint?"

"Neither," she admitted honestly. "And both."

He looked away across the meadow, toward the multitude of fluttering pennons that marked the boundaries of the jousting fields—anywhere to avoid the shy confusion shimmering in the violet of her eyes.

"Well, rest assured," he said at length, "you will undoubtedly return to your original opinion of me before the day is through."

She was startled by the pronouncement, even more so by the anger that sawed across his voice as he said it.

"And now you had best go. Before your brothers send out a search party."

Her heart stumbled again at the gruffness in his voice, but knowing it was not an idle warning, she struggled with her hair a few more moments and gave her belt a final adjustment. When she turned away, about to follow the bank back to the Amboise encampment, she heard him curse and felt his hands on her shoulders.

"Brenna—"

"Yes?"

He was studying her face by the growing light, memorizing it almost, as if he might never see it again, and although his lips were parted and there was some kind of dilemma waging a small war in his eyes, he only clamped his jaw tight again and let his hands fall away from her shoulders. "Are you certain you do not want me to walk you back?"

She shook her head. "Half the camp is likely awake by now. If I am lucky, I can convince them I was only gone a few minutes to the river."

He nodded. "Well then . . ."

"Well then," she whispered, still fighting the tremor in her chin. On impulse, she leaned forward and kissed him, not very hard and not very well. She turned then and started running back along the riverbank, not stopping until she was directly below the sea of black-and-gold pennons.

She was just wading her way through the thick fringe of reeds when Sparrow's head popped up above the grasses.

"You are not in your tent," he charged.

"I needed a few moments of privacy."

"To do what? And why so privately you could not call out to the guard?"

"Because I was only gone a few minutes and it becomes tiresome to have someone watching over your shoulder every time you crouch down in the bushes! As well *you* should know," she added, pointing to where the rucked-up hem of his tunic exposed the gap in his leggings.

Red-faced, he cursed and spun on his heels, tugging at hems and closures until his appearance was restored. By then she had walked past him and gained the top of the embankment.

"You willfully disobeyed an order," he persisted. "I could have you sent home."

"You could." She sighed. "But you won't."

"Ho, ho! And why would I not?"

She stopped and turned and the two glared at one another, hands on waists, mouths set, eyes flashing warnings.

"Because Robin needs me," she said finally. "And anything Robin needs, Robin gets, whether it sits well with you or not, whether it serves him well or not, whether it costs the sun, the moon, the stars, and all the heavens above or not. The rest of us"—she waved a hand to include the camp and everyone in it—"could beg a cup of water from you to ease a parched throat and we would be hard-pressed to get it, but if Robin wanted the merest drop, you would cross deserts and mountains and fight your way through hostile armies to fetch it for him."

"Ho," he said in a softer voice, his chest deflating and his arms wilting down by his sides. "And where is this coming from? Never have I ever denied any of you anything you asked of me."

"No. But you sit in judgment over us and search for the smallest flaw to pounce upon, whereas Robin . . . Robin shines in your eyes like a bright light. He could be missing from his tent for days and come back with some tale of picking daisies and you would not question him."

"Only because if he said he was picking daisies, likely he *was* picking daisies. The rest of you"—Sparrow's eyes glinted and his hands crept back up to his hips—"would as likely be out picking trouble and *tell* me it was daisies."

Brenna was too close to tears to argue. And Sparrow, knowing she had a fine temper and a foot to stamp it with, saw the water in the corners of her eyes and melted again.

"It is Dagobert," he concluded grimly. "You are worried about him?"

"Dag?"

"The joust. The lummock who challenged him at the *fête* last night."

Brenna had no idea what he was talking about, but it was easier to pretend she did, for it diverted Sparrow's thoughts immediately.

"The whole château has been abuzz with the news that Robin is injured and will only fight in the mêlée, yet this crackbrain struts forth and challenges Dagobert to answer for an insult delivered to his former harlot, who has only recently become his lady by virtue of poisoning the wife and breeding up a brat to offer as heir!"

It sounded like just another of Dag's indiscretions and Brenna sighed. "Could he not refuse? He is not even registered in the roles; he did not have to accept the challenge."

Sparrow scowled again. "Name one member of this accursed family who would refuse to fight after a glove is thrown at the feet and an insult at the face?"

He had a point and she frowned. "Who is this fool?"

"Roald of Anjou. The larded codshead with ears so big he sleeps on the one and uses the other as a blanket. Hopefully the size of them will help him listen to reason, for Richard and Geoffrey have gone to see if there is some other way to cool his blood and appease his wounded heart. Hark! Behold the young wastrel himself," he said, hooking a thumb to show where Dag was standing with Robin by a firepit. "Laying his burdens on someone who has not the first notion of what would drive a man to such foolish lengths."

Brenna looked down at him in shock, certain she had

misinterpreted his meaning. "Are you saying that Robin has never . . . that he is still . . . ?"

"Chaste? By Cyril's sword he is indeed, ever since he pledged to remain so on the meadow outside Kirklees Abbey. And there, you see? I have not been able to get him everything he wants, for he has wanted only Marienne FitzWilliam lo these many years of watching his two addled brothers swiv every wench in sight."

He strode on ahead in a kick of dust, letting her know he was still smarting from her accusation, and for all of two seconds Brenna was sorry she had said it. But then her gaze was drawn to Robin's handsome face glowing in the firelight, and she forgot everything as she pondered the impossibility of anyone ever guessing her big virile brother, defender and champion of all Europe, was a virgin.

Her footsteps slowed as she approached the fire but her brothers barely looked up to acknowledge her presence.

"You are up and about early" was Robin's only comment.

"I . . . could not sleep," she answered truthfully enough.

"You heard about Dag?"

She nodded. "Sparrow told me. What are you going to do?"

"Fight the bastard, of course." Dag grunted. "And tup his trull of a wife when I am finished."

Robin frowned. "He is not so easy to unseat as he looks, despite the size of his girth. I know. I fought him in LeMans last summer and came away with more than a few loosened buckles. He is as sly as a weasel and aims high, for the collar. If he happens to hit the visor—which is an illegal foul—he cries his innocence and claims his grip faltered."

"Charming. How do I block him?"

"Your only chance is to hit him equally hard and high. Let him *know* on the first pass that you *are* aiming for the visor without pretense; surprise him thus and you may be able to unsettle his wits enough to make his grip truly falter."

"When he does, you drop the lance and aim for the gut," Sparrow advised, smacking his belly to show the exact spot, just under the breastbone. "Drive the air out of him and the excess suet he carries will do the rest."

The crunch of bootsteps brought their heads swinging around as Richard and Geoffrey LaFer emerged from between a row of tents.

"By the happy looks on your faces, I gather the appeal did not go well?" Robin asked.

"Anjou's father sends his apologies for his son's rashness," Richard said concisely, "and asks if Dag would care to defer the match to a more convenient time and place. He asked it with a grin on his face and a tickle in his throat that made him cough loudly enough for anyone within bowshot to overhear the conversation."

Sparrow rolled his eyes heavenward as if he knew what was coming next, and Richard, for his part, did not disappoint.

"I told him to defer his apology up his arse, that I was only come to recommend the skills of a good coffin-maker."

Sparrow glared at the normally level-headed Geoffrey LaFer. "And you, Brain-Biter? Where were you whilst the happy exchange was taking place?"

"I was seeing to our family's interests." Geoffrey held his hands out to warm them over the fire. "I took the liberty of wagering four hundred marks against the possibility of Anjou remaining in his saddle beyond two passes."

Sparrow groaned while Dag gaped at his brother, then his brother-in-law. "Two passes! The fellow is an ox! He has to send to Flanders for horses large enough to carry his weight."

"And a helm big enough to hold his ears," Sparrow added glumly.

"The perfect target," Richard said, giving Dag a hearty clap on the shoulder. "Be of good cheer, little brother; it could have been worse. It could have been the Prince of Darkness who took offense at where you put your pisser." He looked up as Robin cleared his throat and saw Brenna half hidden by the smoke and shadows. "Bren! Forgive my candor, I did not see you standing there." His gaze raked the length of her surcoat and leggings, and Brenna felt the skin start to shrink everywhere on her body. Her hair was a mess, her clothing rumpled and dampened beyond what a few moments by the river would have allowed; her lips felt red and swollen to twice their size. She was certain there must be some outward sign of lost virtue, and if anyone had eyes sharp enough to notice those signs, it was Richard.

"Surely you are not attending the day dressed like that?" he asked. "You know, of course, we are expected to sit in the royal bower with Prince Louis and the Count of Saintonge."

"I was merely delaying the horror of a wimple for as long as possible," she said on a soft expulsion of breath.

"Even bound in linen, you will draw the eye of every warm-blooded churl on the field," Lord Geoffrey predicted gallantly. "You had best bring an extra pair of sleeves to toss to the poor swains."

"Very funny," she muttered, and Robin reached out to tug on a loose curl.

"Come now, it will not be so bad as all that. You have borne up under silks and velvets before. Just remember to keep your knife handy. Gerome de Saintonge will likely be vying for a seat near you in the dais."

She cursed with enough eloquence to cause all four men to clear their throats and take their teasing elsewhere.

Richard draped an arm over his younger brother's shoulder. "Four hundred marks is a deal of money, brother dear. We had best get your armor sorted out and start discussing strategies. Rob?"

"I will be along in a minute."

Geoffrey crowded Dag on the other side, and together he and Richard led him off. Sparrow lingered behind as well, his agate eyes burning as hot as the flames.

"All right, what is it, Puck?" Robin sighed. "You are hopping from one foot to the other as if the ground was a bed of coals beneath you."

"Richard's tongue often gets in the way of his brain, but this time he has raised an interesting question. Why is it this vaunted Prince of Doom-and-Gloom has *not* put forth a challenge against the Wardieu name?"

Robin frowned. "Perhaps he has more couth than Roald of Anjou."

"Bah! In a hen's noseful! He has no more couth than a copper groat. And I do not think he has come all the way from Rome to wave his lance at dolts and nithings."

"Well, what would you have me do?" Robin asked mildly. "Ask him why he has not come forth? Ask him why he was not among those who gawped and snickered and whispered behind raised hands last night? I will do it, by God. Put me before him and I will do it, for I would sooner gall myself on a barrel of vinegar as share one more false toast with some oaf who wishes me improved health!"

Sparrow snorted. "Indeed, was it not for my knife being as sharp as it was, the lot of you would have been throwing gauntlets hither and thither at every cock in sight."

"He actually stabbed me," Robin said to Brenna. "He stabbed me and drew blood."

" 'Twas only a prick in the thigh. And only because you were wanting help with your wits. You knew before we came that your *injury* would be the source of much tongue-wagging. You also knew there would be suggestions that your ribs were troubled more because of the presence of this unholy paladin than an errant tusk of a boar."

"I survived the night, did I not?" Robin said tautly.

"*You* survived it. I did not. My ballocks are itching as if I had a cruck full of fleas roosting there."

Robin stared. "Yes, well, I suppose that would make you a little on edge."

"They shrivel and burn as if a witch's curse has been put upon them. Something evil is in the air. I suffered to know it the instant the château came into sight and never am I wrong. Never have my ballocks failed me. Take heed: something evil has come here and is lurking in the shadows waiting to strike."

Robin looked down at his hands and twisted the dragon

ring, making the ruby eye flash in the firelight. "Two more days in this place and we are free to leave."

Sparrow snorted. "Two more days of keeping tempers cool and wits keen—a task that should earn me sainthood at the least. Well I know how this galls you, Cockerel, for it galls us all. But *think*. *Think* what must be done. When we have done it, aye, *then* we can return to this poxy turnip patch and you can pare the tongues from every swag-bellied rump sore who dared sneeze out the side of his mouth. Od's blood, I will help wield the first blade myself! But only after we have brought our hearts safely home again."

Robin closed his eyes briefly and reached out his hand, laying it on Sparrow's shoulder. "In truth, it was thoughts of Marienne that kept me in my seat last night, but do not stray too far from my side today, Puck. Use your knife again if need be, but do not let me forget my way."

Sparrow puffed his chest and nodded. "Worry not. With me on the one side and the level head of your sister on the other, we should be able to keep your buttocks firmly in your chair." He peered over the fire at Brenna. "Should we not?"

Brenna smiled hesitantly and nodded, knowing she had just spent the night proving she was the least level-headed of the lot.

20

The official events were well under way by late morning. By then the lords and ladies had broken their fasts in due style and ceremony, many of them barely recovered from the festivities the night before. Precisely at ten, heralds lined the parapets and blared a warning to all malingerers; criers read from scrolls of parchment listing the day's activities. The jousting fields started to fill with spectators several hours before the first run between the more popular champions was scheduled to commence. The early courses were between the younger knights who, due to their eagerness and clumsiness, often provided the best blood sport of the tourney. These matches rarely went more than a single pass, and most of the victors trotted off the field, happy just to have survived.

Strong attempts were made to minimalize the actual danger of death on the field. But blunted or not, the tip of a lance striking square in the chest could stove the ribs inward and pierce the heart as easily as it could send the unfortunate recipient tipping out of his saddle to crack his spine under two hundredweight of armor.

Judges were positioned at intervals along the field to signal fair or foul play. Most of the matches were random and usually drawn to avoid pairing known antagonists together, but there were also the personal challenges, like the one between Dag and Roald of Anjou, that kept the excitement of the crowds at a peak and sent waves of delicately predispositioned maidens swooning *en masse* into the arms of their serving women.

Everywhere lances were held aloft, their pennons fluttering in the wind. Men-at-arms stood an attentive guard around the perimeter of the jousting field. They wore full protective armor of *cuir bouilli* and held their pikes and bills at rigid attention to discourage any curious pedestrians from wandering onto the courses. Multicolored silk pavilions had sprouted around the outside of the palisades overnight where knights dressed for combat and waited to hear their names called to the lists. Squires, pages, and servants hustled to and from these war pavilions laying out armor and weapons, inspecting all for the minutest flaws, expending copious amounts of spittle and oil in feverish attempts to have their lords gleaming brilliantly in the sunlight.

The best of the best, the champions of France and Normandy were well known to their loyal followers. Wagers changed hands as fast as fleas when the names of the upcoming ranks of contestants were announced by the heralds, none so fast or feverish as those placed on the outcome of a contest between the Prince of Darkness and anyone foolish enough to challenge him.

The object of so much speculation stood naked in all his muscular splendor, the light from the small iron brazier shivering over the solid plates of molded brawn. The strong, sloped column of his neck was held rigid, the eerie, colorless eyes stared straight ahead as Fulgrin finished the ceremonial bath and began rubbing him with oil of willow ash and camphor. In the background, they could hear the clash of steel and the roaring cheers of the crowd. Periodically, the ground beneath them reverberated with the impact of several tons' worth of enraged horseflesh charging headlong down the tilting course.

Fulgrin, noting his master was even more sullen than usual, peered up from behind the pillar of one limb and offered a scowl. "You could have earned us an extra five hundred marks by now had you roused yourself earlier."

"By day's end, we will have earned more than enough to satisfy even your greed."

"My greed? *I* was not the one who consented to this unholy pact. I was quite content to remain in Orléans, for that matter, dining on rich foods and stroking the thighs of soft women."

Griffyn glared down. "You could try stroking a little softer now. I would appreciate having *some* skin left when you have finished."

"Hah! Oversensitive today, are we? Out all night like a cat, saddle-galled and foul-tempered this morning . . . dare I ask who the lucky wench was—or did you even trouble yourself to learn her name?"

Griffyn twisted his lips in a prelude to answering but was forestalled by the sound of a woman's voice outside the pavilion. She did not wait for the knave to announce her; she lifted the flap of the door and stepped inside, her crystalline eyes going directly and unabashedly to one of the more formidable muscles on Griffyn's body.

"Am I interrupting?"

Griffyn did not trouble himself with a reply, nor did he make any attempt to shield himself from Solange de Sancerre's intimate scrutiny as she strolled forward and walked a full, slow circle around him, close enough the diaphanous veiling she wore over her hair brushed his shoulders and tickled the powerful display of rock-hard flesh across his chest. Her gown of rich red samite had been fitted snugly to the voluptuous shape of her upper body and showed considerably more of the smooth white shoulders than was customary. Wresting the eye away from the ripe fullness of her breasts was a thick gold torque worn around the slender throat, the band a full three fingers in width and studded with rows of glittering gemstones. Circling her slender waist was a girdle of fine gold links fashioned to resemble chain mail, crossed in front to form a deep, shimmering vee over her belly.

She finished her inspection and the startling green eyes lingered a moment on his face, before glancing at Fulgrin. "You may leave us, churl. I would speak a few moments alone with your master."

Fulgrin put his hands on his hips and would likely have challenged her business there had Griffyn not caught his eye and signaled him out the door.

"An impudent devil," she mused after he had gone. "I could teach him some manners, if you like."

Griffyn reached for his braies. "I thought it was agreed there would be no further contact between us."

"The agreement was between you and Bertrand," she murmured. "I would never be so hasty as to promise such a thing."

She watched him step into the undergarment and draw it up to his waist, but before he could pull the thongs closed in front, her hands interceded and did the fastening for him. "Moreover, I thought it only hospitable to let you know someone was cheering you on."

She laid her hands flat on the granite plane of his belly and skimmed them upward, her fingers spread wide to fully appreciate the mass of solidly sculpted muscle. "I had hoped to see you at the *grande fête* last night."

"I prefer not to dine in the company of men I might kill on the morrow."

"An understandable aversion, though I have never suffered for it myself." She pursed her lips and continued skimming her hands across the powerful contours of his shoulders and down his arms. "Still, it would have been the perfect opportunity to rouse Robert Wardieu's fighting ire. He was prickly as a thorn bush, especially after the younger brother had a gauntlet thrown in his face."

"I am surprised you did not arrange to have it thrown in his."

She smiled and let her fingers slide off his wrists and trace boldly onto his hips and around to the juncture of his thighs. "We thought to save that pleasure for you."

"How considerate."

Her smile widened and she gazed down. "Merde," she breathed, "but you are a healthy enough beast. I may have to wager some coin on you myself."

"Was there something *specific* you came to see me about? I have my first match in less than an hour."

"Actually ... or should I say *specifically* ... Bertrand is worried that you might be losing some of your concentration."

"My concentration is fine."

"Nevertheless"—she leaned forward, sending her tongue in a swirling wet circle around his nipple—"he thought you might require a little extra incentive."

"You?" he asked mildly.

She laughed and used her teeth to pinch the sensitive nub of flesh before she straightened. "What I would want to do with you, my lord, would take much more than an hour. No, he merely wanted me to show you this."

Still smiling, she watched his face intently as she unfastened the gold cords that bound the front closure of her tunic. The crimson samite fairly popped wide over the straining swell of her breasts, revealing a layer of embroidered silk beneath. The garment was obviously too small for the task at hand, and most of the ribbons were tied at the outside limits, leaving wide gaps of flesh showing beneath. But there was no mistaking whose it was or where he had seen it last.

The change in his expression was barely perceptible, but to someone accustomed to searching for the slightest betrayal of emotion, it brought forth an exaggerated sigh. "Not exactly my taste, what with all these wretched little ivy leaves and mawkish flowers, but the silk is of exceptional quality and I have no doubt the owner would be grateful for its return."

Griffyn's eyes met hers and turned as cold as hoarfrost. "You have been following me."

"Not personally, no. I find riverbanks too cold and damp for comfort. But I understand it was a demonstration of vigor worthy of an appreciative audience." She started to draw the silk cords tight over her bosom again. "Poor Gerome. He wore out three whores trying to ease his frustrations. He did so have his heart set on being the first to bed the Wardieu bitch. Tell me—" She looked up, her eyes sparkling with polite interest. "Was she a virgin still?"

Griffyn forced himself to unclench his fists. "I hardly noticed. It was a pleasant diversion, nothing more."

"Nothing?"

He reached for his shirt and sneered. "What were you expecting to hear? That we have pledged undying love and plan to marry within the week?"

"God's blood, I hope not. Gerome was vying for the privilege himself. An outlandish expectation, I agree," she added dryly. "But he feels cuckolded nonetheless."

"Tell him my shield is hung in plain sight. I would be more than happy to oblige his wounded pride in the lists."

"Gerome prefers to seek his revenge in dark corners."

Griffyn nodded. "I will heed the warning."

"Heed this as well: Bertrand does not like surprises. This"—she plucked at the chemise before it disappeared beneath the samite—"came as a complete and unpleasant surprise."

"Tell him . . . it was merely a way of insuring Wardieu's cooperation."

The green eyes narrowed. "His cooperation?"

"Can you think of a better way to rouse the fighting ire of a brother than to boast of covering the sister?"

She watched him warily as he thrust his arms into the sleeves of his shirt and pulled it over his head. "Are you saying . . . you deliberately seduced her?"

"I am saying I dislike leaving things to chance. Now, unless you truly would like me to lose concentration"—he paused and stared meaningfully at the voluptuous shape of her breasts—"I suggest you let me finish making my preparations."

He turned his back, dismissing her with a coolness that might have been convincing had she not seen that initial, fleeting glimpse of shock in his eyes. The chemise had startled him, angered him, and unsettled him, and as Solange smoothed her tunic and preened the wings of her veil, she started toward the door of the pavilion.

"It was indeed clever of you to provide such indelicate insurance," she agreed. "Gerome, I think, would feel somewhat appeased if he could recount his midnight adventure to the gathered throngs. It would, of course, be done only if all else failed. But it would be done," she assured him softly.

She smiled at the look he cast back over his shoulder, then lifted aside the flap of the door and walked out into the sunlight.

Fulgrin caused it to be shoved aside again a moment later as he hastened back inside. "Tell me she was the one who kept you out all night and I shall start hunting now for a new master."

"I would not willingly spend time with her unless I emptied her fangs of poison first," Griffyn muttered, still staring at the door of the pavilion.

Fulgrin peered at him closely. "I gather she was not here just to wish you luck?"

"She was here . . . to make certain I was not suffering from a change of heart."

An eyebrow lifted cautiously. "She is under the impression you have a heart to change?"

Griffyn only glared and thrust his legs into a pair of woolen hose. "Did you manage to find out anything about the Welshman?"

"Ahh. A timely change of subject, as always." He started to fasten the forty-odd leather points that held Griffyn's hose snug to his thighs. "You did not give me much of a description: no nose, no ears, no fingers, no toes . . . but the braids helped. That and the fact some of Wardieu's men have been discreetly asking after the whereabouts of a wool merchant named Dafydd ap Iowerth."

"A wool merchant?"

Fulgrin stood and helped Griffyn into the heavily padded aketon, tightening the crampons that ran down beneath the arms. "It seems he was once a guest at Château d'Amboise. A welcomed guest, so I gather, for he married one of the local widows and lived in the village until such time as his wife's death sent him searching for some useful—albeit reckless—way to overcome his grief."

"Are you saying he was a spy for the Black Wolf?"

He prodded a thigh forward into a pair of leather leggings. "Likely used to carry messages back and forth to England."

"Messages? Between Amboise and . . . ?"

Fulgrin straightened and lowered his voice dramatically. "Pembroke."

Griffyn's frown caused a deep furrow across his brow. It was the second time in as many days Randwulf de la Seyne Sur Mer's name had been linked to William Marshal.

"As for Bertrand Malagane's interest in land in Lincoln, it appears to be genuine . . . unless there is some other reason you can conceive of why he would send Gerome de Saintonge to England."

"Saintonge is going to England? When?"

"As soon as the last pennon flutters down over the field on the morrow. What is more, he has hand-picked his troop from the most bloodthirsty vultures his barracks have to offer, including Engelard Cigogni and Andrew de Chanceas—two of the worst carrion-feeding jackals ever to put their swords up for hire. This, of course"—he paused for effect and snapped the last buckle into place—"after they have slit *your* fine throat ear to ear."

Griffyn looked at him askance.

"Truly. 'Tis likely why the count was so generous with his coin; he had no plans to leave you alive long enough to spend it. And before you scoff at the notion, kindly consider it was at great peril to the sanctity of my own throat that I uncovered this information."

Griffyn had no intentions of scoffing; Fulgrin's talents for gleaning knowledge from solid rock had ceased to amaze him long ago. It had also kept him alive more times than he could count.

That Bertrand Malagane had already made plans for his demise came as no huge surprise; he was probably intending to show that he was so appalled and outraged by Robert

Wardieu's death, he had arranged to have the champion's killer slain in retaliation. Moreover, he had probably also arranged to have it "discovered" that he, Griffyn Renaud de Verdelay, had been paid to kill Wardieu . . . and in good English sterling.

"Shall I have the rouncies packed and ready for a hasty departure when you come off the field today?"

Lost in thought, it took a moment for Griffyn to focus on Fulgrin's face. "What?"

"Leave? Rouncies? Tonight?"

"Why would we do that?"

"Oh . . . to keep the blood flowing through our veins, perhaps?"

Griffyn frowned and signaled for his hauberk. "I am not worried about Cigogni or de Chanceas."

Fulgrin's grunt was directed partly at the cavalier dismissal of the two most deadly and dangerous assassins in Normandy, and partly at the weight of the chain mail tunic as he strained to heft it over his master's shoulders.

"I am glad to hear you are not worried," he muttered, and returned to the chest for the mail chausses, which he laced around his charge's thighs and calves with less than his usually precise strokes. "I, of course, will sleep with both eyes open and knives clutched between all my fingers and toes, but I am glad to hear it will trouble you not at all."

"Certes, it will not trouble me tonight . . . since it would make no sense to kill either of us until *after* Wardieu is dead."

Fulgrin's squint-eye watered slightly as he glared in fulminating silence at the tall knight. He helped him into his cuirass—a vest of inch-thick bullhide boiled in wax and molded to fit the shape of chest and back—then bracers for the upper and lower arms, greaves and sabatons to fit over the legs and boots, rounded aillettes for the shoulders that would deflect the force of all but the most powerful blows.

His face was pouring sweat by the time he handed up the padded bascinet for the head and the mail hood with its descending gorget of pennyplate, the links strong enough to shield the throat but flexible enough to raise or lower as required. The final layer was the gambeson—the surcoat of rich hunting green silk emblazoned with the gold falcon in full wingspread.

"And when he is dead," he finally demanded. "What then? Do we wait for them to come to us?

"Either that, or we go to them." Griffyn held his arms out while Fulgrin strapped his swordbelt around his waist and fetched the great serpentine weapon from the chest. He ran his fingers lightly along the warning etched on the surface before he sheathed it, then, with a final adjustment to settle his gear, strode out of the pavilion and into the bright sunlight.

At almost the same instant, Brenna was blinking the sunlight out of her eyes as she crossed the common and approached the entrance to the bowers. Robin was on one side, Richard and Geoffrey LaFer on the other. Will and Sparrow were with Dag, helping him prepare for his match with Anjou; they would join them in the royal dais in short order, hopefully in time to see Dagobert's ceremonial progress around the field.

Brenna had felt clumsy and all thumbs as she had dressed for the spectacle. She was thankful she had not brought Helvise with her, for the maid's sharp eyes would surely have seen the tender pink patches of skin everywhere on her body—conspicuous reminders of rough beard stubble and greedy lips. As it was, her bliaud was altogether too form-fitting and silky over flesh that was too tender to want constant reminders of the equally silky, tender hands that had stroked over her body all night long. Her overtunic was a rich, rusty gold velvet that molded her breasts and emphasized the trimness of her waist, and while she knew the gown was flattering, she would have preferred a plain holland tunic that would not have drawn quite so much attention to her sex.

Convention required her to cover her hair, and at least

the plain white wimple and veil looked innocuous enough, held in place by the thin circlet of unadorned gold. The day was warm and brilliant under a clear blue sky, but her flesh felt unaccountably chilled and her hands clammy as she waited, first with Richard, then with Geoffrey LaFer, as Dag dressed for his match. Under normal circumstances, she supposed she would have been just as excited and full of merriment, just as eager to watch the opening procession of drummers, trumpeters, lords and knights and ladies. She would have been honored to sit in the same bower as Prince Louis and flattered that their host, Bertrand Malagane, kissed her hand and complimented her on her fair countenance. She would have gasped in awe with the rest of the crowd to see the burly champions arriving at their pavilions, surrounded by squires and handlers sagging under the weight of weapons and armor. She would have shivered deliciously to hear the names of the most ferocious contestants who had come together to compete in the pageantry of the Enterprise of the Dragon's Mouth; names like Mauger the Murderer, Eustace the Widow-Maker, Ferrau the Pitiless, Blondel the Damned, as well as the legendary assassin Loupescaire (whose legend had lost some of its luster when a forewarned victim had arranged to have both his feet chopped off).

Into this company had also come the fearsome Prince of Darkness, the self-proclaimed Devil Incarnate, and while Robin was showing remarkable restraint thus far, there was a tautness around his mouth that suggested Sparrow might have to keep his knife unsheathed. He was amiable enough to the Dauphin and answered questions on tactics and strategies with a patient enough demeanor, but there was the underlying impression that he wanted desperately to be on the field, not watching from a wooden bench.

This business with Dag and Roald of Anjou proved none of them was really safe from the recklessness of his own honor.

Tossed into this cauldron of simmering tension was now the specter of Griffyn Renaud. As Will had pointed out, he had not come all this way to sit and watch the pageantry; he had come to fight, to prove his mettle, possibly to try to win the prize of six hundred marks. Before last night, of course, she would not have cared if he threw himself against Lucifer and all the demons of hell. Before last night she could not have cared less who he fought or what the outcome. Now, however, she found herself chilling at the thought he might well end up broken and bleeding under the hooves of some paladin's charger. On the way to their seats in the bower, she had found herself looking anxiously at each pavilion they passed—she did not even know his colors, for pity's sake—hoping to see, hoping *not* to see his broad shoulders clad in mail, waiting for his call to arms.

It was also the custom for a knight to beg the favor of carrying a lady's token—a sleeve or scarf—into the lists and to fight in her honor. This was usually done during the ceremonial progress around the field when the knight stopped and dipped his lance before the lady whose affection he sought. If she accepted, she fastened the token to the weapon and promptly melted, beyond capability of speech and breath, into the waiting arms of envious companions. Brenna did not even want to think what would happen, how she would respond, what Robin or the others would do if Griffyn Renaud chose to single her out in this fashion. She would indeed melt—into a nerveless, senseless puddle on the floorboards where she would remain, fixed by shame and guilt in utter disgrace.

She groaned softly to herself and tried valiantly to concentrate on the jousting.

Dag was to meet his opponent in the west half of the enclosure. The field had been divided in two by a barrier decorated with cloth hangings, and each of these in turn had a low, single-hung wooden tilt to define the course and insure the riders remained in their own lane. Bowers for the spectators flanked the field, blazing with colors and waving pennons. At either end of the huge rectangle were *recets*, designated areas of refuge where knights could catch their breath between runs and rearm. Many more pennons flew there, for lances were leaned upright against the palisades, some painted in the colors of their lords, some banded, some spotted, all hung with a flag bearing the arms of the champion.

The jousts themselves were staggered so as not to detract one from the other, also to provide continuous entertainment and thrills while the one list was being cleared of debris. Each time two challengers took to the field, they rode a ceremonial progress around the outer ring of the entire field to salute the judges and give homage to the Dauphin. Brenna peered anxiously at each contestant as he entered the enclosure and began his progress, but in full armor, with pot-shaped helms obscuring all but a narrow strip of their faces, they were mostly anonymous, identifiable only by the devices emblazoned on their gambeson and shield. There was a herald reading names at the outset of each match, and Brenna listened closely each time he stood and consulted his scroll of parchment, but did not hear the name she sought in the first three contests, and then it was Dag's turn and she temporarily traded one set of fears for another.

"Can you see him?" she asked, craning her neck to see around Richard's broad shoulders.

"There." He pointed to the entrance of the enclosure. "By God, he makes a fine cut of a fellow, I must admit, no thanks to my tutoring."

Sparrow, his attention divided ungraciously among the other burly men-at-arms whose duty it was to stand guard over their masters, heard the comment and leaned forward to glare.

"*Your* tutoring, you great heaving peewit? *Your* tutoring has thrust him into this peril despite all common good sense. *Your* tutoring may earn him a dented head and cracked bones."

His lecture was cut short as Robin hissed him into silence. They were seated two rows back from the Dauphin and the Count of Saintonge, and at the sound of Sparrow's voice, Malagane's silver head turned and he glanced back.

"Lord Robert! You must be proud of your younger brother. He does indeed cut a fine figure. We can only hope it will be as fine at the end of the joust," Malagane added, inviting the Dauphin to share a good-natured laugh, "since he is the only one representing the black-and-gold this day."

Robin and Richard both stiffened and Brenna put a hand on each arm. She felt like a fawn caught between two lions, although she was not entirely unsympathetic to their plight. The Dauphin was narrow-nosed and spent a good deal of time looking down it, while Bertrand Malagane resembled a cobra she had seen once at a fair: sleek and smooth and quick to strike with a venomous tongue. Seated on his right was Solange de Sancerre, and behind was his son, Gerome de Saintonge, whose head swiveled to note the slightest move Brenna made. She caught him staring openly and outright at least a score of times, always with a leering, lopsided grin that made her feel as if she were naked from throat to waist.

Brenna forced herself to ignore them all as Dag approached the dais. He did make a splendid sight. He rode a gleaming black destrier fully caparisoned in an ebony silk saddle cloth trimmed in gold bands and tinsel, the sawtoothed hem falling almost to the beast's knees. The warhorse was a knight's most valuable weapon in battle, and beneath all the rich finery they carried nearly as much body armor as the rider. A *croupiere* molded of cuir bouilli fit the shape of the hindquarters and a fan-shaped *poitrail* guarded the breast and shoulders from a misplaced—or deliberate—strike from a lance. The noble head was covered in a leather *chanfrein* that exposed only the eyes and kept the animal focused straight forward.

Dag's own helm was flat-topped, painted in black with gilding along the seams and joints. It consisted of metal plates bolted and screwed together to surround the head and neck, offering limited visibility through a hinged visor that could be lifted when on parade, or was lowered to signal readiness at the start of a charge. His visor was up now as he rode around the enclosure and caused his beast to dance a caracole in front of the royal dais. Prince Louis nodded to acknowledge the salute, as did Bertrand Malagane, and Dag cantered on toward the Bower of Beauty where a dozen or more hopefuls leaned forward in their seats and drew a collective breath.

The same dozen melted back in obvious disappointment as the youngest—and some may have thought the handsomest—Wardieu rode past, not stopping until he reached the far end of the enclosure, where Timkin was waiting with his shield and lance. Roald of Anjou, meanwhile, had also completed his progress and was waiting, like a large mound of crimson dough, for a cinch to be tightened on his saddle.

In short time, the two challengers signaled the judges they were ready. Visors were dropped and gauntlets adjusted to insure a firm grip on the hilt of the lance. Squires handed up shields and reins were gathered tight. There was a flourish of trumpets as the marshal raised the small linen *couvre-chef* and glanced one last time at each champion before dropping it.

Dag's charger was first off the mark, its powerful hooves carving up the soft turf, raising great clods of dirt and hurling it back as he quickly built to full speed. From the opposite end of the list, Roald of Anjou bolted forward, the point of his lance stretched out across his steed's neck, his massive bulk leaning into the wind to seek the perfect balance.

It was a sight to inspire awe in every breast, regardless of the combatants, for horse and rider moved as one, straining forward with silks and tassels flowing, lances aimed straight and true, bodies moving to the rhythm of power and fury and steel-edged nerve. The ranks shuddered on both sides of the field as the two mighty beasts converged. The tips of the lances passed, the shafts seemed a moment to stream together as one, then the clash, the screech of metal on metal, the flying sparks and screams of the horses as the impact staggered both and sent them rearing up on hind legs.

Dag had missed his mark and, as the two horses churned apart, Brenna could hear Richard bemoaning a lost opportunity and Sparrow cursing all fools to perdition.

The two challengers rode to the end of the tilt and wheeled their horses around, waiting until each was set before they launched themselves down the course again, black-and-gold rushing at breakneck speed toward the streaking blur of vermilion. It was a matter of seconds only until they met at the halfway mark, and this time Dag's lance struck squarely on Roald's left shoulder, wrenching him back with such force the stem of the lance split and shattered. Despite the heightened and reinforced *troussequin* on his saddle, the bulbous lord from Anjou found himself reeling sideways off the leather. His horse spun, further upsetting his balance, and the weight of his upper body armor did the rest, dragging him out of the saddle, spilling him on the ground in a cloud of dust and thrashing hooves. There he stayed, his arms and legs flailing like an overturned bug, and there he remained until the attendants raced out and helped hoist him to his feet.

There was laughter in the crowds and much snapping of fingers as Dag's charger pranced back to his end of the enclosure. It was a clean win and almost anticlimactic to see all the flags in the judges' hands go up to confirm the victory. Roald, in a fury over the humiliation, struck one of the attendants across the face and pushed another to the ground in his haste to clear the field.

"I never doubted it for a moment." Richard chuckled.

"I should have tried for five hundred!" Geoffrey laughed in agreement.

Brenna turned to respond but was caught by the sudden deep hush that had fallen over the crowd. It was so quiet, where there should have been applause and cheering, she could hear the rustle of the silk pennons stirring overhead in the breeze. Searching for the cause, she had only to look at the sea of faces around her and to follow their rapt gazes to where the second of two new contestants were entering the enclosure.

No one needed to ask who he was. Both the dark knight and his destrier were clad in green silks and black leathers, with shield, pennons, and gambeson blazoned with the gold falcon identifying him as the Prince of Darkness.

"So," Robin murmured. "We see the devil in the flesh at last."

"A great hulking bustard," Sparrow agreed in solemn tones.

Unlike Roald of Anjou, whose weight was centered around his girth, the dark knight's power was concentrated across his shoulders and chest, the latter aggrandized further by the bulk of armor and the fearsome gold falcon in full wingspread. He sat straight and tall in the saddle, looking neither to the left nor the right as he took to the field.

"Now," announced Bertrand Malagane in a voice loud enough for those in the back row of seats to overhear, "we shall begin to see some true fighting skills. You have heard, of course, that he has chosen not to restrict himself to three challenges, but has offered his shield to all comers? It should make for an interesting afternoon."

"Interesting and bloody," Richard muttered out of the side of his mouth.

"Who is he fighting first?" Robin asked, straining forward to see around an offending banner that temporarily blocked his view.

"Savaric de Mauleon," Geoffrey LaFer provided from his slightly higher vantage point in the row behind.

Robin nodded approvingly. He liked Savaric, had spent a good portion of the previous evening in the company of the spirited young champion from Gascon, and was generous with his praise for the other man's considerable talents. "He is not afraid to meet a lance head-on and straps himself into his saddle to insure he does not leave it any too soon."

"He might want to reconsider the buckles this time," Richard said quietly. "Have you seen the other's lance?"

A similar awestruck observation was already beginning

to ripple through the ranks of spectators, for the weapon was not blunted by the conventional coronal. Instead, the metal cap tapered to a single point, the only concession to civility being that the tip was squared.

"He is not come to play at games," Sparrow remarked.

Robin's face had hardened into a mask and he said nothing, but the more practical eye of Geoffrey LaFer noted other ominous refinements in the paladin's armor. "His mail, if mine eyes do not deceive me, is double-linked! And the helm is most unusual—I do not think I have seen its like before."

"Nor have I," remarked the Count of Saintonge, proving his hearing was excellent despite the surrounding buzz of conversations. "But I understand it is a style gaining favor in Germany and Flanders, for the plates are almost completely smooth, and the rounded top offers no seams or ornamentation to catch the point of a lance. What do you think of it, Lord Robert?"

"It looks practical," Robin admitted, his teeth clipping every word.

All eyes in the crowd were on the Prince of Darkness as he rode to the royal dais and tipped his lance in a salute to his host and Prince Louis. Up close, he made an even more formidable impression, for the visor had but one slit running left to right, and because he had already hooked it in place, there was only a slash of darkness where his eyes should be. The double linking of his armor made his arms look as if they were encased in solid sheets of steel, heavy enough to daunt all but the strongest of men, thick enough to deflect all but the mightiest of blows.

He seemed to wait until he was certain everyone in the bower had satisfied their curiosity, then turned and rode directly back to his *recet*, forgoing the customary progress around the rest of the field. It was a blatant discourtesy to the rest of the gathering, who began to hoot and hiss and shout their disapproval. By contrast, Savaric de Mauleon, who was good-looking and dashing and everyone's favorite, won rousing applause and cheers of enthusiasm from each bench as he circled the entire field. Nearly every maiden in the Bower of Beauty offered tokens without waiting to be asked, and by the time he had completed his progress, his lance fluttered with every color of the rainbow.

The two knights took their positions. The crowd stilled and waited for the judges, who were still debating furiously among themselves over the legality of the square-tipped lance. The marshal hastened over to the dais and expressed his concerns to the Count of Saintonge, who in turn gave his ruling that the lance was acceptable, but if Savaric de Mauleon chose to decline to fight, it would be perfectly understandable.

The crowd jeered again at the implied slur against their favorite's courage, and whether he would have liked to embrace the offer or not, honor forced Savaric to refuse it. The marshal returned to his seat and raised the *couvre-chef* . . . and without further adieu, dropped it.

The two destriers broke evenly from the line, but the Prince of Darkness's steed was obviously superior in speed and sheer thundering fury. He ran with his head forward and his silks streaming, so swift to gain full gallop, he carried the contest into Savaric's half of the course and was on him before the knight had his lance fully raised and steadied. The squared tip of the paladin's lance slammed directly into the flat of Savaric's shield and jerked him back with such force, the raised backing of his saddle snapped and sent buckles flying off in all directions. Savaric himself was lifted into the air and seemed to hang there, suspended at the end of his opponent's lance for several rampaging paces, finally falling in such a crump of dust and cracking metal, the crowd continued to hold its breath, to sit in stunned silence as if they could not believe their eyes.

"He made it look as if he was plucking a fly off a piece of meat," Richard murmured.

"A dead fly," Sparrow agreed. "Deader now than before, I warrant."

Robin was on his feet. Savaric had not yet moved so much as an arm or leg. The attendants ran out bearing a litter between them, and some of the gawping tension in the crowd was transferred to the almost casual manner in which the Prince of Darkness cantered to the end of the course and turned into the *recet* without looking back, as if he needed no judges or cheers to confirm the results.

It was a win. It was also the first serious injury of the tournament.

Robin's gaze remained fixed on the dark knight and the frown tightened across his brow as Malagane lifted his wine cup in a salute.

"Have you ever seen so straight a lance, so determined a course? God's blood, I dare swear we could declare him champion now and save a deal of broken bones and barber's fees."

The proclamation won a laugh from the Dauphin and several of the other guests.

"Who does he fight next?" Solange inquired, feigning a yawn.

"The Castilian, Pedro the Cruel," another provided helpfully.

"Unless, of course, he has *injured* himself since his boastings last night," said a familiar voice.

Robin's gaze was pulled away from the field and settled on the grinning face of Gerome de Saintonge. Sparrow, sensing trouble in the air, moved closer to Robin and curled his hand around the hilt of his eating knife.

"Sit you down," he hissed. "The man is offal. Dung. Wormrot. He is a frog turd, not worthy of being scraped from your boot!"

There was a call for fresh wine to fill the Dauphin's cup, and Sparrow took advantage of the distraction to tug openly on Robin's tunic and literally haul him back down onto his seat.

On the field, meanwhile, another pair of combatants were beginning their progress, neither of them drawing more than a polite spattering of applause from the spectators. The entire crowd seemed poised on the edge of their seats, waiting in breathless anticipation for another chance

to see the Prince of Darkness in action. He had not left the
enclosure after his match, which signified another upcoming in short order. His squire was with him and a handler
for the horse, but overall he looked confident, almost a
little bored as he watched the pageantry.

Brenna could not have said who the challengers were,
what colors they wore, how many passes they made or who
emerged the victor. She shared Sparrow's uneasiness, especially when she looked around at one point and saw that
Will had joined them on the dais, but instead of taking the
empty seat she indicated, he shook his head and remained
at the rear, staring hard at two men who were lounging
against the barricades. Their faces were not familiar to
Brenna, but they obviously were to Will, for he stood as
tense as a bloodhound, his hand resting on the hilt of his
sword.

The crowd broke her concentration again as a general
stir and swelling of noise indicated the interim match was
over and the Castilian was entering the tilting grounds.
His horse was caparisoned in gold and blue, a magnificent
roan with thickly feathered fetlocks and a high, proud step.
His armor was gilded and ornamented in the Spanish style,
complete with a tall, sky-blue cluster of ostrich plumes in
his helm. He had dark, intense eyes that glowered boldly
through the raised window of his visor as he passed the dais,
and when he stopped in front of the Bower of Beauty, he
dipped his lance like an accusing finger toward his be-
trothed, a petite, ashen-faced girl of no more than fourteen
years who could only stare in terror at the dark knight
waiting at the far end of the field. She tried to tie a length
of purple scarf to the end of her lover's lance, but her hand
shook so badly, the silk slipped and drifted to the ground.

The crowd gasped and groaned, for it was a bad omen.
The girl fainted into a crush of sympathetic arms, and it was
just as well she remained unconscious during the next ten
minutes, for her affianced fared no better than Savaric de
Mauleon. The Prince of Darkness struck him hard and high
on the first pass, the tip of his lance catching the Castilian

at the base of his helm, shattering his collarbone and nearly ripping his head from his shoulders.

A third challenger managed to remain astride for two passes, but only because his destrier veered at the last minute—which earned resounding jeers from the spectators and a subtle shift of favor toward the champion from the east. The shift became stronger with the next blare of trumpets, for Draco the Hun was well known for his underhanded tricks and fouls, and was rarely anyone's favorite. He gave the Prince his best challenge thus far, stretching the joust into three passes, but even then, there was a sense that he was only being toyed with, like a mouse being tossed around by a cat to prolong the pleasure and the play. And in the end, he went the way of the others, carried off the field on a litter dripping blood. By the time it was Ivo the Crippler's turn to enter the tilt, the crowd was on its feet, stamping and cheering for their awesome new champion.

By this time also Robin was tight-lipped and white with frustration. Richard was in little better condition, and Dag, who had joined them in the dais after stripping out of his armor, merely sat shaking his head each time the judges ignored an obvious foul. Many more flagons of wine had been consumed in the royal bower and the snickers were growing louder, the glances bolder, the questions more brazen as the Wardieus were consulted on the methods they might have used to unseat the usurper—had they been disposed to fight him, that is.

For this, his sixth and final joust of the afternoon, the Prince of Darkness acquiesced to the demands of the screaming spectators and took a full progress around the enclosure, his silks rippling like green fire under the late sun, the gold threads of the falcon almost blinding where it flew on his breast and shield.

He had changed horses after his last bout, and it was not until he had rounded the far end of the palisades and started down toward the royal dais that Brenna found herself staring more at the beast than the man. The main body of the destrier was concealed beneath the cloths and armored paddings, but it could be seen that this charger, like his last, had been gray in color—not uncommon in itself. But what drew her attention now, and what shocked her like a bucket of ice-cold water thrown on a hot day, was the sight of the single snow-white cuff banding the left foreleg.

Desperate to be mistaken, frantic to be somehow faulty in her memory, she looked up at the knight's visored face as he drew abreast. The steel of the helm creaked softly as he turned to face the honored guests. He eased back on the reins and slowed his destrier to a prancing halt, and while every eye in the bowers watched and every breath was held in anticipation, he raised a gauntleted hand and lifted the slotted visor enough to reveal the two black slashes of his eyebrows and the luminous, ice-washed eyes below.

"God's day to you, my lords . . . ladies," Griffyn said casually. "I trust you are all enjoying the spectacle thus far."

21

Robin was plainly stunned.

Brenna would swear later that her heart simply stopped, for she felt nothing. She felt nothing, saw nothing, thought of nothing in those first few shocking moments other than there must be some horrible mistake. It could not be Griffyn Renaud. It could not be him staring out from beneath the visored helm of the Prince of Darkness.

Her lungs finally insisted on air, though she was unaware of having deprived them. It went to her head in a dizzying rush and she felt as if everything were suddenly submerged in a clear liquid. The sounds from the crowd were muted and dull; the fluttering of the pennons around the enclosure slowed to precise, articulated waves. And Griffyn's voice, when it next came through the barrier of the helm, sounded deep and heavy, garbled by that same liquid distortion.

"You comported yourself well," he was saying to Dag. "Pray accept my compliments."

None of the Wardieu brothers was yet capable of civil speech, but Sparrow suffered no such impairment.

"I knew it! I knew there was something of the sly fox in you the moment mine eyes clapped upon you!"

"Christ Jesus," Richard managed, both awed and angered. "You might have said something."

The pale eyes flicked from one tense face to the next, lingering on Brenna's a moment before returning to Robin. "As I recall, I did. I said at Amboise it would make for an interesting rematch. Instead"—he looked toward the *recet* where Ivo the Crippler was concluding his progress—"I must content myself with green striplings and larded collops who throw themselves at my lance for the sheer sake of saying they have done so."

"An easy day's work for you, I should think," Robin said through his teeth. "You have broken enough bones to earn your six hundred marks."

Metal creaked again. "Did my ears hear it wrong when you said the only true pleasure in life comes when you test your mettle in honorable combat with one of equal strength and merit? Is it only a pleasure for you, then, and simple greed for the rest of us?"

Robin flushed. "None of these men is your equal."

"None . . . with the possible exception of yourself," Griffyn countered smoothly. "And how unfortunate that you were *injured,* for we shall never know who would have prevailed."

Sparrow surged forward, stopped from leaping over the barrier by a rail that guarded against such rashness. "Injured or not he could skewer you like a pullet! With one arm strapped to his side he could have you hanging off his lance like gulled tripe! He could have you fileted and fustioned and smiling out the back of your neck for want of a spine!"

The pale eyes narrowed but it was Bertrand Malagane who turned and addressed the remark. "Bold words, dwarf. Do you issue this challenge on your own behalf, or do you speak for Lord Robert?"

Sparrow's mouth opened, closed, opened again in a good imitation of a fish as he realized what he had said and the horror of it caused every droplet of elfin blood to drain out of his face. It was Richard, whose temper had been held in check by the slenderest of threads anyway, who came to his rescue, exploding to his feet with a curse.

"You may consider it came from me, my lord, to be answered at your earliest convenience."

"Not before he answers me," said Dag, leaping up beside his brother.

"And me," insisted Geoffrey LaFer, standing alongside.

"God's good grace," observed a startled Prince Louis as he

swiveled around in his chair. "A veritable floodtide of avengers, and at such a late hour."

"Indeed," said Malagane, the satisfaction gleaming in his eyes. "A pity we are losing the afternoon light."

"Tomorrow will be soon enough," Richard spat. "If the bastard accepts."

"No!" Brenna cried, jumping up. "For God's sake, no!" She looked at Griffyn, appealing to him with eyes like two pools of drowning violets. "You know full well it would not be a fair contest. How can you be so cold-blooded? How can you willingly take advantage after . . . after everything that has happened?"

"Has something happened we do not know about?" Solange inquired innocently.

The pale eyes were briefly distracted by the movement of Solange de Sancerre's hand as she toyed with the end of a ribbon peeping over the edge of her bodice, but they were hard as ice as they returned to answer Brenna's charge. "It was not I who offered the first insult, my lady, nor issued the first challenge. But I would be willing to entertain an apology if your brothers would care to withdraw . . . ?"

"As well they should," the Dauphin observed over a wine-sodden laugh. "For who will fight the battle royale on the morrow if all of Amboise's armor lies trampled in the dust?"

Richard reached a hand to his sword. He was almost beyond reason now and killing royalty scarcely warranted a thought. Only Robin's fingers closing around his wrist prevented him from drawing.

"We can settle both matters at the same time, if it is acceptable to all. Sir Hugh—" Robin's steely gray eyes sought out the brusque-faced baron from Luisignan. "The dispute we have arranged to settle on the morrow . . . would it not be served as well through a single-combat match?"

Hugh the Brown, as he was known, glowered from Robin's face to Louis's, for an insult against the Amboise honor was like an insult to chivalry itself.

"Honor would be well served," he agreed gruffly.

"Though I would be reluctant to claim such a *champion* for our side"—he glared at Griffyn—"and will not warranty his horse or armor should he lose."

Renaud's only reaction to the snub was a slight twist to the mouth. "Am I at least to have the privilege of knowing which of the Amboise challengers I will be meeting on the morrow?"

The surrounding crowd, unable to hear the exchange but fully aware something of vast importance was taking place, had grown still enough to resemble figures painted on wooden boards. And silent enough for Brenna to hear the roaring of blood in her veins as Robin turned his face into the westering sun and let the last slanted rays reflect the fire in his eyes.

"You may meet as many of them as you like," he said evenly, "if you are still in your saddle after I have finished with you."

"No!" Brenna gasped softly. "Robin, no—"

It took almost a full thirty seconds for the buzz of whispers to spread outward from the royal bower and ripple its way around the entire enclosure. The spectators continued to watch in shock as Griffyn tipped his head slightly and touched a mailed forefinger to his helm in a mocking salute before he lowered his visor again and spurred Centurion toward his *recet*.

Brenna could scarcely believe what she had seen and heard. Sparrow was still red-faced and squirming. Richard and Geoffrey were arguing with Robin, who in turn ignored them and focused all his attention on Griffyn Renaud as he prepared himself to face Ivo. If anything, he looked more at ease than he had since they had departed Amboise.

"You cannot go through with it," Brenna whispered, touching his arm.

He covered her hand with his and squeezed it reassuringly as the challengers set themselves in the lists. Where Ivo fidgeted with shield, reins, and the grip of his lance, Griffyn sat his mount easily, man and horse seemingly carved from stone. He held his lance hooked in the crook of his arm with the point touching the earth so as to save strength while he waited for the heralds to blast their lily-mouthed trumpets and the judge to lift the *couvre-chef*.

"You cannot do this," Brenna whispered again, her voice raw with emotion.

"It is done already," Robin said, narrowing his eyes against the russet glare of the sun.

Brenna swallowed hard but still felt physically ill; the acid taste of bile rose at the back of her throat, thickened by the smell of leather and iron, sweat and sticky-sweet ambergris.

The crowd quieted. At the far end of the enclosure, Griffyn Renaud raised the point of his lance and, as the square of white linen fell from the marshal's hand, dug in his spurs.

It took four men to carry the litter from the field, and the cruel jest followed that he would no longer be known as Ivo the Crippler, but Ivo the Crippled.

Griffyn had won the day, as was expected, finishing with hardly more than a few scrapes and bruises to show for the effort. His arms ached dully from the strain of balancing the weight of the lance, but it was a familiar ache and would be gone by morning. His spine let him know it had supported the equivalent of a well-fed man on his shoulders for most of the long afternoon, and each bony knuckle cracked thankfully as he stripped to bare flesh and bathed in a steaming hot tub. Fulgrin's knowing fingers massaged every joint, muscle, and tendon with a vigor that nearly brought tears to his eyes, but when he was finished, Griffyn could stand and walk and bend without once tightening his jaw in discomfort.

He dressed again in his plain hose and green surcoat, and because few had actually had a close look at his face, he was able to slip unobtrusively away from the area of the jousting fields and mingle with the common crowds. The day's activities ended with the dusk and there was already a mass

migration back up to the château where there would be a
second raucous night of feasting, drinking, and celebrating.
Griffyn had declined all three of Malagane's invitations to
attend, even though the last had come from Prince Louis
and had been phrased as more of a demand than a request.
Even Fulgrin, who was used to his temper and broody
nature, removed himself from Griffyn's presence with all
haste, declaring that he preferred the company of the
horses.

The reason for his coming to Gaillard, the reason for his
entering the tournament in the first place was to fight
Robert Wardieu, yet now that the match was set, he was
angry at himself for provoking it. He should have heeded
Fulgrin's warnings back in Orleans and come straight to
Gaillard. He should never have veered off the main road,
never have catered to his own vanity and arrogance by venturing inside the walls of Amboise. Sheer witless self-
conceit had prompted him to go, like a fox amongst the
chickens, to see his enemy up close. Complete unbridled
stupidity had governed his actions thereafter, for he had
enjoyed the evening of drinking and gaming with the
brothers, he had enjoyed exchanging war stories with
Robin Wardieu.

And Brenna . . .

She undoubtedly loathed him now with all her heart and
soul, and he could not blame her. It was probably just as
well, for he was not all that sure what effect it would have
on him if he ever came face to face with her again. If she
ever looked at him or touched him or spoke to him with the
smallest measure of the emotion that had quivered in her
voice last night.

Griffyn's steps slowed as he approached his campsite. A
fire was blazing outside his tent, the cooler currents of air
carrying glowing bits of ash up into the night sky. There
was another light inside, and as he lifted the flap, it was the
first thing he saw: the stout iron lamp on a low table, its
cake of beeswax beset by flying moths. The second thing he
saw was the enormous platter of cheese, meat, and bread,

evidence his squire had not completely abandoned him to
his own wiles. Griffyn crossed the tent and stood in the
bright halo of light; he cut off a chunk of yellow cheese and
had just put it in his mouth when the cool prickle of an
inner alarm feathered across the nape of his neck.

He turned only his head and searched the darkest
shadows beside the doorway. She was standing there, still as
stone, much like the first time he had seen her, with the
light etching the clean, dangerous lines of her bow, glinting
off the steel arrowhead aimed between his eyes.

He crushed the cheese between his teeth and swallowed
it in a solid lump. It stuck in his throat and he pointed
to the flagon of wine to ease his efforts to cough it free.
"May I?"

Only the tip of the arrow moved, jerking once.

He poured out a cup full and gulped it to clear his throat.
It was strong and sweet, and somewhere in the back of his
mind, where all inane things were recorded, he noted it was
the fine, clove-spiced claret from Auvergne that Fulgrin
managed to lay hands on no matter where they roamed.

"Will you have a cup?"

She increased the tension on the bowstring. "I would
prefer to kill you first and celebrate after."

He nodded consideringly. "A more orderly progression of
events, I suppose. But no questions first?"

"Only one. Did you enjoy humiliating us today?"

His hand tightened on the cup briefly before he set it
down. "It was never my intention to humiliate you or to
hurt you in any way."

"We have already established you are an excellent liar,
sirrah," she hissed. "Do not try my patience by trying to pretend you are human as well."

Griffyn's gaze flicked down to the gleaming length of the
bow. Where it had been held rock steady up to then, there
was now a slight tremor to warn of the depth of her anger.

"All right. I confess, I gave it no thought in the
beginning."

"And now?"

"Now," he said honestly, "I have thought of nothing else all day."

"Surely you have," she insisted. "You have been thinking and plotting to find a way to goad my brother into meeting you in the lists."

"*He* challenged *me*," he reminded her, though the rebuttal sounded lame, even to his ears.

"You drove him to it. You left him no choice. It was deliberate and intentional, and I warrant if he had not taken offense at any of the insults you did throw at him, you would have used me to guarantee his participation. Admit that much at least, and I might be able to find some comfort in the fact that you do not think me to be *utterly* and *completely* stupid."

"I do not think you are stupid at all. I think you are angry—and you have every right to be—and confused, and hurt. And if there was something I could do to spare you any more pain, I would do it gladly."

"Refuse to fight tomorrow," she said flatly. "Send word to Robin that you were caught up in the heat of the moment and cannot, in all good conscience, take advantage of his honor and pride in such a cold, callous manner."

He arched an eyebrow. "Is that all?"

"No. Leave here tonight. Go back to the caves of Burgundy where you belong; your own *reputation* will not suffer for it."

"And if I refuse?"

"I will shoot."

"You would kill me?"

"I would only have to put this through your elbow or your shoulder and not even your arrogance would see you into a saddle tomorrow."

His smile was wry as he took a measured step toward her. "I suppose I should be relieved Centaur is not here to threaten again."

"Stop," she warned. "I will do it."

He took another step. And another. Brenna adjusted her

aim to the shoulder and pressed herself back into the corner as far as the canvas would take her.

"Are you so worried I might defeat him?"

"I am worried his pride might cause him to take foolish risks that he cannot afford to take right now."

"Because of his injury?"

"His injury," she scoffed. "He has fought with worse than broken ribs before and never so much as flinched."

Griffyn stopped and folded his arms across his chest. "Then I confess I am doubly curious to know why he is keeping himself behind the palisades."

Her mouth compressed into a thin line. "He has his reasons."

"We all have reasons for doing what we do."

"I asked you at Amboise if you had come to kill my brother and you said no. Was that also a lie?"

"Had I wanted to kill him then, it would have been easy enough to do. I could have done it that day on the archery range if I had just altered the aim of my arrow at the last minute. But I wanted more. I wanted the satisfaction, first, of seeing him go down under my lance; it was what I have trained for, fought for, worked toward all these years. Ever since Gascon."

"Gascon?" The arrow dropped fractionally on a gust of exasperation. "All of this ... because you lost to him at Gascon?" Then her voice dripped with ten shades of contempt as she shook her head in disbelief. "Did you ever consider there might be more important things in life than cockfights and boasting contests?"

"I did. At one time," he said quietly.

"But not since your heart turned to stone and you sold your honor along with your sword."

"You may think of me as little better than a common mercenary, irreligious and possessing few scruples, willing to sell my sword to whoever meets my price ... and until recently, you might well have been right."

"Until recently? Have the heavens opened, then, and showered you with scruples?"

"I have been more honest with you," he admitted truthfully, "than I have with anyone else in a good many years."

"And that should make me raise my hands and give thanks?"

"No. But I would hope it would let you believe me when I say your brother is in grave danger whether I fight him or not."

"What do you mean?"

"I mean"—he sighed and turned his head away for a moment as if wondering what fine madness was gripping him this time—"if I do not fight Robin tomorrow, there will likely be a brace of assassins waiting outside the tilting grounds for the both of us."

Her fingers curled tighter around the shaft of the bow. "What nonsense are you speaking now?"

"Do the names Engelard Cigogni or Andrew de Chanceas mean anything to you?"

Brenna's initial reaction was to dismiss them with an impatient shake of her head . . . but then she remembered. The two men Will had seen in the bower earlier, the two men who had held his attention even through the exchange of insults and challenges. He had mentioned them later to Robin, and to Sparrow, whose face had blanched even whiter than it had in the bower.

"The names are familiar?"

She nodded slowly. "Will told Robin they were here."

"They are in the employ of Bertrand Malagane. Killers both, with dead eyes and no thoughts of their own behind them."

Brenna shook her head again in confusion. "Why would the Count of Saintonge want my brother dead?"

"First tell me this: is Robin planning a journey to England in the near future?"

Her heart stumbled over several beats and the strength in her arms faltered, nearly causing her to shoot out of reflex. Griffyn was close enough by then to reach out swiftly and capture the shaft of the arrow, angling it downward and to the side.

"How do you know this?" she gasped.

"Then it is true?"

"How do you know?"

"Malagane knows. That is why he has his assassins sharpening their knives . . . and why he has paid me an extraordinary sum of money to insure your brother does not leave Normandy."

"He *hired* you to kill Robin?" Her words were barely above a breath and her eyes, which had only burned with the threat of tears until now, blurred beneath a film of shimmering silver. "But you just told me—"

"That I had not gone to Amboise to kill your brother. And that was the truth. I only wanted to have a close look at my enemy, at the man I had hated for five years and blamed for the death of my wife."

"Your . . . *wife?*"

His smile was bitter. "You say that with such flattering connotations. Is it so hard to imagine?"

She did not answer, but the look in her eyes was eloquent enough to earn a small laugh of self-derision.

"Yes, well, the whole idea of being responsible for another life took me by surprise also." He raked his hand through his hair, not wanting to talk about it now, but finding he had little choice. "We were young. Far too young to take on the world. Adele was frail to begin with . . . so very frail . . . and when she found out she was with child . . . I knew we could not live by traveling from tournament to tournament or survive solely on my winnings. Gascon was the last tourney of the season, and the richest. If I could have won there, we would have had enough to keep us warm and fed over the winter. She was big with child, and terrified, but she insisted I go . . ."

Brenna felt dampness on her lashes but steadfastly swallowed the tears that threatened.

"I wagered everything I had that day, everything I won in the early matches, everything I could ransom from the moneylenders. And I was winning. Right up to the end, when the bold and brash champion from Amboise took to the lists and held off my lance for twenty-three passes. I only had the one horse—Centaur—and the judges decided he had taken enough punishment. They declared the match in Robin's favor and it was over, just like that. I lost everything, even Centaur—though your brother was generous enough not to take him. When I returned to the inn where I had left Adele, I discovered the innkeeper had turned her out because of the monies owed. I tore the village apart and finally found her in a cow bothy. She had died there giving birth."

Brenna blinked and felt the hot splash of a tear on her cheek. "And the child?"

He shook his head. "Someone remembered hearing a baby cry through the night, someone else remembered seeing a peasant wheeling a cart with a wailing child inside, but I found nothing. I searched, I asked, I went to all the neighboring villages, but I could find no trace." He stopped and looked into Brenna's eyes for the first time since beginning his story. "I blamed myself and I blamed the world for Adele's death. Robin was just convenient to focus upon. Over time, he became the reason why I could not put a solid roof over her head or hot food in her belly. But even if I had won that day in Gascon, I doubt a handful of coins would have helped her. Perhaps . . . if I had swallowed my pride and taken her home . . . to England, where she belonged . . . perhaps she would be with me still."

It hit her like a cool spray of water. "England? You are English?"

He nodded as if it was a distasteful admission. "I have not ventured across the Channel in over seven years, though I have no doubt Malagane would be prepared to swear I disembarked last week if he knew. As it is, he knew only we had fought before and were evenly matched. He also knew if Robin fell to the Prince of Darkness . . . there would be no fingers pointed in his direction, no reason for your family to suspect he was behind it, therefore no repercussions. He paid me, you see, in good English sterling, probably with the intentions of 'discovering' I was in the employ of your father's enemies."

"He does not know you are English?"

"No. No one else—not even Fulgrin knows."

"Why are you telling me?" she asked. "And why should I believe you?"

"I do not know," he said quietly. "And God help me, I do not know."

He looked at her until her eyes started to water again, then slowly reached up and curved his hand around her neck. He drew her forward and, to her credit, she did manage to deny his efforts to raise her chin and he had to settle for pressing his lips to her brow. That was bad enough, though. Worse when he began to lay a tender path of kisses along her temple and cheek, for it roused every sensation, every feeling, every emotion she had discovered in his arms last night.

"Bastard," she cried softly. "*Bastard!* Why did you ever touch me? I w-was fine until you touched me."

"And I was fine until you touched me," he countered in a whisper.

"Liar."

His lips traveled the curve of her cheek and his hands tried to work their magic against the stiffness in her neck, tried to angle her mouth up so he could capture it.

"Is this what you want?" Her voice was muffled against his surcoat. "Is this what you want in exchange for my brother's life?"

His lips froze and his body went rigid.

"Is it?" she asked, and pushed out of his arms. "If it is, I will gladly give it to you. Here, look—" She fumbled with the buckle of her belt and let it drop to the floor. She pulled off her surcoat and cast it into the shadows, then lifted the hem of her shirt and started to peel it up and over her head.

"Brenna—"

"No. No, if this is what you want, if this is what it will take—" She flung the shirt after the other garment and reached for the waist of her leggings.

"Brenna!" He grasped her wrists and jerked them around to the small of her back. Her naked breasts gleamed as white as snow in the lamplight, the nipples pink and taut and mocking him for even looking, while the dark violet of her eyes sparkled up at him, shining with desperation.

"Are you saying you do *not* want me?"

"At this precise moment?" His fingers tightened around her waist and the dreadful burden of his self-imposed loneliness was etched suddenly on his face. "I want you more than I have ever wanted anyone or anything in my life."

"Then take me," she gasped. "Take me away from this place. I will go anywhere you want me to go, do anything you want me to do, *be* anything you want me to be . . . just . . . take me away from this place, now. Tonight. We can go to Robin. We can tell him everything. He will know what to do about Malagane and Cigogni and—"

"I cannot do that," he whispered.

"You *can*. If you want me as much as you say you do." She pressed against him, her lips seeking his, and it was a testament to his own desperation that he swore and clung to her heat. His tongue filled her mouth, plunging deep in a rough act of possession, and he brought her closer, crushing her against his chest and, for one wild moment, actually considered doing it. He considered leaving, taking her with him, starting afresh, leaving all the lies, the deceit, the treachery behind him.

But then the initial rush of hot blood passed and he could feel the stiffness in her body. He could feel her heart beating as fast as his own but out of panic, nothing more.

He straightened and eased her gently back to arm's length. He bent over and retrieved her shirt, and when she did not take it from his hand, he sighed and pulled it over her head and shoulders, feeding her arms into the sleeves as if he was dressing a child.

"We can go to Robin," she said again helplessly.

He clamped his jaws tight enough to make his teeth ache. Certes, they could go to Robert Wardieu and tell him everything, but what good would it do? It would be his word against the Count of Saintonge's. It would be the word of a banished Englishman who had lived a less than honest, honorable life these past few years in the guise of a Burgundian mercenary, against that of an important and influential ally of the King of France. "*You* should go to Robin and tell him what I have told you. Warn him to watch his back."

"You are still going to fight him?"

"I have no choice."

The hope faded from her eyes and she pushed past him, snatching up her bow, her belt and surcoat. At the door of the tent she stopped and looked back, and for just a moment, her face was shadowed with such a sense of betrayal and disappointment, he felt it like a fist closing around his heart.

It had been so long since he had felt anything at all in that region, he started to take a step after her. "Brenna—"

But she was gone. The flap swung closed and he was left standing alone in the middle of the musty tent, the halo of tarnished light behind him luring another moth to its flaming death.

22

There had been a heavy dew overnight and millions of sunlit pendants were scattered across the ground and on the roofs of the tents, dusting even the ropes and wagons with fine, glittering spickets of moisture. Many in the camp had awakened well before dawn in order to claim the best seats in the tilting field. Some had stayed there all night wrapped in blankets, their breath puffing out between the folds in soft white clouds. Everyone knew the Prince of Darkness and the champion from Amboise were to fight at midday, and while the sun dried the damp earth and the meadows filled with commoners and nobles alike, eager eyes stayed glued to the cloth-draped barriers that marked the entrance to the field.

Inside the black-and-gold pavilion, Sparrow adjusted the lacings on Robin's chausses for the third time.

"The people are in a surly mood," Richard said, lifting the flap of the door to peer outside. "They smell blood in the air."

"Some will want to see Robin unhorsed simply to show it can be done," Will agreed. "Others will not mourn to see him killed or maimed so badly he would never ride against them again."

"I shall do my best to disappoint them," Robin said grimly, wincing as he tested his range of motion from the waist up. Sparrow had bound his ribs so tightly he could scarcely take a deep breath.

Brenna sat in a corner of the pavilion, quietly horrified to watch her brother dress for combat. She could have prevented it, she reasoned, if she had simply had the courage to loose her arrow last night. What did it say for her nerve if she could not even do such a simple thing to prevent such a potentially calamitous consequence? What did it say for her common sense if she could strip all but naked before a man and beg him to carry her away instead of just shooting him and ending the matter then and there?

You should go to Robin.

How could she go to him without admitting what a fool she had made of herself?

I was fine until you touched me . . .

And I was fine until you touched me . . .

"Liar," she muttered. "Liar, liar, liar."

Dag, who sat glumly rubbing a shoulder he had bruised in his match yesterday, looked over and frowned. "Who is lying?"

"The whole wretched world," she said, pushing to her feet.

"Yes, well." Richard dropped the flap in place again. "The world will be calling upon us soon. What say you, Rob?"

"I am ready."

Sparrow darted after another buckle that looked suspiciously like it might allow some movement, and Robin glared down at him. "It was not your fault, Puck. Ease yourself."

"I will ease myself when you have spitted this arrogant codshead and fed him your dust." He reached down and scratched savagely at his groin. "Not one moment before."

Robin signaled Timkin, who was waiting with his gauntlets and helm. Almost as an afterthought, he asked, "Did any of you notice *any* weakness I might have missed?"

Richard, who was too respectful of his brother's position and prowess to think of offering any advice unless it was specifically asked for, was the quickest off the mark. "He pulls his horse to the left just as he is about to strike."

Dag disagreed. "To the right, I thought. And he leans forward, with his elbow flush against the shield."

"From what I saw," said the ever-practical Geoffrey

LaFer, "he changes his stance to match each challenger. He takes a good long look while they set themselves, and he seems to know just where and when they will strike, and how best to counter it."

Robin nodded grimly. "I saw the same thing. That was what kept us bashing at each other five years ago. The bastard adjusts. He can lean forward or back, to the left, to the right, or straight on. And if you are lucky enough to get your lance on him, it is like ramming into a mountain."

Brenna closed her eyes and tried to close her ears, to no effect. The voices were bouncing around inside the belly of the silk tent, impossible to avoid. She felt sick at heart, for she had never had cause to doubt the outcome of a joust or to dread it. Or to harbor a suspicion that some small part of her was hoping Robin's lance would miss its mark.

A rousing cheer went up, deafening all that had gone before, for the sight of Robert Wardieu d'Amboise riding onto the field of combat drew a roar from every throat. His armor, even his lance was black with gold bands and bordures; his gambeson and the great bat-winged shield glittered menacingly with the snarling figurehead of a prowling wolf atop the three gold bars that distinguished his arms as heir to the legendary Black Wolf. His visor was not yet lowered, and a bevy of faint-hearted damsels squealed with excitement and swooned as his gaze raked the ranks of spectators. Even the faces of the men grew flushed to see that the tip of his lance had been modified during the night, the coronal removed and the point squared.

A thin strip of yellow silk was tied around the hilt, just above the cone-shaped guard. It was old and tattered and had been carried in every joust since he had won his spurs. The envy of every beauty present, it was also the cause of every shaking head and furrowed brow as the question was asked and answered a hundred times. No one knew to whom the token belonged, or who held Wardieu's heart so tightly. They only knew enough to be jealous of whoever she was, for surely there was no knight more handsome, more honorable, courageous, bold, fearsome, and daring . . .

A second roar started the penoncels waving and the feet stamping as Griffyn Renaud de Verdelay appeared at the entrance to the field. He had not yet donned his bascinet or helm and the long, flowing waves of his hair gleamed blue-black in the sunlight. As he cast his pale, unearthly gaze around the arena, the dark, brooding beauty of his face prompted a second chorus of shrieks and a second ripple of swooning maidens.

Neither combatant took the customary progress around the enclosure. Both went only as far as the central dais to tip their lances at Prince Louis and the smuggly grinning Bertrand Malagane. The dais, like every other stand of seats, was filled to overflowing with noble guests who cheered just as loudly as the common rabble. Some felt the shocking effect of those pale eyes as the Prince of Darkness searched the rows of ladies, bundled in their cloaks of ermine, marten, and vair, but if there was a particular face he was looking for, he did not see it there. Both champions returned to their respective *recets* and it was Robin, this time, who waited patient and still at the line while Griffyn donned his padded bascinet and clipped his helm and camail in place. He took up his lance and shield and wielded his big gray destrier to the line, the animal stepping high in his eagerness as he awaited his master's signal.

The heralds raised their trumpets and gave two long blasts. In the absolute dead quiet that followed, the marshal of judges rose to his feet and announced the terms of the single-combat match, namely that it was to take the place of the battle royale and decide the fate of the ill-favored niece of Hugh the Brown. There were a few grumbles from the crowd, for there were those who enjoyed the spectacle of an all out battle between teams of highly skilled knights, but if asked privately which they would rather see—the mêlée or this match between two powerful, undefeated champions—there was no question the match would draw the loudest roar. The marshal's speech at end, he gave both

challengers a long, solemn consideration before hoisting
the silk *couvre-chef*. The crowd held its breath. The two
knights raised the points of their lances. Robin hitched his
shield a little more to the right while Griffyn sat as if carved
from green marble.

The *couvre-chef* seemed to float in the air a moment after
the marshal released it. But then it fell and the ground
shook as the two enormous chargers broke eagerly away
from their lines and sped down the course. In less time than
it took the spectators to exhale their pent-up breaths, the
two beasts had converged at the center of the list. The
unblunted tips of both lances clashed simultaneously,
striking the heart of the opposite shield, the staggering
power behind the impact causing both knights to jerk back
in their saddles and their screaming mounts to rear up on
hind legs.

The two parted in a cloud of dust and pawing hooves and
galloped to the far end of the lists, jolted but unscathed.
Griffyn's lance was cracked and he threw it aside for
another. As soon as he was set, the chargers were spurred
forward again, their silks streaming out behind, their ears
flattened, their tails flowing straight back in the wind.
There was another tremendous, crashing impact, and this
time it was Robin who called for a new weapon, the last one
torn from his grip in the violence of the clash. On the third
pass, the two shafts scraped together in a shower of
cracking, splitting wood slivers, and Robin had no choice
but to raise his shield and pull Sir Tristan to the side to
avoid a strike square on the slats of his visor. He came away
with his shield pocked in the shape of Griffyn's lance and
his rage soaring well beyond what was safe in such a deadly
game of skill and nerve.

Three more charges nearly caused the crowd to scream
themselves hoarse, for each would have been worth the
miles-long trek many had made to see such a spectacle of
chivalry and derring-do.

At the end of ten runs, the knights were given a few minutes' reprieve. Battered and dented shields were replaced,

horses were carefully checked for injuries, and the combatants were given the opportunity to catch their breath. It was then, with his visor raised in order to wipe away the sweat streaming down his face, the Prince of Darkness looked somewhere other than straight down the lists. He turned his head toward the crowded enclosure behind the palisades where an errant beam of hot sunlight had touched upon a long, gleaming gold braid and drawn his gaze like a moth to a flame.

Brenna had not given a moment's consideration to the invitation to watch the match from the royal bower. Nor had she dressed in the fancy silks or cendals that marked her as a lady of noble birth. It was a deceptively safe feeling of anonymity that allowed Brenna a momentary lapse as she found herself watching Griffyn Renaud prepare himself for the next course. Her heart had been in her throat since the first pass and while it was true her first thoughts, when the dust cleared and the destriers parted, were always for Robin, she could not help but watch Griffyn as he retired to his end of the *recet*. Nor could she prevent a small clutch in her belly each time she saw him sway or shake an arm to relieve the numbing effects of a freshly earned bruise. Neither man was unhurt. Both had taken devastating blows that would have shattered lesser men. Now, as she watched him fasten his camail in place and signal the judge he was ready, she found herself caught and held by the luminous green eyes. In that fleeting moment, she could have sworn the look he gave her was the same as the one he had given her on the archery range when he had not troubled himself to follow the flight of his arrow.

Griffyn dropped his visor. A split-second later, he spurred Centaur forward and thundered headlong into yet another screaming, tearing, smashing encounter with his opponent. It was a matter of a few seconds only until he saw the looming point of Robin's lance, and it took a fraction less time, the span of a heartbeat, to adjust the angle of his shield downward, leaving the slimmest of pathways free for a solid strike to the shoulder. He could see little more than an approaching streak of black through the slats of his visor, but he imagined he saw the surprised look in Wardieu's eyes as he saw the opening and struck for it. He braced himself for the blow, every instinct in his body screaming to defend against it, and at the last possible instant, he did raise his shield, too late to completely blunt the agony of brilliant white pain as the steel-reinforced tip slammed into his shoulder, tearing him sideways and out of the saddle.

To the crowd's utter horror and delight, the enormous gray stallion emerged from the confrontation riderless. The Prince of Darkness was down! The brazen challenger from the East was unhorsed, the green-and-gold was cartwheeling in the dirt, and Robert Wardieu d'Amboise had stayed upright to emerge the victor, the undisputed champion of the Enterprise of the Dragon's Mouth!

The crowd went berserk.

Hats, pennons, gloves, and any other loosely guarded garment was thrown high in the air. Men burst through the barricades and swarmed Robin where he cantered into the *recet*. Richard, Dag, and Will were capering like fools, and Sparrow came flying down out of nowhere to land in the saddle behind his ward, the impact of his sudden, splatted landing nearly managing to do what a dozen thrusts of a lance could not.

Only Brenna, of all the shouting, jubilant Amboise supporters, looked back in horror to the field where Griffyn Renaud was being assisted to his feet. He staggered a moment under the weight of his armor and stood with his hands braced on his knees until Fulgrin could prise his helm off his head and allow the spitting out of a mouthful of foul-tasting dust. But then he shook off the hands that were helping to steady him and stood straight. Centaur had come back when he realized his saddle was empty, and he approached his master with a bowed head and dragging steps as if the humiliation were somehow his fault.

Griffyn swept his hood and bascinet off his head and shook the sweat-soaked waves of his hair free. He did not look in Brenna's direction again. He did not look anywhere but straight ahead as he took up Centaur's reins and led him off the field.

The blow he had taken to his shoulder had not broken any bones or ripped apart any muscles, but it had been hard enough to drive the links of his armor through the many layers of padding and into the flesh, leaving several bloodied pocks and a bruise as black as his mood. Fulgrin, wary of his master's temper, had not uttered so much as a single word. The only sound he made was a clucking of the tongue as he picked the broken and embedded links of iron out of Griffyn's wound.

He had just finished applying a thick balm and was starting to bind the shoulder in strips of linen when the door of the pavilion was pushed open and Bertrand Malagane strode through, furious enough to kick aside the basin of bloodied water.

"I assume you have an explanation?"

"I offered no guarantees. The bastard is good. Damned good. He gave his best and won the day."

"I paid you a great deal of money to *succeed*, not to fail."

Griffyn's eyes narrowed. "You paid me a great deal of money to come to Gaillard. You *offered* more if I should succeed, but unfortunately . . . I did not succeed."

There was another brief slash of sunlight from the door and Griffyn glanced over as Solange de Sancerre, flanked by Gerome de Saintonge and two burly men, stepped inside the pavilion. He recognized both men from past encounters; Engelard Cigogni was an Italian, swarthy in countenance with a chest like an oaken barrel and arms as big around as truncheons. His companion, Andrew de Chanceas, was deceptively handsome and soft-spoken, but there was no life in the black eyes, no mercy in his soul, no conscience whatsoever that might deter from his being one of the most dangerous and deadly assassins in Normandy.

"It did not look to me as if you were as determined as you should be," Malagane said angrily, drawing the pale eyes back.

"From a comfortable seat in the bower, I warrant nothing looks the same as it does on a field of battle. I see you brought your pet dogs with you. Andrew . . ." He gave the handsome assassin an exaggerated wink. "Still getting down on all fours for your oafish friend there?"

Cigogni took an angry step forward, but de Chanceas stopped him with a smile and a languid wave of his hand. "I am sure I could be persuaded to share if the mood came upon you. And I *know* Engelard would dearly love to have the virile Griffyn Renaud de Verdelay on his knees before him."

Griffyn turned to pour himself another cup of wine. "Some day, when we meet in hell, I should be happy to teach both of you some manners. For the time being, however—"

He did not get to finish the sentence. He sensed the movement behind him and barely had time to brace himself before he was struck across the base of his skull with the stout iron hilt of a falchion. He lunged instinctively for his sword, but Andrew de Chanceas was already there, kicking the blade beyond his reach. The assassin launched a hammerlike fist at Griffyn's jaw, snapping his head sideways with enough force to send him into the waiting arms of Engelard Cigogni, who hauled him upright and braced him for a series of blows that left him slumped in a bloody sprawl across the floor.

When it looked as if the two men would continue beating the unconscious knight, Malagane stepped forward and signaled a halt. He peered down through the shadows, a satisfied smile on his face. "Arrogant bastard. I will show him what happens to men who think to play me for a fool."

Solange glided eagerly forward, her eyes shining with

anticipation. "May I have him now, my loving lord? I can teach him lessons in manners that will have him screaming your praises!"

Malagane petted her cheek for a moment, but his smile, evil and promissory, was not directed at her when he turned his head, but at the corner of the pavilion where Fulgrin was standing, huddled against the side of the tent as if he could make himself small enough to disappear.

"Someone will be screaming soon, my dear," Malagane allowed silkily. "If I am thwarted again, they will be screaming very loudly indeed."

23

Brenna paced outside the black-and-gold pavilion and chewed savagely on a fingernail. Something had happened out there on the tilting field. She was not sure exactly what, but something had happened that put her in no mood to celebrate along with the others. As she paced, her bow slung over her shoulder, she glowered at the throng surrounding the Amboise pavilion. Well-wishers for the most part, it was a crowd composed of knights, nobles, and commoners alike, the latter the noisiest and slowest to depart for they kept hoping the champion would make another appearance. It was the custom for the victor to share his triumph by way of distributing largesse, and Robin had already scattered several fistfuls of coin among them. He was inside the tent now, having his bruises and cuts tended, his privacy safeguarded by a ring of Amboise guardsmen who stood shoulder to shoulder in a glowering circle around the pavilion. Will and Sparrow were with him; Geoffrey was making arrangements to break camp, Dag and Richard were standing inside the cleared circle, grinning like jackanapes, accepting the claps on the back and hearty hand-clasps as if they had been the ones who had defeated the Prince of Darkness.

Defeated? Nay. Some dreadful feeling inside told Brenna it was not so much a defeat as it was a sacrifice. It was nothing she had seen, nothing she could put her finger on or swear with any certainty she had read in Griffyn Renaud's eyes in that one split second before he had lowered his visor. Yet the feeling was there, churning in her belly, chilling her skin, refusing to go away, that he had done something no black-souled, self-serving hireling would ever dream of doing. And if he had done what she suspected he had done, then it must mean he *had* a soul, he *had* a heart, he *had* a conscience. It must also mean that everything else he had told her last night about Bertrand Malagane and the plot to kill Robin must also be true.

If it was, she had to tell Robin. Of course she had to tell him; he had to be warned. But how? How, without confessing her own transgressions? She could almost picture his face before her, hear the disapproval in his voice, see the disappointment in the slate-gray eyes that were so much like their father's. It would be like confessing her shame to the Wolf himself. Perhaps if he wasn't so pure and noble himself, it would be easier. Richard and Dag would not have any difficulty understanding what had happened; they were governed by their passions and emotions. But Robin . . . an avowed celibate, for pity's sake . . . would not begin to comprehend how the heat and temptation of the moment might cause an otherwise sane and level-headed person to behave intemperately and irrationally.

Intemperate and irrational. That was exactly how she felt each time her gaze strayed in the general direction of the green silk pavilion. She could just see the domed peak of it on the opposite side of the enclosure and the wind-teased pennon that indicated he was still inside.

Was he hurt? His armor had been torn over the left shoulder, and he had seemed to favor the arm as he walked off the field. Was it broken? Was that beautiful body maimed or twisted in some way? Was he in pain? Was what he said about the assassins true—that if he failed today, they would be going after him as well? She doubted if he would have attracted a crowd around his tent or if he had guards to keep them from intruding on his privacy, yet she knew it would be nigh on impossible for her to go to him or even be seen anywhere in the vicinity of his camp.

In an agony of indecision she paced and scanned the faces in the crowd. Half of them looked surly and unwholesome; most looked as if they would kill their grandmothers for a copper groat. Will claimed to have seen the two assassins yesterday; she had been too preoccupied to notice. She could be staring one of them in the face right now and not even know it.

The thought stopped cold, half formed in her head as she took a second, slow perusal of the faces pressing up against the ring of guardsmen. Something had caught her eye the first time she had scanned them; something that made the hairs across the back of her neck stand on end and her fingers tighten reflexively around the shaft of her bow.

He was staring at her, waiting for her to find him. His one eye was half closed in a squint but the other was black and penetrating, boring into her like a spike with a message nailed on the end. His face was not familiar . . . yet it was. And as she followed the beck of his head and started walking over to where he stood, she remembered where she had seen him.

"Your name is Fulgrin, is it not?"

He nodded curtly, wary of the two guards who stood between them.

Brenna tapped one on the shoulder. "Let him pass."

When the wiry squire was inside the circle he became suddenly shorter, and she realized he must have been standing on his toes for some time trying to catch her eye. He wasted no more now, however, as he plucked at her sleeve and spoke in an urgent, scratchy whisper.

"You know my name so you must know my master."

"Did he send you here?"

Fulgrin gave his head a violent shake. "My lord . . . has himself been sent to perdition. Alas, they have beaten him, bound him hand and foot and stuffed him in a cart."

"*What?*"

He flinched at the sharpness of her outburst and seemed to shrink a little more.

"I barely managed to escape a similar fate myself. Look—" He leaned forward and lifted the greasy wisps of his hair to display a bleeding lump behind his ear. "My master has always said my skull was too thick for aught but a mangonel to damage, and for once I am happy to applaud his judgment. They clouted me and left me for senseless while they made their plans and sent for their cart, and while their backs were turned, I was able to crawl out of the pavilion and lose myself in the safety of the crowds."

"Who are you talking about? Who beat him?"

His face was gleaming wet with sweat and his eyes darted constantly around the crowd as he whispered the name. "The Count of Saintonge. He came to the tent after the match, him and two hulking brutes who owed my master no favors." The good eye narrowed to as tight a squint as the other as he peered at her. "It seems he gave you a warning yesterday but forgot to heed it himself. Now he is all trussed up like a goose and being hauled into the forest."

"The forest?"

"Beyond Les Andelys, where the road divides. Anyone with a thought to turn west to the coast will have to follow the tract that passes through a narrow gully. 'Tis the perfect place to set up an ambuscade, which Malagane is planning to do, and to leave a certain body there—indeed, there should have been two but for the thickness of my skull—where it might be made to look as if my master took offense at being defeated today and sought to take his revenge."

"Why have you come to me with this?"

"Why?" He thrust his tongue into his cheek and glared. "Because I knew the minute I clapped eyes on you that you were the one making him act like a cat with his nose rubbed in mustard. Because he was up all blessed night long . . . *again* . . . walking to and fro, to and fro. Not in the five long years I have been with him has he lost a moment's sleep over a woman, but last night he near wore a trough in the ground, he did. And today? How many times have I seen him run the lists and never . . . *never* has he dropped his shield like that!"

Fulgrin was actually trembling, he was so incensed, but Brenna could think of nothing to say; the flood of color in her cheeks was expressive enough. She took him by the arm and started toward the door of the tent.

"You have to tell Robin what you just told me. He will know what to do."

Fulgrin drew back, digging his heels into the earth so that they skidded slightly. "Frankly, I would as soon not meet any more angry champions this day."

She shoved him through the door of the pavilion without further ado. Robin was seated under the dome, his face moist and drawn with pain as Will—with Sparrow hovering and giving orders—rebound his ribs and dressed a multitude of scrapes and bruises. He was naked but for a linen breech clout, and it was the first time in recent memory she saw his shoulders sagged with utter exhaustion.

"Robin? This is Fulgrin. He would beg a word with you."

"By St. Cyril's ghost," Sparrow cried. "Are there not enough beggars outside? Can he not wait his turn with the others?"

Fulgrin, who had been somewhat sagging himself, stiffened his spine with an indignant squawk. "You think me a beggar? Me? Squire to the Prince of Darkness? You insolent little toad, you should beg my pardon before I part your tongue from your mouth!"

"Ho!" Sparrow dropped the roll of bandaging in Robin's lap and stalked around to the front of the stool. "Squire to Prince Doom-and-Gloom, are you? Come to arrange the paying of ransom for your lord's armor and pennons? Faugh! We want no ransom, lout, not in coin by any rate. We want the pennons, the shield, the armor, even the shiny bits of saddle trappings that carried your vaunted lord onto the field. In truth, were you not skrint-eyed and troll-necked, we would take you as well in payment for the insults delivered against the noble name of Wardieu!"

Fulgrin's complexion turned a livid, mottled red. "It seems I have made a grievous error after all! I should not have wasted my time—nor my master's—by coming here!"

He made as if to leave but Brenna's fist around the fringed edge of his collar stopped him—that and the sudden appearance of Richard and Dag behind them, blocking the exit.

"Something wrong?" Dag asked.

"Sparrow is venting air again," Brenna said and turned to Fulgrin. "Please, will you not tell Robin what you told me? Will you not let him help?"

"Help?" The squire scowled and glared back at Sparrow. "Such help as I see here will more likely get my master killed . . . if he is not dead already."

"Brenna—" Robin pushed painfully to his feet as Will handed him his shirt. "What is the matter here?"

She held Fulgrin's gaze a moment longer, then answered her brother. "Bertrand Malagane is planning an ambush for us on the forest road. He has taken Griffyn Renaud prisoner and intends to make it look as if he attacked you in an act of revenge."

"Why the devil would the Count of Saintonge want to ambush us?"

"For the same reason he hired my master to kill you," Fulgrin said bluntly. "To keep you from going to England and spoiling the plans he has made with Prince Louis."

There was a subtle whisper of leather closing around steel as both Richard and Dag put hands to their swords. Sparrow, to whom subtlety was a foreign affliction, leaped forward to plant himself like a shield in front of Robin and, in a wink, had two small axes clutched menacingly in his fists.

Robin finished pulling his shirt over his shoulders and calmly reached for his hose. "Where would Bertrand Malagane come by the idea I was making plans to go to England?"

"He came by them through the screams of your man—Iowerth?—who was a guest in his donjons for two days and two nights. I warrant he knows exactly where it is you are bound and why."

Richard took an angry step forward. "He has Dafydd?"

"*Had*, my lord. When my master saw him, he was already dead. Mercifully so," he added, quickly crossing himself, "to judge by what he told me. And now the same thing will happen to him, because it was plain to anyone with eyes—and the Count of Saintonge has those of a hawk—that my lord did not fight to win today."

"Not fight to win?" Richard exclaimed. "What tripe is this? Robin—let me take this bag of bones outside and rattle a few loose!"

He did not wait for Robin's consent, but grabbed a gloved handful of Fulgrin's jerkin and started dragging him to the door.

"Wait!" Robin shouted. "*Wait.* Tripe it may well be, but let us hear it anyway."

"Robin!"

"I said, *let him speak!*"

Richard thrust the squire away from him as if he was a bag of steaming offal. Fulgrin stumbled awkwardly onto his knees and recovered his balance only to find himself staring eye to eye with Sparrow, the razor-sharp blades of both axes pressed to either side of his throat.

"Now then, Skrint," the seneschal warned. "Have a care what you say, or the words you hear will be the last you utter through your God-given mouth."

Fulgrin glanced up at Brenna from a stretched neck and managed only to stammer, "M-my lady?"

"What do you know about this?" Robin demanded.

"Not much more than what Fulgrin just told you," she said quietly. "I saw Lord Griffyn last night, but he never mentioned Dafydd. Perhaps if he had, I might have believed him . . ."

"Last night? You saw him last night?"

She looked helplessly into Robin's handsome face, a face that had turned as hard as granite and twice as cold.

"I . . . went to his tent. I had hoped to persuade him not to fight today."

"Christ Jesus, how were you planning to do that?" Dag blurted.

"I took my bow," she said flatly. "I had every intention of shooting him, especially when he told me the count had paid him to goad you into fighting . . . but then he started talking about assassins and told me that it would accomplish nothing if he left or even refused to fight, and—"

"Wait . . . wait . . ." Robin held up his hand again. "What assassins?"

She let out a huff of breath. "He gave me their names, but—"

"De Chanceas and Cigogni?" Will asked. He answered Robin's frown with a nod. "I told you I saw them in the bower yesterday. And today, they were lurking in the shadows like carrion."

"They have been sent to the forest road now," Fulgrin croaked. "To lurk there with the purpose of collecting the thousand marks that went unearned by my master."

Robin absorbed all of this, but his eyes had not left Brenna's face. "Why did you not come to me before now, whether you believed him or not?"

"I did not come to you . . . because I did not want you to know what a fool I have made of myself."

He saw the shine in her eyes and frowned. "How big of a fool?"

"Big," she admitted quietly. "The biggest, I suppose."

"Did you know he was . . . ?"

"No! *No*, I did not know he was the Prince of Darkness until he lifted his visor on the field yesterday. That was another reason why I wanted to shoot him—because he made such fools of us all."

"Yet you believed him enough to let him live. And enough to be convinced he deliberately offered me an opening today in the lists."

She started to lower her lashes, lower her chin . . . but then she raised both again, slowly, and searched the solemn gray eyes for a long, revealing moment.

"You believe it too?" she whispered.

"I fought that man for the past five years in my dreams. Not once did he make the smallest error in judgment."

"Then you will help him?"

"Help him?" He turned to Will and signaled angrily for

his hauberk and chausses. "I may just kill the bastard myself."

Sparrow grumbled in agreement even as he spared Fulgrin's throat and fit the axes back into their special belt loops. He was not so quick to exonerate Brenna, however, and while Robin finished dressing and Richard and Dag sent for their armor, his agate eyes bored into her with the wrath of a man fated always to watch the ones he deemed to possess the most common sense show the least when it came to matters of the flesh.

Will was no less subtle as he brushed past her to fetch Robin's hauberk. "You picked a hell of a time to turn female on us," he murmured.

"I have not turned anything other than what I was already," she murmured right back.

"Perhaps I just phrased that wrong. Perhaps I should have said: you picked a hell of a bastard to throw yourself away on."

Griffyn's head felt as if someone were jumping around on the inside with wooden-toed boots. He had regained consciousness on the bed of a small cart, smothered under a pile of moldering, stinking hay. The dust sifted into his mouth and nose, throat and ears, making him cough incessantly. His wrists and ankles were bound so tightly his extremities were numb, swollen beyond pain, and whoever was driving the cart paid little heed to the deep ruts and rocks that jolted the wheels and caused him to bounce unmercifully on his wounded shoulder. He judged, by the sound of hoofbeats on either side of the cart, there were at least a score of outriders, one of whom was Gerome de Saintonge, whose nasally voice was unmistakable even through the muffling thickness of hay. Someone had dressed him in his tunic and hauberk, and he thought he felt an empty swordbelt buckled around his waist, though there was nothing that could be used as a weapon within reach.

He squeezed his eyelids tightly shut before opening them

again to the torment of burning dust, but he could see nothing through the hay. One of his eyes was blurred by more than dust and as he squinted to try to clear it, a fresh trickle of blood flowed down from his eyebrow to hamper his vision more. His jaw felt swollen and bruised and he could fit the end of his tongue into a bleeding gap where a large molar had been broken off at the gumline.

He had no idea what had happened to Fulgrin. He might, for all Griffyn knew, be trussed in the cart beside him . . . or dead.

He heard a muffled order to halt and a moment later the terrible jolting stopped. The hay shifted and rough hands reached into the cart, hauling him upright and pitching him down onto the road. Someone bent down and cut the ropes around his ankles, but his wrists were left painfully fettered at the small of his back.

He blinked to clear his eyes and spat out a mouthful of broken straw, and when he could see past the pinkish grit, the first face he saw belonged to Gerome de Saintonge, the second to Solange de Sancerre. She was dressed in tunic and hose, with a molded leather byrnie armoring her upper body. She wore a falchion strapped around her waist and a brace of daggers thrust into her belt. The two were pointing into the woods and discussing the best vantage for the ambush, but when they saw him struggling to sit upright, they walked over and smirked down at him with obvious amusement.

"Well, well, and so we see how the mighty have fallen."

"Untie my hands," Griffyn spat, "and I would be more than happy to bring you down with me."

Gerome laughed. "Oh, I intend to untie you, all right. I may even put a sword in your hand"—he glanced at the stiff, swollen fingers—"not that I imagine you will be able to use it to any good effect."

"I have heard that is how you fight best," Griffyn spat. "When your opponent is bound and helpless and cannot fight back."

Saintonge's dull blue eyes glittered and he lashed out

with his boot, kicking Griffyn on the upper thigh where there was no armor to protect him. The force of the blow sent him into a tight curl of pain, and, laughing again, Saintonge leaned over to grab a fistful of the ebony hair.

"You will not find yourself possessing half so much wit by the end of the day."

"Even half"—Griffyn gasped—"is a full share more than you can claim."

Saintonge tightened his grip on Griffyn's hair and smashed his fist across the handsome face, reopening the split in his lip and the cut on the inside of his mouth. He would happily have added tenfold to the bruises and gashes delivered in the first beating if not for Solange putting a restraining hand on his wrist.

"Gerome, dear, he will be of no use to us dead."

Saintonge snarled and delivered a last savage kick to Griffyn's unprotected flesh before he called upon Cigogni and de Chanceas to tie him to a nearby oak tree.

Panting, coughing out blood and dust, Griffyn was hoisted upright and dragged to the side of the road. A rope was passed around his chest several times, the final loop adjusted by Solange so that it circled his throat and held his head flat against the trunk. The slightest pressure, if he attempted to twist or turn his head, would crush his windpipe. Even swallowing was difficult, and he nearly gagged on the blood flowing from the split in his lip.

Solange's sympathy extended to tipping his head forward so that the blood spilled outward.

"You will have to forgive Gerome's . . . enthusiasm," she murmured. "He wants nothing to go wrong this time."

Her hand slipped beneath the hem of his tunic and rubbed him with a measure of her own enthusiasm. "I am so hoping we could spend more time together. Perhaps when this is over?"

Gerome de Saintonge interrupted her musings with a scowl as he brought her horse forward.

"You had best leave now and rejoin Father. The view should be adequate," he added, shielding his eyes to look up at the jagged dome of a hill that rose above the treetops nearly half a mile away. It was as thickly wooded on the crown as the surrounding hills and gullys, and anyone standing at the top would not be visible to those below. Only a careless glint of sunlight sparking off metal would betray their presence, and Malagane was anything but careless.

"Fight well, my bold lord," Solange whispered, reaching up to press a kiss over Gerome's mouth. "Bring us the head of Robert Wardieu and I will come to you tonight. I will come and you shall know pleasure beyond your ability to comprehend."

A small bead of saliva formed at the corner of Saintonge's mouth as he watched her being handed up into the saddle. When she was gone, he grinned and cupped a hairy hand over his groin then turned and glared at Griffyn Renaud. He came slowly back to the oak tree and stood staring for a long moment before he drew his sword. It was Griffyn's own blade with its polished steel surface and serpentine hilt.

"A beautiful weapon," Saintonge murmured, running a thumb along the exquisitely sharp edge. He saw the writing on the shaft and tilted it to reduce the glare, his fat lips moving as he read the Latin inscription and translated it. " 'You . . . need not hope . . . that you will ever see heaven . . . for I have come . . . to take you to the other side.' " He grinned and glanced sidelong at Griffyn. "How prophetic. And heavy too. One stroke, I should think, would part a man's head from his shoulders. I will test it on Wardieu, then leave it thrust in his corpse so that no one will doubt whose hand wielded it. But first . . ."

He brought the gleaming edge of the blade up and rested it just beneath Griffyn's jawline, in the same place a scabbed stripe marked his own throat. He slid the blade slowly across the skin, parting the edges of flesh, sending a fresh sheet of blood down onto Griffyn's collar.

"I owed you that," Saintonge murmured. "The rest of your debts will be collected in full when our business here is done. Perhaps"—he leaned forward so that the rancid heat of his breath stung Griffyn's nostrils—"I will even let Engelard have his fun with you. Right here. In the grass. With the other men cheering and vying for a turn."

Cigogni grinned through black and furry teeth and, mimicking Solange's caress, shoved his hand beneath Griffyn's tunic and closed his fist around the bulge of flesh.

Griffyn strained against his ropes but was limited to a futile contortion that only increased the pressure on the rope at his throat and brought a gust of laughter out of Cigogni's mouth. The fist tightened around his flesh and Griffyn could not think, breathe, or move through the blinding sheet of agony that tore through him. Only when the clawing fingers released him could he see clearly enough to acknowledge the leering grin on the assassin's face.

"I look forward to it, my sweet," the Italian hissed.

Laughing, Saintonge thrust the point of the sword into the ground beside the oak, temptingly close, impossibly far, then, aware of the pale eyes burning into his shoulders, he ordered his troop to conceal themselves in the trees.

Blinking his eyes to clear them of the sweat and blood that drenched his face, Griffyn saw that only a half dozen or so were knights; the rest were men-at-arms who carried pikes and thick-stocked crossbows. The latter weapon was cumbersome, armed by hooking a foot through the stirrup and drawing the string back by means of a pulley to hook around the trigger-release. The quarrels they fired were less than a foot long and stout; they would not carry far, but in the dense wood, they did not need to gain distance. Shot at close range, they would have enough force to knock a knight out of his saddle, where, in the first few minutes when he fought to regain his senses, he would be easy prey.

Saintonge had set a fine trap for Robert Wardieu and did not anticipate anyone walking away from it with the ability to decry his lack of courtesy. The location was ideal, for the road took a sharp turn just before entering the gully and Wardieu's party would be fully in the sights of the bowmen before he suspected anything amiss. Moreover, Griffyn was tied in plain view, halfway up the far side of the leafy gorge, where the trees were thinner and therefore less threatening than what lay behind.

He tried to curse, but the rope cut into his throat, limiting his effort to a hiss; he doubted if he could rouse more than a crushed whisper. His head was a blister of agony, and he could barely move his eyes high enough to see the tops of the trees or low enough to see the inches-thick bed of decayed leaves that surrounded the base of the oak. He fought through the waves of pain and nausea to stay conscious, though he thought he lost the battle several times. And once he thought he had lost his mind completely when he pried a blood-crusted eye open and stared at a misty shadow so long, the watery shape began to materialize into a face with huge violet eyes—one of them aimed down the shaft of an arrow pointed directly at his heart.

24

Brenna snapped her fingers away from the string and a split second later was rewarded by the solid *f-bungg* of the steel tip striking wood. It quivered in the bark of the oak not two inches from Griffyn's throat, cleanly severing the rope that was pinning his neck to the tree. At the same time, she heard another *slish* and a cry from across the gully, and she guessed correctly that Will had reduced the number of their adversaries by one.

She drew another arrow and nocked it, stepping out from behind the tree to take aim at a second crossbowman who had been startled out of his hidey-hole in the bushes. She loosed the arrow with almost graceful ease, yet the force behind it punched through the bullhide and byrnie and sent the man twirling on his heel to land facedown in the brambles.

She set another arrow and held it at the ready even as she bent low and ran toward the tree where Griffyn was tied. She had to stop once as a crossbow bolt kicked into the dirt at her feet, but her aim was more accurate and another victim fell to the side. The gully came alive then with an eruption of thrashing horses' hooves and clashing swords as Robin and her brothers surprised their would-be ambushers from behind. She and Will had pinpointed their locations with laughable ease, and because the majority were on foot already, crouched behind bushes and tree stumps, relying on the crossbows to unhorse their intended victims, they were no match for the mounted knights. What few quarrels they did manage to fire were easily deflected off shields, but because the weapons required almost half a minute to reload, they were all but useless after the first flight. They were cast aside with curses, and the bearers were reduced to using swords against the fearsome might of the knights who came out of nowhere and bore down on them like furies.

Dag and Geoffrey LaFer each took two apiece, not by choice, but because the men-at-arms had huddled together hoping to present a greater threat in numbers. The pair in the forefront stood defense while the two behind struggled feverishly to reload their crossbows. Fully armed and armored, however, a knight mounted on a seasoned warhorse could easily account for ten, twenty men on foot, and four terrified Brabançons posed no threat, offered no challenge.

The fiercest fighting was at the far end of the gully where Gerome de Saintonge and his knights had mounted quickly and raced into the fray. Richard, quickest to find trouble, charged into their midst, his lance aimed at the closest of the three helmed challengers. He struck the first in the throat, ousting him from the saddle, and because there was no room to turn or mount another charge, he threw down his lance and drew his sword. He fought like a fiend, standing high in the stirrups, bellowing loudly enough to startle a flock of rooks out of the treetops.

Robin set his spurs to Sir Tristan and thundered after a burly knight with two entwined snakes painted on his shield. He caught the man square and high on the hip, shredding the iron links of his hauberk, driving the point of his sword through flesh and bone and muscle. The knight screamed and wielded his own weapon, but it was too late. The blade struck Robin's shield and glanced off without harming more than the surface of the paint.

Robin turned and rode toward two crossbowmen who were winding their weapons to reload. One saw him coming and threw himself sideways, abandoning the fray with a scream. The second man froze as Robin's charging steed ran him down and the quarrel he loosed flew high up into the treetops, nearly startling Sparrow from his perch higher up in the boughs.

Dag was engaged in swordplay with another knight when Gerome de Saintonge thundered out of the trees beside him. He managed to duck the first swipe of Saintonge's weapon but, in so doing, leaned into a strike from the second knight. He went down, cursing and bleeding, as he fought to keep hold of his sword and avoid the thrashing hooves of all three destriers. Robin rode in, bellowing as loudly as Richard, trying to work the fight away from Dag. Geoffrey did what he could to help, slashing his blade across the rump of Saintonge's horse to send him into a bolt.

Gerome turned with a snarl and rode back into the crush. He saw Robin and shouted a challenge, one that was met with steely gray eyes and ice cold nerve. They had room now, with Dag down and Geoffrey driving off the horses. Without a pause to exchange insults, Robin and Saintonge flew at each other, swords slashing, shields raised to absorb the shock of the blows. They wheeled, unhurt, and bashed at each other again . . . and again, until the sheer might of Robin's sword arm forced Saintonge out of the saddle. It was in the act of falling that he swung his shield against the side of Robin's head, tearing off his helm, camail and all.

Robin's vision darkened under a rush of blood as the departing metal opened a cut on his temple. He was not down, though, and after a split-second delay to wipe his sleeve across his eyes, he found the floundering Saintonge and slashed his sword in a downward arc, catching the fallen knight with enough force to dent the back of his helm and knock him senseless.

Their leader undermined, the remaining crossbowmen scattered and the two surviving knights put their heels to their steeds and fled, their shields raised to ward off the pursuing hail of Sparrow's six-inch arblaster bolts. One of them veered onto the road hoping to make better speed, but he cleared no more than a dozen galloping paces when a shaft from Will's longbow brought him down. The other escaped and overtook the men-at-arms who were running in a panic without weapons, without any thoughts other than escape.

Sounds of sporadic fighting still echoed through the greenwood, but the battle, such as it was, was over.

Brenna, one eye on the surrounding woods, cut through the ropes that held Griffyn pinioned to the oak. He staggered heavily forward into her arms and they both went down onto their knees, with Brenna attempting to brace him while she reached around to the small of his back and sliced the cords binding his wrists.

Once freed, he gasped as the pressure on his shoulder was eased and groaned as he cradled his pain-wracked hands to his chest. His face was a mass of purpling flesh. The front of his tunic was liberally splattered with blood; his hair hung forward in thick, matted strands over his shoulders. There was more blood on his thigh where the point of Saintonge's boot had torn his hose and gouged the flesh, but despite the bruises and the battering, he managed a weak smile.

"When I saw you standing there," he murmured, "I thought I was dreaming."

"You will think it a nightmare when you see yourself," she chided gently, using her cuff to wipe at the blood over his eye. She could not keep herself from looking at his mouth, or from touching her sleeve to the split on the lower lip, nor could she keep the overwhelming sense of relief from spilling down her spine and pooling at the base of her belly.

"Can you stand? Is anything broken?"

"Only my pride," he answered, draping an arm over her shoulders as she helped him rise. The pale eyes were still glazed with pain, but there was a glimmer of something else in their depths as he looked long and hard at her face, and once they were on their feet again, he drew her forward into the circle of his arms. The embrace lasted only seconds before a crashing in the woods beside them had Griffyn flinging Brenna to one side and leaping himself to avoid the red-eyed, screaming charge of Engelard Cigogni's rampager.

The horse's flanks brushed Griffyn's shoulder, spinning

him around and thrusting him hard against the trunk of the tree, but he shook off the pain and lunged for his sword, grasping it in both swollen hands as the Italian wheeled around and came back for a second charge. The assassin's weapon of choice was a starburst, a round, spiked metal ball swung overhead at the end of a length of chain. A single swipe could tear away a man's face, especially if that man was without a helm or armor of any kind.

Cigogni roared and came at Griffyn, the starburst wind-milling overhead, the spikes shredding the air, causing a small hurricane of sound as horse and rider leaped into the charge. The one did not lean far enough, however, and the sheer unbendable bulk of his armor kept him straight in the saddle, causing him to clip a low-lying branch with the spikes of the starburst. The branch was ripped away from the trunk and exploded into splinters, but the split-second delay caused by the strike was enough for Griffyn to swing his sword up and catch the stunned assassin high under the upraised arm. The force behind the blow severed the links of Cigogni's hauberk and bit deeply into the flesh and muscle. There was a brief glimpse of white bone at the heart of the wound before that too shattered and split away, and then it was the weight and the momentum of the swinging starburst that changed Cigogni's roar of triumph into a high-pitched scream of pain. Armless, the assassin rode blindly into the woods, the blood gushing from his shoulder as if from a fountain.

Griffyn spun around, braced for another attack, but Cigogni was finished. Brenna was still lying in a crush of spongy leaves, and for one heart-stopping moment he thought she had been struck. But no. The air had just been knocked out of her lungs when he had pushed her out of the way, and even as he went down on his knees to help her up, she was cursing, spitting dirt and decayed pine needles out of her mouth.

Robin came riding across the road then, the side of his face streaked in blood but otherwise unhurt.

"We have accounted for twelve," he said, swinging out of his saddle.

"There are more," Griffyn cautioned roughly. "Twenty at least."

"They are likely half way back to the château by now," Robin guessed. "And if so, we had best not waste any more time than necessary. Is anyone hurt?" He looked around. "Where is Dagobert?"

"Here" came a grunted response. "I am here."

He emerged from the woods, his arm slung around Will's shoulder. The sleeve of his hauberk was torn, the shirt beneath showed bloody, but he was just winded, he was quick to point out, "From learning how to dance with my horse."

Richard and Geoffrey appeared a few moments later, both of them showing minor wounds but grinning ear to ear as they squabbled over strikes and misses. Sparrow swung down out of the trees, landing with a boastful caper to show himself free of the smallest bruise. There were six other Amboise men in their company—to have brought any more would not have been sporting, Dag had declared— and these six also emerged from the greenwood and converged on the forest road, two of them dragging a semi-conscious Gerome de Saintonge between them. He was missing his helm and his yellow hair was plastered to his skull with pink-tinged sweat. At the edge of the road he lost his footing and went down hard on one knee. No one moved to help him up again, and after a small struggle to regain his balance, he stood, his eyes dull and glazed as they went from one face to the next.

"What should we do with him?" Richard asked casually. "Hang him?"

"A single arrow," Brenna said, drawing one out of her quiver, "would do just as well."

Saintonge curled his lip in a sneer. "Murder me, and my father will stop at nothing to hunt you down."

"I would enjoy giving him the inconvenience," Robin said. "But no, I have no intentions of murdering you. The lowly curs you brought with you . . . aye . . . I have no compunctions about teaching them a lesson in chivalry."

He glanced pointedly at the severed arm lying a few feet away in the leaves. Saintonge followed his gaze and his eyes widened as he recognized the starburst and the gloved hand that clutched it. He found Griffyn then and saw the bloodied length of the serpentine sword, and before anyone could stop him, he drew his dagger and lunged for Renaud's throat.

The six-inch bolt from Sparrow's arblaster caught him high between the shoulders, punching through mail and leather and cutting the spine with an audible *cra-ack*. Saintonge froze, his arm still raised, his dagger gleaming in his fist . . . then fell facedown, almost in slowed motion, dead before he struck the ground.

For a full ten seconds no one moved or made a sound.

"Actually"—Robin pursed his lips and frowned—"I was hoping to make use of him if Malagane sent more troops after us."

Sparrow snorted wetly and shouldered his arblaster. "Fine. The next time a viper sets himself to strike, I will ask your leave first."

"He will send more men," Griffyn warned quietly. "You may count on it. He knows where you are going and why."

One by one the Wardieu men turned toward him, their faces showing a combination of curiosity, wariness, and open distrust.

"Your man already warned us," Robin mused. "But we would hear it from your own lips."

"Fulgrin? He is alive?"

"Alive . . . and most insistent about leaving nothing of value behind. We might have been here sooner had he not been so adamant about collecting horses and armor . . . and saddle pouches that make a fine tinkling noise when shaken."

Griffyn's gaze touched on each hostile face before he sighed and nodded. "I suppose I do owe you an explanation."

"It had best be a good one," Robin said, smiling faintly. He gave orders to have the bodies collected and hidden beneath a layer of leaves, then pointed the way, politely enough, to the river. "You can clean yourself up and at the same time give us a good reason why we should not leave you here with the other corpses."

Obeying her brother's glance, Brenna and Sparrow followed, and while Griffyn waded knee deep into the water, Robin took a seat on a convenient boulder on shore.

"First," he said, "I would hear what you know about Dafydd ap Iowerth."

Griffyn sighed and plunged his hands into the cold water. "He is dead."

"That much I know already."

Griffyn nodded and related his initial meeting with Malagane and Solange de Sancerre, omitting nothing, including what details he could recall about the sight that had greeted him in the donjons of Château Gaillard. When he recounted his part in the devil's bargain, Robin's jaw tightened, but he said nothing until the end.

"So he told you we were bound for England to lay claim to my father's lands—lands in Lincoln that he wants for himself—and you did not believe him?"

"On the contrary, I do believe him. I believe King Philip has promised him a prominent position in England when and if the barons support the Dauphin as king. I also happen to believe there will be a good many rich tracts free for the taking since Louis has made no secret of the fact he intends to execute, banish, or imprison those same barons when he takes power."

"Why would he do such a thing?"

"He is convinced any noble who would betray his king once would readily do it again. Malagane, on the other hand, has always fought against John in favor of Philip and stands to become a very wealthy, very powerful individual

. . . providing there is no further obstacle to Louis taking the throne."

"And he thinks such an obstacle might exist?" Robin asked carefully.

"I think your friend died in great agony trying to keep a secret that has been well guarded for over a decade. I think Malagane has discovered what that secret is and is making his own preparations to insure it does not interfere with his plans."

"You seem to know a great deal about matters I would not think would have concerned you in Burgundy."

Griffyn studied his hands a moment, then used them to splash water over his face and throat to rinse away the blood. "I am English by birth. My family has had holdings in Leicester for twelve generations."

"A purebred Saxon champion?" Robin mused. "A rarity indeed. I should think you would rejoice in seeing the Norman conquerors humbled."

Griffyn offered up a wry smile. "As rare as true Saxon blood might be, it would be even more difficult to find pure Norman blood in England. The conquest succeeded only because the invaders intermarried, raped, and impregnated the women of Saxon nobility with Norman bastards. Peasants, people in the forests and in the far north, whisper of a time when a Saxon will sit on the throne of England again. They swear they have seen and heard the great king, Arthur Pendragon, leading an army of ghosts through the greenwood in search of a man strong enough to take back the throne. But that is all it is: stories and whispers. The Normans in England do not even regard themselves as being Normans anymore. They call themselves English and look to the French—the ages-old enemies of the Normans—to help them oust their Norman king."

He stopped, raked his fingers through his hair to squeeze out the excess water, and shook his head. "I dare swear it confuses the hell out of me. I chose to make my home in the mountains of Burgundy because I have no particular affection for the Normans or the French or the Spaniards, all of whom seem bent on conquering each other. I keep to myself and see to my own needs and make a point of avoiding any and all commitments to noble causes."

Robin matched his wry smile. "Which makes me doubly curious to know why you would have put yourself at such risk to warn us of Malagane's treachery."

The gray-green eyes flickered ever so briefly in Brenna's direction. "As I told Malagane, I dislike being used as a pawn in any man's game. More so if I am not told all the rules and all the players."

"You appear to have guessed a few players on your own."

Griffyn acknowledged the supposition with a tilt of his head. "It was not that difficult to do, especially if you remember being a young, impressionable lad of thirteen who still believed in romance and chivalry and the nobility of men who would risk everything to rescue a princess from the donjons of a cruel king. At the time, of course, there were no names given to any of the rescuers; it was not until Malagane inadvertently mentioned that your brother— Eduard?—was especially close to Arthur of Brittany that I was able to fit the pieces together. I gather the Lost Princess is not as lost as everyone presumes her to be?"

"She is a helpless and innocent pawn," Robin replied quietly, "who never wanted to be part of *any* man's game. Nor does she want to be one now, despite those who would parade her before the world, a blind and vulnerable woman committed only to serving God."

Griffyn straightened slowly. "Blind?"

"By her uncle's hand, eleven years ago. It is one of the reasons why he has never troubled himself overmuch to find her; he has known she has posed no threat to his crown."

"I gather no one else is aware of this . . . impediment?"

"By no one, you mean Malagane? No, I doubt he knows. I doubt Robert FitzWalter or any of his dissenting barons know either."

Griffyn lowered his hands and let them drip by his sides. "Then why not simply tell them? Why go to all the risk and bother to rescue someone who would not need to be rescued if the truth came to light?"

"Because it is not Eleanor who needs rescuing," Robin said softly. "It is her son."

Both Sparrow and Brenna turned their heads to gape at this, for the existence of a child was news to them as well.

"He will be ten years old this spring," Robin explained with a sigh. "No one knows about him. Not even Eduard. Only Marienne and a few of the older nuns at the abbey . . . and the child's father, of course."

"Henry de Clare," Brenna guessed on a breath.

"An unexpected lapse on both their parts. It happened during a storm, when they were caught out in the forest. The storm lasted several days, during which time Henry had no means of lighting a fire to dry their clothes or keep them warm and . . . one thing led to another."

"How do you know all of this?"

"Marienne ran out of excuses to give me why she could not come home to Normandy. She finally had to tell me the truth, if only to keep me from crossing the Channel and carrying her away by force. She has claimed the child as her own thus far, and is fairly certain no one suspects his royal lineage, but she says he grows to resemble his great golden uncle Richard more and more each day and they have all began to fear for his safety. I was already making plans to go to England when the dragon ring arrived. I thought . . . I hoped perhaps Dafydd might have had some other *specific* message for me."

"If he did, it died with him," Griffyn said, coming slowly out of the water. "But who is Henry de Clare? Surely, if the child is common and base-born it can pose no threat either."

"Henry de Clare's bloodlines are as pure as you claim your own to be; his ancestors rode at the side of William the Conqueror and, before that, held claim to a vast portion of Gascony. Neither is the child base-born, for they were secretly wed when the results of their indiscretion became known. It has been a marriage in name only these past many years, for Eleanor is committed to the church, but their vows were made before a bishop and no court in the land could declare them false."

"No court in *John's* England?" Griffyn queried sardonically.

"No court that would dare question the word of Stephen Langton."

Sparrow groaned and struck his head with the flat of his palm. "Do not tell me it was the Archbishop of Canterbury who witnessed the wedding vows. Do not tell me this even in jest."

"He was not archbishop at the time," Robin said mildly. "Indeed, he did not even have aspirations of ever becoming Seer. His election came as much of a surprise to him as to anyone else—most especially John Lackland, if you will recall, whose refusal to accept him as the Pope's choice caused Rome to place England under an interdict for six long years."

"And now this same Stephen Langton knows of the existence of a legitimate heir to the throne of England?" Griffyn arched an eyebrow. "A boy-child, no less, one whose claim is stronger than either John's or his weakling babe of a son."

"Langton vowed, with his lips on a crucifix, the knowledge would die with him, if that was what Eleanor wanted."

"And is that what she wants?" Brenna asked quietly.

Robin looked at her. "She wants peace. She saw her brother die as a sacrifice to other men's greed. She saw the ruling barons of England stand by and do nothing while God's laws of descendence were ignored and another was chosen king in Arthur's place. And she sees them now, trying to rally the people behind a French king because the corrupt and brutal king they chose over Arthur turned out not to be to their liking. How loyal would they be to her son if they decided he was not to their liking either? She does not want him to be the cause of yet another spree of bloodletting and rebellion, nor does she want him to live out his days under the threat of an assassin's knife."

"Does this family ever trouble itself with simple matters?" Sparrow sighed. "Like wars and plagues and famines?"

"It is not a burden I have enjoyed carrying alone all these years," Robin declared.

"Then why share it now?" Sparrow demanded.

"Because I realized today—in the lists and here in the forest—that it is not the kind of secret that can simply die with me. There are men who would stop at nothing to kill the boy should his existence become known. Still others who would use him—like a pawn," he added, staring directly into Griffyn's eyes, "to further their own ambitions."

"Even so," Griffyn pointed out, "you have chosen odd company to share it with."

"Not so odd, I think. Unless I am wrong in guessing the reason why you lowered your shield this afternoon—and why my sister thought you were worth saving."

Griffyn looked directly at Brenna for the first time. "She did, did she? And you thought you would test her judgment by revealing information to me that could plunge England into a civil war?"

"You said you liked to be apprised of all the players in the game."

"I also said I avoid any and all commitments to noble causes."

"How do you feel about reckless adventures?"

Griffyn's eyes narrowed. "That would depend on how reckless and how adventurous."

"Reckless enough to have a prince of France and an English king vying to see who can catch us first. Adventurous enough to ride into the heart of middle England and spit up the noses of those who would stop us."

"It is a tempting offer, I assure you, but"—he paused and peered intently into the slate-gray eyes—"how would you know you could trust me?"

"I would know . . . because you would give me your oath of honor."

Sparrow made a choking sound in this throat. "Did you

not just hear him say he was an Englishman? A *Saxon*, no less? You might as well heed an oath from a Celtic bog-fiend!"

Griffyn glared down at the outspoken woodsprite. "As it happens, I was going to say . . . it might prove a greater risk to you to invite me along rather than let me go on my way. The last time I heard there was a reward of some four thousand marks on my head—and it may be even more by now."

Robin was as impressed as he was surprised. "What the devil did you do to warrant it?"

"I took offense at the king offering me hospitality in my own donjons and escaped," he said blithely, "killing a dozen or so of his royal guard and giving his mistress a vigorous serving of Saxon *droit du seigneur*. It was when I was younger, of course, and went by another name."

"Another name?"

He shrugged his big shoulders. "It carries little worth now, but I was the Earl of Huntington until the king discovered my Saxon lineage and sought to eradicate it."

Robin's handsome face broke out in a slow grin. "An outlawed English earl, a Saxon champion, and a dark prince of Burgundy . . . by God's teeth, I would call it an adventure indeed just to travel in such illustrious company! Brenna? Sparrow? What say you both; shall we have him along?"

Brenna was too dumbfounded to say anything. Her brother had been hoping to expose the inherent sense of honor he had recognized in Griffyn Renaud and, instead, had shocked them all by uncovering genuine blooded nobility.

Griffyn had obviously arrived at the same conclusion, and his own smile was tempered with a frown. "I have not yet agreed to *come* along."

"You will," Robin said jovially, "when you realize your only other choice is to go under the leaves with the rest of the corpses and wait for the carrion to sniff you out in the morning."

Griffyn's brow arched again and he gave Sparrow's arblaster—and the itchy fingers that longed to tickle it—a measured look. "Put that way . . . I suppose it *would* be churlish to refuse your invitation."

Robin nodded. "I was hoping you would think so."

Sparrow shook his head and groaned. "Madness. It runs rampant in this family. I knew it the first time I took up company with your father, and there has been no relief of it since."

Robin clapped him on the shoulder. "Yes, but are your ballocks still itching?"

The little man cast a frown in the direction of his crotch. "No," he said, somewhat reluctantly. "In truth, they are not."

"Then away, Puck, and bring up the horses; we have wasted enough time already. Brenna?"

She looked up and held her breath, for she was half convinced he would have changed his mind by now about taking her along.

"Be sure to retrieve all of your arrows; we may have difficulty replacing them once we cross the Channel."

She nodded and darted off to comply, and was not quite out of earshot when she heard Griffyn's startled query.

"She is going to England with you?"

"The island is nine-tenths forest. And in the forest, with or without a bow in her hand, Brenna has few equals. If that is a problem for you . . . ?"

"The problem," Griffyn said evenly, "is that the forests of England are like no other forest in the world."

"Do you speak from experience . . . or fear?"

"An honest measure of both. Ghostly armies aside, you could hide an entire kingdom inside the greenwood between Lincoln and Nottingham and never know it was there."

"With God's help, we will not need to keep a kingdom hidden, only a king."

Half a mile away, camouflaged by trees and dense bramble, Solange de Sancerre gripped Malagane's arm tightly as she counted the number of horses and riders that were leaving the gully below. Six of the knights turned back and retraced their route to join up with the entourage returning to Amboise. Nine continued west, on the road to Rouen, including the girl, two squires, and Griffyn Renaud.

They had enjoyed the perfect view. From their vantage they had been able to watch Wardieu's men approach from the east while two of their number—Solange thought she saw the flash of a long golden braid on one of them—scouted the woods ahead and targeted Gerome's men. The resultant skirmish had them on their toes some of the time, trying to observe it all. Malagane had cursed almost continually to see how easily the ambush had been foiled, but after all, they were Gerome's men. Hired thugs, for the most part, and crossbowmen who were always considered expendable.

"Do you think it worked, my darling?" Solange asked in a breathless whisper. "Do you think the ploy was convincing?"

"I lost count of the bodies, but I expect there was enough carnage to persuade Wardieu the ambush was real."

"A pity about Gerome."

"Blundering oaf; he as good as killed himself. Could you not have controlled him any better? All of this would have been for naught if he had killed the Burgundian—or worse, damaged him too much to make the journey."

Solange dismissed his concerns with a shrug. "Renaud is a strong beast, he will recover. And I doubt it would have looked quite so believable had he merely suffered a slap on the cheek. Besides which, he has his loving little bitch now to tend his wounds. She will nurse him back to health if only to show her appreciation for the noble sacrifices he made today."

"Indeed, I want him back in perfect health," said a low, ominous voice behind them. "I want him healthy so that when I tear his heart from his chest and stuff it down his throat, he will appreciate the true taste of revenge."

Both Solange and Malagane turned to admire the fury

blazing in Andrew de Chanceas's soulless eyes. His tunic was lavishly stained with the blood of Engelard Cigogni, who had died in his arms not ten minutes after leaving the gully.

"You will have your chance at him," Malagane promised. "After he has outlived his usefulness. For now, we have arrangements to make."

"What arrangements?" Solange asked. "The men are ready to leave at a moment's notice. The ship is waiting in Rouen. And we were told there was no need to risk venturing too close." The green eyes sought the distant crust of trees again. "He has assured us he will leave signs telling us where they have been and where they are going. All we have to do is follow our happy company of heroes at a discreet distance."

"Even so, I would have been happier if Wardieu's interference had been eliminated on the jousting field today."

"I suspected your anger at our Dark Prince was not entirely feigned. To be sure, poor Gerome was induced to believe he was bait and nothing more. And think how much happier you will be when you are able to tell Prince Louis you not only witnessed the demise of Eleanor of Brittany personally but that you have brought him proof the Black Wolf is a traitor and has been plotting all along with his sons and his English allies to overthrow the French king. Who knows?" She tipped her head up and offered the luscious pout of her mouth for his consideration. "Perhaps he will reward you with Amboise."

"Perhaps he will," Malagane agreed in a murmur, his eyes gleaming with avarice. "In which case, we must take steps to insure there are no troublesome witnesses left behind. And if the shire of Nottingham is indeed our final destination, I know just the man who would raze the forests to the ground if he thought Robert Wardieu d'Amboise was within his grasp."

PART THREE
Nottingham

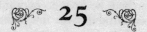

25

Robin's tiny band passed through the city of Rouen without further incident and, riding hard, reached the port town of Fecamp in time to admire the sunset the following night. Jean de Brevant, who had gone on ahead to arrange their passage, was not overly pleased to hear of their troubles at Gaillard. He was even less humored to see Griffyn Renaud and Fulgrin in their midst. The former had bruised splendidly throughout the night and day. One of his eyes was blue and swollen completely shut. His jaw was cut, his lips puffed out of any recognizable shape. But he had kept pace with the others, remaining in his saddle through sheer strength of will.

Brenna's heart had been in her throat each time they halted. She was afraid to go to him, afraid of what she might give away if she touched him or offered to tend his wounds. It was bad enough sensing Robin's displeasure each time he caught her looking in Griffyn's direction; bad enough to know he was aware of what she had given away already.

The ship Littlejohn had found was barely big enough to house the horses belowdecks and the men above. It was a single-masted cog, old enough, leaky enough, it had probably been used in its prime to carry Crusaders to the Holy Land.

Richard, Dag, and Geoffrey, after the first flush of bravado wore off, spent much of the time at the rails, their faces as green as the sea. Sparrow convinced himself the masts were trees and made a perch for himself in one, while Robin and Littlejohn preferred to huddle miserably against a bulkhead. Griffyn kept to himself, although he was never left entirely alone. Will FitzAthelstan was never very far from the dark knight's side, and if Griffyn suspected he was being closely watched, he gave no outward sign of taking offense. He brooded more over the necessity of leaving Centurion behind than the circumstances aboard ship. The stallion had come up lame on the last few miles of their approach to Fecamp, and it had been considered wise not to risk further injury in the cramped hold of the carrack.

Fulgrin had generously offered to remain behind to care for the destrier, but since there was only Timkin to handle the rouncies and supplies (and because he knew as much about where they were going and what they were setting forth to do), his submission was refused. He made no attempt to conceal his indignation and stated bluntly that he preferred the company of the horses. He stayed below-deck for most of the crossing, only surfacing when the stench of offal and wet hay became more overpowering than the sight of the horizon lurching up and down.

Brenna, who had never been at sea before, watched the men falling like nine-pins struck with a guilles stick and waited for her own stomach to protest the chilly, wind-driven passage. Three full days she waited, feeling nothing more than a faint queasiness, and was congratulating herself on possessing an iron gullet when the ship encountered a storm just off the hip of Yarmouth. The wind that had been pushing them along at a brisk pace suddenly blew in from all sides and roared with an unrelenting fury. Waves broke over the deck in solid gray sheets and threatened to sweep away anything not securely lashed to a mast or bulkhead.

In this new shifting, slipping, sliding, careening world, the seas had completely erased any point of reference on the horizon or, indeed, on board the ship, and Brenna quickly changed her opinions of sea travel. Her stomach more than made up for its reticence, and at end of twelve hours of constant battering by salt water and stinging rain, having been one of those objects securely lashed to a capstan, she was never so happy to see land, regardless who ruled or how bitter the ale.

Damaged, the cog had to put in at Lowestoft. Robin had been hoping to sail as far north as the Wash before landing, and he estimated this would add as much as three days to their journey. The men seemed to recover their spirits as soon as they set foot on solid land, proving to be ravenously hungry and insatiably thirsty, eager to be on their way. The horses were not so quick to adapt, however, and one of the rouncies had to be left behind.

The sky did not lose its gray, sullen appearance, not even after the storm had blown itself far out to sea. It remained a dull pewter color, heavy with slow-moving clouds that drizzled a constant, fine mist over the land day and night. Clothing that had become soaked on board ship had no opportunity to dry properly, and Sparrow, whose mission in life, as always, was to remind people of how truly wretched they could be, carped continually about the frozen state of his nose and toes, and about the sanity of any king who would not only choose to conquer such a godforsaken place but actually fight to keep it.

"Give it away to the first passing trull, I would," he muttered for the umpteenth time. "The land is too sour to grow anything but cabbages. The wine is like vinegar"—here he burped to prove he had given it a fair test—"and the meat so foul, a man must needs check his breeks each time he passes wind to insure there are no unwelcome surprises. In truth, I had forgotten how dreary and woebegotten a place is this England."

His opinions included the people as well. They were a forlorn, frightened lot, most of them cowering before the sight of the armored knights like dogs who expected to be beaten. At the odd village they were greeted with the respect due their rank, but these were few and the number of amiable people fewer still, with none inclined to extend more than the barest courtesies to passing strangers.

It was here, in the small vills and hamlets, where Griffyn Renaud proved his worth again. His French, perfect on the Continent and seeming to be tainted with only a hint of the coarser dialects of Burgundy, lapsed easily and fluidly into plain Saxon English when the need was required, startling his companions as well as the peasants he addressed. Robin and the others knew enough of the heathen tongue to get by begging a cup of water or lodgings for the night. But Griffyn could talk like one of them—something even Littlejohn found he had difficulty doing, not having spoken the language in over a decade.

Renaud's fluency saved them on more than one occasion when surly peasants deliberately sought to give them wrong directions as they worked their way inland toward the Great North Road—the main artery from London that passed through Nottingham, Lincoln, and York. It saved them on another occasion, when they were passing through a densely wooded forest and came upon an old man skinning a young, fat doe.

He must not have heard them approaching, for his left ear was missing and the right needed to be tilted toward the speaker's mouth to catch every other word. When he did eventually see the riders coming through the woods, he dropped the bloody knife and threw himself down on his knees, his head bowed, his hands clasped through a fervent prayer that lasted until Robin and Littlejohn dismounted. By then his face, hardly more than wrinkles layered upon wrinkles, had drained to pasty yellow-white and his eyes refused to lift above the level of the swords the two knights wore belted at their waists.

"Good fellow, rise," Robin ordered genially.

"I will stay here, be it all the same to ye, my lord," the old man muttered, "to save my poor head the trouble o' falling so far."

Robin looked askance at Littlejohn, who translated and pointed to the dead doe.

"Indeed," Robin said. "A fine, fat deer you have brought

down this day, and you see before you hungry men who would gladly buy whatever meat you could spare."

The old man cowered further, his belly almost rubbing the ground. "Take it all, yer worship, I need none o' it. They eat my turnips, ye see. I try to drive them off, I swear it to ye, worship, I do, but they keep coming back. This one, I only meant to scare off with my arrow, in truth I did, for I could not shoot my own foot if I rested the broadhead on it first. I like the deer, truly I do. But they eat my turnips, an' without my turnips, my family would starve an' this small plot o' land, poor as it is, would be taken away from me."

"Is this your freehold, then?" Littlejohn asked.

"Aye, worship. As it was my father's an' his father's before him."

"Then surely you have the right to kill any animal that trespasses upon it, especially if they have come to eat your turnips."

Griffyn, who had by then dismounted as well, came forward. "Not if that land is surrounded by royal forest," he said quietly in French, for the benefit of his companions, and again in Saxon English for the old man. "And not if that forest is full of wardens and verderers who earn an extra bezant for every hand they chop off a man who was only trying to keep his family from starving ... or his turnips from being eaten."

A watery brown eye peered up from beneath the folds of wrinkles and gawped. "Ye speak like a son o' the land. Has the king turned the children against us now?"

Griffyn smiled grimly. "Not in this lifetime, Father. We are only travelers seeking to make our way as peacefully through the forest as possible. My giant friend here was not trying to trick you; his belly speaks only the truth when it needs filling."

The old man seemed to inspect them closely for the first time. While they wore mail hauberks and chausses and carried their weapons and shields in plain sight to discourage too close a scrutiny, their tunics were plain, without cresting or colors, and their shields had been draped in gray bunting, in the fashion practiced by those knights returning from pilgrimage. Brenna wore her hair bound in a tight coil and stuffed beneath an oversized cap. She wore no mail but, like the two squires, was protected by a short leather byrnie and a well-padded surcoat that camouflaged any hint of her sex.

"Ye're not the king's men?"

Griffyn shook his head.

"Ye're not wardens?"

He shook his head again.

"Not wringers?"

"Only hungry travelers who would be willing to pay thee well to share a portion of your venison." Griffyn drew a couple of marks from his belt, possibly the first the old man had laid eyes upon in some time, for he stood, wobbling on weak legs, his gaze fixed on the twinkling silver coins.

"Aye, I need only a portion o' the haunch myself; but ye mout take the whole chine if ye have a belly as big as this"—he glanced at Littlejohn—"to fill."

He licked his lips and his bony hand seemed to stray toward the coins a moment before he controlled the impulse and withdrew it, wiping the palm on the greasy fabric of his tunic. "But I'll take no coin for it. Killing the royal deer would only cost me my hands, but if the wringers came an' found the coins, well . . ." He shook his head mournfully. "It would be the gallows-tree for me an' all my kin, innocent as they may be o' any crime."

It took a moment for the translation to win a reaction from Robin. "Wringers? Who are they?"

"Tax collectors," Griffyn explained with a frown. "Of the worst sort. They travel in packs, like wolves, and concentrate on the poorest farms and farmers, tearing a hut apart board by board and breaking the occupant's head if they even suspect him of hoarding an extra grain of wheat they have not listed in their rents."

Robin flushed, for his father had never condoned brutality or violence when dealing with his tenants, and those tenants, in turn, rarely betrayed his trust by trying to cheat their lord of his due. They were, in fact, happy to keep the storerooms at Château d' Amboise bulging. More than once over the past years harsh winters and poor crops had seen the Wolf open his doors to his people, even to sending wagons to neighboring demesnes to purchase grain and meat for those who would have starved otherwise.

"It makes little sense to beat, maim, and starve the very men who work the land and provide the rents that keep the manor lord in comfort."

The old man, who must have known more French than he had initially let on, smirked at Robin's naïveté. "Not if that lord is the Earl of Huntington an' *his* lord is John Lackland who seeks to take every last morsel o' bread out o' every man's mouth to satisfy the hunger in his own." He straightened and puffed out his chest. "An' ye may stab my heart with yer dagger for saying so, if ye will. I'll not beg to recant."

But it was Griffyn who looked suddenly stabbed. "The Earl of Huntington, you say?"

"Aye. Though I warrant he calls himself *god* in his private chambers."

"Does he have a name?"

"Aye. Gisbourne. Guy o' Gisbourne. He were awarded the Huntington claim some years back after the old earl's son disappeared—murthured by the king's men, some say, though there are others who swear he'll come back one day to seek his vengeance. If yer horses be as strong as they look, ye've been riding on Gisbourne's land since yesternoon, an' if ye keep riding hard, ye'll not pass out o' it before another three days hence, well ayont the Great Road. Owns a fair piece o' Nottinghamshire, he does, an' lords over it as high sheriff to make his thievery sound like justice. Like as not, he would own all o' Lincoln an' York too if not for the King o' Sherwood."

"The King of Sherwood?"

"Aye, a brave man. A hero." The brown eyes blazed a moment. "A bold an' stouthearted lad who showed himself not to be afraid o' the king's men an', by his example, fit

spines back into the men who followed his ways an' kept
the forests safe for humble fools like me. First thing Gisbourne did when he came to Nottingham was to put his soldiers on the road an' in the forests—looking to purge it o'
outlaws, he claimed. Looking for pennies to steal an'
women to rape, mores the like. Honest farmers had to hide
their grain in tree stumps just to keep their families from
starving, an' honest husbands had to hide their wives an'
daughters an' sisters in dung heaps to save them being carried away to whore for the guards in Nottingham Castle.
Then one day, a troop o' these black-souled monsters were
waylaid on their way back through Sherwood. Claimed the
devil stopped them, for he were dressed all in black an' wore
a hood over his face, as did the dozen or so disciples who
sprang out o' the trees an' bushes behint him. Took back
the women, they did, an' took back the chickens an' grain
an' pennies, then sent the guards on their way well blistered
to show the sheriff his thievery would not go unpunished
thenceforth. Aye, an' it has not." The old man chuckled.
"Even though Gisbourne threatens to hang every taxman
who comes back with his purse empty an' his mouth full o'
pitch an' feathers." He stopped and laughed so hard, he had
to slap his knee and stamp his foot. "Paints them in hot
pitch, he does, then rolls them in chicken feathers afore he
puts them back on the road. More 'n one has been mistaken
by the sheriff's own wardens an' shot for the castle
kitchens."

"These outlaws must be rich fellows by now," Robin
suggested.

"Nay!" The old man sobered and spat with enough vehe-
mence to startle the horses. "They keep not one cutting o'
one copper groat! What they takes, they gives back to those
it was stolen from—an' more besides! My own son—" He
stopped and chewed on his tongue, as if he had said too
much already, but then he cursed and continued. "He were
beaten by the wringers—so bad he lost an eye an' half a
foot. When he heard about it, the King o' Sherwood found
the wringers an' demonstrated a mort o' Saxon justice. Eye

for an eye, foot for a foot. He gave my Barth more than what was took, as well as the satisfaction o' knowing there are six o' the sheriff's men walking with sticks an' seeing half what they did afore."

"This outlaw king does indeed sound like a stout fellow," Littlejohn agreed. "I trust he will not take offense to our passing through these woods or mistake us for the king's men."

"In fact," Robin said, "we should like to meet him, if you can tell us where he may be found."

The old man looked instantly suspicious, and his gaze went from face to face, studying each with renewed wariness and fear.

"We are not come in search of any reward or bounty," Griffyn assured him.

The turnip farmer wilted again and shook his head sadly. "Would do ye no good even if ye were. Some yellow-livered, fish-pricked swine has already collected it, for he has been locked away in the sheriff's donjons this past month, an' Gisbourne has set the hanging for Saturday next."

"That is"—Littlejohn counted on his fingers—"four days hence. Has no one tried to free him before now? What of these brave men you say follow him?"

"They would follow him to hell if he asked it o' them, but they'll not do the sheriff's work. Nottingham is a fortress. In the woods, aye, they move like ghosts an' know how to cause a man to melt with fits just by whispering his name. But a castle with a full garrison? Few o' the foresters ever held a sword afore *he* put one into their hands."

Dag, whose common sense was often the victim of his impulse and passion, looked at his brothers. "We have swords, and know well how to use them."

"Day an' night," the old man said, "we have prayed for another brave man to step forward and don the lincoln hood with enough boldness an' courage to rescue him."

"You see before you the bravest man in all of England,

France, and Normandy," Richard declared. "His name is
Robin W—"

"—*of Locksley,*" Griffyn interjected hastily. "His name is
Robin of Locksley and he would need to know a great deal
more about this outlaw king before he would commit his
sword to the fight."

"Locksley?" The brown eyes watered under the folded
wrinkles of a frown as they peered intently at Robin's
face—a face that was turned to look askance at Griffyn.

"*Locksley!*" The old man's brown eyes bulged out of their
creases, and he fell onto his knees again, grasping Robin's
gloved hand and pressing it over his head as if he was
seeking a benediction. "The bard was right! Ye did not die
by the king's sword! Ye did come back . . . and ye've
brought Albion with ye!"

This time Robin glared at Griffyn, who only shrugged
and murmured, "I thought it might as well be a good Saxon
name that takes credit for any prayers we might answer
between here and Nottingham."

"Yours, of course?"

Griffyn smiled. "You invited me along for the adventure,
did you not?"

"Not four thousand marks' worth."

"An extravagant gesture and a risky diversion, I grant
you, but look upon it this way: When Gisbourne hears the
real Earl of Huntington is back in Nottingham, how much
attention do you think he will pay to a small abbey at
Kirklees?"

Robin frowned and looked down at the old farmer's
bowed head. "And who the devil is Albion?"

"Not who. What. It is a sword, reputed to have been carried by the Saxon king, Alfred the Great, when he prevented the Danes from conquering all of England."

Robin glanced at the huge serpentine blade strapped to
Griffyn's side. "And now I suppose you are going to tell
me . . . ?"

Griffyn followed Robin's gaze and laughed. "It belonged

to my great-grandfather, aye, but the only legend attached to it has to do with the Prince of Darkness."

"A legend that may be somewhat tarnished now due to an . . . untimely tumble from the saddle."

Griffyn looked up and saw the question hovering unspoken behind the statement, but a faint smile was the only answer he gave as he turned and walked over to the horses. Robin stared thoughtfully after him, then helped the wobbly old farmer back to his feet.

"Come, old man. Share your fire along with your venison and tell us more about this bold King of Sherwood."

26

Brenna was appalled and almost too angry to wait until after nightfall when the others were asleep and an opportunity arose to steal a private moment's conversation with Griffyn Renaud.

"Are you mad? Are you *completely* insane?" she demanded.

The accused, who had been sitting by the side of the small brook that coursed its way past the turnip farmer's freehold, glanced over his shoulder at the sound of her voice.

"And a pleasant good evening to you too," he replied.

"Tell me one thing pleasant about it."

"Well." He looked up at the night sky. "The rain has stopped and the moon is out. For another, the river is sweet and cool, the forest so quiet you can hear the leaves breathing."

Brenna took a moment to look grudgingly around, not even aware of the moonlight until he mentioned it. As for the stream—did he expect it to be hot and bitter? In truth, she found the silence more oppressive than comforting. The trees were taller than those in the forests around Amboise and most had thick vines twined around the trunks to distort their appearance. They wore their foliage up high, while below, their bases were veiled in an opaque, knee-deep layer of mist that undulated like a pool of white cream with every movement. The farmer's cottage, a hut of mud and wattle, was set like a hazy jewel well back in the moist darkness of the woods. And try as she might, the only breathing she could hear was her own, dry and angry and too fast for rational thought.

Those same moments Brenna used to contemplate her surroundings, Griffyn used to steel himself against her nymphlike appearance in the moonlight. The farmer's wife, discovering a woman in their midst, had insisted she take off all of her sodden clothes and lay them out in front of a blazing fire to dry. She had replaced them with a plain tunic of coarse, cream-colored wool, shapeless and inches too short, then boiled enough hot water to allow Brenna to wash the sea salt out of her hair and restore it to its natural golden resplendence. The result, illuminated by the intense streamers of blue-white moonlight, made her look like a druid goddess come to scold him for daring to have human thoughts.

"*Are* you insane?" she asked again, each word crisp and precise.

He tossed aside the stick he had been using to stir up silvered ripples on the water and pushed to his feet. He unfolded his over-six-foot frame with a measured precision that caused Brenna to retreat a discreet step as he turned toward her.

"No," he answered with equal precision. "I am quite within my own mind."

"You do not consider throwing yourself to the wolves to be a touch addled?"

"I have been doing much the same thing for seven years now. It has almost become a way of life."

"Whatever you have done, you have done for yourself. What you propose to do now—putting yourself forward as bait for Guy of Gisbourne—"

"I do for myself as well," he interrupted softly. "And for you, oddly enough."

"*Me?*"

"In truth, for something you said: that some things were more important than simple cockfights and boasting contests."

"Some things are, but—"

"You doubted I would have the character to see them?"

She flushed. "I did not say that."

"No, not in so many words. But you did accuse me of having sold my honor along with my sword."

"You are doing this because of something I said in a fit of anger?"

"No. I am doing it because it needs to be done. I *am* the Earl of Huntington. I *should* have been the one to stand up and fight for my people, not skulk away in the dark of night and hide behind the anonymity of a new name, a new guise."

"You said yourself you were very young. The king would have hunted you down and killed you."

"Would I not then, in your eyes, have died with some shreds of honor draped about me?"

"You twist everything I say, and now you try to twist what I think." She looked away a moment. "You are mocking me, sir."

He took a casual step closer to her. "I am mocking myself, dear lady. Something I have been doing with alarming frequency lately . . . ever since I saw you standing by the river at Amboise, in fact. It was a disconcerting sight, to say the least, for I rather prided myself on my ability to avoid traps and pitfalls. But I never heard you, never saw you coming, never had the faintest inkling of the danger I was in the moment I decided to challenge that look in your eye."

"I . . . am sure I do not know what look you mean."

"You should. It is a formidable weapon and pierced clean through my heart like no mere arrow could. Fool that I was, I thought I had built up enough armor to protect me, but I could not have been more wrong."

This last was said so softly, it startled Brenna's gaze up to his face again. The moonlight was streaming through the trees, hazed blue by the mist, but bright enough she could see his face in all its stark beauty. He had moved to within arm's reach, close enough for her to feel the sworls of displaced mist curling around her ankles.

"You were wrong?"

"As ever a fool can be who thinks he has hardened himself against thinking that someone could care for him again, despite all his flaws."

"But"—her chin quivered and her heel scraped the root of a tall oak as she back up against it—"I do not care for you," she whispered. "I do not even like you, sir."

"Yet you convinced your brother to rescue me from Saintonge's clutches."

She watched his mouth form the words and felt the echo of them shiver along her spine.

"Saving you from Saintonge was the least we could do," she stammered. "Robin does not like being indebted to anyone."

"That would explain his reasons for charging into the woods at Les Andelys. But what about yours?"

Softly: "Mine?"

"You were on the verge of shooting me at one point. The next, you were offering to go anywhere with me, be any manner of companion I wished you to be."

"I w-was not in *my* right mind," she stammered, lowering her lashes. "I was desperate and frantic and—"

He tucked a finger beneath her chin, coaxing it upward again. "And I wanted you so badly I almost agreed."

She took two full breaths before she regained the ability to speak. "But you did not agree."

"No," he mused. "I did not. And I shall probably regret that decision for the rest of my life."

"Wh-whereas I shall probably regret making the offer for the rest of mine."

"Meaning . . . you would not propose it again?"

"No."

"Not under any circumstance?"

"No. You play too easily with people's lives. You play too easily with your own for that matter, and I could not imagine what a life with you would entail."

"You *cannot* imagine it . . . or you are too *afraid* to imagine it?"

"I am not afraid of you, Griffyn Renaud."

"I did not say you were afraid of *me*." A darkened spiral of hair had sprung forward over her forehead and he brushed it aside with a breath of a kiss. "You are afraid of this," he whispered, trailing the caress to her temple and down to the curl of her ear. "And this." He bent his head and she felt the black silk of his hair on her cheek. His lips were on her throat, in the crook of her neck, and she closed her eyes, her breath coming even hotter and faster than before. Her heart beat with a wildness that frightened her, and she felt as if she were standing on the edge of a cliff, the hypnotic lure of danger pulling her forward and the safe sanctuary of solid ground calling her back.

"How . . . can you expect me to believe you?" she gasped. "After everything that has happened . . . the lies, the dishonesty, the cruel games—?"

"The night we spent together at Gaillard was no game."

A hot, stinging liquid blurred her eyes and she shook her head again, helpless to counter the heat of his arms, the ravaging tenderness of his lips. She wanted to believe him. She wanted it more than anything, but the rational part of her mind—the part that cried out to her to step back from the edge of the cliff—was still reluctant to trust him with something so fragile as her heart.

Feeling her resistance, his hands cradled her face and his eyes blazed with the same searing intensity as the moonlight. "What will it take to convince you?"

With her tears spilling faster than she could blink them free, she watched the dark outline of his face bend toward her. Like wax before a flame, she melted into the heat of his mouth, wavering, shimmering, turning soft and malleable inside, lacking any strength or substance to hold her firm against the tenderness of his assault.

She felt his hand sliding down her hip, catching and dragging the hem of the wool skirt upward to uncover the smooth, yielding flesh of her thigh. She felt the dampness of the moss-covered bark against her back as he lifted her bared leg and seated it around his waist, and she felt his hand between them, tugging at and loosening the points of his hose. His own flesh sprang hot and free, and she moaned beneath the pressure of his mouth, but it was too late. He was there. He was touching her, he was inside her, pushing upward into the sleek, moist warmth, groaning as the silky muscles tightened greedily around him and sucked him deeper . . . deeper still.

"Tell me," he rasped, "you do not believe this."

Her reply was a breathless sob and the softest of oaths took his mouth away from hers but only long enough for him to bare her other leg and urge it up around his waist. His hands went beneath her bottom and he lifted her, the muscles in his arms trembling where she clutched at them for support. She felt the driving shock of his strength, the tightening within herself that held him all the more possessively, and with a swiftness that took her breath away, her need became as fierce, as primitive as his own. She pushed herself onto him, her flesh aching-wet, abandoning all of her senses to respond to the force of his passion. Her skin flamed and her blood sang through her veins. A streaking heat shuddered through her with each powerful thrust, its intensity pushing her beyond common sense, beyond all ability to deny the pleasure, the hunger, the need to feel him surging and thrusting and gasping her name against her throat.

His body stretched and throbbed and filled her with a wet, pulsating heat, and the ecstasy lifted her, sent her soaring through one exquisite crest after another, each spasm splintering her body into tiny fragments of pleasure. Her fingers curled into his hair and she had to clench her teeth together to keep from screaming as the shivers ran down her thighs, spiraled through her arms, coiled between her thighs, her belly, her breasts. Her hips continued to meet each savage thrust, though she did not know where she found the strength to do so. The tightness inside her would not relent until she felt him stiffen a second time and a third, the pleasure flooding out of him in long, sweet bursts of shuddered relief.

She gasped for air and found his mouth. Her body was glowing, almost steaming from the extravagant release of pent-up emotions, and she groaned, burying her face in his throat, mortified to feel the proof of their excesses slippery on her thighs.

Griffyn was in hardly better shape. His one hand was braced against the trunk of the tree for support; the other was still cupped beneath her hips. He was afraid to let her go, afraid to move at all in case his knees gave way and sent them both tumbling onto the ground. She was still a very real threat to his senses, for she continued to pulsate softly around him, to hold him in the warm, velvety grasp of her womanhood as if the thought of his leaving her did not even warrant consideration. And for the moment, no thought was further from his mind.

"One of these days," he murmured against her ear, "we really must try doing this in a bed."

Since he was more or less echoing her own thoughts, Brenna felt compelled to lift her head from his shoulder and gaze up into the silvery glow of his eyes. His gentle smile closed like a fist around her heart and she uttered a helpless gasp as yet another silky wash of sensation rippled through her body.

"Or in the clouds," he mused. "Where it will be my pleasure to make you faint as many times as you wish it."

He shifted his hands, sending one up beneath the tunic to circle and engulf her breast even as he sank carefully onto his knees in the mist. He managed, somehow, to keep her firmly in place on his lap, even to move her gently to and fro so that she could feel his heat still deep within her. His arms tightened around her and his lips were on her temple, on her cheeks, on the salt-bathed warmth of her mouth, and she returned his kiss with shameless fervor, her body leaning into his, pressing into his, eager to feel the strength of his passion engulfing her once more.

* * *

Brenna's sigh shivered the entire length of her body. Her
head was pressed back into the moss, her hair was scattered
in a damp tangle beneath. Her body was sprawled in a
puddle of moonlit mist, her limbs immodestly spread, bent
at the knee, one bare foot still draped indolently over
Griffyn's shoulder while the other was being gently lowered
and warmed by his breath and his hands.

Able to think of nothing that made a modicum of sense
at that precise moment, she tilted her head to one side and
peered down at him from beneath a small frown.

"Locksley. Is that your real name?"

He kissed her instep and frowned as if he had to think
about it a moment. "Rowen Hode of Locksley. A name
I have not thought of or used in too many years to
remember."

"Rowen?" She arched an eyebrow in surprise.

"A name conferred upon me by Hern the Hunter, so the
story goes," he murmured in acknowledgment. "My mother
gave birth to me in this very forest and claimed the ghost of
Hern led her to shelter in a sacred cavern. She told me later
it was actually just a hole beneath two rocks, but it was a
good enough tale to make my father think I should become
moderately proficient with the bow and arrow."

"*Moderately* proficient?"

"I have been known to miss the mark occasionally. At
any rate, he sent me to Wales when I was ten, where I was
given my first introduction to the longbow—a weapon I
confess at first was more terrifying to me than it was to any
hare in the forest. I had also thought it a weapon native to
that land alone, which makes me admit to some curiosity as
to how one ended up so far away in Touraine, wielded with
such expertise by a golden-haired minx hardly as tall as the
bow itself."

Brenna rested the warmed foot in the crease of his belly
while he lowered and massaged the other.

"Will's mother—Lady Gillian—was the daughter of a
Welsh bowyer. She taught us both . . . all of us actually,
though it was only Will and I who became . . . moderately

proficient. Robin has a fair hand and eye, but he is too impatient. Richard and Dag . . . well . . . they disdain any weapon that does not allow them to feel the splash of their enemy's blood."

He smoothed his hands absently down her thighs and stroked his thumbs over flesh that was still flushed and dewy from his recent ministrations.

"I would have thought Sparrow to have the least patience of all," he remarked, lowering his mouth to the top of her thigh.

"The least patience," she agreed with a small start, "and the least tolerance. But the most love for my father and, in turn, all of us."

"And Littlejohn?"

"Littlejohn has"—she sucked her breath in through her teeth as his tongue swirled and explored, and finally relented to lick a meandering path up onto her belly—"has been known to tear a man apart with his bare hands."

He laid his own hand on the little fluttered contractions he could feel skittering beneath the surface of her skin and grinned. "I will keep that in mind."

"You should. I do not think he likes you overmuch."

"Neither does Will. Have I . . . intruded on territory he was hoping to claim for himself?"

"Will'um? Good heavens, no. We slept in the same cradle when we were babes, and if ever we gave a thought to sharing something bigger now, my sister Rhiannon would behead us both. No, Will is just . . . Will. He is very much like his father, who can often see things hidden behind a man's demeanor that no one else can."

"Between him and your brother-in-law I feel like a bug in a bottle."

"Geoffrey? He is the easiest-natured of the lot."

"That may well be," he said, molding his mouth around her breast. "But of the lot, I warrant he would be the most dangerous if he found himself pressed into a corner."

Brenna's frown only lasted through the first shudder as she felt her nipples quiver and flush with eagerness under the skilled tutelage of his lips. It seemed so easy, so natural, so instinctive simply to open herself to him, to welcome his big body between her thighs and sigh against his mouth as he filled her with ecstasy.

"What will you do now, Rowen Hode of Locksley?" she asked on a shiver of breath.

"Now? Right this instant?"

She dug her nails into his buttocks by way of a reprimand. "When we leave this place? When we reach Sherwood?"

"You heard the old crone say he would lead us there and introduce us to the outlaws. After that, assuming they accept our help, and assuming my name will have tickled Gisbourne's ears by then, I will endeavor to keep the king's men occupied while your brothers spirit the Princess Eleanor and her son to safety."

"I want to stay with you."

The languid stroking of his body ceased. "Did you not just call *me* mad for my delusions?"

"You *are* mad. And you have already proven you need someone to watch your back."

"What about your brother? Do you think him addled as well?"

"Robin would see the sense of it, especially if it saved him the aggravation of having to rescue you again."

Griffyn shook his head. "Even if he allowed it, I would not."

"Why not? I am perfectly capable of looking out for myself and you know full well I would be more help to you than hindrance."

He groaned and sank into her clinging heat. "You are a hindrance each time I look at you and think only of being where I am now."

"Perhaps"—she bit her lip at her boldness—"if you were there more often you would not think of it as much."

He stopped himself again—with somewhat more difficulty this time—and peered intently at her. "Is that a woman's logic? Or is that simply how you imagine *you* would come to feel after the ravages of boredom set in?"

She curled her nails into his flesh again and squirmed to maneuver him where she wanted to feel him most.

"Boredom"—she gasped into his ear—"is not a fear just yet."

He laughed softly and obliged her urgent whimpers and, when they had both settled again, kissed her soundly on the mouth. "But it does not change my mind."

"Perhaps this will," said a gruff voice from the darkness above. Griffyn flinched as the cold bite of an arrowhead touched his neck and Brenna's cry was cut short as she saw the silhouettes of five, six men emerge out of the mist to surround them. None of them were familiar. None of them were her brothers, and none, save for the one who had his arrow nocked and held against Griffyn's throat, looked the smallest part amused by the sight of the naked lovers twined together on the forest floor.

27

Brenna smoothed a hand over the disheveled mass of her hair and stumbled slightly as her toe caught on a half-buried rock. Griffyn's hand was on her elbow to steady her, and he gave her an additional squeeze for courage as they were prodded in the direction of the farmer's cottage.

She had been permitted to dress, at least, though she had felt the leering eyes of the strangers on her the whole time. Griffyn's clothing had been tossed at him a garment at a time after it was given a thorough search—one that resulted in a small collection of blades and concealed weaponry. Only the one man spoke to them, his orders blunt and to the point, emphasized with a threat from his bow if they were not met quickly enough. Brenna waited, her heart in her throat, for Griffyn to explode into the same kind of lethal violence she had witnessed against her attackers at Gaillard, but he remained oddly calm and kept looking at their tall, lanky leader out of the corner of his eye.

The first to mark their approach to the cottage was Centaur, whose gray head swung up and around with a snort of suspicion. The cottage itself had been far too small for the men to crowd inside, and they had rolled themselves into blankets on the ground around the fire, enjoying the first dry night in several days.

"Brenna?" Robin's voice was rusty with sleep as he lifted his head and peered across the flames. "Is that you?"

"We have visitors," she said unnecessarily as the surly-eyed strangers fanned out in a circle, each picking a sleeping form to stand over with bow and arrow.

Robin propped himself on one elbow and knuckled his
eyes. "So we do. Are there any among them who speak
something other than Saxon English?"

The lanky man nudged Griffyn forward, then stepped
into the ring of firelight himself. He was tall—taller even
than Littlejohn, with most of his seven feet owing to legs as
long and thin as the stilts used by jongleurs to walk above
the crowds at a fair. His face was hidden behind a ratted
beard and there were signs of a childhood disease pocking
the skin that was visible. His eyes were as dark as the
midnight sky and burned with a mixture of contempt and
insolence.

"I speak the Norman language of your king," he said,
curling back his lip with disdain.

"Are you the leader of this motley group?"

"They have been known to obey an order or two."

"Good." Robin smiled. "Then we shall have no mis-
understandings between us and you will be most precise
when you advise your men to lower their weapons before
they find their heads sadly parted from their shoulders."

A second rustling of branches and boughs brought
Richard, Dag, Will, Geoffrey, and Littlejohn out of the
shadows behind the archers, their swords drawn, the
gleaming edges of the blades resting against the newcomers'
jugulars.

The leader was impressed but not worried as he looked at
the rolled and stuffed blankets positioned around the fire. A
moment and a soft whistle later, and the reason for his
bemused expression came clear. A dozen or more silky
swooshes brought as many more foresters sliding down vines
suspended from above, while an equal number emerged
from the mist surrounding the cottage, seeming to fill every
gap and firelit space in the clearing with frowning faces and
glittering arrowheads.

"You mentioned something about lowering weapons?"
the leader commented dryly.

Robin pushed carefully to his feet and cast a cold gray eye
around the crowded glade. They were outnumbered four to

one—not normally cause for concern to a knight facing forest bumpkins—yet while his hand itched to reach for his sword, he agreed with the cautionary look in Will's eyes as he noted the steady bowarms. These men were not unfamiliar with their weapons and, unlike the turnip farmer, would not cower on their knees and beg mercy for killing one of them.

Robin acknowledged a second subtle glance from Will, one given to indicate the trees overhead and remind him that Sparrow was up there somewhere. It was small comfort, to be sure, but they had all been amazed on more than one occasion by the woodsprite's ingenuity, and so he nodded to the others and, one by one, grudgingly, they relinquished their weapons to the foresters.

"May I ask to what do we owe the pleasure of such an unexpected surprise?"

"We were curious to know who you were and what brought you into our forest. You ride with enough arrogance and make enough noise"—he glanced pointedly at Griffyn and Brenna—"to be the king's men, yet you cover your shields with bunting and wear the hooded cowls of humble pilgrims."

"If we were the king's men?"

"We would expect you to pay a generous toll before we let you go any further."

"And if we were but humble pilgrims?"

The outlaw grinned. "Your armor is too rich, your horses too well fed. You would still have to pay a toll in order to pass through our forest."

"That is the second time you have called it *your* forest," Griffyn noted. "May we assume your name is Guy of Gisbourne and you hold title over the lands of Nottinghamshire?"

The forester glared at Griffyn—having to tilt his eyes down at least a hand's width to do so—and spat rather vociferously on the ground at his feet. "There is the toll we pay to Guy of Gisbourne, for the only title he holds has its boundaries in hell."

"An amiable overlord, is he?" Robin asked, drawing the midnight gaze back. "I had an occasion to make his acquaintance once, several years back, and do heartily share your opinion. If I am not mistaken, we too have met, and under somewhat similar circumstances."

The outlaw's eyes narrowed suspiciously. "We have met? When?"

"I do not doubt you have no memory of it, as I was a mere lad at the time. I recall it most clearly, however, for I thought you were surely as tall as one of the spires on the cathedrals we had recently seen in Angers."

It took almost a full minute for a glimmer of recognition to dawn in the outlaw's eyes and when it did, it came with a grunt and a frown. "That was half a lifetime ago, Norman."

"Half a lifetime," Robin agreed. "And I see you have not mended your ways overmuch, despite the promise you gave my brother Eduard when he let you go."

"It has not been by choice, I assure you."

Richard whuffed out an impatient breath. "Would someone care to let us in on the conversation?"

"We met," Robin explained, "in another ambush set in another forest much like this, only the company he kept was far less proficient at skulduggery. Our friend here took an arrow in his arm for his trouble—one of Eduard's, I believe—and his name ..." He paused and rubbed a thoughtful thumb across his chin. "... is Alan. Alan, son of Tom, yeoman of the Dale of Sherwood."

The other villains shifted uncomfortably on their feet, an indication that Robin's memory was without fault.

"I was only thirteen at the time and squire to my brother," he added. "Your courage left a strong mark on my mind, although when you thrust that arrowhead through your own flesh and handed it back to Eduard ... I very nearly lost my stomach right there on the forest floor."

Alan of the Dale hesitated a further moment before offering up a rueful smile. "It hurt like hell. And I *did* lose my stomach, though not until after I was prudently out of sight." The half smile gained a curious twist as he regarded the firelit group of knights with new eyes. "You were bound for England then . . . and you are come again now. I should warn you, we take no kindlier to spies of the French king."

"We are not spies to any king," Robin assured him. "Nor have we come to your forest to cause you any trouble."

"Fresh graves are rarely any trouble. But tiresome to dig, nonetheless."

Robin laughed. "Will you and your men share our fire? There is some venison left and a pot of stew pieced with hare if the cotter can be persuaded to part with it."

The dark eyes flickered to the inch-wide slit in the door of the cottage, which instantly creaked shut again.

"We are too many and my uncle's stew tastes of too many turnips for my taste. Moreover, so many feet leave too many tracks on the ground, and he would be hard pressed to explain the crush once we are gone. Why not come with us instead? Our main camp is but a few hours from here and better suited to entertaining such noble guests."

Robin was not misled by the politeness of the invitation; he doubted they would have a choice even if he declined. So polite were the foresters, in fact, they helped the knights pack up their belongings and saddle the horses. And so swift were they in removing all traces of any visitors to the turnip farmer's cottage that Brenna's clothes were snatched up from the fire and hastily packed away with the rest of the blankets and clothing before she could change. Her protest died on her lips as Griffyn put a cautionary hand on her arm.

"Let it go. Let them think of you as a mere woman awhile longer."

"What?"

"Look . . . they do not even know what to make of them."

She followed the tilt of his head and saw two of the foresters examining the longbows. They were frowning, scratching their heads and comparing them to the much shorter, English-style livery they wore slung over their shoulders.

"Are your men good archers?" Griffyn asked Alan of the Dale.

"The best in England. Nay, I warrant the best in the world."

"Yet they look in amusement upon the best bows ever fashioned in all of Christendom."

"Those poles? You would need the arms of a Hercules to shoot them!"

"Not if you know how. Tell your men to have a care how they handle them and we will ask the lady here to give you a demonstration on the morrow."

Alan of the Dale looked down upon Brenna, who returned his gaze with a directness that made him blush.

"We would happily invite her to demonstrate other talents," said another voice nearby, coarsened by laughter. "We would handle her with care indeed."

And that was all he said. Griffyn's fist came up and caught him square in the face, smashing his nose and knocking him clear across the firepit to land unconscious in the arms of two startled companions. It happened so swiftly and with such exquisite violence, none of the foresters had time to react, not even Alan of the Dale, who found himself staring down the blade of the small but extremely sharp misericorde that was depressing the skin below his left eye socket.

"You will advise your men," Griffyn murmured in guttural Saxon, "to hold their tongues in the presence of my wife . . . lest her brothers and I decide to add their livers to the stew pot."

"They meant no disrespect. I am sure they thought she was just—"

"Just what?"

The forester blinked and clamped his jaw shut. "I will advise them."

Griffyn's pale, unearthly gaze continued to hold the outlaw pinioned while he lowered the misericorde and resheathed it in a hidden fold of his belt. The forester watched the blade disappear but wisely made no attempt to relieve him of it.

Brenna, who had understood only a few of the whispered words, waited for Griffyn to turn toward her before she hissed up at him herself. *"Wife? You said I was your wife?"*

"What else would you rather they think you were, considering where they found us and what we were doing?"

She did not have an opportunity to do more than splutter, for two of the foresters were trying without much success to saddle Centaur. The huge warhorse reared, pawing the air with his forelegs, lifting one man off the ground and sinking his teeth into the arm of the other. Griffyn whistled shrilly, which brought the stallion to a snorting standstill, but neither of the two men would go near him again.

"Where the devil is Fulgrin?"

"Fainted behind a tree, the last I saw him," Littlejohn remarked casually as he passed by.

Robin was coming the other way and clapped Griffyn on the shoulder. "A wonder you ever survived a season in the lists with such a stout fellow as that at your beck and call."

Griffyn cursed and took up the stallion's reins himself.

The outlaw leader, meanwhile, ordered his men to lead the rest of the horses out of the clearing. As they disappeared one by one into the darkness of the forest, they were followed by half the foresters, some of whom spread out on either side and some who ran ahead to insure the way was clear.

"For someone who worries after a few crushed tracks," Robin observed, "you travel in large numbers."

"Necessity breeds unusual circumstances."

"The eminent demise of your leader?" Robin guessed.

Alan of the Dale grimaced and glanced at the cottage. "My uncle has a loose tongue, but aye. He is the reason why we are in the woods in such numbers, and the reason why we will be even stronger in three days when he is to be moved to Lincoln for the hanging."

"They are taking him out of Nottingham?"

The forester nodded. "John Plantagenet is in Lincoln and wishes to be entertained by seeing the King of Sherwood executed."

The Wardieu men stopped what they were doing and listened intently. It came as unpleasant news to them to hear that the English king was so close by, and their concern was reflected on their faces.

" 'Tis the chance we have been hoping for," the outlaw continued unawares. "The only one Gisbourne has offered thus far. He will be moved under heavy escort, to be sure, and there is every good chance the sheriff is using him as bait, hoping to draw us out of the greenwood. But we have no choice. He has risked all, forsaken everything, taken immeasurable risks himself to save each of us from certain death. We must try to save him, regardless of the cost in lives."

"How many men do you have?" asked Will FitzAthelstan.

"By tomorrow eve, if our runners have been successful, we should have near four score in the main camp, more if you count the women who are willing to throw stones and wield staves."

"What of Gisbourne? How big of a garrison does he keep at Nottingham?"

"Forty knights, thereabout, and over a hundred men-at-arms."

Will whistled softly under his breath. One hundred forty trained fighting men against eighty foresters and women. It would be a slaughter.

"It would be a lively challenge," Dag said, his eyes gleaming with enthusiasm.

"It would require delicate planning," Richard agreed. "But aye, it would be a worthy contest."

Alan of the Dale was not overwhelmed by their zeal and said as much. "With no further offense intended, my lords, we have only your words that you are not here to aid the French king. And here in the greenwood, we have not survived as long as we have by accepting someone's bond on blind faith alone."

"What will it take to convince you we are on the same side?" Robin demanded.

"Perhaps just your amiable company over the next few hours."

"We are not come into these woods to be amiable," Littlejohn growled. "Nor do we have the *time*," he added with as much sarcasm directed at Robin and the other young hot-bloods, as to the outlaw leader, "to waste helping you save the neck of this Prince of Thieves."

The outlaw stuck out his jaw. "In the first place, we have not asked for your help. In the second, we are none of us thieves. We are merely men who have become weary of the beatings, the maimings, the raping of our women, the blinding, crippling, and starving of our children. We have had our homes burned over our heads and the food stolen from our babes' mouths. Our skin flayed from our bones and our hands, feet, and tongues chopped off for daring to protest the king's greed. We came together in the forest because we had no where else to go. And we stay together, we will fight together *to the last arrow* if need be because of one man's courage and selflessness."

"Does this noble paragon have a name?" Littlejohn scoffed.

"That he once had a noble name, none of us doubt. For reasons of his own, however, he keeps it to himself and prefers to be addressed by a more humble designation. Tuck, is what he goes by. Friar Tuck."

28

Discovering that Henry de Clare was the elusive King of Sherwood did not come as an earth-shattering revelation to any of the Wardieu men, least of all Robin. It did, however, hasten their footsteps through the forest as Alan a' Dale led them deeper into the wood, into the very heart of Sherwood where their main camp was located. Few outsiders were permitted to venture so close to the pulse point of the outlaw band, and those who did were usually blindfolded and led on a merry chase before being taken to the actual camp. Since the moon was now gone and it was as black as a cat's maw, there was little need for such precautions, although every so often, a distinct *thwang* and *whoosh* could be heard coming from the trees overhead. When asked about it, Alan merely shrugged and allowed that they had sentries who sat watch, and had Robin's band been approaching uninvited, they would likely be dead by now or at least questioned sternly about their purpose for being in the woods.

They walked for the better part of the night, through stretches of wood so thick and dense, they could only move in single file along what passed for a path. They used neither torchlight nor lantern to find their way, and on more than one occasion, it was suspected the silent wraiths moving through the trees on either side were as much to provide direction as security.

It was tiring work, for knights do not march well, especially burdened under mail hauberks. At one point, Robin bade the leader of the outlaws halt that they might strip out of their iron link suits and Brenna, who cursed and stumbled at every entanglement of her skirt's hem, might change into more comfortable clothes for walking.

Alan a' Dale agreed and it was only then, by chance, that Robin and Griffyn managed to exchange a few private words.

"Eighty men and women against one hundred and forty? Even if these foresters were seasoned fighters, I doubt this villain has the knowledge how to best deploy them against such odds."

"And you think we would?" Robin asked.

"You are still fresh from the battlefield of Roche-au-Moines, where the odds were no better in your favor."

"Yes, and though I had experienced knights under my command, we still suffered heavy losses for it. These are like babes in the woods. Pikes against swords, cudgels and hoes against starbursts and mace." He finished securing his armor to Sir Tristan's saddle. "Be that as it may, you heard what he said. He does not want our help, nor does he trust us enough to ask for it."

"In which case, I strongly doubt he will be too eager to let any of us forage off on our own, searching for lost princesses."

"What do you suggest I do? Ask *him* for help?"

"It would seem to be the logical solution."

"Logical?" Robin grunted. "What is to say he would not consider a Plantagenet princess to be as much of an enemy as a Plantagenet king?"

Griffyn's shallow chuckle was laced with irony. "You ask this because he is an outlaw or because he is a Saxon?"

Since Renaud had admitted to being both, Robin took an extra moment to consider his answer—long enough for a six-inch iron bolt to find its mark and *f-thunk* into the soft earth at his feet.

He bent over quickly to retrieve it and peered into the misty woods around them. "Sparrow?"

"I am here, Lummock," came a whispered reply. "Rot my nose if I can leave the lot of you alone long enough to piss up an alder bush."

368   *Marsha Canham*

"You should content yourself with more earth-bound tree stumps and your nose would be where it belonged when we needed it."

"Faugh! Had it been thus, I would have been caught farting at the moon along with the rest of you who can boast only feathers and dung for brains."

Robin sighed and bowed his head. "You are absolutely right, of course. We need you more where you are now. Have you any idea in which direction we are bound? North? South? West?"

"North and west, as far as I can determine, led there by the runners sent out on either side. They are good, by Cyril's toes. Twice I have nearly flown right up their heels."

"Are you having any trouble keeping apace with us?"

There was a pause while Sparrow plainly considered the extent of Robin's weariness and decided it was not worth the sympathy. "If I was, Pillock, would I be where I am now?"

"Well . . . be careful. You may have to show us the way out of this place if the foresters object to our leaving."

He straightened at the sound of footsteps behind him and tucked the bolt under his tunic.

"Time to move out again," said Alan a' Dale, glancing upward into the boughs of the tree. When he looked back, he addressed Griffyn. "The horses have slowed us down and there are still some two or thee hours ahead of us. Would your wife prefer to ride the rest of the way?"

Griffyn barely acknowledged the look on Robin's face as he replied, "I thank you for asking, but she has a stubborn streak as wide as this forest and I strongly doubt she would ride while the rest of us walk."

Alan shrugged and moved away.

"Wife?" Robin said through his teeth.

"I thought it best, under the circumstances, if she appeared to be traveling under the protection of a husband as well as several hale brothers."

Robin's brows crushed together in an ominous glower. "What circumstances?"

"One woman traveling unchaperoned in the company of nine men? What circumstance would you make of it?"

"It would depend upon what that woman was doing if I found her alone in the woods with one of those men at night."

Griffyn's eyes glowed luminously out of the dark.

"When this is over, Renaud . . . or Locksley"—Robin's eyes narrowed—"or whatever the devil your name is . . . there are matters that need resolving between us."

"I look forward to it," Griffyn said, blithely touching an ebony forelock. "Providing fate does not resolve them first."

The camp was come upon suddenly, with no warning of distant fireglow or soft bloom of light bathing the undersides of the boughs overhead. Not until full light of day would they realize why, for the outlaw stronghold was set in the belly of a steep-banked ravine. To reach it from either side required the agility of a mountain goat, and even then, the earth was too soft to support any great weight and would spill the interloper head first onto the piles of jagged stone set deliberately below. To gain entry by the north or the south one had to follow the course of a deep, noisy stream that rushed through the ravine with bristling importance. There was no footpath across this stream, but a log that had to be crossed with care in order to safely approach the mouth of the ravine. Anyone not intimately familiar with the footing could find themselves tipped over rocks and logs and swept several hundred yards downstream before a toehold could be found again. Not that anyone could reach the log or the ravine without being noticed by the guards and sentries peppered strategically throughout the greenwood. The last fifty yards of the approach, arrows zinged by overhead like bits of conversations being passed from tree to tree.

The space between the walls of the ravine was surprisingly extensive, as flat as a meadow and divided in equal halves by the stream. The reason why the fireglow had not been seen through the woods was because the top of the ravine was literally roofed with a tight lacing of boughs and branches, creating an almost cavernlike effect from the bottom looking up. The saplings and ferns that populated the forest floor elsewhere had been stripped away and crude huts erected in the cleared spaces. Some of the trees were ancient, their branches as wide as small roads, and in some of these, enterprising outlaws had built more habitats, linked by rope bridges and a functional system of tough vines.

The biggest tree by far—and likely the oldest in all of Sherwood—was referred to fondly as the Major Oak, and it was there, under the majestic sweep of its gnarled branches, where the communal meals and meetings were held. Here were tables and benches made from logs, and an enormous firepit with fully a dozen huge cauldrons strung over tripods, their contents steaming lazily into the night air, readily available to any hungry sentries who might be returning to camp in the small hours of the morning. At one end of the pit there was an oven, built of stones mortared together, and because it was already dawn somewhere up above the canopy of leaves, there were women busy pounding dough into bread, men washing their clothes and themselves in the stream, others chopping wood for the fires or trussing hare and quail onto sticks for cooking. They all looked up or paused in what they were doing as Alan a' Dale entered the mouth of the ravine leading his weary, footworn guests behind him. But it was obvious they had been alerted well in advance of their approach for the tables were already set with the makings of a meal. Bread, cheese, ewers of ale greeted the weary outlaws, who exchanged a few greetings with fellow fugitives before they started filling the benches and eyeing the platters of food.

As welcome a sight as it was—food and ale after so many hours trekking over uncertain footing in the darkness—it was not the sylvan, cathedrallike setting of their surroundings, or the steaming cauldrons of aromatic food, or even the thought of finally lying down and resting his weary bones that made Robin stop dead in the middle of the broad common.

Brenna, nearly asleep on her feet, stumbled to a halt beside him and followed his frozen stare. Richard and Dag, close again behind, stopped on the other side and looked instantly for some treachery arranged for their welcome.

There was no treachery, however. What brought Robin to a dead, breathless stop was the sight of a slender, plainly dressed woman standing as still as a statue at the wide base of the Major Oak. His eyes, as sleep-deprived eyes will do, had passed over her in the first sweeping appraisal of the ravine, but something had drawn his gaze back. Something had made him hold his breath and brace himself through the thunderous, pounding beats of his heart.

The girl was as pale as candlewax, her face surrounded by a glossy chestnut mane of curls that fell in soft profusion around her shoulders and halfway down her back. Her eyes were impossibly large and dark and round in a face blessed by the angels with such sweet beauty, even Richard and Dag found themselves holding their breaths and growing warm.

"Saints preserve us," murmured Littlejohn. " 'Tis the little maid. 'Tis the maid Marienne."

Robin drew more than one startled look from brothers and a sister who had never seen him look so utterly, helplessly defenseless against the rush of emotions that flooded him. His hands hung limply by his sides. His chest labored to catch and hold a breath. His cheeks flushed every shade of red from pink to crimson, the color ebbing and flowing like tides gone mad.

"Marienne," he whispered.

She was obviously unable to respond or to move other than to sway slightly, side to side, in disbelief, and it was left to Robin, on legs hardly more steady, to walk across the remaining thirty feet and stop a body length away from touching her.

"Marienne? Is it really you?"

Though she still had not moved so much as a fingertip, her soft doe's eyes had become flooded with tears, making her lashes so heavy, they drifted shut at the sound of his voice. So absolutely still and pale had she become, and so piously plain the linen of her tunic, that for one terrible instant, Robin feared he was too late. He feared she had grown tired of waiting and resigned herself to taking her vows.

But then the smallest tremor of a smile spread across her mouth and when she opened her eyes again, they were brimming with such joy, he felt the effects of it wash over him like a warm wave of nectar.

"You are . . . well, my lady?"

She lowered her eyes again and managed a timid nod. "And you . . . my lord?"

"Better now that I have seen you. And . . . your mistress?"

"She is well also. Perfectly well," she emphasized, raising her downcast eyes again. "It was almost as if . . . she felt your presence for she bade me come here just yesterday."

Robin swallowed hard but could not dislodge the lump in his throat. "The child?"

"He is here, with me. He is . . . off hunting for berries . . . or acorns . . . or . . ." Her voice faltered to a whisper and a shimmer of fresh tears welled along her lashes. "Robin. Robin . . . you came . . ."

"We made a promise, you and I," he said, drawing closer, his voice shaking with emotion. "Did you doubt I would keep my part?"

"It was so long ago . . . I thought you might have changed your mind. I thought you might have found someone else, someone beautiful and wealthy and . . ."

He raised shaking hands and cupped her face, forcing her to look up and see the emotion burning in his eyes. "You are the most beautiful creature on this earth, Marienne Fitz-William. As for wealth, if there was but you and I in this world and naught but a wooden cup between us, I would not dare ask God for more happiness."

With the strength of his love shattering every accepted social convention that separated the nobility from the base-born, the most honored and celebrated champion in all Europe stunned the gathered assembly by dropping humbly down on one knee before her. He took her ice-cold hands into his, pressing them first to his forehead, then to his lips, holding them there long enough for her fingers to warm under his breath as he repeated the pledge, word for whispered word, that they had made to each other in the midnight shadows of Kirklees so many long years ago.

When he had finished, he pressed a kiss into the palm of each small hand then held his breath and waited—not long, for she sank down onto her knees before him, crumpling in a pool of spread linen and tremulous sobs that could not be stopped, not even when he gathered her into his arms and held her tight against him.

"That was the promise we made, was it not?"

She nodded, her face buried in his neck.

"Then you hold the fate of my heart and my life in your hands, my lady, for I would have your answer now, before I draw another breath."

"Yes," she whispered. "Oh, yes . . ."

Smiling, almost giddy with emotion, he bent his head and, uncaring of the dozens of eyes gawping at them, he kissed her.

The kiss was long enough and passionate enough to stir the outlaws into clapping and hooting. Even the brothers Wardieu, who had never seen their older sibling bestow more than a chaste kiss of peace on the cheek of a woman, put their hands together and grinned ear to ear. Brenna, watching from the common, felt someone beside her and looked up to find Griffyn observing the reunited lovers with something akin to amusement playing about his lips.

"So," he murmured. "He does have his human failings after all."

"Do not even think to mock him," she warned tautly.

"Mock him?" He glanced down at her in surprise. "My lady, I do not mock him. I am merely glad to welcome him to the fold. Indeed, I am even tempted to join him in giving these louts something to buzz about the rest of the day."

He said this while staring at the ripe fullness of her lips, and Brenna, acutely aware of his penchant for accepting challenges, refrained from having them say "You would not dare." But only just.

He laughed anyway, for the words were in her eyes, plain as ink on parchment, and despite the precautionary step she took away from him, his arm came out and his hand slipped around her waist. He drew her to his side and held her there long enough and with enough familiarity for Will, who was closest, to notice and send a bristling frown in their direction.

She managed to extricate herself just as Robin brought Marienne across the common to make formal introductions.

"These are the upstarts I have told you about in my letters," he said as he presented Richard—who bowed gallantly over Marienne's small hand—and Dagobert, who was still grinning like a mad fool in Bedlam.

"Allow me to be the first to truly congratulate you," the latter said, "for we have never seen Robin brought to his knees before, nor blush half so bright a shade of red as to rival Will'um's scarlet hair."

Robin smote him good-naturedly on the shoulder and did indeed turn a most glorious shade of vermilion as he turned to Brenna.

"Our sister Brenna. Bren . . . my Marienne."

Up close, Marienne's sweet oval face fairly radiated her happiness, and it was contagious. She started to offer a curtsy, as was expected from someone of lesser birth, but Brenna stopped her and put her arms around the young woman's shoulders, bestowing a warm, sisterly hug.

"We have heard so much about you, I already feel as if you are a part of the family."

"Which she has just agreed to become," Robin announced proudly. "As soon as we can find a priest to marry us."

Brenna laughed and hugged her again, then hugged Robin until he begged for mercy. Geoffrey, Will, and Griffyn added their congratulations in a moderately less boisterous fashion, and then there was only Jean de Brevant, standing apart from the others, a pillar of muscle and brawn that wilted down on his knees when the dark-eyed Marienne smiled in his direction.

"Petit Jean," she whispered. "How truly good it is to see you again."

"You look well, Little One. The last time I saw you, you were but a child, so thin and gaunt and worried, I felt sure your face would never catch up to the size of your eyes. But now . . . look at you. A beautiful young woman. I could not be more proud if you were my own daughter."

Marienne stifled another sob behind trembling fingers and, following Brenna's example, cast propriety to the wind and hugged the huge captain of the guard so hard he turned nearly as dark a mottlement of red as Robin. He stood to cover his embarrassment and yielded his place to Alan a' Dale, who had been watching the proceedings with frank astonishment.

"My lady . . . you are acquainted with these knights?"

"Happily so," she said, slipping her hand into Robin's as he came up beside her.

"Does this mean you will accept my future wife's word as a bond against our character and our intentions?" Robin asked.

The forester read the happiness on Marienne's face and allowed a rueful smile to soften his features. "If I doubted Lady Marienne's word, I would have to doubt my own."

He extended his hand in a tentative gesture of apology and Robin took it immediately, clasping it with a firmness that roused another cheer among the men and women gathered around the base of the Major Oak.

"I would say this calls for a toast," Alan declared. He indicated the tables, laden with food and drink, where impatient foresters were already beginning to pick and pilfer. He took his seat near the middle, inviting Robin and Marienne to sit close by, then called for one of the men to fetch a large cask from the stores.

"Wine from the Aquitaine, my lord," he explained, laughing as the bung was unstoppered and the contents spouted forth in a rich red stream. "The very best intended for Nottingham's cellars."

"Only the best should be used," Robin agreed, "to toast newfound friendships and future alliances, but I would ask one favor first."

Alan sobered slightly and called for a hush amongst his men. "A favor, my lord?"

"Aye." Robin nodded grimly. "That we be treated with equal measure while we are guests in your greenwood. That there be no lords or knaves or lackeys or villeins to distinguish us one from the other." He paused and grinned at the startled looks on his brother's faces. "That I am called Robin and my brothers are Richard and Dag and Geoffrey. That Littlejohn is . . . well, Littlejohn and Will . . . may be Will Scarlett by the fire of his hair." The outlaws laughed and thumped Will genially on the shoulders, bringing a smile and flush to his cheeks. "As for that black-haired devil at the end, you will have to check beneath his hood upon waking each morning to see what name he prefers to go by that day, but for the time being, we shall keep it Griffyn for ease."

Another laugh dispelled some of the tension that seemed to be an instinctive response to the pale, other-worldly gaze as Griffyn raised his cup and saluted Robin's humor.

Even Brenna found herself smiling, completely at ease with his outrageously handsome features for the first time since stumbling across the half-naked satyr she had found in the woods outside Amboise.

29

Brenna ate until her belly ached, and drank a tasty forest brew until her head spun and the treetops threatened to change places with the forest floor. She had no memory of leaving the table, but when she wakened several hours later, she knew she would not soon forget the bludgeoning boots that were dancing around on the inside of her skull.

"Here," Griffyn said, handing her a cup of diluted wine and water. "Drink this. It will help."

"God love me," she gasped. "What was I drinking before?"

"A rather potent concoction they ferment from juniper berries. According to Alan a' Dale, you should have another healthy dollop of it to clear your head, but, judging by the color of your skin—or lack of it—I warrant another dollop might do you permanent damage."

"Are you saying . . . I was intoxicated?"

"Quite splendidly so. You even insisted, as my wife, that we should be given our own hut with our own bed instead of having to share lodgings with 'forty farting foresters.' "

Brenna cast about her in horror. The hut she was in was made of bound staves and thatch, no bigger than the width of the rush-filled mattress, but obviously designed for privacy.

"I did not really say that, did I?" she squeaked.

He smiled. And watched a spray of freckles rise dark against the paleness of her skin before he said, "No. You were quite beyond saying anything when we were shown to our accommodations. It was just assumed we might not enjoy an abundance of company."

Brenna groaned and squeezed her temples. He laughed softly and moved around behind her, sitting so that she was positioned between his knees. He loosened her braid enough to enable his fingers to stroke the back of her scalp, to knead away the tension and knots across her shoulders and down her neck.

"Relax," he commanded. "As soon as the blood is flowing properly again, you will feel better. You will have to look a lot better too, since your brother and I have arranged for you to give these wolfheads a demonstration on the longbow."

"What?"

She tried to turn her head but he stopped it and raked his hands deeper into her hair, curling his fingers into her scalp and winning instead a small shudder of relief.

"Will could always show them if you are not up to it, but Robin and I thought the lesson would be more effective coming from you."

"Lesson?"

"They boast of having the best archers in England in their midst. We thought they might like to see what they could do with a *real* weapon in their hands."

"Why would *you* not show them?"

He ran his hands down her slender arms and up again. "Because you would be far more convincing."

She bowed her head forward, obeying the gentle command of his hands. The tugging and kneading of her hair and scalp was having the desired effect: the bludgeoning faded like magic and she could actually feel her blood tingling with new life. Unfortunately, it was also starting to tingle in places not intended, like her breasts, her belly, her loins, and she found herself sighing with each stroke, bemoaning the helplessness of it all.

A word, a look, a simple touch of his hands and she was lost. Even worse, he could sense it, feel it through his fingertips, and he tilted her head back, drawing it against his shoulder as he brought her mouth around to his, kissing her with a thoroughness that completed the work his fingers had begun on her body.

"Now you know how I felt that first night at Amboise, *Margery*," he murmured against her lips. "All oiled and warm and ready to come out of my skin every time your hands skimmed down my body."

She slid her hand up and around his neck and pulled him back, her mouth parting beneath his in a lush invitation. The gentle rolling motions of his tongue matched those of his fingers and she would gladly have come out of her clothes had he not tempered her eagerness with a soft, husky laugh.

"Unfortunately, Robin is waiting. But do not drink anything stronger than water with the evening meal," he warned with lusty menace. "We will have a bed beneath us tonight, by God, and a long afternoon ahead to plan best how to use it."

He kissed her again, then helped her to her feet.

The ravine, when they stepped outside the hut, was spackled with darting points of sunlight, brightening the camp more than she would have expected from remembered first impressions. It seemed as if more men had arrived and the common bustled with activity. There were more fires scattered around the encampment, filling the air with lazy fingers of smoke. More women in evidence, too, and even several children who ran screeching from an outlaw dressed in a deerskin robe, imitating some forest ogre.

Alan and four of his henchmen were seated under the Major Oak with the knights from Amboise and while it was surety everyone in the stronghold was anxious about their animated conversation, the outlaws all went about their normal business, trusting they would be privy to the results in due time. Some were staging mock fights with staves and broadsticks. Others were practicing with slingshots, with bow and arrow. Brenna was starting to feel guilty over being the only one to sleep away the morning until she saw the red creases in her brothers' faces and the bloodshot veins in their eyes that suggested they had only just been roused themselves.

Robin acknowledged her arrival in their midst with a slight frown as he finished what he was saying to Alan a' Dale.

"Gisbourne will be expecting you to ambush them on the forest road, as has been your habit thus far. While his troops are in the forest, therefore, they will be as alert as bloodhounds, with every conceivable defense at the ready."

"So, you are telling us it is impossible for an attack to succeed."

"They have only to move in a tight pack, with their shields raised, and your efforts will go for naught," Will advised. "The men-at-arms will flush you out of the trees and the knights will ride you down and those of you who survive will likely be hanged alongside your Friar Tuck to save them the trouble of soiling their donjons."

Alan spread his hands. "Then what do you suggest we do?"

"The very last thing they would expect you to do. Attack them in the open, on a meadow or a field. It would have to be the *right* meadow or field, of course, preferably with hills on either side and a small stand of wood to conceal us before the attack, but . . ."

"Attack Guy of Gisbourne's forces in an open field?" The outlaw stared at Will as if he had suggested doing it naked as well.

"They will be even more shocked at the improbability," the younger man promised. "And because they will have left Sherwood behind, they will also have eased their muscles enough to let the sweat run out of their sleeves. They will have shouldered their shields, unwound their crossbows, even spread themselves carelessly along the road to applaud their courage against your cowardice."

Alan shook his head. "We are successful because we can move like ghosts through the trees. We can strike and run and disappear into places the king's men would never dare venture near. These men are all as brave as brave can be"—

he looked around the camp, his face reflecting the agony of leadership—"but we have no more than a dozen swords among us and not half that many who can use one to any good effect."

"But you have archers by the score," Robin pointed out excitedly. "And archers are most effective and most deadly from one, two hundred yards away."

"From two hundred yards away," Alan retorted dryly, "our arrows would bounce off their armor like drunken maybugs."

Robin smiled. "Not if you use these."

Littlejohn came forward at his invitation and produced a large leather pouch bulging with twice-tempered arrowheads.

"Unlike the softer iron broadheads your men use, these will pierce through mail and bullhide like a knife through cheese."

The outlaw fingered the bright, sharp arrowheads but still looked dubious. "At fifty yards, maybe . . . and if every one of my men had the strength of Littlejohn in their arms."

"Would you dispute the fact that my sister is by far the smallest member of our party?"

Alan shrugged, not knowing where the question was going. "She is a woman, not overlarded to be sure."

"And therefore likely to be one of the weakest?"

All of the outlaws seated at the table exchanged glances and nodded warily.

"Choose a target," Robin said, and took up one of the longbow staves that lay on the table in front of him, handing it to Brenna.

"Do not make it too easy a mark," Dag cautioned, "or she will choose her own and it may come as a painful surprise."

There was a tree standing at the mouth of the southern end of the ravine, a distance of some fifty yards. Someone had been gathering acorns and a small pouch of them hung from one of the lower branches.

Dag shook his head and gave the outlaw who chose it an I-warned-you look, but Brenna nocked an arrow, raised the

enormous bow and drew back on the string, firing all in the
same fluid motion.

The outlaws' heads swiveled and saw the acorns jump
violently as the arrow struck, pierced clean through the
sack, and tore it off the branch, carrying it another twenty
yards or more into the stream, leaving the foresters gaping
at the weapon in her hand.

Geoffrey LaFer cleared his throat to break the stunned
silence and pointed casually to an oak high on the lip of the
ravine. "Perhaps a more challenging target?"

The tree had been hit recently by lightning and had one
half of its trunk split to one side. Some bird or animal had
chewed through the charred bark and opened a bare patch
of raw wood. It was smaller, perhaps, than the painted eye
of an archery butt placed a similar distance away—at least
two hundred and twenty yards—but with the sunlight
gleaming on the peeled wood, it made an acceptable mark.

The outlaws—two of whom could not make out the spot
even though they squinted and shielded their eyes against
the glare of the sun—balked and declared that such a shot
was a good joke but impossible to make.

"She can make it six times," Griffyn said quietly, "in
under a minute."

Brenna looked at him, and he looked back with his best,
seductive smile, and the outlaws were quick to pull out
their pennies to match the ones Dag tossed to the center
of the table.

Brenna selected six long ashwood arrows and checked
the vanes of the fletching for any breaks or flaws. Five of
them she stuck upright in the soft earth at her feet; the
sixth she nocked carefully in the string. She stood with her
head cocked a moment to follow the gliding path of a hawk
overhead and to gauge the currents of the wind where they
blew stronger at the top of the ravine. She drew the
fletching slowly back to her chin, then further still to her
ear as she sighted along the shaft. With a snap of her fingers
she loosed the arrow and reached for a second one,
nocking, drawing, and firing before the first had struck its

mark. The four remaining shafts followed the first two in awe-inspiring succession, but it was the shrill echo of a distant scream that brought the outlaws surging to their feet.

Brenna's smile froze, half formed on her face, and for one dreadful moment, she thought she had missed the designated target and hit another, for at the last possible second, a round elfin face had popped out of the foliage beside the charred oak to spy on the assembly below. It had disappeared again, his scream ricocheting off the opposite wall of the ravine as he dove into a cradle of cracking branches and flying leaves. One after another, almost without a break, the six arrows thudded into the trunk of the tree, narrowly missing the mop of curly dark hair by a mere hand's width—a shockingly slim margin of error that brought Sparrow tumbling down from branch to branch, vine to slithering vine until he landed like a bat-winged squirrel in the midst of the startled encampment.

Several of the foresters scrambled for their bows, many more scattered behind the sheltering trunks of trees as the bandy-legged seneschal stalked over to Brenna and stood before her, his hands planted on his hips, his cap askew over one dark, accusing eye.

"See you this ear, Missy? I have grown fond of it over the years and would like to keep it thus, pinned to the side of my head! If you wanted me to come forth, you could have called my name and I would gladly have joined you! There was no need to throft me hither by the skin of my ballocks!"

"I swear, I did not know you were there," Brenna gasped, her hand covering the laugh that refused to be contained. "It was Geoffrey who chose the target."

Geoffrey, prudently, was not in his seat when Sparrow whirled around to confront him. He was making haste to put the trunk of the Major Oak between himself and the red-faced woodsprite, who set off after him with a quarrel drawn and nocked in the string of his arblaster.

Alan a' Dale signaled his men to lower their weapons and resumed his seat, scratching his head over some distant memory as he followed the farcical pair running around the tree. "I thought I had only imagined seeing a gnome that day in the forest of Angers."

"Sparrow is very real," Robin assured him. "And so is the power of the longbow."

Alan cast an eye in Brenna's direction with a new gleam of respect kindling in the midnight-blue depths. She, in turn, saw the wisdom of Griffyn's caution back at the turnip-farmer's cottage, especially when the outlaws quickly made room for her on their bench and asked if they might try pitting their strength against the bow.

"Do you have bowyers among you?" Robin asked. "And fletchers?"

Alan nodded and indicated several wide-eyed foresters edging closer to the table to have a better look at the Welsh weapon. "Though in sooth, will it not take more time than we have for my men to learn how to use one of these things?"

"We have a dozen bows with us. Pick your best archers and give them over to Will and Brenna for the rest of the day. They may not be able to make as fine a shot as you have just witnessed, but certes, they will be able to hit one of Gisbourne's fine fat coystrils from a hundred yards away. If we can cut down half the knights while they are blinking the confusion out of their eyes, the rest will scatter and run before your arrows like hens in front of a fox."

For the first time, a glimmer of real excitement touched Alan a' Dale's eyes. "Then we have a chance?"

Robin lifted his cup of ale. "With God's good luck, we have an excellent fighting chance . . . if we can find the right place along the road to set up our attack."

One of the outlaws looked up from the bow he was admiring. "Hills on either side, you say, and a wood nearby?"

"Do you know of such a place?"

"Aye. An hour's walk beyond Sherwood—the Witch's Teats, we call it."

"Could you show me this place?"

"Aye, could do."

Robin reached out and snagged Sparrow by the fringe of his collar as he chased by. "Enough fun, Puck. We have much work to do over the next two days. Saddle the horses," he said to Timkin, who was lounging nearby with a dozing Fulgrin. "Hopefully we can find this place and be back by nightfall."

Richard whistled low to catch his attention. "Rob?"

He turned to follow his brother's gaze and saw Marienne coming across the common. There was a young boy walking by her side, no more than ten years old to judge by the smooth face and wide, innocent blue eyes. He was not very tall, nor very broad across the shoulders yet, but there was promise in the long, easy stride. The promise of a future king.

Robin's instincts started to send him to his feet, but a warning flash from Marienne's eye caught the gesture and bade him keep his seat. She had her arm draped in a motherly fashion over the boy's shoulders and, by the look of it, had to use it to encourage him to cross the last twenty or so paces.

"Robin . . . I wanted you to meet my son Eduard. Eduard"—her breath and courage almost failed her as she placed both hands on the boy's shoulders—"this is the man I told you about," she whispered. "This . . . is your father."

30

"**Y**ou might have warned me," Robin said later that night. "I dare swear a bird could have flown into my mouth it fell open so wide."

"It was not something I could tell you in a letter. And in truth, when my lady first begged me to claim the child as mine, we gave no thought as to naming the father."

It was well after dark and the forest was silent save for the constant burp and burble of the stream. Robin and Sparrow had returned hours ago from scouting the Witch's Teats and pronounced it more than adequate for their needs. Since then, the outlaw band had laid out a fine banquet of roast venison served with stews and steaming platters of carrots, turnips, and onions to honor their guests. There had even been entertainment to break the solemnity and tension—a man who boasted some talent on the gittern had strummed chords while another soft-voiced lad had filled the cavernous glade with the lyrics of several ballads he had begun composing that afternoon. He sang of Robin, Marienne's long-lost love, and of how this boldest of champions had come to them, willing and eager to don the outlaw hood and lead them in a valiant battle against the villainous Sheriff of Nottingham. He sang also of the giant Littlejohn and the bowman Will Scarlett, and of the fierce, long-limbed beauty who had fired her arrows into the sky and brought a faery tumbling to earth.

Richard and Dag had been quite put out not to be included in any of the *chansons*, but they were promised mention in the next composition should they accomplish something more heroic than relieving the outlaws of their hard-won pennies.

After the feast, when the fires had died down to beds of glowing red coals and the men had talked themselves sleepy, Robin and Marienne had slipped away hand in hand for a walk in the moonlight.

"Maids are . . . often victims of such anonymous carelessness," she said, stopping beside the bright ribbon of the river. "It was Tuck . . . Lord Henry . . . who loves the child better than his own life to be sure, who suggested—nay, *insisted*—the boy not have any scar of bastardy sitting on his shoulders for the rest of his life. He could not claim the child himself and it just seemed natural, somehow, when young Eduard started asking questions, that I name the bravest, boldest champion I knew as his father. Even Tuck agreed I would never be able to speak of any other man with as much love or conviction, and . . . and it would give the boy something to be proud of, knowing he was the son of Robert Wardieu d'Amboise, grandson of the Black Wolf of Lincoln. I"—she bowed her head and showed a trace of shame as she admitted—"I told him we had exchanged our vows before the eyes of God, and that you had returned to Normandy without knowing he was in my womb. I told him also that it was too dangerous for you to come back just yet, but that when you did, you would . . . you would take him back to Amboise with you."

"What about the princess? How does she feel about all of this? He is her son. He is the rightful King of England. Would it not be more fitting for him to think of himself as the heir to Richard the Lionheart?"

Marienne shook her head. "She does not want to think of him as a future king; she only thinks of him as a small, helpless boy who would have his throat cut if his uncle John knew of his existence."

"But once John is gone? I have heard he has grown so fat and bilious, he reeks of putrefaction. And the doctors, when they listen for his heartbeat, hear only wheezing and bubbling eructations."

She sighed. "If the king died tomorrow, what would happen? His son is seven years old—too young to have learned the thieving ways of his father, yet young enough to be molded into a king the barons could control and govern. Robert FitzWalter would likely be named to the king's council until he reached the age of majority, a responsibility that would be shared by my own father, William Marshal. It could, conceivably, mean peace for the first time since John Lackland murdered Arthur of Brittany and snatched the throne.

"But what would happen to this tentative peace," she continued, "if the existence of another heir became known? The Marshal and FitzWalter are not without enemies. There would be more strife, more war, more political intrigues. Eduard's heritage would come into question, as would his legitimacy, even though my lady and Lord Henry are legally wed.

"And then there is my lord's outlawry. Granted, he is born of a noble family, but there are those who would condemn him for turning his back on his own kind and debasing himself for the sake of helping simple people survive the tyranny that has reigned over their simple lives."

"What, then, do Henry and Eleanor want for their son?"

"They want him to live a free man, unencumbered by the past. They want him to learn that courage and honor go hand in hand with kindness and mercy. They want him to grow old and live in peace. To marry a woman he loves and have a dozen children who carry the Lionheart's noble blood in their veins, but not the violence of his ambitions in his heart."

Robin looked down at his hands and was surprised to see they were shaking. "It is a weighty responsibility to place on one man's shoulders."

Marienne smiled and drew close. She ran her hands up the front of his surcoat and across the solid breadth of his shoulders, resting them finally on the stubble-roughened planes of his jaw. "They suspect you will be more than adequate to the task, my lord. As do I."

His hands circled her waist and urged her comfortably closer. "He would need brothers and sisters, of course, to achieve this . . . normalcy you advocate so strongly."

"The sooner the better," she agreed on a breath, leaning forward to touch her forehead on his chin.

The tremors spread up his arms as he skimmed his hands higher up her back, beneath the dark, glossy mane of her hair.

"Sooner, indeed," he murmured tautly, "if there was but a priest nearby. Do these heathen outlaws not believe in the benefit of keeping a confessor in their midst to safeguard their souls?"

Marienne's lips found his throat. "The nearest one is at Edwinstow; he visits once a week, thereabouts, to carry away their sins."

His long fingers stroked the soft hairs at her nape. "How long before the next visit?"

"He was just here."

"How far to Edwinstow?"

She rose up on tiptoes. "How fast are your horses?"

"Not nearly fast enough, I fear."

The warm pressure of his lips made the breath catch in her throat. A shudder of expectation opened her willingly to his tender explorations, but in the next instant, he grasped her by the shoulders and eased her away, holding her out at arm's length, as if any further contact would scorch them both to cinders.

"I confess . . . I do not trust myself, Marienne. In truth," he blurted, "I came overly close to ravishing you this morning on the green, and"—he cast around, almost in panic—"you should not have allowed us to stray so far from the camp alone."

"But I did not allow it, my lord," she said calmly. "I did it deliberately."

He looked stricken. "Deliberately? Surely, you were aware how much I . . . how badly I . . . how *desperately* I . . ."

She placed her hands over his and gently pried them away from her shoulders. With a soft wash of moonlight filtering through the trees and the pinpoint reflections of light refracting off the surface of the river beside them, she unfastened the thong binding her tunic and let it slip down her arms, past her waist, her hips, her thighs . . .

Underneath, she wore nothing but a small gold crucifix suspended between her breasts.

"Marienne—"

"Robin . . . you have always had possession of my heart and my soul, but my body has been virgin far too long."

His breath choked him again as his eyes devoured the pale, moonwashed splendor of her body. Her breasts were high and firm, her waist small enough to form the shape of an hourglass, her legs were slim, smooth as ivory with an enticingly dark thatch of curls at the juncture.

His hand came slowly up from his side, slicing through a beam of moonlight to touch with unholy reverence the tautly gathered crown of her breast.

"Such bold words I spoke," he murmured. "Yet I stand before you with hardly more courage than a fool."

She smiled and moved forward so that his hand was invited to engulf her whole breast.

"Only love me like a man," she whispered. "And all will be forgiven."

She came into his arms and their sighs blended together in a rush of unchecked passion. Several broad paces away, a shadow moved, melting back from whence it had come, having heard all he needed to hear.

Brenna shifted on her mattress of husks and pine boughs, alerted by the soft crush of leaves outside her door, followed by the sound of the canvas being lifted to one side.

"Where have you been?" she asked sleepily. "It must be well past midnight."

"I wanted to check on Centaur," Griffyn said. "And I thought I should at least wait until the others had retired into their blankets before I came creeping into yours. Little-john sleeps with one eye open, I swear it."

She purred and stretched out full on the bedding, her body naked beneath the single layer of wool. She could not see anything in the utter blackness, but she could hear the leathery scrape of his belt being loosened, the rustle of his surcoat and tunic being lifted over his head, the soft snapping of points as he unfastened his hose. And then he was beside her and the blanket had been tossed aside. His hands were sliding up the length of her body, cool company next to the heat of her skin. His palm cupped her breast and lifted it into the hungry wetness of his mouth and she sighed, her head tipping to one side as his tongue rolled languidly over and around the nipple.

"You could at least spare a moment for conversation."

"I have been talking all blessed night long."

"Not to me."

His mouth released her flesh with a moist sucking sound and he turned onto his back, breaking all contact as quickly as he had initiated it. "Very well, my lady. What would you care to talk about?"

She pushed herself up onto her elbows. "You. But I know that to be a prickly subject."

He was so quiet, she swore she could hear his lashes blinking. "What would you like to know?"

"Everything. Anything you would care to tell me."

"Repent my many sins?"

"Good heavens, no. That would likely take all night. And besides, Sparrow says the deathbed is the place for repentance. Before reaching it one should endeavor to commit enough sins to make the groveling worthwhile."

Griffyn laughed. "A wise man, Sparrow. I could grow to like him."

"I could grow to like that sound."

"What sound?"

"You. Laughing. You do not do it very often."

"I have not had much to laugh about the past few years."

She felt through the darkness for his eyebrows, which were, not surprisingly, pleated together in a frown. "Even the bard noticed: 'a face as black as thunder / a mood as dark as rage' . . ."

"He had a vivid imagination."

" 'Eyes with a thousand ghosts inside / such fearsome, frightening pride.' "

His frown shifted under her fingertips. "I do not recall those lines."

"I just made them up."

"In that case, pray do not trade your bow for a lute."

He was lying with his arms folded beneath his neck as a pillow, and it made for a temptingly warm bulge of muscle on which to lay her head. Her hair was unbound and spread teasingly over his flesh; her body was smooth and soft and molded easily to the harder angles of his hip and thigh as she pressed against him. She could hear his heart beating deep within the chamber of his chest and she could feel his flesh shiver ever so slightly as she danced her fingers over the ridge of his breastbone and down the muscle-clad rack of ribs.

"Do you think this attack will succeed?"

"A politic change of subject," he noted.

"Since my singing talents were called into question, I thought I might as well return to more familiar ground."

"Did you make any new archers today?"

"A few took to the weight and balance of the bow easily enough, though I warrant the sack of acorns would have proved too much of a challenge just yet. But they are keen and we still have tomorrow."

"They have good teachers, you will succeed. Who are your two best, do you suppose?"

She traced a circle around the velvety disc of his nipple and pondered the question a moment. "A rather stout, jovial Welshman named Derwint," she decided. "He has actually had some experience with the longbow before. And . . . Eldred of Farnham. He shows promise. But you did not answer *my* question."

"You have distracted me. I forgot it."

"Do you think the attack will succeed?"

"I think . . . your brother has raised their hopes."

"Without justification?"

"Possibly without thinking there are those who actually go into battle being less than certain of absolute victory at the end. It is the curse," he added, softening his words with a kiss on her brow, "of most men who cannot see the darker side of chivalry, honor, nobility, and justice."

"Whereas you do?"

"I have seen it up close," he admitted quietly. "I have lived in its shadow too long not to know it is out there somewhere waiting like a living, breathing thing for something too recklessly good and valiant to ride into its maw."

"You say that as if you are expecting something terrible to happen."

"I do not *expect* it. I *assume* it. That is how I have kept one step ahead of the devil all these years."

"I believe I know something of the devil myself," she murmured, "since coming upon him in the forest one day."

He drew a measured breath as her hand skimmed lower onto his belly. "And what have you learned about him?"

"Oh . . ." She leaned over and pinched his nipple between her teeth. "That he is unpredictable. Dangerous. Without a conscience or care. Difficult to understand. Impossible to satisfy." She sighed, letting her lips rove lower. "As for trusting him, or loving him . . ."

She heard his quick intake of air and felt his big body stiffen out of its casual nonchalance as her mouth trailed her hand onto the flat board of his belly.

". . . it is probably not safe to do either . . ."

"Christ Jesus," he muttered, freeing his arms and reaching down to bury his hands in her hair. She shook off his attempts to restrain her and continued to chide him through caressing mouthfuls.

"This, regardless if he is merely a rogue or an outlawed earl . . ."

"Brenna!"

". . . or a prince of darkness . . ."

He groaned around a silent oath and arched his head back into the rushes.

". . . or a Saxon greatheart of undiluted bloodlines."

She straightened suddenly and a groan shivered the length of his body. But she was *so* still and *so* quiet, he pushed himself upright and groped in the darkness for his dagger.

"What is it? What is wrong? Brenna?"

"You seem quite proud of your pure bloodlines," she said solemnly, "yet I do not have the smallest drop of Saxon in my veins."

"*What?*"

"My ancestors. They were some of those same rapine conquerors you so disdained."

He released a gust of breath and shook his head. "It was not a personal dislike." He threw aside the dagger and caught her up around the waist, pulling her down onto the mattress beneath him. "As for you not having a drop of Saxon in you, my lady, it will be my happy pleasure to remedy that. Again and again. As many times as it takes to fill you."

31

Henry de Clare was a mass of bruises, cuts, and raw festering weals. He had discovered, over the past weeks of his incarceration, that if he did not move, the pain would sometimes relent and turn into a sort of dull throb. There was nothing he could do about the stench, however. It filled his nostrils with every breath, coated his throat, soured his belly—not that there was anything in his stomach to rebel. A crust of moldy black bread and a small cup of scummed water were thrust into his cell now and then when the guards remembered him. Even so, sometimes they did not push it far enough inside the door and his chains would not permit him to reach it.

The cell was tiny, six feet by six feet, if that. No window, of course, for it was far beneath the main keep of Nottingham Castle, and thus below the level of the moat surrounding it. Water constantly seeped through the roughly mortared walls, turning to slime long before it collected on the floor and mixed with the decay and rat droppings. Screams echoed throughout the honeycomb of corridors day and night, along with the moans and whimpers and weeping of grown men. Rats clicked and squealed as they moved from unfortunate to unfortunate, gnawing on old wounds, opening new ones.

The only relief in the absolute darkness was the dim bloom cast off by a torch somewhere well down the corridor and around a stone corner. The only reprieve from the agony was sleep, which he seemed to be doing more and more as he grew weaker—often too weak to fight off the rodents for his crust of bread.

He had begun to pray this past week that he would simply not wake up again. Until a week ago, he had wondered why they had even kept him alive this long and he had had the naïveté to be grateful for small mercies, for they had not tortured him. Beaten, yes; flayed with spiny ropes, yes; whipped with chains and scorched with hot rocks on the soles of his feet and hands, aye. But he had not been dismembered piece by piece or peeled in strips like some poor screaming bastards. Foolishly, he had thought perhaps it was because he was, despite everything, a member of the nobility. He was Henry de Clare, nephew to William Marshal, heir to one of the most prominent names in the Welsh Marcher country.

Foolish. Naïve. He should have known from the evil laughter in Gisbourne's eyes that he was being saved for something special. He should have known, when he refused to answer any of Gisbourne's endless questions, that there would be some heinous punishment for his stubbornness down the road. He should have known, when they started chaining him hand and foot to the wall, that they did not want him doing harm to himself to cheat them of their final entertainment.

A week ago, Gisbourne had come to the donjons, carried there on a litter like some Roman emperor, bathed in a blaze of torchlight that had blinded Henry for nearly eight hours afterward. He had come to ask one last time where the outlaw stronghold in Sherwood was located and where, in the interest of a merciful death, Eleanor of Brittany had been taken after her rescue from Corfe Castle so many years ago. There were rumors she had died shortly thereafter. Rumors she had been spirited to Wales and had married another outlaw prince, Rhys ap Iowerth. There were rumors also that she had been seen in Scotland holding royal court behind the mud-and-timber bastions of Edinburgh. Was she dead? Was she alive? Had William Marshal been involved in rescuing her? If Henry would only answer his questions and sign a confession . . . he would die quickly and painlessly under an executioner's axe, as befitting a knight of the realm.

Henry had remained silent and Gisbourne had laughed. He had not changed much in the decade since their last encounter. He was still thin and ferretlike in appearance, with a long hooked nose and eyes too narrow and too close together to encourage any hope of compassion or sympathy. He dressed as if he ruled the world and not just the outlaw-infested shire of Nottingham. His robes were the finest velvets, heavily crusted with jewels and embroidery. The plaited gold sallet he wore on his head was fashioned like a crown and glittered atop straight dark hair that was oiled and groomed to a perfect roll just below the ear. When he talked, he continually stroked his bejeweled fingers over the manicured point of his beard, and when he laughed, he revealed two crooked front teeth, forked like gleaming white fangs.

Ah, but when he walked—or attempted to—he had to do so with canes, and that was Henry's one consolation. His rich velvet robes hid the damage well, but his legs were bent and twisted, the knees broken, the bones warped. And higher up, where there had once hung an instrument of perverse pleasure, there were now only two small sacs with naught between but a nub and a scar.

It was this Henry remembered and this he tried to envision in his mind each time Gisbourne's wine-soaked breath washed over his face. And it was this he was thinking of when Sir Guy announced, almost casually, that he was to be moved to Lincoln the following week's end that the king might have the pleasure of watching him hung, drawn, and quartered.

Since then, he tried to think only of Eleanor, his love, his life. She had learned to laugh again over the years, and had found peace with her God. Just sitting with her in the garden of the abbey had been his greatest pleasure in these later years, and he hoped she would sit there still and think of him fondly. She would grieve for him and, for that, he was sorry. She had had enough pain in her life and he did not want to be the cause of any more. He remembered what she had suffered at the hands of her cruel, vindictive uncle, how she had been strapped into a chair and had her brilliant blue eyes seared out with hot iron pokers. She said there were still days when she woke up and wondered why she could not open her eyes, or see the birds that sang on her windowsill. And there were nights when Marienne had to hold her and comfort her through the nightmares and pain she relived time and time again.

At least he would not have to suffer that. The unimaginable pain, yes, of being hung until almost dead, then revived enough to appreciate the artistry of some brutish bastard severing through the joints of his arms and legs, then splitting him open down the middle so that when they tied his wrists and ankles to four horses and spurred them into a gallop, his body would tear apart easily. But it would all be over in an hour or so and then he would have peace.

When Gisbourne had announced the method of his execution, Henry had managed to hold onto his bowels, but only just. And only until he had been hauled back to his cell and manacled to the walls. To his shame, he had soiled himself then, and wept like a child, for he had witnessed the barbarous method of execution once in Wales and he knew—he *knew* he had not a tenth of the courage needed to endure such excruciating agony.

They came for him in a *crump*ing of heavy boots and creaking mail. Six guards, two bearing torches that dragged ribbons of black smoke behind them, came to his cell, unlocked his manacles, and towed his filthy, emaciated body back along the corridor, up a steep corkscrew flight of steps and out into the gray, foggy morning.

His eyes had grown weak from lack of sunlight and even though the sky was cloud-ridden and dull, it took several minutes to blink away the crusted filth and water, and to see what awaited him in the cobbled bailey.

It looked, at first, like an army. A host, to be sure, comprised of ranks upon ranks of knights in full mail mounted on caparisoned warhorses. Many sat with their lances raised and pennons hanging limp in the gray, misty air; a few—a very few—glanced furtively at Henry de Clare, ashamed to be part of such an ignominious escort. Behind these helmed and blank-faced knights were the men-at-arms. Dozens of them. Scores of them. All wearing thick bullhide armor and carrying pikes, crossbows, and shields. Pacing back and forth at their head was the gravel-voiced Reginald de Braose, shouting orders, issuing warnings, threatening any who failed in their duty this day.

Henry heard a familiar, sly cackle of laughter and, though he did not have the strength to stand entirely on his own, he struggled to pull himself upright that he might glare defiantly at the High Sheriff of Nottingham one last time.

Gisbourne was not laughing at him, however. Nor did he even appear to notice the bag of rags and bones that stood wobbling between the arms of two burly guards. He was laughing at something a tall, silver-haired man was saying. Laughing, and at the same time casting a lascivious eye over the buxom figure of the red-haired woman who stood by the nobleman's side.

"An ambush at the Witch's Teats, you say? And you have this on good authority?"

"The best," said Bertrand Malagane. "We have had a man with them since they left Normandy. He managed to slip away during the night and found our own encampment not an hour ago. As you can see, I have come straight here with the warning."

Gisbourne's eyes glazed over as he stared out over the crowded bailey. "Robert Wardieu d'Amboise, here in Sherwood. You can have no idea how long I have waited to renew our acquaintance, how desperately I have wanted to offer him the hospitality of my donjons." He looked back at Malagane. "Where is this man who dares to have done what none of my men have managed to do thus far? He should be rewarded for his ingenuity!"

"He has remained behind with my men. To help plan a little surprise for our mutual friends."

Gisbourne's mouth twisted suspiciously. "What is your interest in all of this?"

"Strictly personal," Malagane lied smoothly. "Wardieu was responsible for the death of my older son."

"Well." Gisbourne signaled brusquely for his horse to be brought forth. "If there is anything left of him when I am finished, I gladly bequeath it to you."

"In that case, perhaps I can offer the services of Lady Solange. She is deliciously adept at leaving just enough left over for one last poignant scream."

Gisbourne regarded the curvaceous beauty with an eye that recalled, many years ago, another lethal female in the guise of Nicolaa de la Haye. She had been in the employ of the Dragon of Bloodmoor Keep—the half brother to Randwulf de la Seyne Sur Mer—and later discovered to be the mother of Eduard FitzRandwulf, the Black Wolf's son. The irony was almost too exquisite, and he threw his head back and laughed.

He cuffed a lackey out of the way and limped over to where Henry de Clare was standing. His fine pointed nose wrinkled with displeasure at the odor that clung to the prisoner's clothes as he thrust the edge of one cane under Henry's chin, forcing him to look up.

"Of course you heard your friends are planning to attempt a rescue. What you may not have heard was that a mutual acquaintance of ours has come back to Sherwood after all these years away." He leaned closer, his eyes almost crossing as he peered into Henry's face. "What do you suppose we should do? Cringe in fear? Take another road? Delay until another day? Unfortunately the king awaits our arrival in Lincoln and there is no other road suitable for our needs. Alas, we shall simply have to ride out, then, and meet them." He straightened and laughed again. "But not without a few surprises of our own, eh?"

He laughed even louder as he swung his walking stick across Henry's shoulders and back. He swung and struck until his arm grew tired, then ordered the bleeding body thrown into the back of a small cart.

"Come along then, my friends," he said to Malagane and Solange de Sancerre. "Our bait is loaded, our swords are sharpened. Let us see how many wolfheads we can catch in our traps today!"

In the outlaw's camp, less than five miles away, the foresters were also making last-minute preparations to leave. Runners had already been dispatched to watch the road, but because of the size of the escort and the distance they had to travel before they cleared Sherwood, it was not supposed Gisbourne's troop would reach the Witch's Teats before noon. It would give Alan a' Dale's archers plenty of time to shake out their nerves, although they had delayed their own departure long enough to avoid giving them too much time to ponder the risks.

Brenna and Will had worked all the previous day with the archers who showed the most skill with the longbows. They would be positioned atop the crests of either hill, while the vast majority of bowmen would be situated halfway down, at a distance that promised devastating results even with their less powerful weapons. Fletchers had worked day and night to make arrows, and there were impressive bundles of steel-tipped shafts waiting to fill the quivers.

The knights from Amboise were fully armored for battle and moved with quiet intensity among the horses, checking girths and straps for any sign of weakness. They were not overly worried about the foot soldiers; it was the company of knights—forty against seven—that was cause for concern, and they were counting heavily on Will and Brenna and their small team of elite archers to cut the odds to more comfortable numbers.

"Have you seen Griffyn?" Brenna asked, coming up behind Robin.

"Not since last night." He paused and straightened from tightening the buckles on Sir Tristan's *croupiere*. "Was he not with you?"

She supposed she should have had the humility to blush, but there was simply no time for it now and her breath puffed white in the mist as she turned and glanced at the activity taking place around them. "No. And his horse is gone."

"What do you mean gone?" He twisted around, frowning, and took a quick head and beast count. The outlaws had a dozen or so animals of their own, palfreys mainly, that they had dressed with bits of confiscated barding and accoutrement. The men themselves were wearing pilfered coats of mail, tunics, and carrying knightly arms to make it seem as if their force of mounted fighters were more formidable than it was. Littlejohn and Geoffrey LaFer had worked as hard with them as Brenna and Will had worked with the archers, and Robin saw them moving among their protégés now patting backs and giving words of encouragement for a sword well buckled and a shield impressively painted to resemble real coats of arms. But there was no sign of the big gray destrier caparisoned in hunting green and gold. No sign of his master either.

"I mean . . . gone," she said quietly.

The violet eyes were waiting for him when he finished his count and he could see that she was angry. Very angry. On a day when any emotion that might distract her or put a tremor in her hand could jeopardize the entire venture.

"Perhaps . . . perhaps he rode on ahead with some of the others to check the road."

"I have asked everyone. No one has seen him since late last night."

Robin abandoned the girth and turned to face her.

"Perhaps," she said with quiet intensity, "he realized there was no profit in risking his life for such an *ignoble* cause. Perhaps he has had all the adventure and reckless-ness he cared to enjoy."

"You do not really believe that, do you?"

She looked off into the trees, obviously too hurt to put her emotions into words. "His horse is gone. His squire is gone. The two bulging sacks of coin he so generously donated to the outlaws' coffers ... they are gone as well. What would you have me believe?"

"Bren ..."

She shook her head. "No. I should have known better. We all should have known better."

She turned and went back to where her archers were waiting. They were leaving in groups as soon as their quivers were filled, setting off through the mouth of the ravine at an easy loping gait. Will was there. He saw the mutinous set to her mouth and the flush that sat high on the crest of her cheeks, as if she had already run the dis-tance and back again. Her throat was working frantically to swallow some tightness gathered there and her actions were brusque, all but vicious, as she slung her bow over her shoulder and grabbed up a bundle of arrows.

He looked, as Robin had, to where the horses were being led toward the forest path.

"Where is Griffyn?"

"Gone."

"Gone? What do you mean gone?"

"How I do grow tired of repeating myself," she hissed through the grate of her teeth. "I mean gone. Fled. Tucked tail and run. He is probably halfway back to Burgundy by now where the profits are larger and the women"—she had to stop for a catch in her throat—"the women ask nothing of him but the charity of his smile."

"Bren—"

She glared at him across the top of her saddle. "I do not want your sympathy or your understanding. I was a fool and I paid the price."

"But are you in the proper frame of mind to do what must needs be done today?" he asked softly.

"I will do what has to be done," she insisted. "And likely take pleasure in doing it."

Will watched her snatch up the reins and lead her horse to the mouth of the ravine, and the only sympathy he felt was for the men who would come within range of her arrows this day.

32

The fog had thickened to rain by the time they arrived at the Witch's Teats, a cold, cutting drizzle that turned the road to mud and the grass on the meadow into slick, gray-green waves. Robin rode back and forth across the stretch of meadow checking the position of the archers concealed in the long grass that grew down the slopes of both hills. It was an ideal place for an ambush. The mist-shrouded tree-tops of Sherwood were just barely visible low on the southern horizon and the ground was relatively flat from there to the Teats, where the two gently rising mounds of earth forced the road to zig and zag between their bases. There were no trees and few bushes on either slope, and an unobservant eye would skim right across them without contemplating what mischief might lurk in the natural pocks formed by earth and overgrown rubble. There were more woods to the north, in the direction of Lincoln, and to the east, but they were neither as dense nor foreboding as Sherwood. The easterly wood was closest—no more than five hundred yards beyond the hills—and, if things turned sour, offered a handy escape route to take the men back to the safety of Sherwood, while hampering any horses or foot soldiers who tried to follow.

The heavy mist was an annoyance, but better than the strong sun in a midday sky that might reflect off bits of metal to betray their presence. Even so, as a precaution, the men on horseback were positioned behind the hills well out of sight of the road. Lookouts were posted as much as two miles away to give plenty of warning, and it was one of these men who came galloping along the road now, his horse's hooves kicking up clods of muddy earth.

"Robin! They are nearing the edge of the forest." He panted. "They are coming."

"How do they look?"

"Fearsome." He was bluntly honest. "Too many to count."

"Knights? In the van or at the rear?"

"Rear, with the wagon."

Alan a' Dale came loping toward Robin and the lookout, a bow slung easily over his shoulder. He was dressed, like the others, in the simple brown leather jerkin and green woolen hose that had become their uniform of sorts. A wide, hooded collar sat on his shoulders, the hood raised to keep the dampness from sliding down his neck.

"They are come?"

"We should be able to see their steam in a few minutes," Robin said casually. "Are the men ready?"

"As ready as ever they will be, with God's luck."

Luck, Robin thought grimly, had nothing to do with it. And everything. He glanced at the top of the westerly hill where Brenna was positioned with half the longbow archers, and to the east, where Will waited patiently with the others. Two of their protégés had deserted the camp during the night and taken the longbows with them as mementoes, but there were ten stout weapons with eager hands to draw them, and they would open the first stage of the attack.

"Lady Brenna near took my head off," Alan said ruefully, "when I reminded her there were no vows, no chains binding these men to our cause. We had hoped for four score, we have nearer a hundred counting those who came in yesterday from the nearby vills and villages. Yet we lost some we had counted on." He shrugged and spread his hands. "Some have families. Others want them."

It was the same on any battlefield and most leaders held their breaths on the day of the actual fight hoping to see the same faces behind him that were there the day before.

Knights were different, of course, for they carried their honor onto the field. But these were not knights and, as Alan said, not bound by any oath of service. They were farmers and cotters and turnip-growers (the old man was even here, crouched behind a boulder with his scythe in hand) who had never fought an open, pitched battle before. Their hopes lay in speed and surprise, and a goodly part in the slender arms of a woman who had had her heart crushed by a callous, cowardly rogue.

Robin did not want to think about that now. There would be time afterward to debate the ways and means of avenging his sister's honor, and he would do it gladly if it meant following the black-hearted bastard to the ends of the earth. For now, he had to concentrate, to focus on the impending attack, and to hope the men—his brothers most of all—would set aside the rules of battle etiquette and follow his orders precisely. Chivalry dictated the knights should show themselves first and allow their enemy ample time to prepare a defense, but this they could not do without forfeiting their biggest advantage. Chivalry would have also blanched at the thought of women arranged beside the men in the front line of battle, but Alan had brought forth a score of them the previous night who insisted they were just as capable (and some more so) of drawing a bow as any of their menfolk.

Nor was it considered an honorable ploy to attempt to cut down as many mounted champions as possible with bow and arrow before the actual fighting began. His brothers had grumbled loudest at this, at being set back behind the hill until they were called forth, claiming it was unmanly. Conversely, the foresters trusted him so completely, he was afraid their enthusiasm would cause them to break cover before he had given the signal.

Not by his choice had they started to look upon him as their leader, for he had been careful not to intrude on Alan a' Dale's authority, but even the lanky archer had seemed glad to relinquish the responsibility, far happier in the role of second-in-command. Richard and Dag had contributed to the subtle shift the first night in camp when they had been asked about the way of things in Normandy. The stories they told of their recent victory against the king's army in Maine had every man on the edge of their seat. Further tales of Robin's successes in the tournaments had brought their eyes nearly popping out of their heads, no more so than when they recounted his most recent triumph at Château Gaillard against the ferocious, flesh-eating Prince of Darkness.

The camp bard was kept busy composing his ballads, which were turning out to be such thrilling and exaggerated testaments of Herculean feats, Robin had found himself listening in awe. Now that the time had come to live up to their expectations, however, he found himself breathing a little harder, fighting to control the tightness in his chest. It was not the dying that mattered, he had always believed, but the manner of it, and to die on any battlefield was to die courageously and honorably. He had never given death much more than a passing thought before. But now he had Marienne, and the thought of losing her so soon after he had finally found her again . . .

"My lord?"

His mind had wandered and he brought it back out of Sherwood with an effort. It was Timkin holding out his shield and helm, regarding him with grave and trusting eyes.

Robin had almost forgotten the boy was there, as faithful and dutiful as he had been at Roche-au-Moine. He wore a suit of mail and tunic emblazoned with the Amboise device, for it was expected a squire should remain by his master's side to guard his back against attack and defend with his life, if necessary, that of his liege lord.

How old was he? Fourteen? Fifteen? A man already seasoned to war, yet a boy still who had never felt the scrape of a blade on his hairless chin.

Robin took his helm. "When this thing starts," he said, pointing up to the crest of the westerly hill, "I want you up there."

"My lord?"

Wary of pricking the boy's pride, Robin nodded grimly. "It is most important—*vital*, in fact—to the efforts of us all that you see no harm comes to Lady Brenna. If she and her archers have any measure of success, you can be sure the sheriff's men will try to cut her down or stop her. If I thought I could trust either Richard or Dag not to be distracted in the heat of battle, I would put one of them there, but since I have more faith in you, I will take your vow instead, that you will defend Lady Brenna as you would me, to your last breath, if need be."

The boy flushed and nodded. "You have my most solemn vow, sire. Nothing will get past me!"

"Good." He fitted the helm over his head and hooked the pennyplate camail under his chin. He took his shield in his left hand, sliding his forearm through the grip until it was seated snugly. Alan was dispatched back to take his place with his archers, leaving Robin to take one last pass down the road, Sir Tristan's saddlecloth flowing black and gold with each high, prancing step. It was more for show than any need to check on the men's placements; he hoped if he appeared calm and unworried, the confidence would spread to those crouched on the slopes.

Brenna kept one violet eye on Will, the other on the slow-moving procession of guards and knights who were beginning to plod into range. The ranks of footmen who came first moved in rippling waves, their conical helms bobbing in uneven lines. They walked without any apparent vigor in their step and carried their pikes and crossbows by their side as if the relief of leaving Sherwood in their wake was too much weight to bear at the moment. Lady Gillian had bred an early contempt for crossbows into both Brenna and Will. Where, in the heat of battle, was a man to find the time to set the thing nose down, place a foot in the stirrup, then wind the string back by means of a pulley in order to fit a new quarrel onto the stock? In the same amount of time, a somewhat less than proficient archer could loose four or five arrows—if he took extra care in aiming. To someone like Brenna, who aimed almost by instinct, twice that number was not impossible.

Behind the men-at-arms were the knights, and while there looked to be considerably less than the number they had expected to see, they still seemed to present an unbroken line of flowing colors, armor, crests, and pennons. They rode in a protective, boxlike formation around a wagon that appeared at first to be empty. As it drew closer, however, Brenna could see there was something inside. It looked like a stained pile of canvas sacking, but then her keen eyes picked out bony legs and arms, and she knew it must be Henry de Clare.

Not a blade of grass on either hillside moved. No curious heads poked up out of cover. They had all made their prayers and placed their quivers nearby, adjusting the arrows just so and just so again for ready grasp. The air bristled with so much determination the rain actually stopped, as if whoever was squeezing the clouds had paused to observe the drama unfolding below.

Brenna had a full quiver of arrows resting on her hip and a spare bundle lying at her feet. She was hunkered down in a crouch now, waiting for Will to give the signal. When it came, she was expected to spring to her feet, have the bow raised, and fire within a few seconds.

It will not be like hunting game in the forest, her mother had said. *You may find yourself having to fight living breathing men whose only goal is to survive, and you may have to face them so close, you will see the fear in their eyes.*

On the road outside of Gaillard, she had not had time to debate what she was doing. Her thoughts had all been on Griffyn Renaud, and she had shot at Malagane's men without any conscious thought. But this was a deliberately planned, cold-blooded assault. In a minute or two, she would see Will stand and loose the first shot, and a man would die, just like that. She would join him in firing more arrows with similar detachment and precision, and more men would die or be horribly wounded before they were fully aware an attack was under way.

It had seemed easy enough to agree with the plan when Robin and Will proposed it using bits of wood and stone around the firepit. But the men winding their way along the road, miserable and cold in the falling drizzle, were flesh and blood. Perhaps they had families. Perhaps one of them was riding with his mind distracted by thoughts of the woman he loved. Perhaps he would not see the danger until it was piercing through his armor, his chest, his heart, ending all thoughts forever.

Brenna's eyes swept the line again, slowly and carefully, her breath jammed in her throat, her heart pounding in her ears. She wiggled her fingers to ease the tension and glanced over at Will again. He had nocked an arrow into his bow and was balanced lightly on the balls of his feet, ready, waiting . . .

He stood up.

He drew and fired and a knight two hundred yards away clutched his chest and fell backward off his horse.

Brenna sprang to her feet. She shouted to the rest of her motley band of snipers, who were but a beat slower in jumping up and setting themselves. Immediately they began to shoot, choosing their targets amid the sudden eruption of confusion taking place in the rear of the cavalcade. Knights split from formation and galloped off the road searching out the source of the sudden and terrible destruction that struck down their comrades with swift, almost graceful precision. They raised their shields to ward off the unseen death that fell from the sky and, at the same time, screamed to the crossbowmen to return fire.

Brenna kept up a steady, smooth barrage of arrows, each finding its mark on an unprotected arm or thigh or shoulder. In little over a minute, she was grimly pleased to lead her archers in taking credit for a dozen or more knights who were out of the saddles, writhing in the mud. Will was having similar success—it was almost too easy!—and she paused a moment to observe what was going on in the rest of the panicked escort.

The crossbowmen were firing blindly at the slopes of the hills, but their ideal range was fifty yards and the closest of Alan a' Dale's men was twice that distance. He was in command of his outlaws, and he waited until the first wave of quarrels had fallen harmlessly short in the grass, then gave his men the signal, all of them rising out of the green like a spray of porcupine quills to nock, draw, and fire. A shocking number of Gisbourne's men screamed and fell backward, their feet still in the stirrups of their empty crossbows, their hands winding furiously on the pulleys to reload them. Another wave of arrows sent them scrambling for what cover they could find, many of them abandoning their weapons, flinging them into the mud like so much useless deadweight.

Alan's archers broke from cover and started running down toward the road. At the same time, Robin and his brothers led the mounted foresters out from behind the hill, their silks rippling, hooves pounding, their destriers thundering into the heart of the fray.

Robin set his spurs to Sir Tristan and rode straight for a party of three knights who had turned to make a stand. Their lances were unstrapped, their shields held forward as they put spurs to the flanks of their own beasts and rode out to meet him. One never made it. An arrow caught him high, just beneath the rim of his conical steel helm, and he toppled out of the saddle in a spray of blood. The other two kept coming, however, one a few roaring paces behind the other, and Robin knew he would have mere seconds to aim the point of his lance at the first and swing his shield up to defend against the second. When they came together, he felt the satisfying jolt of a solid strike as his lance shredded through mail and bullhide. He had his shield up, braced for the full brunt of a solid thrust, and managed to retain both his seat and his grip on his weapon while Sir Tristan wheeled about, his turn much quicker, his training taking his master right back into the path of the two knights, leaving one floundering in the mud, the other jogging crookedly away, his arm hanging limp by his side.

Robin saw Richard on his left, standing high in the stirrups as he fought, and Dag on the right, riding gleefully into a crush of Gisbourne's mounted henchmen. Again, the graceful *hiss* and *thunck* of an ashwood arrow lowered the odds, and Robin gave silent thanks for the quick eyes and steady hands high on the crests of the hills.

Geoffrey LaFer was in trouble. He had attracted a swarm of four knights to his side and had lost his lance already, shattering it on the first charge. Two of the knights were working in close with swords, bashing and hacking at his head and shoulders; two others stood back and shouted encouragement, waiting to take their turn when arms grew tired and swords heavy. Robin snarled and cast his own lance aside, riding in at full gallop, his sword drawn and slashing down in a mighty arc across the skull of one observer. Richard rode in screaming from the opposite side and drew off the second vulture, whose quick demise sent the others scrambling away to regroup.

"Are you all right?" Robin shouted to Geoffrey.

His helm dented in several places, LaFer nodded his thanks.

Of the mounted foresters, two were down and three more had retreated with bleeding wounds. The rest stayed valiantly in the midst of the fighting, slashing away with a ferocity that opened the way for Robin to reach the wagon that held Henry de Clare. The ground between was slippery, churned to mud and littered with cast off pennons, broken lances, gear, even bodies. Riderless horses screamed and pawed the empty air, and the crossbowmen, who were having no better luck fending off outlaws, began to scatter and run.

Robin plowed through the chaos with a roaring Littlejohn close on his heels. The latter wore a glittering hauberk of jazerant work, rows of flat steel plates attached to a vest of mail and canvas so that each plate overlapped, like the scales of a fish. He carried no ordinary sword, this fearsome behemoth, but a long, axelike glaive with a curved head and wickedly hooked spine, which he wielded with the ease of a starburst, hacking through arms, necks, skulls as easily as chopping the ripe fruit off a tree. Seated snug against the broad armor of his back was Sparrow, who fired his harp-shaped arblaster with the glee of an elfin demon.

Together they reached the wagon and saw Henry slumped against the rope-and-timber sides. The cart was being jostled by the movement of the panic-stricken beasts that drew it, one of which had taken an arrow at the base of its throat and was bucking wildly in an attempt to dislodge it.

There was no sign of life from the badly emaciated prisoner. His face was bloodied beyond recognition, his head lolled on the coarse planking, smearing it red on every twist and turn. Robin might have guessed him to be already dead if not for the flicker of one swollen eyelid and the gasped warning that went all but unheard amid the clash and clatter of battle.

Robin swung out of the saddle and clambered into the wagon. "Henry? Henry! Can you hear me?"

De Clare's bloodied lips moved, but again the warning came with no sound.

Sparrow, meanwhile, had jumped off Littlejohn's horse and taken up the reins, intending to drive the cart off the road and onto the meadow. But the wounded animal only gave a groan in reply to the shrill, snapping command and sagged down onto its knees, collapsing heavily onto its side.

Sparrow cursed and Robin, without missing a beat, turned his attention to Henry's shackles. They were bolted to the bed of the wagon with thick chains, and, although he struck the iron repeatedly with the hilt of his sword, the rings held.

"Heave over," Littlejohn ordered, hardly waiting to see if Robin obeyed before he brought the glaive smashing down like a thunderbolt, shattering the links of chains, the planking of the wagon, even the single axle that ran beneath the bed of the cart.

Sparrow gave a loud squawk as the wagon collapsed and sent him tumbling into the mud. He came up brown and dripping just as Robin and Littlejohn were hoisting Henry's deadweight over the front of Sir Tristan's saddle. Robin mounted behind him and Littlejohn, with a sigh and a dismayed grimace over the state of the muddied seneschal, was in the process of grabbing him up by the scruff of the neck when his eye caught sight of movement from the direction of the forest—the same nearby forest that was intended to be their escape route—and his mouth dropped open in shock.

"Holy sweet Jesus . . . Robin!"

It had been part of the original plan for Will and Brenna's archers to join the rest of the foresters when the initial flush of surprise was over. It was agreed they would be of more use, once the bulk of Gisbourne's mounted forces were pared down, driving off the crossbowmen and defending a retreat if one became necessary. At that point, also, Will was to ride to the opposite crest and join forces with Brenna, where it was supposed the two of them, firing with lethal accuracy, could wreak enough havoc to discourage any of Gisbourne's men from following them into the woods.

It was a sound plan and Brenna saw Will give the signal that he was coming to join her. She glanced at the spare bundle of arrows at her feet and estimated she had about three dozen left, plenty if supplemented by a similar number from Will. She still had Timkin by her side, and one of the more clumsy outlaws who could not shoot for saving his own life, but stood back with the warhorses and kept them from answering the call of bloodlust.

Will was down the slope and riding hard. Neither he nor Brenna saw the crossbowman until his horse was past the camouflaging clump of bramble and the man broke from cover, took aim on FitzAthelstan's back, and fired.

At twenty feet, a quarrel carried enough thrust and power to pierce readily through bullhide; Will's leather jerkin (he had loaned his hauberk and chausses to one of the mounted foresters, thinking the armor would better serve him) presented as much resistance as paper against a knife. It was also a fact, however, that a quarrel shot from a *wet* crossbow at the same distance is lucky to even reach its mark. While the drizzle may have temporarily let up, the effects on the arbalest had not, and the quarrel flew on a shortened arc, striking Will's upper thigh instead of his back. It still went deep into the muscle and carried enough punch to startle Will sideways in the saddle. He jerked on the reins, sending his horse into a confused stumble, and the next thing he was going down, landing hard enough on the wet grass to temporarily knock him senseless.

Brenna had taken her eye off him only for a second—for as long as it took to loose an arrow at a knight who was threatening Dag's unprotected back. She snatched up another immediately and had the crossbowman wilting onto his knees even as she started running down the slope toward Will. Timkin shouted something at her back but she did not stop. She reached Will a few moments later, skidding onto her knees beside him, and it was only when Timkin ran up, breathless and pointing anxiously at the westerly end of the meadow, that Brenna heeded his shouts and turned to look.

A solid line of mounted knights had emerged from the woods; a second host of fresh fighting men clearly held back to await the outcome of the initial encounter.

It was a trap! Gisbourne had somehow been alerted to the ambush!

Alan a' Dale had told them there would be forty of Gisbourne's guard riding escort and Robin had thought it an error of ignorance (to an uneducated cotter, ten knights looked like forty) that less than half that number had accompanied the wagon through Sherwood. It was clear the number had indeed been in error, but to the lesser side of evil.

Now there appeared to be thirty, perhaps as many as forty knights charging out of the woods, all with lances thrown forward and saddlecloths streaming back over the powerful, galloping strides of their destriers. Robin, Littlejohn, Dag, Richard, and Geoffrey were trapped near the wagon, vastly outnumbered even though the valiant foresters were swiftly closing together to form a line of defense in front of their wounded leader. Some of the archers cut back for the slope so as not to be run down beneath the hooves of the rampagers. Some became moving targets and the knights mowed them down like so much chaff underfoot.

Brenna struggled to help Will to his feet. Her arrows were at the top of the hill; she had only one in her quiver. Will's horse had bolted halfway down to the road again with his spare arrows and Timkin, understanding the desperate look on Brenna's face, set off at a run after it.

"Leave me," Will gasped. "Get back up the hill and do what you can to—"

He stopped and squinted hard against the glare of the gray skies. Brenna followed his gaze and froze as well, for silhouetted on the crest of the hill, his long black hair flowing loose around his shoulders, his armor glinting dully beneath the hunting green silk of his tunic . . . was Griffyn Renaud de Verdelay. In his hands he held a longbow, with an arrow nocked, the steel broadhead aimed straight for Brenna's heart.

33

"**B**ehind you!" he shouted, loosing the arrow. Brenna's head whipped around as she followed its flight and saw it strike the breast of a crossbowman who had seen them and was attempting to cut them down.

Griffyn was already firing again, and, like magic, two more silhouettes appeared by his side, outlined against the low gray ceiling of cloud. Derwint the Welshman and Eldred of Farnham took their stance and started firing, choosing their targets with much more care than Griffyn, but counting nearly every one a hit.

"Where, by Christ's toenails"—Will gasped—"did he come from?"

Brenna shook her head, still in shock. She slung Will's arm around her shoulder and hauled him up to the top of the hill, where she propped him against a boulder. The blood was oozing between the fingers he held clamped around his thigh, and with an urgent "*Go! See to Robin!*" he tried to work the quarrel free.

Brenna ran over to where Griffyn was calmly loading, aiming and firing. He paused for the briefest of moments to read the question in her wide, dark eyes, and smiled grimly. "Like I told you: I always *assume* the worst."

She fit an arrow to her bow and fired, striking the arm of a knight whose sword was about to cut Sparrow off the back of Littlejohn's horse.

"Here," he said, shoving another full quiver of arrows into her hands. "I have told Derwint and Eldred to try mainly for the horses. Despite your confidence in their ability, I am not sure I trust them aiming for anything smaller."

"Where are you going?"

"Where I am needed more," he said, glancing down at the bloody mêlée. He half turned and gave a shrill whistle, which brought Centaur galloping across the grass, his proud head held high, his nostrils flared wide with the scent of battle. "You must hold this hill; can you do it?"

It was Will, limping up behind, the quarrel broken but still wedged in his leg, who took Griffyn's bow from his hand and nodded. "We can do it."

"Good man." He fit his helm on his head, clapped Will on the shoulder and, almost as an afterthought, tucked a freshly gauntleted hand under Brenna's chin and kissed her. Hard. "As for your faith in me, my love," he murmured, "we will discuss the matter later."

Brenna watched him swing up into Centaur's saddle. Her eyes widened, grew round as two glittering coins as he slid a hand beneath his surcoat and withdrew a flimsy slip of rose-colored silk. It was the veil she had worn into the bath house at Amboise, and he had been carrying it next to his heart all this time!

He tied the scrap of silk to his arm, put his spurs to Centaur, and rode down the hill, his sword drawn, his roared challenge causing several of Gisbourne's men to veer toward him. She felt Will's eyes on her but before she could say anything, he was nocking another arrow to his bow.

"He picked a hell of a time to turn human. But I am damned glad he did."

It was an awesome, awful sight, and it had happened so quickly, going from the pulse-racing anticipation of victory to the heart-sinking realization it had been a trap, that Robin met the oncoming rush half blinded by rage. The foresters had fought bravely, his brothers like courageous fools willing to follow him anywhere regardless if they agreed with his tactics or not.

He had no choice now but to unsling Henry from his saddle and lower him as gently as possible to a patch of wet grass beside the road. His brothers and Littlejohn had already ridden out to meet Gisbourne's men; Geoffrey, with more blood than skin showing behind the nasal of his helm, had attracted a swarm of ten or more crossbowmen who had detected his weakened condition and sought to pull him down out of the saddle.

Sir Tristan reared high and obeyed the command from Robin's knees, charging headlong into the crossbowmen, trampling two underfoot while his master's blade scattered several more. Something struck Robin from behind and he whirled in time to get a gauntleted hand around the long metal tip of the pike being smashed across his back. A moment later he was holding the pike without resistance; the man was sinking to his knees, his hands clawing at the arrow between his shoulder blades.

Robin was struck again and although he saw the sword and anticipated its coming, his shield slipped and the blade slashed across his shoulder with enough force to split the links of mail and open a gash in his arm. Cursing between gasps, he shook off the pain and tried to maneuver Sir Tristan clear and regroup his senses. Something was blocking his way now. Another knight! He wheeled again in time to see a large kit-shaped shield with four red lioncels painted in the quadrants loom before him.

Andrew de Chanceas brought his sword smashing down over Robin's head, denting the side of his helm, driving a sharp edge of steel into his temple. The blow was stunning and Robin grasped instinctively for the pommel with his right hand, blinded instantly by the profuse flow of blood. He heard Sparrow's voice behind him and saw a blur of brown-and-green leather fly past him, axes glittering in the dull light, and he wiped as best he could at the blood filling his eyes, clearing them in time to see the seneschal flung aside like a pesky gnat.

Another blow was coming, a savage chop and slash that would have hacked through bone and flesh and brain if not for the bright stroke of steel that came down like a crack of lightning and halted the assassin's blade in a screaming shower of hot sparks.

Robin recognized the serpentine hilt and followed the mailed arm to the pale, luminous eyes glowing out from beneath the unvisored helm. That was all he had time to see, for Griffyn grasped the hilt of Albion with both hands and put all the might of his powerful shoulders into reversing the momentum of both swords, forcing de Chanceas's arm back and down, twisting the assassin's shoulders hard enough to bring forth a sound of screeching mail and popping crampons.

Seeing who it was who had interfered, de Chanceas roared and struck again, aiming this time for the gold falcon. Griffyn was ready for him, and the two blades came together, neither giving way. It took a third and fourth smash before Griffyn saw his opening and sent his blade slashing across the assassin's throat. The streak of steel silenced the knight's raging vengeance and sent de Chanceas's horse bolting away to fling the headless body onto the grass in a welter of gore.

"Your timing"—Robin gasped—"is most impressive."

Griffyn laughed. "I thought you could take care of this paltry business without my help, but I see I was wrong."

"Robin . . . are you all right?" It was Dag, pounding up behind them.

"I am intact, brother. How do the others fare?"

The others were still fighting like madmen and, like madmen, were turning away their opponents with the sheer force of their indefatigable frenzy. Littlejohn's glaive still windmilled over his head, causing any who ventured too near to shrink back in terror at the destruction it wrought. Arrows still found their marks and several of Gisbourne's men tried to ride up the hill where Brenna and Will ruled supreme, but they died before they covered half the ground.

Griffyn's sword flashed again and again, bloodied to the hilt, and with Richard, Dag, and Robin forming up beside him, they drove Gisbourne's troops back . . . back . . . until they retreated to the edge of the wood as quickly as they had come, with the foresters running after them, flinging arrows and insults in their wake. The sheriff's knights rode clear to the verge of trees where they regrouped around a small party of observers. Sir Guy was among them, identified by a keen-eyed forester from his black velvet robes and gold sallet.

"Will he send them again, do you think?" Richard gasped.

"I doubt he will give up too easily," Robin said grimly, and glanced around the bloody field. There were bodies everywhere, man and beast alike, some well dead, others wounded and groaning in their misery. Some of the injured outlaws, heeding Alan's orders, were already beginning to limp back along the road toward Sherwood. But there were more who walked, ran, or pulled themselves into a determined line that stretched out on either side of Robin and his brothers, exhausted, battered, but resolved to fight to the last man if need be.

Brenna, with Derwint the Welshman clinging precariously to the saddle behind her, came riding down the slope, her hair flown loose from its braid, her eyes searching out her brothers, Littlejohn, and Geoffrey, settling briefly on Griffyn before she came to a mud-splattering stop in front of Robin. She helped the forester slide off before she asked the same question and received the same answer.

"How are you set if they come again?" Robin asked.

"Will has been hurt. He says he shoots with his arms, not his leg, but he has lost a great deal of blood and the arrow is wedged fast against the bone."

"Christ! Arrows?"

"I left most of what we had with Will. I have sent Derwint to retrieve as many as he can."

Robin cursed again for not thinking of that first and dispatched more men to search along the road and the meadow for spent arrows. He tried to sound confident, but he was not hopeful of fending off another full attack if it came any time soon. The men were sapped. Even though the heat of battle could sustain a false strength for a while, injuries and armor took a heavy toll; his own arm was folded across the pommel of his saddle, not because it was convenient, but because his sleeve was soaked with blood and he could not lift it. His head was clearing, however; the loss of blood had helped that. And he had the further fore-sight to send several more men to fetch the swords and crossbows left behind by Gisbourne's men. Such weapons would come in handy throughout the long outlaw winter ahead.

"What of Lord Henry?" Brenna asked. "Is he—?"

"He is alive, but barely. Alan's men have him."

Brenna searched the line again. Geoffrey's face was pale as snow beneath bright splotches of blood. Dag's chausses were torn and stripes of blood flowed freely through the mail, dripping onto his boot and stirrup. Richard looked bashed but was still a formidable threat with his blazing eyes and grim, compressed lips. Littlejohn looked the least affected of the lot, but his fine suit of jazerant plates was covered in gore—whose it was, she could not tell. And Griffyn . . .

Her gaze lingered on him the longest after Robin. He had claimed no prominent place in the line and stood a little apart, magnificent in his green-and-gold.

She frowned and sought Robin's attention again. "Where is Sparrow?"

He turned his head. "He *was* with Littlejohn."

"I saw him by the wagon."

"No, by the boulder," said Richard.

"I last saw him attached to the shoulders of one of Gis-bourne's men." Dag chuckled. "Trying to fell him like a tree."

Robin remembered the blur of leather he had seen flying to his rescue and he stood higher in his stirrups, twisting around to see more of the field. The first pass went unre-warded but he thought, on the second careful sweep, he saw a scrap of buff jerkin poking out from beneath a clump of gorse.

He flung himself out of the saddle and hastened over to the bushes, his footsteps slowing when he drew near the last few feet. It was Sparrow, and Robin felt his stomach slide down to his knees and his knees to the ground, for the little man was dying, and dying fast. The side of his neck had been torn open from throat to shoulder and blood pulsed onto the grass, thick and dark and not able to be staunched, regardless how tight and close Robin pressed his hand over the wound.

The huge agate eyes were opened wide, searching for an explanation in the gray vastness of the sky, as if he could not believe his own end was near. And yet he knew it. He knew it even as he saw the blood and tears flowing down Robin's face.

"Do not weep for me, Master Robin," he gasped weakly. "Only tell me we have won the day."

"Aye, Sparrow. Aye, we have won it. Gisbourne has crawled back under his rock where he belongs."

"And your brethren?"

"All are well."

"Littlejohn? Will? Lady Gillian?"

Robin saw death beginning to cloud the dark eyes and let the error go unchecked. "Everyone has come through it."

"Good. That is good." His eyes drifted shut and Robin thought he was gone, but a moment later, they opened a squint. "I would ask you grant me but one boon, my lord."

"Anything, Sparrow. Anything."

And the voice came out surprisingly insistent. "I do not want English worms growing fat on my flesh. I would sooner sweeten the orchards at Amboise."

Robin clasped his hand. "It shall be done."

"And . . . tell my Lord Randwulf . . . tell him I loved him well. Tell him . . ."

Robin squeezed the pudgy hand tighter, as if by sheer strength of will, he could keep the elfin soul earthbound a little longer. He had never passed a day of his life without Sparrow's wit and wisdom by his side, nor had it ever occurred to him he might one day lose him. It had just never occurred to him.

"Cyril save me," came the merest gasp of breath. "I see her there, waiting for me."

"Who?" Robin asked, leaning his ear closer. "Who do you see?"

His lungs deflated on a sigh of resignation. "Old Blister. I should have known . . . she would not even let me rest in peace . . ."

The black wings of his lashes fluttered closed a final time and Robin shook his head. He squeezed the cold hand harder and when there was no response, he took the tiny body into his arms, rearing back with a cry filled with such rage and sorrow, it echoed across the field and shivered up into the sky.

Richard and Dag bowed their heads and balled their hands into fists. Littlejohn's face remained hard as granite, but his eyes grew round and wet and turned slowly to stare menacingly across the meadow. Brenna stood behind Robin, feeling helpless and useless and ashamed for every harsh word or thought she had ever had for the fiercely loyal villein who had always been there and never would be again.

"Robin! Look!" Alan a' Dale hurried over. "The white flag. Gisbourne seeks a parlay!"

Robin lay Sparrow gently on the grass. He wiped his eyes and stood, then stared hard at the small group of riders who were venturing forth from the trees. Gisbourne rode in front, strutting his finery and arrogance. By his side was another man with silver hair, and behind were five guards, one of whom carried a lance with a white flag.

"Has he come to offer his surrender, do you suppose?" Richard asked grimly.

Someone handed Robin a cloth to clean his face of blood. Brenna held out his helm, but when she started to move back to rejoin her brothers, he stopped her.

"No. I want you with me. And bring your bow; they may have some treachery in mind. Besides"—he gave his mouth a wry twist—"it should warm the cockles of their brave hearts to know a woman has wreaked so much havoc."

"Will it not only anger them more?"

"I sincerely hope so," he said brusquely, and called for his horse. "Angry men make stupid mistakes."

Griffyn nudged Centaur forward and produced a scrap of bloodied silk emblazoned with the device bearing four red lioncels. "I thought perhaps I was affected by the heat of battle when I saw de Chances. But he was here, and so is Bertrand Malagane."

Robin nodded, recognizing the silver-haired noble who rode by Gisbourne's side. "He wasted no time . . . but how did he know where to come?"

Griffyn returned his steady gaze and smiled tightly. "Permit me to ride out with you and we can ask him."

Robin delayed his answer long enough to give his brow a final swipe with the cloth. The bleeding had stopped, but the pain was setting in and he hoped the fiery stinging would keep his senses sharp. He put on his helm and fastened the linked camail beneath his chin.

"All right. The three of us then." He kept his eyes fastened on Griffyn, but turned his head slightly to address Alan. "Have your men take Lord Henry . . . Tuck . . . to Kirklees. If aught happens to separate us . . . we will meet there." He paused and glanced down. "And if you will see to Sparrow as well? I would be in your debt."

"Any debt you owe me could not amount to a tenth of what we owe you," Alan said gravely.

"Your men," Robin declared, looking around him, raising his voice so all could hear, "are the bravest I have ever had the privilege to fight beside. The honor is all mine."

Brenna mounted and kept her bow held loose in her hand. She started to pull a cap over her head but it was Griffyn who stopped her this time.

"Let them have a good look. It may be the last beautiful thing they see."

Brenna's heart soared and she lifted her head proudly. She reached around to tug away the thong that bound the remnants of her braid in place. A few quick strokes of her fingers loosened the golden mane completely so that there could be no doubt, at any distance, the deadliest of the snipers had been a woman.

Robin spurred Sir Tristan forward, matching the pace of Gisbourne's advance across the field. The High Sheriff arrived at the midway point before they did and the five guards he brought with him fanned out in a semicircle behind, leaving himself and Bertrand Malagane to observe Robin's approach in glowering silence. The smile he wore was one of sheer malice, the gleam in his dark eyes as Sir Tristan pranced to a graceful halt less than a dozen feet away was serrated with pure loathing.

"If I was not seeing this with mine own eyes," Gisbourne murmured, "I would not believe it. Robert Wardieu. In England again."

"Sir Guy. It has been a long time."

"Eleven years," Gisbourne hissed, his cheeks flushing. "Nearing twelve. And not a day has gone by that I have not thought of you."

"Fondly, I trust?"

"Oh . . . very fondly. I am looking forward to renewing our acquaintance. I have your accommodations prepared and waiting for you already, the chains polished, the knives sharpened, the pincers warmed."

"Ah. Yes, well, I am sorry to disappoint you, but I have not the time to spare on such pleasantries."

Gisbourne smiled and his gaze shifted to Brenna. "God-strewth. My men swore there was a *grisette* raining arrows down upon their heads; I assumed she would look more like a Medusa or a Hippolyta. But hold—do I detect a resemblance?"

"Lady Brenna Wardieu," Malagane provided helpfully. "Sister to the cub, daughter to the Black Wolf."

Gisbourne's chest swelled at the thought of such bounty within his grasp. He bowed his head in a mocking imitation of civility while his eyes raked down the front of her leather jerkin and settled lewdly at the crux of her thighs. "Indeed, I have no doubt my men will be most enthusiastic to offer you their hospitality as well, dear lady."

"Since I have yet to see any real men in your company, Sir Guy," she said easily, "I shall not endeavor to hold my breath until one appears."

His gaze slid to the third member of their party and reacted visibly to the calm, gray-green stare. Griffyn had not worn his helm and his black hair rested loosely on his shoulders. He had not shaved in three days and the lower half of his jaw was heavily shaded with stubble, making the lines of his face appear more stark, the frost in his eyes more penetrating.

"Another healthy beast," Gisbourne murmured. "Do I know you, sirrah? The look of you seems vaguely familiar."

"Renaud," said Malagane. "Griffyn Renaud de Verdelay. A Burgundian whose acquaintance *I* am looking forward to renewing."

"Lord Bertrand." Griffyn allowed an insolent dip of his head. "I see you managed to find your way without my help."

"Oh, but I did have help, my lord. The very best, I assure you. My youngest son: Lothaire. He has been guiding our footsteps all the way from Gaillard."

Robin frowned. "We have no one named Lothaire in our company."

The blue eyes sparkled like chips of broken glass. "Forgive my presumption. Of course, you knew him better as . . . Fulgrin."

Griffyn's sharp intake of air widened the smug grin on Malagane's face. "A rather clever fellow, would you not agree? And *so* resourceful. We had both seen you in the lists at Gascon, and it was my thought if ever there was a man who might serve a useful purpose one day, it was you. How glorious your rage that day when you were cheated of your victory over Robert Wardieu! And how magnificent that rage became as you worked to transform yourself into the Prince of Darkness."

"Your son is a dead man," Griffyn said quietly. "You may tell him that for me when you see him again."

"Why not tell him yourself?" Malagane said generously. "He is just over there."

Griffyn looked past the count's shoulder to where the main body of Gisbourne's knights had formed a solid line against the trees.

"When we have concluded our business here," Gisbourne said on an impatient sigh. "You may deliver messages to the devil, for all I care."

"What business?" Robin demanded.

"You have my prisoner, Henry de Clare."

"Lord Henry . . . is dead."

"Dead?"

"You may come and view the body if you wish," Robin said blithely, mimicking Malagane's munificent offer. "He is just over there."

Gisbourne glanced toward the road and the ominously silent line of foresters. "I am sure that is not necessary. But you do appreciate my predicament. The king is in Lincoln and he expects to see the hanging of an outlaw on the morrow."

"You could volunteer your own neck," Griffyn said quietly. "As High Thief of Nottingham."

Gisbourne turned a cold eye to the sarcasm. "I was thinking more of offering him the pleasure of watching Lord Robert Wardieu dance upon the gallows boards. In exchange, I would order my men off the field, grant amnesty to all of your wounded, and, further, issue writs of safe passage to those of your kin who would, naturally, quit England as soon as possible."

The generosity of the offer was surprising—too surprising to be believed, and Robin scoffed. "Your writ of safe passage would be as worthless as the integrity of the signature that would bind it."

Gisbourne's nostrils flared at the insolence but his smile remained intact. "Your arrogance is admirable but ill-timed."

"And your 'offer' is no offer at all."

"Shall I present another, then? One more worthy of your precepts of chivalry." He turned and raised a gloved hand, signaling someone back in the line. "Do you play chess?"

"Not when lives are at stake."

"But you do appreciate the finer points of necessary strategies? The sacrificing of a knight, for example . . . for a queen?"

Robin's gray eyes turned brittle as he saw the solid line of Gisbourne's men shift apart to allow two figures to pass through. One was a man, tall and burly and gleaming with armor; the other was a woman, a slender, hooded splash of white against the glowering threat of guardsmen.

"She is the reason you have come all this way, is she not?" Gisbourne asked quietly. "She is the reason you are here, to uphold the family tradition of rescuing the poor, tragic Eleanor from harm? Another admirable quality, to be sure, but again, ill-timed, for as you can plainly see, she is *surrounded* by harm now, and standing presently in the company of my captain of the guard, Reginald de Braose, who is most eager, I promise you, to avenge his own humiliation suffered at the hands of your brother Eduard all those many years ago."

He saw the hard sparkle in Robin's eyes and added, "I will give you one hour to discuss the proposed exchange amongst yourselves. After that, I will take *her* to Lincoln instead and make a present of her to her royal uncle."

Robin's jaw clenched and unclenched, his lips turned bloodless as he pressed them into a taut, flat line. "Do the conditions of your original offer still stand? Parole for the wounded and safe passage for the others?"

"Yours is the only neck I seek this day," Gisbourne agreed blithely.

"Then we do not need an hour. We can make the exchange here and now."

Brenna gasped. "Robin!"

He glanced her way. "There is nothing to discuss."

"What do you mean nothing? There is *everything* to discuss." She turned to Gisbourne. "Will you allow us a few moments of privacy, Lord Sheriff?"

Gisbourne gave the outline of her breasts another thoughtful glance, then bowed his head with princely generosity. He and Malagane turned their horses around and retreated a short distance, whereupon Brenna turned frantically to confront her brother.

"You cannot do this thing," she whispered urgently. "You cannot sacrifice yourself!"

"We have no choice. He has Princess Eleanor, he will take her to the king, and the king will have her killed."

"He will have you killed as well."

"Aye. More than likely he will."

She glanced helplessly at Griffyn. "There must be something we can do!"

"There is," Robin said, reaching out to grasp her hand. "You can tell the others to waste no time in making their retreat. I would sooner trust a promise from a snake as one from Gisbourne, and he will not waste time in debating the ethics of honoring his word."

"Robin, *please*—"

"Yes." He squeezed her hand so hard the pain prevented her from interrupting again. "Please tell Marienne that . . . that I love her beyond life. That . . . I will have her name on my lips with the last breath I draw."

The declaration drew Griffyn's attention away from the verge of trees, and he looked from Robin to the wide, shiningly desperate gaze that was fastened on him as if he was the last thread of a fraying lifeline. "Do you not think it odd that Gisbourne would make such a trade if he had two valuable prizes within his grasp?"

Robin frowned. "What are you saying?"

"I am saying . . . he just signaled his captain to bring 'the princess' forward, but she had already started forth on her own . . . and stepped carefully around a boulder to do so. Did you not tell me she had been blinded?"

Robin's gaze shifted slowly to the trees. "Are you certain?"

"My eyesight is quite excellent," he assured them. "For instance . . . what color hair does she have?"

"The princess? It . . . it was pale. The color of moonlight."

"Moonlight? Not a bloodred moon, by any chance?"

Robin searched for the answer to the grim smile that spread across Griffyn's lips and swore softly. "Solange de Sancerre?"

"Not even the vestal robes of a virgin could conceal the way she walks when she has an audience of lusty men following her every footstep."

"What are we going to do?" Brenna asked.

Griffyn stared thoughtfully at the longbow slung over her shoulder. "Let them know we have changed our minds."

He took the bow and drew an arrow from her quiver, careful to keep his actions concealed until the arrow was nocked in the string.

"Surely you are not going to shoot the woman?" Robin exclaimed in an anxious whisper. Despite who and what she was and the infinite agonies she had caused in her torture chamber, the thought of cutting down a woman in cold blood appalled him.

But Griffyn's attention was not focused on Solange de Sancerre. It was on the line of knights behind her, on one figure in particular who was doubtless watching the proceedings with smug satisfaction.

Brenna read his intent. "You will waste the shot. It is too far. And I only have two arrows left," she added in an urgent whisper.

But he did not take his eyes off the target, he only murmured a quiet, "Centaur. *Stand.*"

The stallion, who was battle-trained to respond to his master's every command, lifted his tapered head and seemed to turn to stone. Griffyn raised the bow and eased the fletching back to his chin, then to his ear, adjusting the angle of flight to allow for the distance to the trees. He drew farther still, bending the mighty bow almost beyond its limits before he released and sent the ashwood shaft *whoosh*ing across the expansive sweep of grass.

Both Malagane and Gisbourne heard the distinct *twang* of the bowstring and whirled around in time to see Griffyn straighten. Their heads swiveled again and they saw, nearly three hundred yards away, Fulgrin jerking up and falling back in his saddle, his hands clutching at the arrow where it had punched through his chest. The knights on either side of him skittered out of the way, men and beasts alike startled by the sound of Fulgrin's scream—a scream that came echoing back across the field in a thin, watery wail of incredible pain.

Malagane roared and spurred his horse back across the meadow, thundering past a stunned Solange de Sancerre.

Gisbourne passed a moment of shared incredulity with Robin and Brenna as all three turned slowly to stare at Griffyn Renaud.

"Not one man in a thousand could have made that shot," he gasped.

Griffyn acknowledged the compliment by calmly nocking another arrow and aiming it between Gisbourne's eyes. "I can guarantee this one would pose no difficulty either."

The sheriff stiffened and called out to the five guards who had accompanied him onto the field. When there was no response, he glanced quickly over his shoulder only to find they were already halfway back to the trees, spurring their horses into a gallop to catch up with some of the others who were making haste to put a thick shield of trees between them and the knight wearing the gold falcon.

"Robin?" Griffyn's voice sounded almost casual. "Perhaps you have some new terms you would like to discuss with Sir Guy?"

A slow, wide grin spread across Robin's face. "Personally, I couldn't care less if you shoot the bastard here and now . . . but I am sure we have some friends who would be most eager to offer the lord sheriff their hospitality while matters of mutual concern are discussed."

Gisbourne's face glowed red. "This is an outrage! I will see you both hang before this day is through!"

He pulled up on his reins intending to wheel his horse around, but before he could complete the command, the arrow was loosed and sliced hotly past his ear, taking away the fleshy pad of his lobe. He screamed and clapped a gloved hand to his neck, and when he removed it and stared at the blood-smeared leather, he screamed again.

Brenna was quick to hand her last arrow to Griffyn, who was equally quick to bring it to bear on Gisbourne again. "As I understand it," he murmured, "you have not many such useless appendages of flesh left to spare, Sir Guy. Would it not be prudent, therefore, to come with us as a whole guest rather than leaving parts of you scattered behind you on the field?"

"You will not get away with this!"

"I think we have already. Kindly wave the rest of your men off while they are still of a mind to obey your orders."

Gisbourne stared at the blood pooled in his palm, then raised his arm and jerked it once to order his men to remain in the wood. Robin brought Sir Tristan trotting forward and leaned over the sheriff, relieving him of his reins.

The dark, ferret eyes flicked past his shoulder and scanned the amazed line of foresters who were still murmuring among themselves over Griffyn's shot and were beginning to suspect something even more amazing was about to happen.

"I am a noble, an earl, a baron for pity's sake," he hissed. "You cannot simply hand me over to those peasants and outlaws!"

"Whereas I," Griffyn said evenly, "am Rowen Hode of Locksley, twelfth Earl of Huntington, and those peasants you speak of are my loyal tenants and villeins whom I absolve completely of any charges of outlawry. You would be wise to hold your tongue whilst you are among them, lest you find yourself missing it."

"Locksley!" Gisbourne gasped. He looked pointedly at the longbow and something flickered behind his eyes a moment before the dark centers rolled up into the back of his head and he slumped forward in a dead faint over the pommel of his saddle.

Robin caught him by the sleeve before he slid off into the mud and peered narrowly at Griffyn as the latter smiled the smile of an indulgent Lucifer.

"Something else you have not told us?" he inquired dryly.

"A trifling incident from my youth." Griffyn shrugged. "But if you care to count his fingers, you will see he only has nine."

Robin's grin was cut short by another scream and the sound of pounding hoofbeats coming up fast behind them. It was Bertrand Malagane. He had donned a conical steel helm and drawn his sword, and he was streaking back with vengeance on his lips and loathing blazing in his eyes.

Robin had his hands full keeping Gisbourne upright in the saddle, and it was with no small gleam of pleasure in his own eyes that Griffyn wheeled around. He tossed the longbow to Brenna and spurred Centaur on to meet the ravening Count of Saintonge, drawing his sword as the two destriers closed the distance with deadly purpose. As Griffyn raised his blade, a stray beam of light caught the steel and flared blue-white along its length, causing the burnished metal to glow like a fiery beacon. The blade slashed downward, the arc smooth and graceful, striking Saintonge with explosive force. The count's sword shattered in two. His wrist snapped in a spray of blood and splintered bone, but even that could not deflect the power of the blow.

There was a look of utter disbelief in Saintonge's eyes as he crashed to the ground. Centaur danced around for another pass, but it was not needed. The count rose halfway to his knees, his hands clasped over the bloodied front of his tunic, but the effort cost him his last wailing breath and he collapsed facedown in the grass, his life pulsing into the grass beneath him.

That left only one screaming threat on the meadow, and Brenna, who was not bound by the same chivalric codes as the men, nocked, drew, and fired the last arrow.

34

The abbey of Kirklees sat upon the crest of a gentle hill, with meadows and orchards spreading out from the base of its gray stone walls to the verge of trees that marked the boundary of Sherwood. It was not large and had no fortified barbicans to guard against uninvited entry, but it had protected the sanctuary of the meadow for over one hundred fifty years, its inhabitants cloistered against the turmoils of the outside world.

The small group of knights and foresters was admitted through the low postern gate where the mother abbess, flanked by several sisters of the order, was waiting. Two of the foresters carried the litter bearing a half-conscious Henry de Clare through the ivy-covered arch. He had seemed to be more dead than alive when they had left the meadow, but at the first touch of the mother abbess's hands, his eyes opened and he managed to whisper something that only the abbess heard and was able to muster a smile over. The beating he had suffered that morning had all but finished what a month in Gisbourne's donjons could not, and Robin, watching solemnly from the shadows as the abbess ran her hands tenderly over the swollen, bruised, torn, and ravaged parts of his body, spared a moment to give thanks that in this instance, at least, her blindness was a blessing.

It was almost full dark in the courtyard and the nuns had only two hooded candles between them, so Robin had to rely a good deal on his memory of Eleanor of Brittany's face to distinguish any of her features. Once regarded as being unquestionably the greatest beauty in Christendom, the years had been kind. Despite the raw ugliness of the scars that marred the sockets where her eyes used to be, her skin was still smooth and unblemished. There were lines on either side of her mouth and a certain looseness beneath her chin, but these inevitable signs of aging only added a kind of dignity not found on the faces of women desperate to cling to their youth. Marienne had said her once silver-blonde hair was pure white now beneath the nun's cowl, and had been since the night she had given birth to young Eduard. She had always been slender and delicate of form, but her wrists, where they peeped out from her sleeves, were beyond fragile; they looked as if the slightest pressure would snap them. Surely, the strength of Henry's grip, when he first opened his eyes and saw where he was and who was tending him, should have crushed her fingers at the least.

"For eleven years he has defied all of God's efforts to remove him from this earth," she said when his men had followed the nuns inside with the litter. "I warrant he will survive this just to prove his stubbornness."

Robin moved forward, the metallic clink of his hauberk seeming to desecrate the peace of the garden as he went down on one knee before her.

"Highness. It was good of God to keep you so well over the years."

She urged him to stand again. "It was graciously good of God to bring you here safely, Robert, and for him to bless my . . . to bless Henry with such loyal and steadfast friends. Your family is well? Lord Randwulf, and your mother?"

"They are very well, Highness. I thank you for asking."

"And Eduard? We heard he was injured in Maine."

Her voice carried the soft concern of a lifelong friendship and Robin reassured her. "Lady Ariel has him securely bound, hand and foot, or he would have come himself. He is much like Lord Henry. Too stubborn by far to leave this world just yet. But you will see that for yourself when we return to Amboise."

"Return to Amboise? No. No, dearest Robin, I will not be returning. This is my home now, I have no wish to leave it."

"But, Highness—"

"Please." She smiled and pressed a finger over her lips. "Do not address me thus. To the sisters, I am but a humble daughter of the church. And thus I will remain until I have served out my time here on earth. Here, Robin, at Kirklees, where I have found peace and happiness."

"The king—"

"Is a broken man. He is ill and desperate and he knows his kingdom is in jeopardy. He fears the barons because they grow stronger every day and he knows his army of mercenaries and misfits cannot hope to defeat a host of zealots calling for change. He also knows I am no threat to him. In truth, he even visited me here once, begging my forgiveness."

"He knows you are here?" Robin was shocked.

"He has known almost from the beginning and has never breathed a word of it, not even to his confessor. Guilt, I think. My brother's murder weighs heavier on his mind than he would ever admit, and I must believe he has difficulty at night washing the stain of royal blood off his hands."

"Well," Robin said with raised eyebrows. "Then it will just be Marienne and the boy returning with us?"

She nodded and clasped her hands solemnly together. "You have seen Marienne?"

"Yes, most happily. And the child," he added carefully. "A handsome, clever boy. Courageous too. He wanted to fight with us today."

She reached out to touch Robin's arm. "You did not allow it, I trust. Oh!" Her fingers found the wetness on his sleeve and traced it up to the gash in his armor. "You are hurt!"

" 'Tis but a cut, nothing more."

"Nonetheless, you must let Sister Goneril see to it. Are there other wounded among you?"

"Most have gone back to the camp in Sherwood. I myself cannot linger, for we have a guest of some importance waiting for us there, and the foresters may grow impatient to heat the pitch and pluck the feathers."

"A guest?"

"Aye. Sir Guy of Gisbourne was invited to come along and listen to some of the foresters' grievances."

Her eyebrows arched slightly in surprise. "He did this willingly?"

"Willingly enough. I gave my word he would be returned to Nottingham unharmed. A little *ruffled*, perhaps, but unharmed."

Eleanor tilted her head once more toward the postern. "I am also told you have a bold lady archer in your company."

Robin beckoned one of the two shadowy figures forward. "My sister Brenna."

Brenna dropped awkwardly in a curtsy. "Reverent Mother," she whispered. "I have heard so much about you for so long, I . . ."

"You were beginning to wonder if I was real?" The abbess laughed softly. "It is an affliction suffered by many outside these walls, and I can only hope it grows stronger as the years pass. But you should not be the one to speak of legends and reality. They are saying you can shoot faeries out of the sky."

Brenna exchanged a startled glance with her brother and the abbess, sensing her puzzlement, smiled again. "Did you not know that Sherwood is a magical place? Did no one tell you the humming you hear high in the boughs is the trees speaking to one another, whispering to those farthest away what is going on at the heart? Within a sennight, every tree in England will rustle with the tales the bards are singing— of Robin in his pilgrim's hood, and Will with the scarlet hair, and . . . and a great Saxon warrior who calls himself the Prince of Darkness."

This last was said with some curiosity, and Robin beckoned once again into the shadows. "That would be Griffyn Renaud de . . ." He stopped and corrected himself with a small shake of his head. "Lord Rowen Hode of Locksley."

The abbess seemed to draw a careful breath as she pressed

a hand over her breast. "Surely not ... Wystan Hode's son?"

Griffyn knelt before her as Robin had done and bowed his dark head. "You are kind to remember him."

"The earl was a good man. When I first came here, he used to deliver us grain and meat through the long, harsh winters. Your arm," she added hesitantly, reaching down to trace her fingers lightly over Griffyn's scarred left hand. "Does it still pain you?"

Although Robin had thought himself beyond reacting to any more surprises where the dark knight was concerned, he found himself gaping.

"You two have met before?"

"The earl brought his son here," the abbess explained, "hoping the sisters might know enough of herbs and medicines to undo the terrible thing the king's men had done. The young lord was half conscious and burning with fever, so it would not surprise me if he does not remember."

"I remember," Griffyn said. "Though I did not begin to suspect whose gentle hands helped me until Robin mentioned that you were ..."

"Blind?" she provided delicately. "In truth, I may have lost the sight of my eyes, yet my uncle did not take away my ability to see the goodness in men's hearts. Your father was a brave and honorable man. We all grieved when he died, and felt the loss as deeply as your own people when you and your young wife were forced, shortly thereafter, to flee England."

"Huntington was too rich and tempting a prize for the king to leave it in Saxon hands—especially those of a seventeen-year-old hothead who came close to killing him the once and likely would have succeeded had he been given a second chance."

"And have you come back now, then, to join the other barons and nobles who fear they will also have their birthrights stolen, their sons tortured and imprisoned, their lives torn asunder by the ambitions of an unjust king?"

"I hold no such lofty ambitions, Highness. Huntington

has been disseized these past seven years; I do not even think of it as mine anymore. Today I absolved the villeins and woodcutters of all charges of outlawry, but they were empty words, spoken in arrogance by a man who has no home now except the one he has made for himself in obscurity."

"Oh," she mused, "not so obscure, I think. And these lofty ambitions you speak of, they are more a part of your destiny than you may realize." She smiled gently and tilted her head in Brenna's direction. "Has he told you how his hand came to be scorched?"

Brenna looked from Griffyn to the abbess. "No. He has not, though I have asked."

The abbess nodded, as if she expected as much. "When I first arrived, the old mother abbess took me in without question. She was doughty and kind and wise, and we never thought there would come a day when she would not be ringing the bell to come to chapel, never be there to share our whispered fears late into the night, never be there to stand in the gates and defy the soldiers to set a single foot across God's threshold. After I had been here for several years, the king's men came to the gates and wanted to search the abbey, but she withstood their threats and their shouting. I had taken refuge in the chapel, preparing myself for what I suspected was my return to prison, but the abbess was successful in telling them to chase their rumors elsewhere; that this was a house of God and their immortal souls would be in jeopardy if they defiled it with their presence.

"A few days later, the earl—who was himself very ill at the time—brought his son here to Kirklees and begged a private audience with the abbess. None of us knew what they discussed until some time later when she suspected the pains in her chest would soon be fatal. She had already chosen me to be her successor and confided in me many things about the abbey, but now it was time to share one last secret about the history that bound Kirklees and Huntington together."

She paused and laced her fingers tighter. "It seems the king's men had not come for me at all. They had been chasing a rumor of a different kind—a rumor that had to do with the existence of a great charter drawn up almost a century ago by the son of William the Conqueror. He was young, and in love with the daughter of a Saxon noble, and in an attempt to make peace between the two peoples he would eventually rule, he compiled a list of a hundred promises to be made into law when he became king. True to his promise, he signed and affixed his seal to the great charter on the day of his coronation and dispatched one hundred copies around the kingdom, but he had not predicted the violent reaction of the Norman conquerors—those men who had eagerly followed his father across from France and fought to defeat the Saxons, only to be told by a lustful son that they should now consider themselves equals.

"Fearing this violence could turn into open war, Henry recanted at once and recalled the charter, managing to retrieve all but two of the one hundred copies. Of those two copies, one was said to have burned in a fire, but the other . . . was rumored to have been stolen by his Saxon mistress, who in turn, and at great risk to her own life, had it spirited away into safekeeping. Over the years, kings would periodically hear the rumor of its existence again and send their spies out in the hopes of finding it and destroying it. My dear, brave Uncle John was no different. He tore apart the house of every Saxon peasant and noble, determined the charter would be found or the rumor set to rest once and for all.

"When his men came to Huntington, they arrested Wyston Hode and accused him of being in possession of Henry I's charter. They tortured him cruelly and, when that failed, they declared they would leave the ultimate judgment to God."

"He was too weak," Griffyn whispered. "He could barely stand."

"And so the son took his place," the abbess said quietly.

"He suffered the trial by ordeal in his father's stead, and when he reached into the boiling oil and retrieved the crucifix, he held it out before the tribunal, defying the bishops to question God's judgment."

"My father died anyway a few months later," Griffyn said through his teeth. "And a few months after that, the king came back for Huntington, so the *nobility* of the deed went for naught."

The abbess shook her head. "You cannot know the pride your father felt as a result of your courage. Nor could you comprehend the depths of agony he suffered, knowing it was his secret you were guarding."

"Are you saying"—the pale eyes glowed out of the darkness—"the charter exists?"

"He intended to tell you," she said softly, "but at the time, you were too ill, and later, you were too full of rage. He was afraid of what you might do. Tell me . . . do you still carry Albion?"

Griffyn looked as puzzled as Robin and Brenna as he reached haltingly to his side and unsheathed his sword. The abbess took it gingerly, the weight of it too great to balance without resting the tip on the cobblestones. Her fingers probed carefully around the base of the serpentine guard and, finding the small indent she sought, pressed a hidden catch that allowed her to twist the rounded cap of the hilt to one side. It did not twist easily, especially to fingers more accustomed to praying than handling weapons of war, and, for a few probing moments thereafter, was still reluctant to give up the secret it had protected inside the hollow grip for so many years. But then she caught hold of something and extracted it with some difficulty, the object having been wrapped securely in cloth to prevent betraying its presence in the hilt of the sword.

She held it out to Griffyn. "Your father entrusted you with the sword, knowing you would never part with it; that it would stay in your keeping until you drew your last breath. He confided his sacred trust in the abbess, hoping she would find the right time to tell you, praying you would understand that he could not risk letting the secret die with him."

Griffyn stared at the small bundle she had placed in his palm. He began to unwrap the layers of cloth, so old the threads had disintegrated at the creases, but identifiable by its shape long before the glint of metal appeared.

"A key," he murmured. "But what does it open?"

"There is an old stone altar in the chapel at Edwinstow. On the bottom, near the back, there is what appears to be a crack in the stone, but I am told if the dust and mortar is scraped away and the key fitted to the crack, it will open and a secret chamber may be found therein. The charter is there, in a gold tube, stamped and sealed with the insignia of Henry I."

Griffyn turned the key over in his long fingers and shook his head. "I thought it was just another legend, like King Arthur and his army of ghosts waiting in the forests, biding their time until England can be reclaimed from the Normans." He looked up, mystified. "What am I expected to do with it?"

"It is not for me to tell you what to do," said the abbess with a sigh. "But the king who rules this land now is a cruel and unjust monarch; he believes himself to be above all laws, even those decreed by God. There are other men, good men, at their wits' end, desperate to find some way to end the tyranny and treachery, to put an end to the injustices and cruelty without having to resort to civil war. The promises contained in this charter are wise and fair; they would make a king accountable to his own laws, to his people, to his God. With a document such as this, the good men of England might be able to find a way to bring the king to justice."

"Robert FitzWalter," Robin murmured. "He has the ear of Stephen Langton, and the archbishop, in turn, could use these laws of Henry I to rally the barons into confronting the king. He was able to bring Lackland to his knees once. With the church, the law, the barons, and the people of England behind him, he could do it again."

"Then you take it to him," Griffyn said gruffly, offering the key.

"Oh, ho-ho, no, my friend," Robin said, laughing as he held his hands up and backed away. "This is your country, not mine. Your destiny. You are going to have to play the hero yourself this time, I am afraid. By midday tomorrow I intend to have myself a new bride and be halfway back to Lowestoft."

Griffyn's hand curled around the key. "I am not a hero. I am not a leader or a savior or a Spartan wielding a sword of fire. I do not even think of this place as my home anymore and doubt I would ever have come back here had *your* destiny not interfered at Gaillard. No," he said, handing the key back to the abbess. "I want nothing to do with saving a king or a country that destroyed my family, destroyed my life."

"He destroyed mine as well," she said softly. "And my brother's."

"For that I am truly sorry. But there is nothing I can do about it."

He turned and strode out of the garden, exiting through the postern, leaving three silent figures staring after him.

"You will have to forgive him, Highness," Robin murmured at length. "He is not yet accustomed to wearing this mantle of virtue."

"There is nothing to forgive," she replied. "Perhaps it is still just my own fear speaking, for the archbishop is the only other man outside these walls who knows about Eduard. He gave me his word, pledged it with his lips on the cross, but he has defied a king and angered a pope by siding with the barons. Imagine how strong their position would be if they could produce a legitimate heir to the throne?"

Robin drew a deep breath and reached over to gently ease the key from her cold fingers. "Eduard will soon be too far out of their reach to strengthen anyone's position. And if this charter is as important as you say it is, perhaps Langton will accept it in his stead."

"You will take it to him?"

"Actually, I will have Richard and Dag deliver it. They are considering staying in Sherwood awhile longer . . . to help Alan a' Dale make proper fighters out of his woodcutters. They think it would be a worthy adventure to harass Lackland on his own territory for a change."

It was the first Brenna had heard of it. "They are staying?"

"Will has mentioned it too. He would not be able to travel for a few weeks anyway with his injury, and thought he might as well make the best of it by training some new archers."

"Geoffrey?" she asked sardonically. "Littlejohn?"

"Geoffrey misses Isobel too much, and Littlejohn knows Father will need him more than ever now with . . . Sparrow gone. That only leaves you and . . . ?" He lifted a hand to indicate the postern gate.

Brenna found him by following the flattened path his long, angry strides had cut through the dew-wet grass. He had walked all the way down the slope into the belly of the valley and stopped by the banks of a small brook that coursed a lazy path through the apple orchard.

He was just standing there, his one hand braced on the trunk of a tree, the other planted on his hip. His head was bowed and his hair was fallen forward over his cheeks, rippling slightly each time he kicked the toe of his boot into an overgrown root.

"I brought you your sword," she said, holding the heavy blade awkwardly in front of her. "Robin is just having his arm bathed and bound, and then we can leave."

He straightened and turned. His jaw was rigid, fierce with pride . . . and something else . . . as he took the weapon from her and resheathed it.

"I suppose you expect me to play the hero as well?"

"No. No, I do not expect it all."

"Because it is not in my character?"

His voice was brittle with sarcasm and she almost smiled

at the effort he was making to try to shrug off the dreadful weight of that mantle.

"On the contrary," she said softly. "I think it is very much in your character."

"Because of this?" He held up the scarred hand. "It was not nearly as brave or heroic as the telling of it would lead you to believe. The monk in charge of boiling the oil was my father's retainer and made the cauldron look to be hotter than it was."

"Did you discover that before or after you volunteered to take your father's place?"

He glared, giving no answer, then cursed under his breath and turned away again. "You were quick to believe I betrayed you today."

She opened her mouth to deny the charge, but bit the pad of her lower lip instead.

"The look on your face," he murmured. "In that one split second. It accused me of everything from cowardice to deceit to betrayal to a willingness to commit cold-blooded murder."

It was not an excuse, but she said it anyway: "You snuck out of camp while it was still dark—"

"I did not want to disturb you. It was my fault you had little enough sleep the night before."

"You told no one where you were going. Your horse was gone, your squire was gone. The money was gone," she finished lamely.

"I knew Fulgrin had left but not that he had taken the money," he admitted. "I thought perhaps he had just decided I had gone a little too mad this time, spurning all those years we had worked so hard to make me into a bastard. I assumed he'd had enough adventure for one lifetime—either that or he knew we did not stand a chance today and thought to cut his losses. He was always clever that way, knowing when to leave a place when it became too warm."

He plucked a leaf—rather, he tore it savagely off the branch and began shredding it between his fingers. "I have no one to blame but myself, of course. I have been living a life of deceit, betrayal, and cold-bloodedness for so long . . . it has formed bad habits that are hard to break. I suppose . . . I have not given you any good reason to trust me thus far."

Trust me, he had said. *Let yourself go.*

"You gave me reasons," she said haltingly. "I just chose not to see them."

"Yes, well." He cast aside the scrap of leaf. "You see me for what I am now. A noble without nobility. A knight with tarnished spurs. A man who has made a fine reputation for himself by killing without conscience or qualm."

"A truly villainous sort," she agreed, moving closer to where he stood. "Not at all the kind of husband my family envisioned me spending the rest of my life with."

He drew a breath and held it for a long, dragging moment. "I was not aware I had asked. Or that you had answered. In fact . . . were you not most adamant when you said you could not imagine what a life with me would entail?"

"I cannot imagine it now," she murmured with genuine consternation. She was close enough to touch him, to raise her hand and gently trace the strong line of his jaw. She could feel the immediate tensing of his muscles, hear the coarse exhaling of breath as his lips parted beneath the whisper-light pressure of her fingertips. "But why is it you always remember the things I say in haste . . . or in anger?"

"Because you always seem to be speaking hastily. Or angrily."

She considered that for as long as it took her to sigh and ease her arms around his waist and rest her cheek on the plush green chamois of his surcoat. "If that is the case, then I shall say this very slowly and very calmly so that when the time comes, it may be quoted with even greater authority. I love you, my lord. I love you as Griffyn Renaud. I love you as Rowen Hode. I even love you as the glorious Prince of Darkness. And if you do not ask me to marry you, I shall have to settle for some large-nosed lout who would want to teach me manners and modesty, who would insist upon a well-ordered household and a wife who demurred always to the lord of the castle."

His arms trembled as he slid his hands up into the tawny crush of her hair and forced her to tilt her head upward. "What makes you think I would not demand the same things?"

"Because you know I would not obey you. And besides—" She stretched up on tip toes and brushed her mouth over his. "How orderly a household could you expect me to make of a mountain cave?"

He looked at her blankly for a moment, then began to laugh. It started as a deep rumble in his chest and grew to a lusty and exuberant sound that echoed around the valley and caused Brenna to frown up at him as if he had indeed gone a little mad. In short order, however, he was kissing all such foolish thoughts out of her head. He kissed her fiercely, tenderly, passionately, lifting her off the ground and spinning her around so that the ringing sounds of their laughter reached out and touched the magical trees of Sherwood.

When he settled her again, he did so with the sigh of a reluctant hero. "I suppose I shall have to go back and fetch the key?"

"Actually, my lord." She smiled and reached for his lips again. "I brought it with me."

❦ *Epilogue* ❦

Brenna groaned as an exquisitely warm curl of pleasure rippled slowly down the length of her body and back again. She opened her eyes with a soft sigh and looked up at the bronzed, naked flesh of the man kneeling over her and wondered if the smile he wore was a threat or a challenge.

After nearly ten full years of wondering much the same thing, it still amazed her that such a simple thing as a smile could set her pulse racing and her heart pounding in her ears. It amazed her that the challenge to see if he could make her faint had not yet worn off, though he was clearly cheating this time. He knew she was weakest on mornings like this when she threw open the shutters on their tower window only to find the clouds had engulfed the keep overnight.

One day we will make love in the clouds, he had promised, and she had thought at the time he was only being poetic. Little did she know then or suspect later in the valley at Kirklees that his "cave" was a magnificent castle perched high on the crest of a mountain like an eagle's eyrie and boasted a keep that rose another breathtaking eighty feet into the sky. Its sheer gray towers and battlements and steeply pointed turrets encompassed the entire top of the mountain, and on a clear day, the view from windows and walls left her dizzy with awe.

She groaned again and pressed her head back on the pillows, shuddering deliciously each time his oiled hands glided over her flesh. It was his favorite method of torment, massaging every inch of her body until she was a quivering mass of sensitized nerve endings. He used oil scented with ambergris and just the faintest whiff of it, caught when he was taking the stoppered bottle out of the spice chest, could weaken her knees and make her incapable of motion until he prowled up behind her like a big cat and fetched her back to bed.

"You should be ashamed of yourself," she whispered. "We have guests."

"Robin and Marienne are not guests. They are family."

He slid his hands up from her hips to her waist to her breasts, stroking his slicked fingers around the plumped flesh and circling the nipples until they were hard enough to abrade his palms like small pebbles.

"They have their children with them."

"Our children will keep them amused."

"They have—" Her mouth flew open and her breath stopped somewhere in her throat as his fingers slithered down to her belly and delved into the golden thatch of tight curls.

"Yes? They have . . . ?"

She could not answer for almost a full minute and, even then, could not remember the question or complaint.

Ten years, she thought. And it was always the same feeling of helplessness. She could feel it warming her thighs if he looked at her—just looked at her, for pity's sake, across a crowded room. He still wore his hair long and carelessly loose over his shoulders. He still practiced every day in the tilting yards so that his body was hard with muscle, his belly flat as a board. He had earned a few more scars over the years, to be expected in a man who still wore the infamous gold falcon on and off the field of battle. His stark beauty still drew the hungry eyes of every warm-blooded female east of the Loire, although they were soon discouraged by the obvious and open love he held for the tall, slender lady archer who walked proudly by his side.

It had been that way since the day they had ridden to Edwinstow with Robin and Marienne and exchanged their vows before the village priest. Oh, now and then he tried to order her to stay at home while he tended to border disputes or quarrels with the other dark lords who inhabited the mountains around them. But only once, when she was a month away from birthing their first child, did she obey. And then only because he conducted a most thorough search of the wagons and rouncies that rode in his escort.

They had four children; two boys and two girls. Robin and Marienne were keeping apace, though Eduard was the only young lord among a bevy of sweet-faced ladies. He had grown into the very image of his lionhearted uncle, with hair like summer wheat and eyes so piercingly blue they put the sky to shame. The Wolf had stared long and hard at the boy when he had first been introduced, for he had fought alongside the great golden king and knew Richard's face better than any other man alive, with the possible exception of William Marshal and King John. But the question was never asked and the boy was welcomed with such ease, he had trouble later remembering a time when he was not part of a thriving, boisterous family. He was in his twentieth year now and already wore the gold spurs of a knight, a fact that made his father, the former champion from Amboise, proud enough to burst the seams of his surcoat.

Robin had come to Burgundy specifically to speak to Brenna and Griffyn about a matter of some delicacy, for they were now the only two living souls who knew for certain the secret of Eduard's bloodlines.

Lord Henry de Clare, though not as strong as Robin had predicted, had recovered from his wounds and remained a faithful sentinel, watching over the walls of Kirklees for another six years. It was then, while tending some villagers who suffered from a debilitating fever, that both he and the abbess fell ill. They died within a few hours of each other, and at his request, wary to the end of safeguarding his beloved's whereabouts, a single arrow was fired into the forest of Sherwood to mark the place where both should be buried. There were no telltale signs or crosses left behind, and even before the first summer had passed, it was said the greenwood had grown up around the sylvan glade, distorting the memory of anyone who might have tried to find their resting place again.

"What will you advise him?" Brenna asked, purring beneath her husband's hands again.

"What are his choices? King John has been dead for eight years. The boy, Henry III, will soon be reaching the age of majority, and the articles of the great charter his father was forced to sign at Runnymede not only safeguarded his throne but insured that, once he is king, he will never be able to abuse his powers again. The barons have a puppet they can control. What good would it do to raise the specter of war again?"

"But Eduard has matured into such a fine young man," she said languidly. "So handsome. So bold. So courageous."

"Reducing the rest of us to old, ugly miscreants?"

"He is a prince of England, my love. You are only the prince of my dark desires."

His hands stopped stroking for a moment. She gazed into his face, smiled, and opened her arms.

Griffyn accepted her invitation with a hapless smile, suspecting the only one who would come near to fainting this day was himself. He slid deeply inside the warm sheath of her flesh, savoring the volley of tiny shudders that welcomed him and held him fast. That, combined with the ambergris and the slick evidence of her passion, threatened to be his undoing. Ten years and four children. If Brenna found the notion of wedded bliss difficult to comprehend, he found it nigh on impossible. He had expected—hoped—for a kind of contentment after so many years of brooding isolation, but this . . . this feeling that clutched around his heart every time she whispered his name or touched his hand . . . he had not expected that at all.

Her arms, her legs twined around him and she started moving slowly to his rhythm. Her eyes were wide and dark and filled his vision, telling him how much she loved him, how much she believed, utterly and completely, in this life they had made together.

"The clouds are coming in," she murmured against his lips.

He glanced over at the window embrasure and saw the opaque wisps drifting through the opened shutters.

"Trust me," he whispered. "I will not let you fall through."